CLUB LLITHIUM

by

C.R. Allen

First edition published by Rich Pageant Media

Cover design created with assistance from AI

Editing and layout by Lupi Docs & Designs/Rich Pageant Media

ISBN: 978-1-7339561-5-4 (paperback)

ISBN: 978-1-7339561-6-1 (ebook)

for Tara

Contents

PART ONE

Ilyana rolled her eyes for what felt like the hundredth time that night. Her date didn't even notice. He had been too absorbed talking about himself, explaining to her how he had made a fortune in the stock market. He seemed to enjoy using jargon and acronyms that meant nothing to her.

Ilyana had only been listening to every other word, but the more he described it, the more it rang of exploitation and downright fraud. Not that the legality of it bothered her, she was born in Russia after all. However, most Russian criminals didn't brag to their dates in detail about how they had committed their crimes.

She did find solace in the familiar martini the bartender had made for her. It was made with Russian Standard Vodka, her favorite brand back home and while traveling abroad. She remembered ordering it extra dirty, and seeing her date's eyes flicker with excitement at her muttering the word. She was fairly certain his jaw had hung open for almost a full minute before the impatient waiter's grunt interrupted whatever speculative fantasy he had been entertaining.

"Jack Daniels," her date said quickly. "With extra Jack." He had laughed at his own joke.

The waiter did not bother to check her ID when she had ordered. If he had bothered, he would have had the same trouble reading her Russian passport as the other, more attentive waiters had been while she was visiting America.

"Ain't no stopping Chaz when he's on a roll!" he said rather loudly and obnoxiously, breaking her chain of thought.

"Clever," she said in response, figuring that the flattery would mask her complete lack of interest in anything he had said thus far.

"So, um," Chaz stumbled as he searched for something else to talk about. "What's Russia like?"

"Cold, very cold," Ilyana responded, smiling at him and setting down her drink.

"I bet," Chaz replied. "I'm from California and let me tell you, it's nothing but fun in the sun out there. Beaches, bikinis, margaritas. My parents have a beach house in Malibu. I can take you there some time, it's really nice. We can have dinner at the club."

His voice continued but she no longer heard it. She was peering across the bar into the mirror behind it, checking herself out in her reflection. She was skinny and short, like all the girls in her ballet group. Her blond hair flowed over her shoulders and stopped just below her collarbone. This, combined with her perfect posture (thanks to years of training from her overbearing mother), gave her a narrow physique that limited much of what she could and couldn't eat.

Maybe one day she could eat what she wanted, drink what she wanted, and do what she wanted. But that was not today. The salad she ordered remained untouched. Smothered with thick creamy dressing, layered with cured meats, and infiltrated by fatty cheeses; the Americanization of her meal likely would lead to an upset stomach and a distraction before her next performance.

Chaz, meanwhile, had inhaled his cheeseburger like one who had just returned home from a deserted island after living on coconuts for months. He began piling handfuls of fries into his mouth, barely breathing between boastful statements about his family's wealth.

His profile picture on the dating application had been attractive, but it was clear that the picture had been taken many years beforehand. His eyes were more sunken, his shoulders and build lumpier, and his bulging belly gave him the appearance of a large gorilla from Africa. His Ed Hardy jeans with their obnoxious embroidered plastic jewels and designs only squeezed the fat to hang over his belt.

In the end, she didn't really care. This was her last night of freedom in America, her last night to experience things she usually only got to watch on TikTok. They were booked to fly back to Russia after their next performance, her homeland anxious to have its prized ballet group returned. Though Chaz's self-absorption was no different than every other typical American male she had met, he had indicated he knew the best nightclubs in town and that was an invite she could not have turned down.

"How was your salad?" she heard Chaz say from across the table.

She turned back to him, only to find him staring at his phone and frantically texting with some unknown contact.

"It was ok," Ilyana replied.

"What?" Chaz said loudly in reply, clearly not paying attention either.

"It was disgusting," said Ilyana with a smirk.

"Glad you liked it," Chaz said, never slowing or pausing his text message.

"I'll be right back," Ilyana said, standing and scooting her chair back from the table.

"Sounds good," said Chaz with disinterest, as he was writing a short novel on his phone.

Ilyana noticed their waiter taking the drink orders for another table near the sign that indicated where the restrooms were located. She slid the slit on her silver silk dress to one side so that her leg was exposed as she walked.

The waiter definitely noticed, his eyes darting to steal glances at her.

"I'm sorry ma'am, what was your drink again?" she heard him stutter to his table as she passed.

She smiled, it felt good to have this kind of control over men.

The ladies room at the trendy restaurant was decorated with a Chanel theme. Framed art with recreated prints of Chanel advertisements going back 100 years adorned the walls. Chanel perfumes, scented soaps, and lotions stood on the white marble counter next to the sinks. The iconic double-C logo was projected onto the wall while a white crystal chandelier hung from the ceiling.

She took her seat on a chair in front of the vanity embroidered in a brilliant pattern that resembled a checkered race flag. This was the part of America she absolutely enjoyed, the luxurious and elegant style that was a requirement for any half-way decent restaurant. It was a stark contrast to the dilapidated and aging cafes she had grown up with in her small hometown outside Moscow. There, her family had barely enough to afford even the most basic toiletries. While here in America, samples of perfumes and the like were left out for anyone to take as if they were candy from the dish by the door.

From her clutch, she pulled a small makeup kit and began to touch up her cheeks and eyes. Content that she looked perfect once again, she leaned forward to check under the stalls for any other visitors to the restroom. Relieved to not see any legs sticking underneath, she reached back into her clutch to produce a small vial that she placed to her nostril and breathed in hard. The immediate rush of the cocaine was a welcome relief from the night's monotony.

After checking herself in the mirror one last time, she exited the restroom to find the same waiter from earlier nearby entering an order onto a tablet. He couldn't resist the urge to look up at her and smile. A smile she did not return. She kept walking right past him like he wasn't there at all and only until he was behind her did she smile at herself. She enjoyed the thought of the waiter thinking about her all night long, knowing he would never have her.

She imagined later that evening his distraction causing him to mess up another order, maybe his manager would find out, maybe they would fire him! Maybe he couldn't afford rent, and would have to live on the street until he died of an overdose, hunger, or the cold. The thought that her beauty could trigger a chain of events that eventually lead to the waiter's demise excited her greatly. *Maybe looks can kill.*

Arriving back to the table, she was relieved to see her date had already settled the bill and was ready to go.

"Hey, I got us an Uber," said Chaz. "Figured we could head back to my place and..."

She interrupted him.

"You told me you would take me to the club," she said sharply.

"Yeah, I know," Chaz said shakily. "I just thought since I took you out to dinner, you'd want to... you know, just head back."

"I want to go to the club," Ilyana replied, as she peered at him wide eyed. "You can get us in can't you?"

"Umm, yeah," said Chaz unconvincingly. "I know a guy, I can get us in."

"Then let's go," Ilyana said, walking past him and to the door.

Their driver was Arabic and listened to a Middle Eastern pop song that Ilyana did not recognize. As they drove, she could tell Chaz was feeling uncomfortable, he kept looking into the cash compartment of his wallet then putting it away, then pulling it out and checking again. As if he were some magician and more cash would appear every time he re-produced it.

In between obsessively checking his wallet, he would check his phone. Ilyana stole a few side glances to see what he was looking at, only to see the logo for a bank on the screen. He must be checking his balance and counting it with whatever cash was left in his wallet to see if he had enough to cover the cost of the club. Chaz looked a little nervous.

"Can you change that music to something American?" Chaz said irritably to the driver.

The driver turned down the music slightly.

"At least he understands English," Chaz muttered to himself as he counted the cash in his wallet for a fourth time.

Ilyana just looked out the window, enjoying the lights of the tall buildings as they passed.

She had first been told about Club Llithium by a fellow dancer who had read about it online. It was one of the oldest and most exclusive nightclubs in the city. Redditors had raved about how it was one of the most amazing experiences of their lives, though details about the club were typically vague and scarce. When asked for advice about how to get in, many posters had indicated they knew someone who had gotten them in.

Chaz had been the only man she met on the dating app who claimed he could get her into the club. It was really the only reason she had agreed to go out with him in the first place. However as he fumbled between his bank account and wallet, she was starting to doubt the truth to that.

Several minutes passed, but eventually they pulled up to a rather large, dark building.

"This can't be it," said Ilyana aloud.

"This is the address," the driver said with a heavy accent and pointing to the phone on the dash where the screen indicated they had arrived.

"But it's an old church," she replied.

"We could go back to my place instead," Chaz said tentatively, pulling the app back up on his phone.

"No," Ilyana replied. "Let's check it out first."

They both exited the car and the Uber pulled away, the music much louder now that the driver no longer had any passengers to satisfy.

"Two stars," Chaz said aloud as he tapped away at his phone. "Music was too loud."

Ilyana ignored him and studied the building towering over them.

It was an old church alright, three large crucifixes adorned the peaks of three large steeples. Stained glass windows, thirty feet tall, nestled underneath the rises. The walls were made of rough stone blocks that gave it an almost natural appearance, as if the whole place had emerged like a volcano from under the ground. It felt ominous, as there was not a single light on the exterior at all. The only illumination was the faint glow of the nearby downtown lights that seemed to be absorbed by the church itself.

"You said you knew this place," Ilyana said with anger in her eyes.

"I didn't say that," Chaz said defensively. "I said I could get you in."

"And how did you intend to do that if you don't even know where the club is?" she replied pointedly.

"Don't worry about it, babe," said Chaz, pulling out his wallet and retrieving his remaining cash. "Money is a universal language."

They were both startled when a black SUV appeared from the darkness of the quiet street and stopped nearby.

Two women and a man emerged from the vehicle, talking and laughing. Ilyana watched closely as they crossed in front of her like she didn't exist, and disappeared down the alley next to the church. As they did so, their voices disappeared along with them and the silence of the street returned.

"They must be going to the club," said Ilyana.

"How do you know?" asked Chaz.

"They were dressed like it," Ilyana said, walking in the direction of the alley.

"Hey, where are you going?" Chaz said, trying to catch up.

"We are going to find this place," she replied.

As they approached the alley entrance, it appeared devoid of any signs of life. Ilyana only temporarily felt a twinge of anxiety, it was quickly extinguished by her urge to find the entrance.

"I don't know about this," Chaz said fearfully.

"Shut up and come," Ilyana said, grabbing his shirt and dragging him around the corner and into the alley.

They were nearly blinded by a bright light that appeared above them. As their eyes adjusted, Ilyana lowered her hands from her face and was amazed at what she saw.

It was as if an invisible barrier had existed and once they had passed it, the entire world around them changed.

The alley was suddenly brightly lit, flame-like sconces adorned the walls of the church's exterior and cast an orange and red glow on the ground. Two lines fifty feet long snaked along the alley, crammed with people standing shoulder to shoulder.

Music boomed from an open double door at the end of the alley where two muscular bouncers dressed in suits stood letting people in.

"This line is going to take forever," Chaz whined from behind her. "Let's just go back to my place."

"No, I want to go in," Ilyana replied defiantly. "You said money talks, right?"

"Yeah, but..." he trailed off.

"Then let it do the talking," said Ilyana, grabbing his arm at the elbow and dragging him toward the open double doors of the club.

As they walked past the line of people waiting to get in, they were greeted by dirty looks and sneers from the crowd. Ilyana didn't care, she didn't know them and she was determined on her final night in America to spend it at the most exclusive club in the entire city.

Ilyana took a moment to check out what the people in line were wearing. As expected, she spotted the typical knockoff designer jeans and outlet rack Bugatchi button-down shirts for the men, women in scantily clad dresses or short skirts with bare-all tops.

Stranger though, she found several wore full suits and formal dresses. Their style more attuned to a Victorian ballroom. Ascot ties, lace frills, handkerchiefs, top hats, bonnets; all clothing items that hadn't been in style in decades or centuries. What were they thinking trying to get into a club like this?

Chaz and Ilyana arrived at the front of the line and Chaz stepped forward towards the two bouncers.

"Name," said the bouncer, not even looking up and just staring at a clipboard.

"Brian," Chaz said furtively.

"Last name," the bouncer said with an annoyed tone.

"Roberts," Chaz replied with palpable uncertainty in his voice.

Ilyana said, “I knew there was no way this was going to work.”

"You're not on the list," the deep voice of the bouncer replied. "Back of the line."

Chaz looked at Ilyana. Ilyana stared back at him with an expression of annoyance that let Chaz know the night would be over for her and he'd be going home alone.

He seemed to muster up the courage finally and from his pocket he took out all of the cash from his wallet and set it down on the bouncer's clipboard.

"Are you sure you can't check again?" Chaz said as confidently as he could.

The bouncer opened up the slightly crumpled wad of money, Ilyana could distinctly see a tangle of $5 and $10 dollar bills.

The bouncer looked at his partner and laughed.

"What is this crap?" he said looking back at Chaz.

It was then his expression changed as he noticed Ilyana standing nearby.

"Come on man," Chaz said. "Help a brother out."

However the bouncer's attention was completely focused on Ilyana.

After a minute of studying Ilyana closely while Chaz watched nervously, the bouncer leaned over to his partner and whispered something into his ear.

His partner nodded and swiftly disappeared into the doorway.

The bouncer looked back at Ilyana and Chaz.

"ID's please," he said.

"Shit," Ilyana thought to herself. She could tell the bouncer was no idiot and would be able to tell that she wasn't of age.

"Here you go," said Chaz, handing his driver's license to the doorman.

"Not yours," the bouncer retorted to him. "Hers."

"Got it," said Chaz, recoiling.

Ilyana fished in her clutch for her passport, dreading the inevitable.

Eventually handing it to the bouncer who took it and proceeded to read it carefully under the overhead light.

She prepared herself for the eventuality of being turned away because of her age; though back in Russia, seventeen was old enough for just about any activity you could imagine. She was shocked when the bouncer handed her passport back to her and unhooked the rope that blocked them from entering the club.

"Ladies first," the bouncer said.

Ilyana stepped forward with a smile, relieved that she had finally gotten what she had wanted.

Chaz took a step forward after her.

"Hold on there, champ," the bouncer said with a large muscular hand blocking Chaz from moving inside.

"What do you mean?" Chaz said, confused. "I'm with her."

"We are at capacity," the bouncer replied, standing up now to his full height that loomed almost twice as tall as Ilyana.

"Come on man," Chaz pleaded. "This is bullshit, I paid you!"

Ilyana didn't care anymore, she wasn't stopping to wait for Chaz. She walked through the double doors, away from the pathetic pleading of Chaz from behind her.

The corridor was dark, very dim sconces providing just enough light to see where you were going but not enough to make out much detail. The walls were adorned with full length antique mirrors the entire way, she cheated a glance at her posture as she walked.

Perfect ballerina posture, her back and neck straight. Her head seemed to float forward as she walked instead of bobbing up and down. She looked and felt as elegant as she moved.

The sound of music that was emanating from the double doors at the end of the corridor grew with each gliding step. Bright lights filtered through the cracks in the door, silhouettes moving among them.

Her heart began to race, the skin all over her body tingled. She reached for the door handle, the music was infusing with her body by now, her insides vibrating to the beat.

The doors swung open on their own, and she was suddenly engulfed in silver and blue light. The music no longer muffled by the barrier between them hit her full force now. Her eyes struggled to adjust to the new lights, movement, and sounds.

"Welcome to Club Llithium," said the other bouncer that had gone inside ahead of her. He welcomed her with an inviting smile.

She stepped forward without thinking, trying to fathom the mass of bodies moving and dancing in front of her. Looking up, the tall ceiling sloped upwards. Catwalks and lighting rigs hovered above her, the motorized lights dancing along to the beat of the music.

The whole club was arranged in the exact same layout as the old traditional Orthodox church she remembered from her hometown. Shaped like a crucifix, the entrance was at the long end.

The porch entrance of the church that had appeared boarded up from the outside, was lined on the inside by a long bar with half a dozen bartenders serving an endless supply of patrons. Glass bottles were flying through the air and being passed from bartender to bartender with perfect fluidity. She creeped forward, overwhelmed, and still struggled to fully grasp the entire scene and atmosphere.

As she approached the bar, the crowd seemed to naturally part for her. She walked right up to the opening.

"What can I get you?" asked the bartender. He was wearing tight, faded jeans with a black t-shirt that showed off his toned arms and shoulders. Decorating his tattooed arms were owls, eagles, and several winged beings that appeared unfamiliar to her. He smiled at her which gave her the feeling of butterflies in her stomach, his strong jaw trimmed with the perfect amount of dark stubble. He sported a close-cropped hairstyle on the sides, while the top was arrayed into a neatly spiked Mohawk.

"Um," Ilyana struggled to put her thoughts in order.

"Let me guess actually," the bartender said with a smirk. He looked her up and down, sizing her up. But to Ilyana, it felt like he was looking inside of her mind and thoughts, prodding through her needs and desires. After several moments he started mixing a drink for her.

"What are you making?" Ilyana asked.

"Martini," the bartender replied. "Extra dirty."

Ilyana smiled.

"Was it that obvious?" she said to him.

"I know a martini girl when I see one," he said playfully back to her.

"Can you make it with Russ," she said before being cut off.

"With Russian Standard Vodka," he said before she could finish her sentence. "I know."

As if perfectly choreographed ahead of time, a large bottle came flying above the bartender's head and he grabbed it midair as if it was magically spirited into his awaiting grasp. Spinning the bottle twice in the palm of his hand, he poured the alcohol into the metallic mixer.

"First time?" He asked as he began to shake the cocktail mixer in perfect rhythm.

"Yeah, how'd you know," Ilyana replied.

"I know everyone who comes here," he said with a smile before tossing the mixer from behind his back over his shoulder and transitioning perfectly into pouring it into the martini glass.

"You could say it's kind of my job," he added before dropping a pair of olives into the drink and sliding it towards Ilyana.

Ilyana opened her clutch and began searching for her wallet.

"How much do I..." she began.

"Don't worry," the handsome bartender replied. "First drink is on the house."

"Thank you," she replied giddily.

"I'm Harper," the bartender said, extending his hand.

Ilyana reached out to shake it, noticing how strong and firm his hand was as it held her small, dainty one.

"Ilyana," she said with a smile.

"Have fun out there," Harper said before disappearing further down the bar.

Ilyana turned and sipped her martini.

"I will," she murmured to herself through her smile.

Where church pews should have been arranged in neat and orderly rows, with God-fearing parishioners on their knees praying, the main area of the church had been cleared out completely, and in its place, was the dance floor. Hundreds of bodies jumped and gyrated amongst each other in time to the music, the lights dancing around them. Lining the walls on both sides were lounging areas where the most beautiful and well dressed club goers sat in low-clearance couches and chairs, sometimes on each other's laps.

Ilyana admired just how beautiful everyone in the club was. From Harper, to those on the dance floor, to those sitting and talking amongst each other, every single person could have been a model in a magazine.

She arrived at the front of the club where the building split into north and south transepts, forming the iconic crucifix shape of the old place of worship. Each transept was cordoned off, only accessible via stairs that lead to a platform guarded by bouncers. The platform of this VIP area was far too tall for her to see in, but she could certainly speculate at all the drugs, sex, and partying that was bound to be occurring just out of view of the common area.

However the most impressive area of all was where the altar should have been. On a raised platform in the apse of the church, a hooded DJ played at a table. On both sides of him, were cages hanging from the ceiling donning half-naked male and female dancers swaying and moving to the music as if in a trance.

Above the DJ, a ten foot tall crucifix hung from the rafters. A projector shined images of forests, deserts, and outer space all across its surface. It was difficult for Ilyana to take her eyes off all of it. The movement, the images, perfectly in time to the music. It must have been a massive effort to coordinate, choreograph, and manage the whole place.

She finished her drink, smiling at how perfectly made it was, and put the glass down on the tray of a cocktail server passing by.

Ilyana didn't come here to watch, she came here to dance. Taking a step forward towards the dance floor, she felt like the crowd parted for her as she moved. Usually she would have to push and jostle her way into the center, but not tonight. As the music took hold of her, she swayed her hips, then moved her shoulders. Eventually it spread to her neck and arms and legs. The warmth of the martini tickled her stomach and her thoughts began to drift to the sound.

“Good riddance Chaz,” she thought. At least was safe now from being awkwardly fondled by the horny creep for the remainder of the evening.

She stopped worrying about her next performance. In fact she felt like she did some of her best ballet after a night of partying. One last night in the U.S., one last night of fun. She was going to use her temporary freedom to its fullest. And she did.

She danced in the center of the crowd, bodies moving around her like waves. She felt like liquid, a water molecule in a river, swirling with the rest of the club in harmony towards the ocean.

Ilyana felt a pair of eyes watching her. Looking up toward the transepts, the haughty VIP Area, and saw a tall man watching her while leaning on the railing. His eyes stood out from the rest of him, they seemed to reflect the light of the club, like a cat's at night. The man's glare gave her an uneasy feeling deep in the pit of her stomach. For a moment, she heard a voice in her head telling her to run.

She pushed it out of her mind, she was just being paranoid.

Someone bumped into her. Ilyana was startled, but could not tell which of the countless moving bodies had knocked into her. It had only been a moment she had looked away, but when she looked back towards the transept, the man was gone.

She caught sight of the bartender Harper. He was serving some cocktails to a group of girls lounging nearby. By the attention and care he was giving them, they must be regulars or influencers of some sort.

"Is that all, ladies?" Harper asked them.

All the girls seemed to look towards the girl at the center for affirmation, a beautiful blonde with blue eyes.

"That's all for now, Harpy," the blonde said with a smile. Her voice carried an air of authority.

The girls returned to chatting amongst one another as Harper noticed Ilyana approaching him and walked to meet her.

"Enjoying yourself?" Harper asked her, smiling.

"Extremely," Ilyana said, returning the smile.

She leaned to her side to see around Harper and look to the lounging girls who were busy clucking like a hen house behind him.

"Harpy?" Ilyana asked playfully.

Harper sighed.

"Friends of the owner," he said. "Unfortunately, they requested I wait on them personally."

Ilyana giggled.

"I don't know, I kind of like it," Ilyana said.

"Like what?" Harper asked with one eyebrow raised.

"Harpy," Ilyana said with an innocent tone.

Harper groaned.

Her mind and body felt truly free for the first time in her life. The oppression of her home country, and expectations of her ballet company, none mattered anymore within the walls of the club. She felt free enough to take a chance.

She reached forward and picked up the martini glass that was on the tray Harper was holding.

"For me?" she asked playfully.

"I screwed up the order," he replied. "Brought them an extra martini by mistake."

He winked very deliberately.

"Doesn't sound so unlucky for me," Ilyana said with a smile as she sipped the drink.

"How about a dance?" she asked, tugging at his free arm.

"I can't," Harper replied. "I'm working."

"Well when do you get off then?" Ilyana replied.

"Not for another couple hours," he said with a smile.

"Come find me when you do?" she asked seductively.

"Without a doubt," Harper replied with a flirtatious tone.

"You'll know where you can find me," she said as she walked back towards the hoard of people on the dance floor.

"I do," said Harper. He grinned.

Some time had passed, she wasn't sure how long. She was happy getting lost in the music. No one seemed to bother her here, no men clumsily bumping into her trying to cop a feel or unwelcome grinding as they passed.

Until suddenly, she felt a presence behind her on the dance floor.

She turned to see standing in front of her, the tall man who had been watching her from the VIP area.

"Hello," he said, his voice deep and soothing.

He was dressed in an elegant black suit, short hair, and face clean shaven. A single diamond stud in his ear sparkled in the light from the DJ booth, but so did his eyes. Two dark coals in the dim light of the club, barely visible except for the bright reflections that danced in them.

It was how broad his shoulders were that gave him an ominous presence at first, sleeves hiding a musculature that could rival an Olympic weightlifter. He looked strong enough to pick her up and throw her twenty yards in the blink of an eye.

From the balcony, he had been foreboding, but in close proximity, she suddenly couldn't bear to move away from him.

He held out a hand to her.

"May I dance with you?" he asked.

Though the club was loud, his voice was as clear to her as if they were conversing in a quiet meadow.

She struggled to find an answer. She wanted to wait for Harper, to dance with him, maybe even sleep with him. This stranger, this tall, dark, and extremely handsome man; something about him, she just couldn't resist.

"Yes," she finally managed to say in a soft voice.

Reaching out, she took his hand.

Immediately, energy began to flow between them. Ilyana felt it right away. A connection, primordial, their essences now brought together by a light speed super highway between their fingertips. She felt the warmth spread all over, like the first sip of coffee on a cold winter morning.

As he brought her closer to him, she felt heat radiating off of him. Her other hand grasped his shoulder, his jacket was cool to the touch. But the heat hit her whole body in waves as he led them in a soft sway to the beat.

Thoughts of Harper evaporated from her mind, replaced by this mysterious man. She felt intoxicated by him, she breathed in his scent, pushed her body closer to his, and began to feel new sensations flowing across her skin.

"I'm Ilyana," she whispered into his ear.

"Cam," he replied.

"Do you come here often?" she asked, his strong hands exploring her hips.

"Sometimes," he said with a short laugh. "When I'm in the mood."

"What mood is that?" she asked.

He paused for a moment before getting close to her ear.

"Hungry," he said softly.

She felt a jolt of electricity run through her entire body. They swayed close to one another and with each movement, the feeling only intensified.

It was almost too much, she suddenly stood up straight and shuddered.

"Are you OK?" he asked softly.

"Yes," she said out of breath. "Yes, everything is fine."

She didn't want to admit to the mysterious man that she just had an orgasm on the dance floor with him, without any kind of direct stimulation.

She took a deep breath and tried to regain her composure.

"So..." She searched for the right thing to say. "What are you looking for?"

His breath was hot on her shoulder as she moved in close to him again.

"Well I was looking for something to slowly enjoy and savor," he replied.

"Savor?" she said with a high pitch. "I'm afraid there's no time for that, I leave tomorrow night."

"Is that so?" Cam said with a wide grin.

The wave of ecstasy hadn't diminished since her orgasm, and she felt nothing but sexual hormones running through her veins. She wanted him, wanted him bad.

"You know you don't have to savor every meal," Ilyana said with her mind focussed on one thing only. "Sometimes, if you know you can't keep it, it's best to just enjoy it fast."

"If you say so," Cam replied, his eyes reflecting the club's light brighter than ever.

He pulled her forcefully closer to himself and continued their dance. She was lost in time again. It could have been minutes, hours, or even days. She wouldn't know, nothing else mattered.

Every few minutes, the tinglings in her body would build again and she would climax once more. Her body was starting to weaken with each one.

She felt her joints begin to swell and ache, yet she continued to dance. Her heart raced at an uneven pace, yet she continued to dance. Her breaths became short and more labored, yet she continued to dance. She was unwilling to let go of the blissful moment.

The song ended, the club went quiet for a moment and the lights went dark. She broke away from Cam for a moment, hoping to catch her breath as the last orgasm had made her feel a bit disoriented.

Ilyana felt something change. She no longer felt warm and at ease; those feelings were replaced by exhaustion and soreness. She felt more tired now than she had ever felt after any of her ballet performances or marathon rehearsals.

She turned to look for Cam, but his tall towering frame had disappeared into the crowd. Just the faceless body people around her all dancing to a new song the DJ started to play. The song didn't sound familiar, in fact she had a hard time hearing it at all. Her hearing felt muffled, like trying to listen to someone talk underwater.

Maybe she needed to take a break. She'd go to one of the lounge areas for a few minutes and collect herself.

Cam must have gone to get them fresh drinks, right?

She took a step forward, and found herself unsteady. Taking another step, she barely caught herself in time to avoid falling. What was going on with her? Why was she having trouble walking?

She stumbled and bumped into another couple dancing nearby by mistake.

"I'm, I'm sorry," she managed to croak from her throat that suddenly felt hoarse.

"Ew, gross," the man said, looking at her with a face of disgust as he pulled away.

"Tim!" said the woman as they both stopped. "Can't you see she needs help?"

Ilyana was speechless and confused.

"This way, ma'am," said the woman, taking Ilyana's hand and leading her off the dance floor.

"Th...Tha...Thank you," Ilyana said, not sure what was going on but finding it hard to speak.

In the distance, she could kind of see Cam talking to two other large muscular men and pointing at her.

He was getting her a drink after all, though she wasn't sure she should drink anymore if she was already stumbling around.

"These gentlemen here will help you," said the kind woman as the two men approached.

"Sorry about this, madam," said one of the men. "Vagrants sometimes sneak-in off the street."

Vagrants? Ilyana thought to herself alarmed. She was no vagrant.

"B...B..." she sputtered but was unable to find the word.

"Please make sure she gets the help she needs," said the woman. The two men held Ilyana's arms and led her toward the front door of the club.

"Don't worry, we will," replied the other doorman.

The lights swirled around Ilyana, the world seemed to swim in circles around her. A familiar face in front of her, Harper was standing by the door waiting for them. Then, she felt relief.

"Har, Har, Har," Ilyana tried to sputter to get his attention.

"It's OK, gents," Harper said, holding up a hand. "I can take her from here."

Neither bouncer hesitated, and much to Ilyana's relief, she found their large brutish grips on her waist replaced by the soft and gentle grip of Harper's. He helped her up and led her towards the double doors and the mirror lined hallway.

"Where's Cam?" Ilyana managed to form into words and ask.

"It's all going to be OK now," said Harper, smiling at her. "Not much longer now."

They went through the double doors, her eyes having trouble adjusting to the dim, mirror-lined corridor that led to the club exit.

Harper was going to take care of her, call her a ride so she could get back to the hotel. She was so tired, so exhausted. Crawling into her warm bed back at the hotel was all she could think about to comfort herself.

Her comfort was replaced by alarm, as Harper stopped halfway down the corridor. The illuminated "Exit" sign glowed above her, confused as to why they stopped.

Harper began to fiddle with a mirror on the wall. He was looking for something around the frame of a large floor to ceiling length mirror.

"What, what, what are you doing?" she asked, somehow completely out of breath.

"Shhh," Harper responded as he continued to feel around the frame. "Soon."

Ilyana looked around, she could make out the intricate details of the mirror frame, the gold engravings. Looking into the reflective surface, she could see Harper's handsome reflection in the mirror. His smile was gone, replaced by one might have as he or she concentrates on a complicated situation.

He was holding up someone, but it wasn't Ilyana she saw. It was an old woman, skinny and frail. Her hair brittle and gray, she was even wearing Ilyana's silver silk dress which hung loosely from her bony skeletal frame. One of the old woman's breasts hung out from the loose fitting dress, it was lumpy and misshapen. Who was he holding?

Ilyana looked down, and she saw her body for the first time since leaving the dance floor. Her skin was no longer soft and smooth, it was wrinkled and blotchy. It hung loosely from her bones, the strong muscles in her legs and arms seemed to have diminished. Looking back into the mirror, she saw a familiar face in the old woman looking back at her. Her own, except her eyes sunken in, her nose crooked, and several teeth missing.

No, this wasn't her. It was an illusion, a trick of the mirror. Or maybe she had taken some drug that caused her to hallucinate. This wasn't real, it was all in her head. It had to be.

"Got it," Harper said with relief.

Harper took a step back as the mirror swung open and revealed a pitch black opening in the wall.

"He...He....Help me," Ilyana managed to say. Every word was difficult for her to conjure up in her head, difficult to grasp and bring forward to her lips.

Harper smiled at her.

"It'll all be over soon," he said. His eyes delivered a sliver of hope, false hope.

Harper shoved her forward.

She fell towards the dark opening. She tried to resist, tried to get a footing, but she was too weak. Her fingers grasped wildly until they managed to grip the edge of the crevice and stop her at the last moment.

Ilyana hung over the cusp of the darkness, trying to find the breath and energy to scream out but finding only gasps of hoarse breath.

"I'm sorry, love," Harper said one last time.

He pushed her again and this time her fingers failed.

Ilyana felt her body fall, the darkness engulfing her. Her body felt nothing but cold air as she dropped. That chilly air was the last thing she would ever feel.

"Bernice, dear," said Professor Mikkelson. "Please collect the quizzes."

A collective groan emanated from the classroom as the scratching of pen to paper suddenly became pronounced and frantic.

Bernice wished the professor would call her by her preferred name, Bea. However, as he had explained when she had been assigned to him as his teaching assistant, he was an old man and he followed the old ways of referring to women by their proper name. At least it was only in class.

Bea walked the aisles collecting the quiz papers from the undergraduate students; she could feel their eyes on her as she strolled amongst them. It made her nervous.

They must really hate you. Since childhood, Bea's innervoice had been an unwanted companion that embodied all of her anxieties and insecurities bundled into one ever-present commentator. When she had escaped her small hometown to go to college, it had bombarded her with reminders of her failure as a daughter to honor her parents' wishes. When she was applying to her Masters, it was whispering paralytic poisons into her ear questioning why she should even bother applying to something she was clearly unqualified for.

Today it reminded her that the teacher's assistant was the most despised member of the classroom. The only question was whether they disliked just because she was the T.A. or because she was ugly and unkempt.

Bea kept her long black hair crimped in a ponytail so she wouldn't have to constantly push the hair out of her eyes. She wore thick glasses that covered her dark brown eyes, much more convenient than having to put in and take out contacts every day. She had on a thick sweater, trying to avoid wearing anything that could be perceived by Mikkelson as inappropriate. The Professor hadn't updated his own standards of female modesty since the 1950s.

She knew deep down it wasn't because of Mikkelson, she wore the same drab and boring outfits everyday. An old habit from growing up in the conservative household of a church deacon.

Having not been allowed to wear makeup at all in high school by her conservative parents, she had long ago resigned herself to being the boring smart girl in class.

Dropping the thick stack of papers onto the desk next to the professor, she did her best to push her anxiety from her mind. Who cared what they thought, right?

But Bea secretly knew. A small part of her knew. A voice somewhere in the back of consciousness was screaming.

I do, I care!

She ignored it and began to pack up the quizzes into a manila folder and handed them to the professor.

She had been lucky to be placed with Professor Mikkelson. He was one of the most prestigious and tenured Professors of History at the university. His resume of published work was truly extraordinary; more than thirty textbooks, over a hundred articles in scholarly periodicals, and countless citations referencing him in graduate student theses across the globe. He would, no doubt, be a vital resource to use as she began writing her own thesis over the next few months.

The downside though, was that he had a reputation of being difficult to work with at times and quite demanding to boot. A relentless perfectionist, every detail was scrutinized, every mistake accounted for. Bea knew she was going to be in for quite a long, but critical semester.

Professor Mikkelson tried to stand up shakily. She rushed to assist him, he held her off with a raised hand.

"Class," he began to speak after what seemed like a colossal effort to stand up straight and proper.

"As you all hopefully know by this point in your lives, knowledge is power. The great historian Henry Steele Commager said, 'History is a jangle of accidents, blunders, surprises and absurdities, and so is our knowledge of it, but if we are to report it at all we must impose some order upon it.' That is what we are doing here, learning the order of our past so that we are not doomed to repeat it. I wish you all the best this semester, class dismissed."

The students shuffled out of the class.

"My dear," said Professor Mikkelson, sitting back down in his chair and breathing heavily. Bea imagined a cloud of old dust billowing out from beneath him as his musty old plaid pants hit the leather bound seat.

"Would you mind grading the quizzes tonight?" he asked, sliding the folder towards Bea.

Bernice held back a groan. She had her own homework to do and she knew Mikkelson would expect the quizzes to be graded completely by the next day.

"Absolutely, professor," she said with her best feigned smile. She watched nervously as Mikkelson began to pack his things into an old faded leather book bag.

"I was wondering, sir," she began. "Could I talk to you for a few minutes about an idea I had for my thesis?"

Mikkelson looked up at her, peering at her through the glasses that hung on the end of his crooked nose. He paused, just staring at her.

"I suppose that would be alright," he said at last, ceasing packing and leaning back in his chair. He placed his interwoven fingers over his stomach.

"Proceed," he added.

"So I was thinking," she said. "A study of the Middle Ages, the impact of the Catholic Church on Feudal Soc..."

"It's been done," Mikkelson replied. "Braun in '87. Do something else."

"Um, ok," she stammered. "Changes to the structure of the Catholic church during the Crusades."

"I really thought you would be more imaginative than this," he replied. He began to shuffle his notes back into his book bag. He stood and began to make his way towards the door at his hunched over, tortoise-like pace.

"Sorry, um," she struggled to think of something else.

She started to panic.

"The Black Death..." she blurted out, grasping for anything she could think of that hadn't already been done by a thousand other grad students.

"And...its..." she was frantically searching for anything that would get his approval. "Its effect on demonic worship."

She immediately regretted it.

It was a silly idea, a stupid idea. Society in the Middle Ages was so strictly managed by the Church, there wasn't any room for actual demonic worship. How would she find anything to write about?

She felt like crying, was she this idiotic?

She was surprised though to see Mikkelson had stopped at the door, his hand grasping the doorknob.

"Yes..." he muttered to himself. "Yes, that could be it."

He turned to Bea.

"Not a lot written on the subject you know," he said, staring into the distance behind Bea and stroking the sparse white hairs that adorned his chin. "It would be difficult, very difficult to find the research materials."

Bea's panic did not dissipate. What did she just get herself into?

"But it would be worthwhile," he added. "Most graduate students these days pick the same old topics, the same subjects hashed and re-hashed by countless other students. This subject, though, no one's written about it in a long time."

"How long?" Bea found herself asking instinctively.

"Start with Christenson, 1874," Mikkelson began speaking excitedly as he paced. "It will give you the basis for where you go from there. Then perhaps, Geoffrey of Monmouth to cover the Isles, William of Malmesbury for the secular point of view. But the French, you'll have to look into Baudri of Bourgueil. He may have written something regarding the subject as well. Dear, shouldn't you be writing this down?"

Bea had been standing at attention and now quickly grabbed a nearby notepad and began scribbling names as best she could remember.

Professor Mikkelson continued for several more minutes, spilling out names and works of Middle Age history at a feverish pace. Bea wrote down each one, hoping Google would correct any spelling mistakes.

Out of breath but with excitement in his eyes, Mikkelson picked up his book bag again.

"Very good, dear Bernice," he said, walking back toward the door. "Very good. Perhaps we will make a true historian of you." And with the speed of a much younger man, he was out the door and down the hall while Bea continued scribbling down the last few names he had fired off to her.

Looking at her notepad, panic and dread returned to her thoughts. There must have been three dozen authors and books on the notepad, some of which she had heard, and knew as long, difficult original histories. The ones she did not recognize scared her more.

Demonic Worship? The Black Death? Her focus and background thus far had been on Christianity and the church. It was what she knew best. She would be starting a new world of study for her thesis, and none of her prior knowledge or research would be applicable to it.

She always did this when she panicked, trying to appease whomever was pushing her. Whether it had been her father, her mother, her few friends back in school.

Bea packed up her bag and slung the strap over her shoulder. It was heavy, weighed down by the thick stack of quiz papers that she would be up all night grading in her dorm room. This day couldn't get any worse.

Arriving at her dorm, she realized that she had been very, very wrong.

The first thing to greet her was the flashing lights of two fire trucks, the red and orange flashes bouncing off the brick walls of the building. The large crowd of dorm residents gathered outside, staring at the building.

"What happened?" she asked, joining the crowd.

She didn't need to hear the answer.

From the front door of the building, the main entrance, a flood of water was pouring out like a river. It ran over the sidewalk, into the grass, and then emptied into the storm drains on the street.

"Water main on the top floor burst this morning," said the onlooker next to her whom she did not recognize. "Started while everyone was at class, by the time they turned off the water, the whole building had been virtually flooded."

Bea didn't know how to respond, she just looked on in disbelief as firemen laden with large yellow boots walked in and out of the building. High stepping above the current of water when they could.

"Excuse me," said a woman's voice yelling above the crowd. "Can I have your attention please?"

She was standing in the front of the large group and wore a pink pantsuit that looked out of place among the t-shirts and faded jeans of the congregation of grad students.

"My name is Heather O'Connell and I'm from the university housing department," she began. "Unfortunately, due to the water damage from the main line break, we are going to be closing this dorm for several weeks to repair the damage."

The crowd burst into a flurry of whispers and commentary that slowly grew to a roar.

"Please calm down," said the administrator, sweeping her hands up and down. The murmur of the crowd softened.

"Now," she continued. "In a few minutes you'll all be allowed to go up with the fireman floor by floor in order to retrieve any necessary personal items from your rooms. We have arranged temporary housing for you in the undergrad dorms."

The undergrad dorms? Bea could not believe what she was hearing. The undergrad dorms were notorious for how loud and chaotic they were, hardly the place to live while trying to write a complicated thesis. This was a nightmare.

"We are going to start with Floor 17," said Ms. O'Connell.

Several onlookers stepped forward and were ushered to the firemen waiting to lead them up.

Bea began looking through her phone frantically, was there anyone she knew who would let her stay with them until she could find another home?

Friends, what friends? The little voice in the back of head mocked her.

Bea knew it to be true, she hadn't made any friends since moving to the university for grad school. She had picked the graduate dorms because they were single-resident living only, no pesky roommates to distract her. She had avoided the various social events organized by the resident assistant, preferring to hide away and study or read. She had even picked this university in part because it would be somewhere no one else would bother her, no distractions; she could focus on her studies.

She put her phone back in her pocket and watched as the first group of residents emerged from the front door. They carried large garbage bags full of belongings, some were crying.

"Floor 16, you're up!" said Ms. O'Connell.

Bea stepped forward and did her best to avoid the puddles that had formed on the walkway up to the building, and she followed the fireman up the stairwell to her room.

❦

After several hours of waiting, Ms. O'Connell had rounded up Bea and the rest of the students and was escorting them to the area of the campus where the undergraduate dormitories were clustered. She felt with each step that the area around her got noisier and noisier. A group of three students skateboarded past them quickly, nearly knocking into Ms. O'Connell.

"Slow down!" the administrator yelled at them.

They either didn't hear her or just ignored her.

This area of campus was busy to say the least. There were at least half a dozen dorm buildings, all arranged in neat concrete rows down a main drag that led to the center of campus; each building contained what seemed like hundreds of residents. Despite it being nearly 8:00pm, a traffic jam of cars lined the entire length of the street. Some honked at no one, anyone, just waiting for the endless wave of pedestrians to clear the road so they could continue on their route.

Bea's head was already swimming in a panic.

At least the dorm buildings themselves seemed nice. They were modern, with thick concrete walls and double-paned windows. She took some deep breaths. Maybe this wouldn't be that bad.

Except they kept walking, drifting past the nice new dormitories. With every few yards the dorms grew older and more decrepit. They stopped and Ms. O'Connell ushered them into a dormitory that looked like it could have been a condemned building.

The paint on the walls of the lobby had long peeled off, the elevator had an "Out of Order" sign hanging from metal doors, half the mail slots were hanging open, no longer able to latch closed.

"You students are in luck," Ms. O'Connell announced to the crowd. "We had planned on tearing this dorm down last year and building a new one, but we ended up delaying it until next summer. As a result, it's only at half capacity this year and you'll be able to finish the semester here."

"When was this place built?" asked one of the other grad students.

"Sometime around when they founded the university," Ms. O'Connell responded with a smile.

A cockroach scurried across the floor behind her.

Bea was in shock, she didn't know what to say or do except follow Ms. O'Connell up the cold concrete stairs. In groups of two, Ms. O'Connell placed the grad students into various rooms and paired them up with roommates. Each new room somehow made the previous one look like paradise.

At last it was just the two of them, the other students already placed into their respective temporary homes.

"Bernice Logan, correct?" Asked Ms O'Connell aloud, reading from a clipboard.

Bea nodded.

"Well, dear," Ms. O'Connell continued, putting a hand on Bea's shoulder. "I have some unfortunate news for you."

They walked down dark and musty corridors, some of which had graffiti on the walls.

"When we re-assigned everyone's rooms," Ms. O'Connell said carefully stepping over a couple day old pizza box laying on the ground. "We had one extra with no single room left for them."

Here it comes, said the voice in Bea's head with an ominous tone.

"We picked at random," Ms. O'Connell said with sympathetic eyes. "And your name was picked for the one who would have to be assigned a roommate..."

Bea used every bit of self control she had to avoid screaming.

When you thought it couldn't get any worse...

Bea breathed deeply, she didn't have a choice. She had to make this work. She had to rationalize her way through it.

Who cares where I sleep, I'll be spending most nights at the library anyway?

She did her best to look at the bright side of things.

They turned a corner and were immediately blasted by loud screaming. After a moment, Bea realized it wasn't screaming. It was music.

Death metal music, maybe someone had left their door open and had their music on too loud. But this was the end of the hall, and there was only one door. And it was closed.

The music which had hit them was coming from speakers inside the room, and since it was the only room left on the floor...

Ms. O'Connell knocked on the door loudly, after a minute there was still no response. She knocked louder, the door reverberating in its frame with each strike.

They both heard from the other side of the door, voices talking frantically.

The music turned down to a dull roar and the door opened.

On the other side of the threshold, stood a skinny pale girl with black and purple hair; wearing nothing but skimpy black lingerie. Her lips were covered in jet black lipstick and she had piercings on both eyebrows and her nose. Two shirtless men were behind her in the room, quickly zipping up their jeans.

"What is it?" the girl said to Ms. O'Connell. "The RA said she didn't care how loud my music was. There's no one else nearby."

"Yes, um, hello," Ms. O'Connell said with a smile. "Things have changed actually. I'm Ms. O'Connell from the University Housing Administration. One of the other dorms has been closed due to a water leak and..."

"Thanks for letting me know..." the dark-haired girl said before closing the door in their faces.

Ms. O'Connell cleared her throat and knocked on the door again.

It opened quickly and aggressively, the lingerie-clad female staring at Bea and Ms. O'Connell with a displeased look.

"Yes?" she said annoyed.

"As a result," Ms. O'Connell continued. "We are placing Bernice here as your new roommate."

"You got to be fucking kidding me," said the girl, not making the slightest effort to hide her displeasure.

"You can call me Bea," Bea said, reaching out a hand.

Her new roommate just stared at her.

"I'm Tess," the lingerie-clad woman said. "These are... I don't remember." She waved a hand at the two nervous men behind her who were now rushing to put on shirts.

Bea peaked around Tess nervously.

"We'll give you three minutes to tidy up," Ms. O'Connell said with a smile.

It wasn't until Tessa had closed the door that Ms. O'Connell turned to Bea.

"I am so sorry, Bernice," the woman said, putting her hands on Bea's shoulders with a sincere expression of concern. "There's nowhere else for you, I know this isn't ideal."

"Thank you," Bea said feebly, still in shock. "Please call me Bea, everyone does."

"Bea, you got it," Ms. O'Connell said nervously looking at her watch. "I'm sorry, I have to get back to the office to process all this paperwork."

Bea smiled at her as the woman handed her the key.

"Thank you," she muttered and the administrator walked away and turned the corner down the hall.

Bea turned toward the door, put the key into the lock, and walked into her new home.

After two weeks of being Tess's roommate, Bea was at her wit's end. She had barely slept, she had missed several deadlines from Professor Mikkelson. She hadn't worked on her thesis paper in the slightest. At this rate, she wasn't going to pass her classes this semester.

Tess listened to heavy metal music day and night, even when she slept, it played in the background like a grotesque gothic rock soundtrack to every waking moment of her life. Even worse, Tess seemed to have a different guy over every day. Bea would return from a full day of classes, just wishing to change before heading to the library to study, only to find a sock on the doorknob warning her to not enter. She'd wait patiently outside the door for the music to eventually die down and a rather exhausted looking male to emerge from the room and stagger down the hall.

Tess also had a strange habit of watching porn for fun. Bea would be reading or trying to sleep, and Tess would be on her laptop watching porn eating a bowl of popcorn or a bag of Twizzlers.

Bea felt like she couldn't catch a break, *should she just drop out now and cut her losses?* Maybe she could claim a medical emergency and go on a leave until she could find somewhere new to live. She debated endlessly with the voice in her head, but every time she couldn't find a solution that didn't involve losing her scholarship and her one chance at a graduate degree.

She just couldn't catch a break.

Or at least, so she thought.

After returning home early to try and sleep while Tess went out to dinner, Bea found the sock on the doorknob of the room once again. Loud screams and moans from the other side of the door told her that it was going to be a long one tonight. Bea decided if she couldn't sleep, she might as well be studying and so she headed towards the library.

Deciding it was now or never to start researching her thesis, she checked out "Demonic Mythology" by Christenson. The book was a reprint of the original manuscript; despite that being the case, the binding was still considerably old and decrepit. It was so dusty, Bea imagined that no one had opened it to read it in over a decade. She blew the dust off with a heavy breath and watched as the cloud settled on the library table.

Reading the first few chapters, she regretted her topic already. The author had written in a style that required careful focus and sophistication to decipher. Each paragraph took work to fully comprehend, and focus was in short supply for Bea who was running on very little sleep already.

It wasn't long before she caught herself nodding off, she took several deep breaths trying to wake up her mind and body. She must have been asleep for at least fifteen minutes when she woke up startled.

"Bea, is that you?" said a familiar voice.

Bea's eyesight without glasses was horrible and she struggled to see who it was that had woken her as she fumbled on the table for her spectacles.

A soft hand handed her something, her glasses, and Bea put them on quickly.

She was relieved to find the smiling face of Ms. O'Connell looking at her from across the table.

"Hello Ms. O'Connell," Bea said excitedly, sitting straight up.

"Please, call me Heather," the woman replied.

"Heather, yes," Bea said, putting her thoughts back in order. "Sorry, fell asleep. Working late again."

"My dear," replied Heather. "It's only seven pm."

Bea glanced down at her phone and indeed saw it was only a few minutes after seven.

"Right, I...um..." Bea struggled to find words. "I haven't been able to get much sleep lately and Tess has a friend over right now..."

Her words trailed off.

"I see," said the administrator sitting down next to Bea at the table.

“How are repairs at my old dorm going?” Bea asked, hoping and praying for good news. “Do you think we’ll be able to move back in sometime soon?”

"Um, about that," Ms. O’Connell paused with a regretful look. "Things aren’t going according to plan. They found some very old mold in the walls, it's been there for years actually. Surprised no one was feeling sick already. The city inspector is having us check the entire building and replace almost all the drywall."

“How long will that take?” Bea asked, holding back her own disappointment at hearing the news. “A few more weeks?”

⸙

Ms. O'Connell smiled, swallowed hard, then proceeded.

"I'm afraid we won't be able to reopen the dorm until next semester," she said.

Bea's heart dropped in her chest.

"I'm really sorry, Bea," Ms. O'Connell added. "It's just there's nowhere else to put you. We have new students transferring in every day and I don't even have places for them."

"I know," Bea said with her best attempt at smiling despite the feeling of helplessness in the pit of her stomach. "I know you are trying. I'm fine, I really am."

"What are you working on?" Heather said, looking at the old book on the table.

"Um, my thesis," Bea replied.

"Great, how far along are you?" Heather asked with concern.

Bea looked down at the book and then gestured to the notepad next to it with pages of scribbled notes. She shrugged.

"Oh dear," Heather said standing up. "That's not very far along at all."

"I know," Bea said as tears formed in her eyes. "It's just with my homework and the demands from Professor Mikkelson; and then Tess's music and boyfriends. I don't feel I've actually slept in weeks. I don't know what I'm going to do."

Heather put her hand on Bea's shoulder trying to comfort her as the tears poured from the poor girl's eyes, dripping onto the table mixing with the dust from the book and creating little brown streams and brooks that flowed toward the table's edge.

"I'm so sorry, my dear," Ms. O'Connell said, rubbing her shoulder. "I wish there was something I could do..."

Her voice trailed off and she stopped to think.

"Actually," the older woman said, fishing into her purse and pulling out her cell phone. "I do know someone looking for a roommate. It's off campus, but it should be comfortable and quiet."

"I don't think the scholarship fund pays for off campus housing," replied Bea wiping tears from her eyes.

"Don't worry about that," Ms. O'Connell replied. "I'll work it out with them, it is extenuating circumstances after all."

Heather picked up Bea's pen and began writing in beautiful cursive a phone number and address.

"Here, it's a friend of mine's daughter," Ms. O'Connell said, tearing the paper and handing it to Bea. "You'll have to interview with them of course before you'd be accepted, but it's a beautiful house just off campus."

"Would it be quiet, you think?" Bea asked as the tears started to dry.

"Absolutely," replied Heather. "Not even a mouse there to disturb you."

“I don't know what to say," said Bea, smiling. "I thought, I thought I was cursed or something. Thank you."

"It's the least I can do," Heather replied, smiling. "You still have to interview, but if I know the girl, you'd be right up her alley as a roommate."

They hugged and Heather departed.

Bea stared down in disbelief at the note with the phone number and address. Above the phone number, Ms. O'Connell had written.

Call Mallory

Chapter Three

Bea walked through the neighborhood toward the address that the housing administrator had given her. Google Maps on her phone had informed her it was only a 15 minute walk from campus, something quite manageable. She was a bit alarmed at first. The neighborhood she had passed through this far was a bit run down. However, as she turned a corner she was greeted by a beautiful gated community hidden away down a side street.

Approaching the gate, a security guard emerged from the guard post to greet her.

"Sorry hun," said the overweight and aged black man. "No solicitors allowed."

"Umm, I'm not a solicitor," Bernice muttered.

"No door-to-door volunteers either," he continued as he stood tall between her and the community call box. "We get our fair share of campus clubs looking for donations here and let me tell you, you're barking up the wrong tree with these people."

"Actually, I have an appointment," Bea said with uncertainty. "With Mallory Phillips."

"Oh, she did call ahead to let me know you were coming," the guard said with a welcoming grin. "Let me give you a ride."

"I really think I can manage," Bea said.

"Nonsense," the guard said, ushering her to the golf cart parked behind the building. "Ms. Phillips asked me to give you a quick tour beforehand."

"Th..thank you," Bea replied uneasily. She wasn't threatened by the man, but recently the kindness of strangers had been few and far between.

The electric golf cart quietly buzzed to life as they approached the community gate. The large wood and iron security wall began to roll away with a squeal from the motor.

A large ornate sign hung from a stone wall above a beautiful waterfall next to the gate. “Murcielago Square”

The guard must have noticed her examining the sign.

"Sounds fancy, huh?" the guard laughed.

"I guess," replied Bea. "What does it mean?"

"I looked it up," the guard said, still laughing. "It's Spanish for Bat. When Mr. Phillips developed it he must have had quite a laugh convincing others that it was some fancy place with a name like that."

"Mr. Phillips?" Bea questioned. "Is that Mallory's father?"

"Yes, ma’am," the guard said as the cart accelerated forward into the community.

"He built this place a few years ago so his daughter would have a nice place to stay while she was in college. He's a big real estate developer around the whole country. Smart man though, he sold the rest of the houses for millions more than he spent. Somehow found a way to make money off his daughter’s college housing."

Bea was barely listening. Her attention was fixed on the beautiful homes that graced the landscape around her. Large front lawns with circular driveways, Ferraris and Rolls Royces parked in them. The houses were gigantic, sprawling across a space that would have occupied half a dozen homes back where she came from in Pennsylvania. Every house looked to be designed by master architects; natural stone structures, brilliant marble fountains, intricately decorated columns. She felt like she was in a movie.

"Impressive, huh?" the guard commented beside her, as he noticed her gawking. "I can't tell you the names of some of the people who live here, because you'd probably recognize them. They pay a pretty penny for their privacy, that's why you have me and several other guards on staff here. At least one of us is always around, we patrol the neighborhood regularly and we make sure anyone who shouldn't be here isn't able to get in. By the way, I'm Barry."

"Hi Barry," Bea replied instinctively. Still in shock at the beautiful houses surrounding her. "I'm Bernice, but everyone calls me Bea."

"Bea...I like it," said Barry. "Well, here we are, Ms. Bea."

The cart stopped on the street in front of the largest house she had ever seen. Somehow it dwarfed the other houses in the community, making the others seem cozy in comparison. The path to the front door was made of beautiful oversized travertine tiles, a stone paver driveway led to an eight-car garage. The house itself was a beautiful white with tall Corinthian columns framing the front entryway.

Bea took a step out of the golf cart.

"Thank you, Barry," she said with a smile, turning back to the guard.

"No sweat," Barry replied. "Now you head on up, I'm sure she's expecting you. You'll do just fine."

Bea turned red, she didn't realize that even Barry had noticed how nervous she was to be interviewed. She knew she had to get this right, it was her last chance to escape Tess and the dorm from hell.

Bea turned back toward the house.

"Oh, one more thing," Barry called out.

Bea turned back.

"I'm always watching," he said, pointing toward the sky.

Bea looked up, on a streetlamp nearby she saw multiple security cameras that pointed in every direction. This was the case for every lamp that ran along the full length of the drive back to the gate. He clearly had visibility to anything that happened on the street.

Bea nodded.

Barry pulled away slowly, the faint whine of the electric motor powering him back to his post.

Bea continued her walk up to the doors, pausing for a moment at the top of the steps that led to the entrance.

The doors to the house were easily three times her height. They were solid wood with iron hardware. She looked for a doorbell, but did not find a button. She considered knocking, but that likely wasn't going to do much against the thick structure. She decided instead to swing the large iron knockers.

Lifting one up, she didn't realize how heavy they were. It came swinging down with a loud bang that made her jump. She closed her eyes.

Was she already screwing this up? That bang was loud enough to wake the dead.

Would they be annoyed at her for causing such a commotion already?

Her mind didn't have long to simmer on her self-doubt, she heard the sound of locks click and the door slowly swung open.

Bea felt dumbstruck at who she saw on the other side of the threshold. It was a girl, tall and blond. She wore a white sundress and had a bright glow around her where she stood, backlit by a massive skylight in the foyer. This gave her a somewhat angelic appearance. Her azure eyes glistened akin to precious gemstones, her nose possessed flawless symmetry, and her petite mouth exuded perfection. She was simply beautiful.

"Well hello Bernice," the girl said with a smile. Her teeth stood in flawless alignment, as straight and pristine as freshly laundered linen.

"Um...Hi," Bea said, trying her best to smile in return but suddenly feeling self-conscious about her own gangly appearance by comparison.

"I'm Mallory, but everyone calls me Mal," she replied.

They stood there looking at each other for several moments.

"Well, don't just stand there, come on in," Mal said at last, beckoning a dainty hand and opening the door wider. Bea followed, clutching her book bag tightly to her chest.

She took several steps forward over the marble threshold and looked up. Her jaw dropped.

The front room of the house was bright and brilliant. Two large curving staircases bordered the left and right sides. They led to a balcony that overlooked the entryway. An exquisite and intricate crystal chandelier dangled gracefully from the ceiling, diffusing the sunlight pouring through the seemingly endless row of windows, suffusing the room with a radiant luminosity.

"Wow," Bea managed to sputter out.

"I know, right," Mal said, standing next to her. "My father did not spare any expense with this place."

"How many rooms is it?" Bea asked instinctively.

"Twelve...I think," Mal said, pausing for a moment. "Most of the rooms are empty, daddy doesn't allow me to have any friends over."

"It's beautiful," Bea added, turning her attention to the dozens of paintings decorating the walls.

She recognized one of them immediately.

"Is that the Garden of Earthly Delights by Bosch?" Bea muttered rushing forward.

"Maybe, I don't know," Mal replied, walking elegantly forward to join her. "Daddy decorates this place with overflow from his art collection."

"This is amazing," Bea said, looking at the painting closely. "I've only ever seen it in textbooks, it's one of three large triptychs. This recreation is spectacular."

"Recreation?" questioned Mal.

"Well it can't be the original," Bea said, still looking closely at the painting. "It's in a museum in Spain."

Mal smiled, "I'm sure it is. Shall we?"

Mal extended her arm, indicating a grandiose sofa positioned adjacent to a nearby fireplace.

"Please sit," she said as they approached. "Can I get you some water or tea?"

"I'm fine, thank you," Bea said nervously. Not sure if it was polite to accept or not, but sure of herself that whatever choice she made would be the incorrect one.

"Very well," Mal said, sitting across from her.

On the coffee table between them was a laptop, Mal opened it and pointed the camera end towards Bernice who felt nervous immediately.

Mal must have sensed it.

"Don't worry about that," Mal said with a reassuring smile. "Daddy just asked me to record the interview so he could watch it later."

That didn't help to alleviate Bea's stress. The little red light from the camera lens flickered on.

"So Bernice," Mal began sitting on the couch with perfect posture and her hands in her lap. "Let's start with telling us a little bit about yourself."

Bea struggled on where to begin.

"Well, um," she began. "First, I prefer to be called Bea. Everyone calls me that."

"Oh I'm so sorry, I didn't know," Mal replied with an unflinching smile.

Strike one, the voice in Bea's head said. She immediately regretted correcting Mal.

"So let's start over," Mal said, sensing Bea's nervousness.

"Bea," Mal emphasized. "Tell me about yourself, please."

"I grew up in a small town outside of Pittsburgh," Bea said, regaining some level of confidence. "I went to the University of Pittsburgh for my undergrad in history, where I focused my studies on the Catholic church during the Middle and Dark ages."

"So you're a grad student right now?" Mal asked.

"I am also a Teacher's Assistant at the University," Bea answered.

A long pause followed that only amplified Bea's anxiety with each passing second.

"Is that ok?" Bea asked nervously.

Mal didn't stop smiling as she stared at her.

"I'm sure it's fine," Mal replied at last. "It's just... We were looking for someone a little bit on the younger side. We had preferred a freshman or sophomore. Ms. O'Connell didn't mention you were older."

Strike 2, the voice in Bea's head said.

"What do you do for fun then?" Mal said after another awkward silence.

"Um..." Bea struggled to think of an answer. "Honestly, I don't do much. I spend most of my spare time working on my thesis."

"Oh come on, you must do something for fun," insisted Mal.

"Well...I guess, I...um..." Bea couldn't think of anything good to say.

Make something up, her inside voice screamed at her.

"I guess I like to drink wine?" Bea's words carried a tone of inquiry.

"Who doesn't, girlfriend?" Mal said slyly back to her. "White or red?"

"Red, I guess," Bea replied. Uncertain whether Mal would grasp that her idea of enjoying wine involved a $3 bottle from the liquor store, intended to ease her nerves before a night of studying.

"Oh yes," Mal said, sounding delighted. "I could go for a glass of Silver Oak right now myself. We've got a couple cases in the wine cellar, but don't you get excited now. We only open those on special occasions."

Bea forced her best smile.

"I understand," she said and held out hope that Mal wouldn't ask her any more questions about expensive wines.

"What about your family?" Mal asked. "What are they like?"

Bea thought for a moment.

"Well, I'm an only child," she began. "My mother didn't work, but my father was the deacon at the local parish."

"Deacon, you say?" Mal said as her eyes seemed to light up. "That's interesting."

"He's really devoted to the church," Bea commented. "I grew up going to church several times a week with him and my mother. You could say I had a very religious upbringing."

Mal's perfect smile faded. She seemed to be nervously glancing at the laptop every few moments, unsure of how to proceed.

And that's Strike 3, you're out of here, the voice inside her head shouted with the resounding authority of a baseball umpire's call.

After another painfully long awkward silence, Mal glanced at the laptop and then her regular smile returned.

"Well, I hope it doesn't bother you," she said reassuringly. "But I don't think I've ever stepped foot in a church before to be honest."

"Oh no," Bea blurted out. "It doesn't bother me at all. In fact I'm not really close with my family anymore, nor the church for that matter."

"Oh dear, I'm so sorry," Mal said, putting her hand over her chest. "Do you mind me asking, what happened?"

Bea struggled to explain it.

"Well, they didn't really agree with me going to college," she began. "They, um, kind of hoped I'd stay home and, you know, maybe start a family. They didn't really believe that, like, going to school and getting a degree would, um, lead to anything good, I guess."

"Well that's not very supportive now is it?" Mal commented.

"No, my dad keeps asking me when I'm going to give up on this place and come home," Bea responded. "But this is what I want to do, so I'm going to go do it."

"I like that," Mal said with a large smile. "You go, girl."

Bea smiled back at her.

"Ok," Mal continued. "Looks like I don't have any more questions for you. So, what questions do you have for me?"

"Well, I mean..." Bea began as her curiosity began to get the better of her. "This place, it's amazing. In fact, amazing may not be a worthy word to describe it. Why would you be looking for a roommate? You certainly don't need the money."

"I know," Mal replied. "Daddy thinks it's best if I have someone around to share this big old house with. A partner in crime so to speak."

Bea wasn't entirely certain about what that implied. If Mal was hoping for a companion to share activities with, Bea felt a bit out of place. She pondered her response: Should she speak up? Should she explain her plan to stay in the room for studying and only come out for classes and meals?

The fear of going back to the dorms seized her. The thought of attempting to study amidst the backdrop of pornography, the constant uncertainty of her room's availability with a sock on the door, and enduring another exhausted night while the cacophony of screaming metal music persisted weighed heavily on her. She couldn't do that, she needed this place. Her entire graduate study career depended on it.

She smiled.

"I'm sure I'd be good at that," she said, kicking herself for lying.

"Excellent!" Mal said excitedly. "Well, I think this is going to work out."

What did she just say? The small voice within Bea's mind whispered hesitantly.

"Really?" Bea blurted out in her own disbelief.

"Absolutely," Mal said with a beautiful smile. "In fact, I think this is going to work out swimmingly for us both. Can you move in tonight?"

"Um..." Bea's thoughts raced frantically through her mind. "Yeah, I can. The sooner the better."

"Splendid," Mal said standing. "Follow me, I'll show you your room."

"Should I call Ms. O'Connell to finalize the arrangements?" Bea asked, sure that the administrator would need to pull some strings with her scholarship program to transfer the money from the University to Mal's father.

"No need," Mal replied, taking Bea by the hand and assisting her to her feet. "My father has people who will take care of all that for us."

Mal's hand felt soft in Bea's, so soft that Bea suddenly felt self conscious over her own neglect to properly moisturize.

"This is going to be fun," Mal said, turning back to her as she led her toward the closest of the magnificent stairwells.

Bea felt like crying when she saw her room. It was the first one on the left at the top of the stairs. The room was embellished with elegant silver and soft baby blue curtains adorning the windows, allowing a flood of radiant sunlight to fill the space. The bed had four posts and matching drapes. The desk next to the bed was solid oak and larger than the community tables at the library.

Every piece of furniture radiated opulence, from the gilded dressers to the ivory bookshelves.

The closet boasted dimensions nearly as extensive as her dorm room, providing ample room for her modest assortment of clothing.

It was the bathroom that nearly floored her. The centerpiece was a freestanding clawfoot bathtub, a sight she had previously encountered only in movies. The shower walls were crafted from a single, impeccably smoothed stone, as though hewn from a colossal boulder and meticulously polished to perfection. Three shower heads adorned each wall, with an additional one suspended from above. Sunlight streamed in through the crystal-clear skylight, bathing the space in natural luminance.

"You could have a lot of fun in that shower with a friend..." Mal said giggling from the bathroom door. "Or two."

Mal turned and Bea followed her out of the bathroom, still speechless.

"Speaking of which," Mal said, turning and sitting on the edge of the bed. "I forgot to ask, do you have a boyfriend? Fiancée?"

A pause.

"Girlfriend?" Mal said with a sinful smile.

"No, no, nothing like that," Bea replied. "I had a boyfriend for a little while in high school, but it didn't work out."

"Bad in bed?" Mal asked, grinning.

Bea didn't know how to reply, no one had asked her anything like that before in her life. Should she be offended? The question was inappropriate, but then again she did not dare offend her new roommate.

"I'm just messing with you," Mal said after the silence extended to an awkward length.

Bea felt immediate relief.

"I myself am between boyfriends right now," Mal said, picking a piece of lint off the hem of her dress and dropping it to the floor. "It's so hard to find a good man these days."

"I bet," Bea said, glad the topic had shifted.

"I'm going to have Barry set you up with a keyfob to access the community," Mal said with a smile that hinted that she knew how to play to Bea's anxiety. "You already have my cell phone number, and... oh yes I almost forgot."

Mal put a key down on the dresser.

"Here's your house key!" she said giddily. "I'll leave you alone to get settled."

Mal glided towards the open door.

"Hey Mal," Bea remarked.

Mal paused for a moment in the doorframe and turned.

"Thank you," Bea said with a genuine smile this time, her first one in too long.

"No, thank you," Mal said. "This is going to be fun."

She disappeared into the hallway.

Bea sat on the bed where Mal had been sitting, still feeling her roommate's warmth on the comforter.

Now that she was by herself, there was nothing holding back tears of joy as they flowed down her face.

After weeks of struggle, stress, and just plain bad luck, she had finally turned the corner.

It's gotta be too good to be true, the little voice returned, ruining the moment like it always did.

But she didn't care, even if she was dreaming and was due to wake up back in her crappy bed with Tess humping some stranger next to her. She felt happy, and that was all that mattered.

It had been three weeks since Bea had moved into her room at the mansion and it may have been the best three weeks of her life. She had caught up on her sleep, she was able to stay on top of homework without pulling all-nighters, and she was back in Professor Mikkelson's good graces. The mansion had been quiet, just as she had hoped.

During the day she would see Mal from time to time in the kitchen, exchanging friendly banter. However at night, Mal left for dinners and parties, often inviting Bea to join her. Bea of course refused, citing the laundry list of excuses from grading homework to her thesis.

The only aspect of her life she hadn't quite gotten back on track was her thesis. The subject matter was still slow going and Professor Mikkelson had been less helpful than she had hoped in guiding her through the process.

Dusk had settled, casting a gentle dimness outside her window. The soft glow of her desk lamp bathed the room in a warm embrace. Seated at her desk, she found herself gazing vacantly at a towering pile of weathered research books. Her assignments and quizzes, dutifully graded for the Professor, were all completed. Now, on this Friday evening, only her thesis remained to be tackled. Yet, her motivation had dwindled, and she made no effort to crack open any of the daunting, dust-covered tomes sitting stalwart before her.

She stared at the books as if they would magically open themselves and perform a little dance in front of her, the words of her thesis magically appearing on the blank page of the word processor. The blinking cursor overlaying the devoid document only intensified as she focused on it. It must have been ten minutes that she just stared at the black line that thumped like a little synthetic heartbeat on the screen.

This sucks, Bea and her inner voice in rare agreement.

Tap, tap, tap. She heard the sound of heels approaching from down the hall. She knew it was Mal, approaching to invite Bea out once again, and to be rejected once again.

A dainty knock on the door and Bea stood up to let her roommate in.

"Hi Bea!" Mal said, walking inside the room and hugging her.

"Hi Mal," Bea responded with a warm tone, unsure of how to reciprocate a hug without appearing peculiar.

Mal looked simply stunning tonight. Her flawless, long, blond hair bore silver streaks intertwined within it. Her lipstick and eye shadow were shimmering silver to match. Her dress was silver and white, fitting her breasts tightly before slimming down to her waist. Her high heels were white and open toed, revealing silver painted toenails.

She must have noticed Bea checking her out.

"Do you like it?" Mal said with a giddy hop.

Bea looked at her dumbly for a moment, still enthralled by her beauty.

"The dress, do you like it?" Mal asked again. "I picked it out earlier today."

"You look beautiful," Bea said, breaking from her trance.

"Thank you," Mal replied with a smile. "Are you ready to go out tonight?"

"Listen Mal," Bea began. "I'm so sorry, I just can't. My thesis, I'm so behind on it."

"Your thesis, huh?" Mal said, walking over to the desk.

She slid a finger along the top book of the pile and then showed the layer of dust to Bea.

"Looks like you've been hard at work on it," Mal said with a smirk.

Bea didn't know what to say. She stared at the pile of books, not wanting to work on her thesis either.

"Listen," Mal began. "It's been three weeks, you haven't come out once. Please, pretty please come out tonight. If you come out tonight, I promise I won't bother you at all tomorrow and you can shake the dust off these old textbooks and work to your heart's desire."

"I don't know..." Bea said trailing off.

"Remember," Mal cut her off. "I really wanted a roommate to be my partner in crime."

Bea remembered, she remembered also being desperate to get out of the dorms and her roommate from hell. She didn't want to go back, she couldn't go back there. She had been miserable, meanwhile this place was just a dream come true.

One night out, couldn't hurt, could it? Her inner voice chirped in her brain.

Bea stared at the stack of books, maybe one drink would be fine.

"I can go out for a little bit," Bea said reluctantly. "But not too late."

"That's the spirit!" Mal said clearly pleased with Bea's response. "I'll order the Uber, you'll be downstairs in fifteen, right?"

Bea panicked, she had nothing to wear.

As soon as Mal exited and closed the door behind her, Bea ran to the closet and began throwing clothes anywhere she could. Searching desperately for anything she had that would be worthy of going out with Mal.

Finding a pink skirt she hadn't worn since high school, she decided that it would have to do. She paired it with a white sweater and looked in the mirror. She looked...like a librarian.

Looking at the clock nervously, she pulled her hair out of the pony tail and let her dark locks pour down over her shoulders. It was messy, split ends everywhere, but like the rest of her outfit it would have to do.

Walking down the stairs to the entranceway, she saw Mal in the front foyer checking herself out in the full length mirror attached to the wall.

Mal turned noticing Bea walking down and smiled.

"That's my girl," she said.

Then her smile straightened.

"Hmmm," Mal said aloud.

"What?" Bea asked, knowing that she didn't quite match Mal, but figured this was good enough for dinner or a bar.

"Well," Mal said, walking around Bea. "You look great, but the place we are going is a little bit on the fancier side. You wouldn't quite fit in."

"Oh, um... I'm sorry," Bea sputtered out. "I think this is the fanciest outfit I own."

Mal's phone beeped at her.

"Oh the Uber driver is here," Mal said with a frown.

"You know, maybe it's best I stay," Bea replied. "I wouldn't want to hold you up..."

"Nonsense!" said Mal with her smile returned. "I'll just tell him he'll have to wait a few minutes."

She texted frantically on her phone.

"Wait for...?" Bea questioned.

"For you to change of course," Mal said with a smile and grabbing Bea's hand. "Follow me."

Before she could protest, Mal had her by the hand and was pulling her towards Mal's room. She hadn't gone into Mal's room before, and she was immediately floored by how luxurious it was.

Though Bea was living in the largest room she had ever lived in her entire life, Mal's room was at least three times the size. A vast bed occupied a prominent position against the wall. Above it, in the ceiling, there was a recessed area housing a mirror. To the right was a couch and a bar area, full of whiskeys and spirits from the floor to the ceiling. On the bed's left side, there lay a petite seating nook, featuring a low raised platform enclosed on three sides by mirrors, much akin to what Bea had observed in the ateliers of seamstresses. Beside the platform, a pair of grand double doors swung open, revealing a closet larger than Bea's room. Every corner of this expansive area was filled with magnificent garments and a diverse collection of exquisite footwear.

"Wow," Bea said aloud without thinking.

"You know what, though?" Mal said as she began to sift through the hangers on the walls. "I still have trouble finding something to wear sometimes."

Bea had a hard time believing that.

"Hmm," Mal said with her hand on her chin staring at the clothing rack. "I'm thinking dark for you today, but still something that lets your gorgeous hair pop. Strip please, I need to know what I'm working with."

Bea's eyes popped wide open.

What did she just say? The little voice in her head asked.

"Come on, hurry up, we don't have all night," Mal said. "Clothes off!"

Bea was frozen, she hadn't stripped in front of another person before. Not even her high school boyfriend whom she had always been in complete darkness with when they had been intimate.

Mal gave her a look of impatience, and Bea, not able to think of another option, reluctantly slipped her sweater over her head and unhooked her skirt till it fell to the ground.

"Thank God," Mal said with a sense of relief. "You look fabulous. Tits could use a little work, but the rest of you is definitely doable."

"My tits?" Bea said suddenly feeling very exposed and wrapping her arms in front of her.

"Yeah, I know a doctor who could take care of those real quick," Mal replied as she started pulling clothes hangers and tossing garments onto an ottoman in the center of the closet.

"That's a conversation for another time, though," she continued. "For now, put this bra on, it'll get you looking good for tonight."

Bea only barely reacted in time to catch the bra in the air as it was hurled at her face.

"Should I, um," she hesitated, "head to the bathroom to change?"

"There's no time, girl," Mal replied. "Uber is waiting. Plus, don't you think I've seen my share of tits before? Nothing to be ashamed of, we're both women."

Mal's attention stayed focused on critiquing different outfits, rather than on Mal's progressively more exposed form.

Not wanting to hold up the driver or disappoint Mal, Bea fumbled with the clasp of her bra before removing it. Trying to cover her breasts as best she could, she slid the new bra on and clasped it in the back.

"There aren't any straps," Bea said with alarm.

"That's kind of the idea," Mal replied, walking over to her. "Try this dress on."

Bea had little time for thoughts as Mal assisted her in slipping the dress over her head and down her body.

"Not enough time to do more with the hair," Mal said, looking disapprovingly at Bea. "But you know what, maybe you can pull off the slightly messy look."

Before Bea could respond, she coughed as a mist of hairspray enveloped her face, followed by discomfort as a brush was tugged unkindly through her tangled locks.

"Hold still, will you," Mal commanded.

Bea did her best but...

Bea winced.

"All done," Mal replied and the pain ceased.

Mal seized Bea's hand and guided her, picking up the pace slightly, out of the closet and out of the room. They stepped into the foyer, and headed toward the front door.

"Dammit, I forgot the most important thing, be right back!" Mal said disappearing back to her room.

Bea took a deep breath and looked into the gold bordered mirror next to the door for the first time since changing. She didn't recognize the girl staring back at her.

She donned a striking, non-reflective flat purple dress that seemed impervious to even the foyer's intense lighting. The gown featured sleek black trim and was strapless, ending just above her knees. Her jet-black hair, a departure from the years of ponytails and buns, cascaded beautifully over her shoulders. Despite its slight dishevelment, it harmonized seamlessly with her overall appearance.

"Like what you see?" said Mal from behind her, smiling.

Bea jumped as she was startled.

"Ok, last thing," Mal said.

Mal reached out her hand and dangling from her fingers were a pair of black strappy high heels.

"I...um..." Bea stuttered. She hadn't worn high heels in a long time.

"Come on, no time," Mal said, pushing the heels into Bea's hand. "We got to go!"

In what felt like only a few seconds later, she was in the back of a large luxurious Escalade with a well-dressed driver in the front seat smiling at her from the rear view mirror.

"Thanks for waiting," Mal uttered as she shut the door behind her and settled beside Bea in the backseat.

"No problem," the driver said, putting the car in drive. "Where to tonight?"

"Club Llithium please," Mal retorted as she began rapidly texting on her phone.

Bea watched out the window as the bright lights of the mansion disappeared behind them and the roar of the city began to grow before them.

Although Bea had been living in the city for several months, she hadn't yet ventured into downtown. She had found the bustling atmosphere of the campus to be exhilarating on its own. Downtown seemed like a far away neighbor, whose porch light was always on and people yelling at each other inside. Approaching in the large SUV, the metropolis loomed larger than ever. The buildings towered over her head, dwarfing anything she had ever seen up close before. The illumination from cars, street lamps, buildings, and shops transformed the night into something resembling daytime.

Bea felt bewildered as they drove straight through the vibrant and bustling cityscape, only to find themselves on a dimly lit road surrounded by aging neighborhoods. She had assumed that the club would be located downtown, amidst the city's vibrant core, where only the most glamorous and stunning individuals frequented.

Mal must have noticed her confusion.

"Club Llithium is in the historical district," she said without looking up from her phone.

As they ventured deeper into the dimly lit neighborhoods, Bea observed a significant transformation in the architecture. The concrete and steel structures gave way to brick and mortar buildings. The once towering skyscrapers were now replaced by two and three-story aged edifices that enveloped her from every direction. Here, many of the shops had shut down permanently, their boarded-up windows and out-of-business signs serving as stark reminders. The houses in the surrounding neighborhoods exuded an eerie and foreboding aura, shrouded in darkness with no street lamps to offer any illumination.

The SUV slowed as they approached a large structure at the corner. Bea recognized it immediately as a church, the three steeples topped by crucifixes were a dead giveaway. In the dim glow of the headlights, she could discern a diverse range of muted hues emanating from the sizable stained glass windows beneath each spire. The grand entrance doors at the front of the church were securely boarded up with wooden planks.

She was getting nervous.

"Have a good night, ladies," the driver said, coming to a complete stop outside the church.

"You too," Mal said, flashing a smile into the rear view mirror. A smile that Bea had no doubt the driver would remember well into the rest of his night and beyond.

Bea followed Mal out the door.

"One second," Mal said as she hurriedly finished a text and hit SEND.

Bea felt a little chilly, the warm summer air seemed to have dissipated and a damp chill gave her goosebumps. Autumn was quickly approaching.

This is a prank, the little voice said in her head.

There is no club, this is all a ruse to get you out of the house so that she can humiliate you. Just like the other girls in high school did, it continued.

Bea's heart quickened, and memories of the frequent high school humiliations she had endured flooded her mind. Finding her clothes missing after gym class, fake notes from boys she had crushes on asking her out, promises of friendship that lead to quick betrayals.

Just like high school, the voice said again.

No, this felt different. No one would offer the kindness Mal had already shown her, only to have it turn out to be a deception. Bea felt compelled to move forward, her only alternative being a return to the dormitories.

Besides, when she had peeked at herself in the mirror on the way out the door, she had looked almost beautiful. She liked that feeling, for the first time in her life she felt pretty. It was a new feeling, it warmed her heart, and made her smile.

Just like high...

"Shut up," Bea said softly to herself.

"What was that?" Mallory asked without looking up.

"Nothing," Bea replied, kicking herself for saying it outloud.

"And I'm done," Mal said. She must have finished her message.

Mal grabbed Bea's arm and half walked, half pulled her towards a dark alley behind the church.

This couldn't possibly be the way inside, could it?

Bea's alarm bells returned to her head, that was until they had turned the corner into the alley when she was suddenly blinded by light and commotion.

A line of a hundred people waited, bathed under bright fluorescent lights, all leading to double doors where music could be heard bumping loudly from within. She couldn't believe her eyes.

The line was quite long, impossible to gauge how long the wait would be. But to Bea's surprise, they didn't join the throngs of people waiting. Instead, Mallory pulled her directly to the doors where a small group of girls stood in a circle next to the entrance. All their faces were bathed in the ghoulish blue light of their phones.

"Mal!" one of the girls yelled, looking up and noticing them. The girl rushed forward and hugged Mallory then to Bea's bewilderment, hugged Bea as well.

"Hi, I'm Adelaide," said the girl. She was about 5 foot 4 inches tall, just about Bea's height but much shorter than Mal. Her hair was blond like Mal's but less well kept, and cropped right above her shoulder line. Her short hair allowed her face to perfectly frame around her brilliant blue eyes. She was of mixed ancestry, Mal guessed Asian and European based on some of her features. She wore a bright green dress with thin straps that showed off her pencil-like figure.

"I'm Bernice," Bea said immediately, wishing she hadn't given her full name.

"But I prefer to be called Bea," she added hurriedly.

"Oh my God, just like Beyoncé!" Adelaide said excitedly.

"Sure," Bea nodded, not sure what that meant.

The other girls rushed over to join them.

"Ladies," Mal said. "This is my new roommate Bea."

Each girl introduced themselves quickly, but Bea was lost trying to remember their names.

"Another one?" remarked one of the individuals in the group, a girl with deep brown hair and dark eyes.

Mal looked at her uncomfortably.

"You girls thirsty?" said Mal quickly after the awkward moment.

"Oh, hell yes," said the girl with dark brown hair. "They wouldn't let us in until you got here, and you're late."

Bea was surprised by how flat and direct she was with Mal.

"I'm so sorry," Mal said with a smile. "We had an emergency we had to attend to."

Mal shot a side glance at an embarrassed Bea.

"Here we go!" Mal said with excitement.

"Good evening, Ms. Phillips," said the bouncer as he opened up the sash barrier to grant them passage.

"Hello Marshall," Mal replied. The bouncer leaned down so that Mal could give him a small peck on the cheek, he smiled from ear to ear.

Bea glanced at the line of people patiently waiting, a hundred jealous faces stared back at her.

At first she felt guilty, that she could just walk in and they had to wait outside in the cold night air.

Then a new emotion took hold of her, something she had rarely felt before. It was satisfaction, satisfaction that for once she wasn't the one waiting in the back of the line, but instead ushered to the front.

She followed the girls through the doors and into Club Llithium.

The group passed through a dim corridor lined with antique mirrors. Bea couldn't help but take a moment to stop and look at herself in one of the particularly large ones. She still didn't quite recognize herself in a dress with her hair down; the only thing that remained remotely recognizable were her thick glasses she had owned since she was 15. Otherwise, she felt like an entirely new person, an entirely different person, one who even goes to trendy nightclubs with friends!

"Maybe I'll get hit on!" She thought excitedly to herself. "Maybe they'll even buy me a drink." She hoped, mostly because she didn't have much money in her bank account to cover an expensive bar tab.

You wish, the voice in her head said.

She ignored it.

Something did catch her eye, the antique mirror she was looking at looked very authentic. It wasn't the artificial, faux-antique facade she had anticipated, but rather, it bore the marks of genuine use and frequent relocation. Delicate scratches and minor imperfections embellished the frame, while patches of worn paint hinted at areas frequently touched or grasped. It must have been very old, yet the glass was virtually flawless.

"Like what you see?" said a voice behind her that startled her.

It was Mal.

Bea looked at her and smiled.

"Yeah. Yeah, I do," Bea said.

"You look great," said Mal. "Thanks to me of course."

She winked.

"Can't stare at ourselves in the mirror all night" Mal grabbed Bea's arm. "Let's let the others do that for us."

As the doors opened, Bea walked through into a fog of bodies, lights, and sound. She felt the music reverberating throughout her entire body, a mist hung in the air, bright stage lights and lasers shot through the cloud. She felt like she was in a movie.

"Your usual table, ladies?" said an extremely handsome man dressed in jeans and a sleeveless tank top. His arms were covered from wrist to shoulder in tattoos of birds of all sorts, their talons accentuated in bright yellow ink.

"Of course, Harpy," Mal said, hugging him.

"This way," he gestured.

Bea couldn't help but get the feeling that the crowd of people dancing and talking parted for him as he led them forward.

"Your table, ladies," he said, gesturing at a lounge area right next to the main dance floor with a great view of the DJ. There were several bottles of champagne in buckets of ice waiting for them at the table.

The girls each picked their seats on the comfortable sofas and lounge chairs, Bea choosing one farthest from the dance floor, as if distancing herself from the mass of dancing bodies would somehow immunize her from having to partake herself. The nicest chair in the area wasn't claimed by any of the other girls, it had a tall back and cushioned arm rests. It resembled a soft pink and white throne.

Mal sat in it after everyone else had taken their places, she looked like a queen holding court.

"I believe I know everyone's favorite drink orders already," the man who seated them said, pouring a glass of champagne for Mal.

"Except this one, she's new," he said suddenly, looking at Bea.

"My new roommate Bea," Mal commented as she took her glass.

The man walked over to Bea and crouched down until he was eye level with her.

Bea felt uncomfortable. His gaze was unflinching and seemed to look through her.

"Um, hi," she said, not sure of what else to say.

"Shhh," the man simply gazed at her, his lips curving into a subtle smile, while his eyes narrowed in focused contemplation.

"I'm sorry, dear," the man said, suddenly standing up. "We don't serve Shirley Temples here."

The other girls giggled.

"Oh Harpy," said Mal, putting her glass down. "You've had your fun, bring the girl a drink. Make it a... surprise."

"Yes, Ms. Phillips," he said before disappearing back into the crowd.

Bea sat back nervously as the girls began chatting loudly, their voices growing louder as they competed with the music.

From her seat she could see the DJ on the stage at the front of the dance floor, playing electronic music she didn't recognize. The rhythm, the pulsating sounds, resonated within her, causing her heart to race. The DJ donned a metallic mask adorned with towering bull-like horns, soaring a full foot above his head. His attire was adorned with a mesmerizing array of LED lights that swayed and flickered in harmony with his music.

The crowd of club goers, dancing on the stage below him was massive. Their arms high above their hands wagging to the music like an excited dog's tail. Some hopped up and down, as if in some kind of trance. They all wore different styles of clothing, something Bea found quite odd. A girl wearing nothing but suspender straps danced half-nude next to someone in a full suit that looked like it belonged in a black and white movie about Dracula.

No one dressed in a pink poodle skirt and an oversized sweater, the voice in her head said.

"What's that?" Bea asked Adelaide who was seated next to her, pointing to the areas that flanked the dance floor and defended by a small squad of security guards.

"VIP Area," Adelaide responded, sipping on a glass of champagne she had poured for herself.

She hiccuped.

"Excuse me," she said, covering her mouth.

"So what happens up there?" Bea asked, growing more curious.

"I don't know, never been," Adelaide answered. "Mal's been of course, but she's only told us it's a bunch of old men sitting up there waiting for girls to sit on their laps for free drinks. Not exactly our scene."

"I see," Bea said, content with the answer. She had seen enough movies and read enough stories to understand that probably nothing wholesome happens in the VIP area.

The man who had seated them returned with a tray full of drinks, all varying in size, shape, and color.

A chorus of "Thank yous" greeted him as several of the girls had already finished their champagne.

He seemed to purposely skip Bea, leaving her for the end while three glasses remained on the tray.

He put the tray on the table in front of her.

"So, Ms. Bea," he said, putting the first glass down in front of her. "As it is your first time at the club..."

He paused to smirk.

"...and drinking something not bought at a gas station," he added.

The rest of the group girls all "ooooo"ed in unison which only amplified Bea's embarrassment at her lack of experience at venues like this.

"Oh, you all were just like her once," he scolded the girls behind him before turning to Bea.

"I've brought you three to start you off on the right foot," he smiled.

Bea was nervous, the entire group was staring at her intently as she eyed the strange clear drink with something that looked like maybe salt on the rim in front of her and a lemon.

"I don't know," Bea said nervously.

"If there's one thing I'm good at it in this world," he said with a reassuring smile. "It's knowing what people like."

"That's the truth," Adelaide said next to her, sipping on a drink with a mint leaf in it.

"This first one is just a teaser," said the man. His words felt sweet in her ear. "Consider it the foreplay, something to loosen you up a bit."

Bea hesitated, unsure if this was a good idea. She should be at home studying, not out at a club drinking. This was wrong, very wrong.

Mal smiled at her intensely from across the table, which only made Bea feel more nervous.

Knew you'd chicken out, her inside voice said.

Fuck you, she replied back. Thankfully not aloud this time.

Grasping the glass firmly, she tilted her head back and swallowed just like she had seen in the movies.

Pleasure ran down her mouth and into her stomach.

"Wow, that tasted like..." she searched for the right flavor. "Chocolate cake?"

"Very good," said the man. “By the way, the name is Harper.”

“Nice to meet you,” Bea replied.

She experienced instant relief when the other girls resumed their chattering, no longer casting her as the center of attention.

Harper placed another drink in front of her, this one was in a tall martini glass. However, unlike a martini the liquid was pink in color.

"What's this one?" she asked.

"Best not to ask, love," he replied. "Best just to enjoy."

The handsome bartender in front of her still made her uncomfortable. As pretty and as charming as he was, she could tell that it was all just an act. A facade of charm meant to woo her.

She drank this one quickly, it was smooth, sweet, and delicious.

"That was probably the fastest I've ever seen someone drink a cosmopolitan," Harper said with a laugh.

He placed the last drink in front of her, it was in a short regular glass and the liquid was an amber color. Bea smelled it, it didn't smell sweet at all.

"I'm not sure about this one," she said, setting it back down.

"Would you go to a fine dining restaurant and return what the world class chef prepared for you?" he said, staring deep into her eyes.

Bea hadn't previously observed it, but now she noticed how his eyes shimmered with the vibrant club lights. The dance floor's illumination played a captivating dance in the reflection within his pupils.

"I guess not," Bea said, picking up the glass. Her body shivered for a moment as she drank, then immediately relaxed. This wasn't that bad after all, nowhere near what she had imagined and dreaded.

It tingled faintly as it traveled down her throat, yet its smoothness surprised her, offering sweeter notes than she had anticipated. Caramel and vanilla flavors gracefully waltzed across her taste buds.

All worries in the world seemed to disappear from her mind after that.

Harper stood up and smiled.

"Which one was your favorite?" he asked.

Bea didn't need to think, she already knew the answer.

"That last one, by far," she said.

"Ah ha!" he said, bowing to the rest of the ladies who all applauded him. "I know a Bourbon girl when I see one."

"I hope Harper here is taking good care of you," said a deep voice from the dark corner behind them.

Bea was immediately startled.

All the girls turned to look.

"Cam!" shouted Mal. She rushed to hug the tall, well-dressed man that had somehow coalesced from the darkness.

"He's teaching Bea how to drink," Adelaide said with a laugh before trying to desperately hide another involuntary belch with her hand.

"Bea?" the man said with a curious tone.

"She's my new roommate who I was telling you about," Mal said, escorting him to Bea and Adelaide.

Bea got her first full look at him.

He was at least six and a half feet tall, he towered over everyone not only at the table but even some of the bouncers. His shoulders were wide. His suit would have to be custom made for him, as nothing off the shelf would likely fit around his burly linebacker-like frame.

He was clean-shaven, his entire face was flawlessly smooth. In his left ear, a tiny diamond stud sparkled. His eyes were dark, like coals against his tan skin. However every few moments they would catch a spare bit of light and reflect brightly, just like Harper's. His hair was dark and combed back, smooth and suave. His watch was expensive and designer, however it was not new; of the old style that was likely passed down from an older generation.

He stepped forward and extended his hand to Bea, who reciprocated the gesture. To her surprise, he elegantly bowed and gently pressed a kiss to the back of her hand, reminiscent of a scene from a romantic novel.

"A pleasure to meet you," he said looking into her eyes. "My name is Cam, welcome to my club."

"Hi...I'm..." Bea felt warm. Not just warm, but hot. Just standing there she felt like she was sitting next to a fire snuggled under a fuzzy blanket.

"Bea," she stammered out.

"A pleasure," he said, still holding her hand and staring into her eyes. "Short for Bernice?"

She turned red, embarrassed that he guessed her full name.

"Yes," she said, pulling her hand away and sitting back down. She avoided eye contact with him, though she could feel his eyes still burning into her.

“My dear Adelaide,” Cam said, turning to Bea’s neighbor.

“Hi Cam,” Adelaide remarked with a disinterested tone. She faked a smile.

“It’s good to see you again,” he said without being deterred.

“Sure is,” Adelaide quipped.

“Have you reconsidered my offer regarding dinner?” he asked.

“Nope,” she replied, sipping her drink.

Cam stood staring at the girl for a long moment.

Bea felt something in the back of her thoughts, a twinge of jealousy. This must be one of the most handsome men she had ever met—he owned the coolest (and the only) night club Bea had ever visited—and Adelaide was giving him the cold shoulder like he was a leper.

“Very well,” Cam replied, with an unflinching level of confidence in his voice. Ending the long moment of awkwardness that had engulfed the table.

“Hey, Adelaide,” a dark-haired girl interjected from nearby. She wore a black sparkling dress with calf-high black boots. “Want to hit the ladies room? Give the slugger here a chance to regain some dignity?”

“Absolutely,” Adelaide replied.

Both girls wandered off laughing with each other, their giggles eventually being drowned out by the music.

This left the charming Cam alone with Bea, as the other girls pretended to have their own conversations while covertly observing his every action.

Cam took a seat in Adelaide’s empty chair.

"You look like a girl with a secret," Cam said with a mischievous smile.

"Me?" Bea said questioningly. "I don't have a secret."

Cam studied her closely.

"Maybe it's a secret you don't even know yet," he replied.

Bea looked to see the rest of the girls glancing at her and Cam sideways, holding back smiles of their own.

"Oh Cam," Mal said, sipping her drink. "Stop flirting with my roommate."

The girls all laughed, Bea faked a chuckle as well trying to fit in.

"My apologies," Cam said, standing up.

"What's the theme tonight?" Mal asked.

"You know I haven't quite decided yet," Cam said, looking over at the DJ who was playing what sounded like music from a club scene in a movie. "Any suggestions?"

Bea was confused as all the girls seemed to chirp all at once different ideas and thoughts for a theme. Bea had trouble keeping up.

"Ladies, ladies," Mal said, putting her hands up. "It's Bea's first time, we should let her decide."

Bea found herself at a loss for words, unable to comprehend the question. She had been unaware of any theme, let alone her choices. Panic set in as the group and Cam fixed their gaze upon her.

"Um, I don't know," Bea stammered. "I guess this is nice."

"Come on, Bea," Mal said with her smile piercing Bea's confidence sharply. "You got to have something, anything that you've wanted to see at a club before. Go wild."

Wild...wild...Bea's mind raced.

"Um...maybe some dancers..." she began to say. The girls all looked at her with faces of boredom.

"Men...dressed in something..." her mind was blocked. She couldn't think, she struggled for any inspiration.

"Dressed as something wild," she blurted out.

The group was silent for a moment.

"You know," Cam said, breaking the silence. "I think I know just what you are looking for. Enjoy yourselves, ladies."

Cam and Harper disappeared into the crowd.

The rest of the girls all began talking excitedly.

Adelaide and the dark-haired girl returned shortly and took their seats near Bea.

"So you're Mal's new roommate," Adelaide stated. "What's it like living in Barbie's dream house?"

"It's great," Bea said. "My room is amazing, it's quiet. I have plenty of time to study and work on my thesis."

Work on your thesis? Are you kidding me? The voice laughed.

"Mal mentioned you were a grad student," Adelaide said, stifling another strange belch.

Bea found her incessant gaseousness strange but dared not ask the cause for fear of embarrassing her.

"Yes, in history," Bea said, pretending to ignore the belch.

"I'm majoring in communications," Adelaide said, downing the last of her drink. "My Vater said I should get a degree and I'd heard it's the easiest one."

"Vater?" Bea asked.

"Sorry," Adelaide replied, her cheeks turning slightly red. "That's what I call my dad. He's from Germany."

"That's cool," Bea said nervously. She wasn't quite sure how to talk to girls. "What does he do?"

"He's an executive at a car company," she replied with a grin.

"Oh," Bea said, realizing that Adelaide, much like Mal, had a family that was likely loaded. She struggled to think of something to say next to keep the conversation going. She was so bad at this.

"I like your necklace," Bea blurted out. "Is that a mermaid?"

"Kind of," replied Adelaide. She put her hand to her neck and fiddled with the chain and pendant. "It's a Nixie. Nixies are..."

"German water spirits," Bea without meaning to, cut her off.

"Wow," Adelaide said with a smile. "You sure know a lot."

Bea leaned in to take a closer look at the necklace; it was silver, inlaid with aquamarine and emerald gems. It depicted a woman with long blue hair that flowed down over her emerald green skin. Between her legs was a tail with a fin.

Bea's eyes seemed to drift on their own from Adelaide's necklace down her body. She blushed when she realized that she was feeling attracted to this beautiful woman.

Adelaide was beautiful, but in a fragile sort of way. Like a ceramic statue of a ballerina, so delicately propped up on a toe that the slightest nudge might break it.

Like what you see? The little voice asked.

Something about staring so closely at Adelaide's body for just a few moments had made Bea feel flustered.

"Well I think it's great Mal is making friends with older girls," Adelaide said, breaking Bea's hypnotic stare.

"Older girls?" Bea questioned.

"Yeah," Adelaide said, pausing to grab a small antacid tablet from her purse and popping it into her mouth. "She usually sticks to being friends with freshmen and sophomores, you're what, 22?

"24 actually," Bea said, growing self conscious.

"Well her last few roommates were total ditzes," Adelaide said, taking another drink before hiccuping. "You're probably smarter than all of them combined."

"Last few roommates?" Bea questioned aloud.

But before she could get an answer, Harper appeared from behind them with another tray of drinks.

"You ladies looked parched," he said, handing Adelaide another drink with a mint leaf in it and another Bourbon for Bea.

Bea took a sip of hers and quickly found that enjoyable sensation warming her again, temporarily forgetting her conversation with Adelaide.

"Ahh-ahh-ahh-ahh-oo-oo-oo!" a Tarzan yell pierced the dense fog of the electronic music building. All the girls looked up, the whole club looked up, to see a man clad in a green camouflage pattern thong swing from ropes above their heads. He swung from the DJ stage all the way to the far end of the club, landing on the bartop. The man had long brown hair, held out of his face by a green headband. He was completely hairless everywhere else on his body, and by the way the club lights glistened on his body, he appeared to be covered in oil.

He let loose another Tarzan yell as the girls at his feet screamed in excitement. They reached forward grabbing and groping at him. He ignored them.

The always stealthy Harper appeared nearby and swung a bottle high into the air from behind his back.

Tarzan caught it midair and immediately began chugging whatever it contained.

The girls were chanting "Tarzan" in time with the crowd. Bea joined them, feeling her body tingle at the sight of the near perfect specimen of a man putting on a show for the whole club. It felt good to be part of it, part of the group. She felt normal, for that moment like she actually fit in somewhere. The alcohol had done its job; her thesis, school...those thoughts were far away now. Buried deep in her mind along with the voice.

A rope swung back toward the bar. Tarzan swiftly released the bottle, and with a flourish, Harper caught it. He poured a round of shots for the still-screaming girls at Tarzan's feet. Tarzan gracefully leaped from the bar, soaring over the heads of the crowd, and effortlessly grabbed hold of the swinging rope, propelling himself back toward the stage.

Landing at the now empty DJ booth, new music bellowed from the speakers.

A Jungle beat, pounding in Bea's ears. The club lights tinted green and yellow in unison. The mood of those still on the dancefloor changed immediately. They all grew suddenly wild...as if under a spell.

They were whooping and jumping high in the air, ripping pieces of their clothing that fluttered to the ground before being trampled. Even those who had dressed in strange formal wear joined in, tearing off the strings of their corsets revealing skin. Several male and female dancers dressed in loincloths similar to Tarzan appeared on the stage, dancing and grinding into each other.

The alcohol must have moved from Bea's body to her head. She felt the inexplicable urge to join the throng on the dance floor, to move her body to the music just as wildly as they were. She didn't even realize that she had begun to nod and move her head back and forth in time to the music.

"Good choice," Adelaide said with her eyes closed. She was swaying to the beat in a trance-like state.

Bea wasn't sure whether it was the alcohol or if her drink had been spiked, but the dance floor underwent a surreal transformation right before her eyes. The dancers vanished, replaced by a gathering of gazelles in the night, with hungry lions circling them with ravenous eyes. Their sharp teeth dripped with an insatiable thirst for the blood of their next victim. The thought filled her with excitement.

"Let's go dance!" Adelaide yelled, grabbing Bea's hand.

"No, I can't," Bea weakly protested. "I don't know how to dance."

"It's simple," Adelade said. With each passing moment, Bea felt the desire to follow her. Where didn't matter. "You just let the music guide your movements, however you desire."

"I don't think..." Bea protested. A brief look at Mal, who observed them from her throne, served as a reminder to Bea of the reason she had agreed to venture out that evening.

Partner in crime... The voice returned to echo in Bea's mind.

"Ok, let's do it," Bea said. Hoping this would cement her status in the group, the group of girlfriends she had never had growing up.

"Yay!" yelled Adelaide as she led Bea to the dance floor, trailed by the other girls in the group.

Bea looked back to see Mal watching them, but she was not alone. Cam was kneeling beside her, and they were engaged in hushed conversation, trading whispers in one another's ear. Both stared at Bea, or it could have been Adelaide. It was hard to tell.

The crowd of dancers engulfed them. Bea felt herself being ushered to the center of the group. Bodies moved all around her, their collective heat combined to create what felt like a steamy, sweaty, jungle rainforest. Everyone was glistening with sweat. With Adelaide nearby holding her hand, she began to let the music take control.

Adelaide guided her slowly at first, but as her inhibitions waned, Bea began to feel more in tune with the beat. It wasn't long until Adelaide's small body was grinding against hers, their hands intertwining as they danced.

Bea's body tingled with excitement as they moved with each other, she looked around to find several men watching them. Their eyes reflected red in the strange lights from the stage. Bea began to feel self conscious.

Adelaide must have noticed, she leaned in close to Bea and whispered in her ear.

"Let them watch," she said softly.

Bea felt the hair on her arms stand up, feelings of excitement overpowering those of self consciousness. She wrapped her arms around Adelaide as they danced, the world around them began to spin.

Adelaide's hands moved to Bea's hips and grabbed them, pulling Bea in closer. Bea's hands cupped Adelaide's bosom, seemingly having a mind of their own. The whole scene felt like they were caught in a hypnotic trance, at the whim of the DJ and the notes floating from the speakers through the air and into their souls.

There was one pair of eyes though that she felt on her at all times, the eyes of a shadowed man in the VIP area staring down at her and Adelaide. No matter how much she danced, she could feel his eyes upon them. Who he was or what his intention, she could not know, was he just some curious onlooker or something more sinister?

Let him watch, her inner voice whispered.

Adelaide's energy had somehow imprinted onto hers.

The crowd parted in front of them, Bea didn't even notice.

Adelaide held on to her hand, guiding her to the front of the stage which seemed to grow larger and larger.

Bea looked up. Tarzan was crouched above them on the stage and his hands were reaching down towards them. His perfectly sculpted abs, arms, and legs still glistened. He smiled at them and winked.

"Should we?" Adelaide asked.

Without a word, Bea simply reached up and seized one of his arms.

Tarzan lifted both of them up onto the stage where they both froze. Before them, a sea of people cheered and roared for them to continue.

"Looks like we're Queens of the Jungle tonight," Adelaide said with a smile.

Bea nodded, trying to hold back expressing her own excitement.

They drew nearer to each other, as the enthusiastic cheers of the crowd grew even louder. Before long, they were dancing intimately, and the entire club seemed to erupt with excitement at the spectacle.

Bea hadn't ever felt this way before, she felt on fire and alive. Time no longer existed, as she and Adelaide danced and danced. The night could have lasted forever. She lost track of anything and everything until eventually the club and music became just a blur around her.

Bea's head was spinning. It was pitch dark in the room. She didn't remember much from the night before. She remembered the club, she remembered it turned wild when Tarzan appeared. After that, her memory became very fuzzy. Dancing, more drinks, the stage...

She heard snoring next to her, something far from expected.

Who was lying next to her?

Are you even sure this is your bed? The voice in her head said.

Bea's panic only worsened as she realized the foreign nature of the room around her.

The only light was a faint ray of sunshine shining from the bottom of the black-out curtains that covered the window. She shifted slightly hoping to get a better view of whomever was sharing the bed with her.

An arm appeared and draped itself across her chest, it was large and muscular.

After a moment of shock, Bea continued to slowly move herself towards the edge of the bed. Maybe she could slide out from under...

She was blocked by something else, someone else. Another body lay on the opposite side of the bed. This one rustled slightly as she brushed up against it.

Bea's anxiety screamed in her head.

Her splitting headache pounded harder, she needed to get out of there. She needed water, she needed an Ibuprofen. She decided that down was the only way out, she slowly slinked under the covers and downward in the bed towards the foot. Lifting the arm over her head, she was relieved that whomever it belonged to didn't stir.

The person on the other side though wasn't quite such a heavy sleeper. They were even beginning to roll over as Bea tried to slide down the bed.

Then Bea froze.

She recognized this person, in the dim light she could make out the features and face of Adelaide.

Had she slept with... another woman?

She didn't have time to think as Adelaide's eyes opened. She looked at Bea and smiled.

"Good morning," she said.

"Good...um...Hi," Bea managed to say back, still stunned.

"Last night was amazing," Adelaide said smiling.

"It...was...fun..." Bea stammered out.

"You want to go again?" Adelaide asked with a giggle.

Bea didn't have time to react, Adelaide leaned forward and kissed her on the lips.

Bea was still in shock, she didn't know how to feel. The kiss felt good; she hadn't been kissed in several years. However, she hadn't kissed another woman before, well, until last night. The kiss triggered more memories of their romp the evening prior. They felt good but also very confusing.

"Should we wake him up?" Adelaide asked..

Bea sat up suddenly.

"I...um...I got to go," she said, jostling out of bed as fast as she could.

"It's Saturday though," Adelaide said, sitting up and stretching her arms. She was completely naked, unashamed to be sitting topless in front of Bea.

"I...um..." Bea struggled to not stare at Adelaide's naked figure. She searched frantically for her clothes.

"Thesis," was all she was able to mutter as she rushed.

Turning on the bathroom light to help her see, she finally found her clothes on the ground and her phone. Looking back to the bed, Adelaide had laid back down and gone back to sleep. The man next to her rolled over in the bed and moved in closer. Bea recognized him... Tarzan!

Bea got out of there as soon as she could, her mind still aching and blurry the entire Uber ride home.

She was relieved that Mal had not woken yet when she walked inside. She hurried to her room and quickly went to the bathroom medicine cabinet to pour several Ibuprofen tablets into her hand. Swallowing them with water from the sink, she crawled back into bed hoping she could sleep.

She couldn't.

She had only had sex with one other person her entire life. She knew the dangers of having sex; years of being relentlessly warned by her parents and threatened with eternal damnation had done the trick.

She didn't remember seeing any condom wrappers anywhere.

She didn't even know Tarzan's real name!

You're such a slut, mocked the voice.

She was so angry with herself, she couldn't believe she had done that.

All for what? A hangover on a day she should be catching up on her thesis.

It was several more hours of paralyzing anxiety until she felt herself nodding off to sleep at last, the exhaustion of the previous night finally taking control.

Bea spent the next two weeks avoiding Mal at all costs. She didn't emerge from her room to eat until Mal had left to go out for the evening. Bea would sneak down to the fridge, make whatever she could find in the microwave and then sneak back to her room.

Though her hangover faded, she found herself struggling to focus on her work.

She had missed one of Mikkelson's deadlines for grading and been given a thorough verbal lashing because of it. She didn't even realize she had missed it because she had forgotten which day of the week it was entirely. In class, she had forgotten something she had studied the night before when attempting to answer a question in front of the class. She knew the answer, but when she raised her hand the answer disappeared entirely from her thoughts.

Bea could only think it was her anxiety, the uncertainty in the back of her mind distracting her from everyday activities.

It wasn't until two weeks later that Bea could no longer wait, and scheduled an appointment on the University's health care portal.

The waiting room was full of other students nursing coughs and runny noses. She tried to stay as far away as she could from them, not wanting to derail herself further by catching whatever flu had been circulating around campus.

To her relief, her name was called quickly and she was escorted to a nearby exam room. The table was cold, the thin sheet of sanitary white paper rustling uncomfortably loud underneath her as she waited. The posters displayed in the University Medical Center's exam rooms were different versions of the same public service announcements (PSAs) found throughout the campus: the dangers of alcohol, tobacco, drugs, and sex.

Back home, Bea had gone to a pediatrician all her life; the office was decorated with Mickey Mouse and Roger Rabbit-themed posters about washing hands and the importance of getting your shots. The walls, equipment, and multi-colored furniture that were all patterned with friendly prints. It had made her feel juvenile, but looking at the cold, drab exam room of the Medical Center she realized she preferred her old pediatrician's office.

A slight knock on the door preceded a gray-haired male doctor entering without much hesitation. His short stature made the bald spot on the top of his head prominent, it reflected the glare of the fluorescent lights in every direction. He stared down at a clipboard in his hands instead of at Bea.

"Bernice Logan," he said without looking up.

"I prefer to be called Bea," she said in response.

"Ms. Logan," the man said without really acknowledging her. "I'm Doctor Tompkins, what brings you in today?"

His voice was monotone and robotic, Bea didn't feel any warmth or empathy from him at all.

"Well...um...." Bea began to speak. "I wanted to get a blood test done."

"Why?" the Doctor asked, pulling out a pen and looking at his clipboard.

"Well," Bea tried to find the words. "I haven't been feeling myself lately. I was out late and I went home with somebody... I just want to know if I'm pregnant or if I caught something from them."

"Do you drink often?" the Doctor asked.

"Not often, every once in a while I guess," Bea replied.

"How many drinks did you have the night you went out?" He asked in follow-up.

"Six...maybe seven?" Bea answered tentatively.

Doctor Tompkins ticked a check mark on his clipboard.

"We consider that binge drinking Ms. Logan," he said without looking at her. "Tell me, were you doing any drugs?"

"No, I would never," Bea replied instantly.

"Are you sure?" Doctor Tompkins raised his eyebrow at her as he spoke.

"I mean I don't remember much," Bea answered.

He ticked another check mark on his clipboard.

"Memory loss is another common side effect of drug abuse," he said flatly.

Bea had hoped for this visit to the Doctor to be more reassuring and less like she was on trial.

"Do you have unprotected sex?" The Doctor asked her as if it was a routine question he asked everyone.

"No, I mean," Bea's anxiety swirled around her thoughts as she struggled to answer. "I don't remember. I'm not sure."

She wasn't sure if he was referring to that one night or in general.

Another check mark.

"It takes just one time for you to get pregnant or catch an incurable venereal disease," the doctor said. It sounded like he was reading off a script, like the safety briefing the amusement park ride operator has to repeat every day.

Please keep your hands and feet inside the ride at all times...

"Are you on birth control?" he asked next.

"No," she replied. "I don't have a boyfriend, so..."

"Didn't your school teach you anything? Your parents?" he said, putting his clipboard down and moving to the cabinets and sink nearby.

“They taught me to not have sex until I was married,” Bea said.

Doctor Tompkins let out a deep sigh.

He rummaged through the drawers, Bea's thoughts drifted to her parents and their discussions with her about sex. “Discussion” was probably too nice a word for it. Their instruction regarding sex had been more like sermons, with elements of demon fire and eternal damnation the focus. She had been scared of even touching a boy most of her life.

While she wasn't a virgin, she had developed an immunity to her parents' fiery and judgmental speeches during high school. Back then, she had only been intimate with her boyfriend.

The doctor handed her a piece of paper.

She struggled to read his atrocious handwriting.

"You want me to go on birth control?" She asked, confused.

"Trust me, I'm doing you a favor," the man said without looking at her. He scribbled away on his clipboard more notes.

Bea grew frustrated and angry.

"I'm not out there screwing everyone I meet, you know," she blurted out.

"I'm not here to judge," the doctor said in the most sarcastic tone possible.

Bea grunted in frustration and crossed her arms.

"Listen," he said. "It's nothing personal, I just see your lot...well...a lot. You get swept up in college life, before you know it you drop out with a baby or because you're on meth. Giving you birth control is the best I can do to help."

"I don't want your help," Bea said as tears of anger began to surface. "I just want a blood test."

"Fine, fine, fine," he replied, turning toward the door. "No reason to get all worked up about it. I'll send the nurse in. We'll call you if we find anything. If we don't call, then you have nothing to worry about."

"Ok..." Bea said to herself, wiping away tears as she realized the doctor had already left the room and moved onto the next patient.

One week passed, then two. Still no call.

Bea wasn't sure which was worse, getting the call or the uncertainty of if she was going to get a call.

It was on week four that she finally started to relax.

"Nothing to worry about right?" She said to herself.

Unless you gave them the wrong contact phone number or they messed up your tests. The voice was louder than usual, as it always was when her anxiety was in full swing.

Her phone buzzed in her pocket during Professor Mikkelson's lecture. Checking the caller ID, it was an unknown number with a local area code. She panicked, could it be the Medical Center? Were they calling her finally to tell her they found something in her tests?

As she stared, horror-struck at her phone...

"Ms. Logan?" the old frail voice of Professor Mikkelson chimed in her ear.

She looked up, the whole class was staring at her.

"The quizzes please," he said with annoyance in his voice.

"Oh yes," she replied. Quickly putting her phone back in her pocket she pulled the graded quizzes from her bag and began distributing them to the class. Some of the students snickered at her.

As the class shuffled out, Bea stood and gathered her bag; anxious to check her voice mail.

"A word, dear," said the old man's voice behind her from his desk.

She turned and smiled at him. Fully prepared for another verbal lashing about not having her phone out in class.

"How's the thesis coming along?" he asked, his eyes piercing from behind his round glasses.

She panicked. Should she tell him the truth? That she had barely made any progress on it in the last month?

"Great!" She found herself saying without thinking. "Moving along nicely."

"That's great to hear," the Professor replied. "I was concerned earlier that you may have bitten off more than you could chew, so to speak. Glad to hear that's not the case."

Bea didn't know what to say, other than stand there trying to hold her smile and not break down into tears.

"I'd love to read what you have so far," he said.

"Oh...um...ya..." she stumbled.

"I know, it's bad luck," he replied. "But I don't believe in that supernatural garbage. To be honest, I'm just very excited to read what you've found. I'm sure it's going to be great."

"Ya, I need a little more time to button things up I think," she said.

"I understand," he said. "Shall we say...by Thanksgiving break?"

She looked at him, he was smiling from ear to ear. He knew she was having trouble with her thesis.

Thanksgiving break? That was like four weeks away. She had nothing. What was she going to do?

"Great, perfect," she said.

"Splendid, have a good day, dear," the Professor said, looking down again at his papers.

Bea walked out of the classroom and out of the building into the bright sunlight.

She didn't have time to think about how she was going to have a draft by the Professor's deadline, she had to figure out who had called. She played the voicemail.

"This is a message for Bernice Logan from the University Medical Center," the recorded voice began.

As soon as she heard it, her heart dropped in her chest.

"We would like to schedule you for a follow-up visit at your earliest convenience, please call us back to schedule at...".".

She wobbled over to a nearby curb and sat down. Unsure of what to do next, jumping off the tallest building seemed like a completely rational next step, right?

They had been able to schedule her for the follow up appointment that same afternoon, something she found strange since they were usually booked at least a few days out. The nurse had told her they would find a way to squeeze her in.

She had arrived early, planning to catch up on her reading for her thesis while she waited.

"Name, please," the nurse at the entrance asked as she typed away at her computer.

"Bernice Logan," Bea replied. "I know I'm early, but I'm willing to wait..."

"We'll see you right away," the nurse replied with a nervous look. "This way."

Confused, Bea followed the nurse down the hallway to an exam room.

Dr. Tompkins walked in and was followed by a tall woman doctor.

"Hello, Ms. Logan," He uttered those words, just as devoid of empathy as he had been when they first crossed paths. "This is Doctor Keeling."

"Hello," said the female Doctor, her voice was soft and friendly. "Thank you for coming in on such short notice."

“Hi,” was all Bea could manage to say before pausing, alarmed about why she was there. "Is...is...is this about my blood test?"

"Unfortunately," Dr. Tompkins said. "It is."

"Oh my God," Bea said, sitting down in a chair next to the exam table. "I'm pregnant. I’ve heard of how forgetful women can get while pregnant and this week I..."

"You're not pregnant," Dr. Tompkins stopped her.

"Then...then...I have an STD?!" Bea exclaimed. "Oh my God, is it HIV?"

Doctor Keeling sat down next to her and put her hand on Bea's shoulder.

"No...no...no, it's not that," the friendly Doctor said. Her touch was sweet and comforting.

"Oh, thank goodness," Bea said in relief. "With everything, I just thought...you know the worst."

Dr. Keeling gave her a reassuring smile, but Bea could tell there was something she wasn't saying, some truth hidden behind her bedside manner.

"Well," said Dr. Tompkins awkwardly. "The good news is that you don't have any sexually transmitted diseases, at least not in the traditional sense."

Bea trembled with confusion.

Dr. Keeling shot Tompkins a piercing glare.

"What I'm trying to say is," he continued with difficulty. "Is that..."

"Just tell me," Bea demanded as her anxiety began to speak for her.

"We found some abnormal genetic markers in your sample," Dr. Tompkins said at last. "You have Huntington's."

Silence engulfed the room.

"What's Huntington's?" Bea said. She had never heard of it before.

"Oh, it's um..." Dr. Tompkins stumbled.

"It's a genetic disease, passed down from your parents," Dr. Keeling said warmly, squeezing her hand tightly. "It's surprising that you didn't already know this."

"Why?" Bea replied, still in shock.

"Well," Dr. Keeling continued. "One of your parents must have it for them to pass it to you. We assumed you would have known, except you didn't list it in your medical history."

"One of my parents has it?" Bea said in disbelief.

"Yes," the friendly Doctor replied. "I'm sure you must have noticed one of your parents' health deteriorating."

"No, not at all," Bea said as she began to feel tears well up in her eyes. "My parents just ran a 5k for their church. What are the symptoms?"

"Lapses in cognitive function, short-term memory loss, personality changes," the Doctor spouted off the symptoms as if reading out of the medical dictionary.

"I've experienced all that already," Bea said.

Dr. Keeling handed Bea a tissue.

"No, you haven't," Dr. Tompkins interjected. "That's just because of the drugs and alcohol."

Dr. Keeling bestowed upon him another penetrating gaze.

"He's right about the symptoms," said Dr. Keeling with a clarifying tone. "Symptoms of Huntington's Disease don't present until someone is into their 30s or even 40s sometimes. In only very rare cases the symptoms present early..."

"No," interjected the doctor, not really listening. "It would have been present when she was a child. Unless she wrote down the wrong birth year on intake, she shouldn't have any symptoms for at least another decade."

"I told you I don't drink or do drugs," exclaimed Bea.

"Sure," said Dr. Tompkins with raised eyebrows.

Bea could no longer hold back her tears, she broke out into hysterical crying. Dr. Keeling held her tight as the tears fell down her face in a flood.

"I'm sorry, but the likelihood of you presenting symptoms this early," Dr. Tompkins said with a smirk, "compared to the likelihood a college student is lying about their substance abuse, it doesn't take a genius to figure out which one is more logical."

"I told you," Bea grew angry. "I have been feeling different the last few weeks but I haven't done any of those things."

"I believe her, Tompkins," Dr. Keeling said to her colleague.

Tompkins thought hard for a moment.

"Very interesting indeed," he said as he seemed to hold back a growing excitement. "If she is telling the truth..."

"I am!" Bea exclaimed.

He ignored her.

"If she is telling the truth," he continued, "then we might have a variation of the disease we've never seen before. An abnormality that needs to be studied and researched."

Bea wanted to yell at the top of her lungs.

Bea wasn't sure what was worse, the hourglass that now would follow her counting down grains of sand until her final breath, or the fact that Dr. Tompkins was more excited about treating her like a lab animal.

Leaving the University Medical Center later that evening, she stood outside in the cold night air for a long time just staring at the stars above her. Her eyes were now dry, having drained the reservoir of tears inside her.

Well, ain't that shitty, the voice said.

She couldn't argue with it, it was right. Everything that had gone wrong up until that point had only been the appetizer. She had done everything she could to do things right, only to be given a death sentence. It was almost ironic that it took a night of her drinking and having sex with strangers to discover she had a terminal genetic disorder.

She wanted to blame someone. But who?

Her thoughts wandered to her father, the rigid deacon of their church. The man who would rather put it into God's hands than go to a doctor. Maybe if he wasn't such a zealot they would have known about this years ago, instead of Bea wasting what she only now knew to be the prime years of her life.

Or perhaps it was her mother's doing. The always compliant and passive wife of the deacon. The doctor had told her the gene could be passed from the mother or the father equally; perhaps it was her mother's side and her descendants. Her mother was always so quiet and reserved, she may even have known, but had covered it up all these years.

Anger began to swell inside her. Her fists were clenched.

"Fuck it," she found herself saying out loud.

"Ooh, fuck who?" said a familiar voice behind her.

Turning around, Bea found the stylishly dressed figure of Mal standing on the street.

"Mal!" said Bea, startled.

"Everything ok?" Mal asked.

"Yes," Bea said with her best feigned confidence. "Everything's great."

"Haven't seen you in awhile," remarked Mal. "Thought you were avoiding me."

"I'm sorry," Bea apologized instinctively. "I've just been caught up with school and everything."

Mal was staring at her up and down.

Bea felt like Mal knew, somehow she just knew what Bea had only just discovered.

"You look like hell," Mal said after a few moments.

Bea did her best to wipe her eyes.

"I know, I know," Bea said.

"You should take a break," Mal commanded in her usual tone. "Go out with us Friday night."

"I don't know," Bea waffled.

"Come on..." Mal said, pulling on her arm. "It's Halloween, the best night of the year and you only live once."

Bea looked at Mal's perfect blue eyes.

She thought about it, another night of partying. The impact it would have on her thesis homework, her studies. She was running out of time to complete her thesis and all...

Fuck it, remember? Or did you already forget? The voice was loud in her head.

"Ok, I'll go," Bea said at last.

"Great!" Mal said with a rewarding smile. "You won't regret it. It'll be the best night of your life."

"Great," was all Bea could manage to say.

"See you at home!" Mal said as she strolled away.

Bea stood there a minute longer, still unsure to what she had just agreed.

It wasn't until she started to feel her arms shiver that she realized how cold it was outside. Reaching into her backpack, she pulled out her old jacket. A piece of crumpled paper fell to the ground.

Leaning down she picked it up and straightened it out.

It was the prescription for birth control that Dr. Tompkins had given her when she had first visited. She had forgotten all about it.

Fuck it.

She put on her jacket and walked toward the pharmacy on the corner.

Chapter Six

Bea looked at the clear plastic bag on her bed and immediately her thoughts filled with anxiety.

She had never dressed up for Halloween before. Her parents had always taken her to church on October 31st as a child and as an adult so far she hadn't ever found a good reason to wear a costume, typically electing to spend the night catching up on schoolwork.

She was going to look ridiculous.

That's what you get for waiting to get your costume till the last minute, the little voice chided her.

The voice wasn't wrong, she had been so anxious about shopping for one that she didn't actually go to the local pop-up costume shop that appeared in the strip mall next to campus until the day of Halloween. By then, most of the stock of costumes had been picked over and only a few outfits remained. Not feeling quite ready to show up to a club barely wearing anything (which a majority of women's costumes exemplified), she had elected something more conservative for her first foray into the holiday.

But a nun, really?

Bea couldn't help but second guess herself as she pulled the black and white nun's habit from the bag and laid it out on her bed.

The historian part of her brain immediately began critiquing the costume. It was hardly historically accurate, most medieval nuns wore gray and browns more often than black and white. The cut of the tunic also revealed cleavage, something that would have never passed a Mother Superior inspection.

Pulling it over her head and down her body, it fit surprisingly well. As she gazed into the mirror, she adjusted and smoothed the fabric until it embraced her figure, and she observed that the length was perfect, revealing only her feet at the bottom. The outfit was tight around her chest, which Bea noticed accentuated the gap of material where her cleavage would be visible. She considered for a moment putting on a t-shirt underneath to cover the provocative bare skin.

You know that wouldn't fly with Mal, the voice knew what it was saying.

What she knew about Halloween, she had learned from movies and TV. Girls were expected to show a little skin, sexifying almost any costume choice; no matter how mundane. It was just a little bit of skin after all.

Emptying the remainder of the costume bag onto the bed, several items fell onto the comforter. A fake plastic Bible that contained a hidden flask, Bea tossed it into the garbage bin next to her desk. That won't be necessary. She planned only on having a drink or two before heading home. Cheap fake, plastic leather handcuffs, little gold crucifixes printed on the material. That went into the garbage as well. Definitely wasn't planning on needing that.

The last item was a plastic beaded rosary with an oversized crucifix adorned to the end. She wrapped it in her hand and looked in the mirror.

Her phone vibrated behind her, startling her.

She turned, but the costume rosary caught on the post of her bed. Without much effort, the cheap string holding it together tore and beads flew in every direction across her room.

"Shit," she said aloud.

She knelt onto the floor and began collecting the beads.

Her phone buzzed again.

Glancing at the message it was Mal.

UBER IS HERE, WHERE R U?

Bea panicked, she'd have to finish cleaning up later.

Standing, she grabbed her purse from her desk and reached for the doorknob.

She paused as she looked at herself in the mirror, without the rosary the outfit just looked like it was missing something.

Without hesitating to think any longer, she rushed to her jewelry box and pulled out the rosary her grandmother had given her.

She was down the stairs and into the Uber within a minute.

Per usual, Mal spent most of the Uber ride texting on her phone. Her silver-colored fingernails tapped on the screen rapidly. She wore a mesmerizing silver gown intricately embellished to resemble the shimmering scales of a fish, she appeared to have a tailfin-like flourish in the back. In the matter of hours since Bea had last seen her, she had miraculously transformed her hair into a pristine shade of white. Complementing her enchanting attire, silver lipstick and eyeshadow.

"Mermaid?" Bea asked, breaking the silence.

"A Siren, actually," Mal replied with a mischievous smile.

"Planning on luring any men to their deaths tonight?" Bea joked.

"Maybe a few," Mal shot her back a look.

Silence returned, Bea wanted to talk to Mal more but wasn't sure what to say.

"Will...um," Bea said at last feeling the awkwardness close in around them. "Will..."

"Will Adelaide be there tonight?" Mal completed her question for her, returning her gaze to her phone. "Totally."

"Great," Bea managed to say. She was unsure how she would feel about seeing Adelaide again in person. Having not spoken to her since they woke up naked next to each other over a month ago despite hundreds of texts and missed calls from her.

"You have nothing to worry about," Mal said comfortingly. "She's excited to see you, we all are. Cam's been asking when you'd be coming back."

"Cam?" Bea said, confused. The owner? Why did he care...

"Don't get any ideas though," Mal said, eying Bea closely. "That man eats women alive, I would hate it if you ended up like my last roommate."

"Your last roommate?" Bea asked, unsure what Mal was talking about.

"Oh yes," Mal said with a scoff. "The poor girl, she got one look at Cam and fell head over heels for him. All it took was one night and she was in love. Didn't last though, she moved out one day all of a sudden. Dropped out of school, apparently too hurt by the heartbreak to go on."

"Oh," Bea said, not sure what to think of it.

She returned to looking out the tinted window as Mal typed away on her phone.

As before, the block that the old church resided on was eerily quiet. None of the businesses or homes were decorated for Halloween, not that they needed it. Many were so dilapidated and run-down that they could have easily passed as haunted houses without any effort whatsoever.

Exiting the Uber on the dark street and without hesitation rounding the corner of the alley, Bea halted in amazement.

The entire alleyway was soaked in flickering orange light. There must have been over a hundred Jack-O-Lanterns lining the path, each bright with candles and ornately carved. Lifelike hooded bodies hung from nooses over their heads, swaying slightly in the night's breeze. Pentagrams of various styles were painted in fluorescent orange, yellow, and white paint on the ground; they glowed and pulsated under the blacklights.

The line of those waiting to get into Club Llithium was longer than it had been the first time Bea had visited. Every one of them in full costume from zombies to werewolves and beyond. Mal and Bea met the girls at the door, all were absorbed in their phones like before.

"Ready ladies?" Mal said as she approached.

They all looked up, their dull expressionless faces replaced with feign excitement.

"Mal!" they seemed to scream in unison and took turns hugging the Siren and kissing her on the cheek.

"You all remember my roommate, Bea?" Mal said.

"We haven't seen you in forever," said one of the girls as Bea struggled to remember her name.

"Sorry, you know, school," Bea said nervously.

"Ya, school," said the dark haired girl sarcastically.

"Oh, be nice for once, Viv," Mal said.

Bea remembered Viv from her first visit to the club, Viv had kept mostly to herself only speaking to make a sarcastic comment or complaint. Tonight she was dressed in what Bea would have considered lingerie more than a costume. A black lace top that showed off her ample bosom, black short shorts layered over thigh-high black fishnet stockings. She wore the same black calf-high boots that Bea remembered, but it was the black cape and the fangs that gave her costume away.

"I like your costume," Bea said with a smile, trying hard to be nice. "Vampire?"

"No," Viv replied with a scowl. "I'm a dominatrix in need of a dentist."

Viv smiled and licked her fanged false teeth at Bea.

Bea managed to force out a nervous chuckle.

One face missing from the group was Adelaide. Bea couldn't tell if she felt relieved or more nervous at the absence.

"I don't feel like waiting any longer," Mal said, putting her phone away. "Marshall, please keep an eye out for Ady."

"Yes Ms. Phillips," the large bouncer at the door said, unhooking the sash barrier to allow their entrance. He was dressed in a brown loincloth, several gold and jade necklaces hung from his neck onto his large muscular chest; on his head was a headdress that resembled a Jaguar. In fact his skin had subtle markings all over it, a pattern that matched that of his jaguar headgear.

"Looking good, Marshall," said one of the girls as they entered.

Marshall seemed to ignore her, standing at attention as they passed him and into the club.

As impressive as the decorations in the alley had been, they were nothing compared to the inside of the club.

Cobwebs and torn drapes hung from the bar and tables, several lit candelabras were rigged to float over their heads from invisible fishing lines. The walls were illuminated with orange and white lights, the ornate stone columns and brick windows casting dancing shadows up to the ceiling. Shadowy apparitions of skeletons and phantoms gracefully waltzed across the walls, each projection individually choreographed and detailed, no two looked or behaved the same.

All of it gave the club the look and feel that you were in a haunted castle from the Middle Ages, if it weren't for the lasers and fog coming from the stage where the DJ was dressed in a full body werewolf costume. Bea smiled. If this is what Halloween was like, she had been missing out all these years. She followed the group of girls to their usual table, where Harper was waiting for them and next to him was...

"Adelaide!" The girls all screamed and giggled at the thin creature standing next to Harper, taking turns running up to her and hugging her.

Bea remembered Adelaide as thin from their first time meeting, but the figure before her now looked even smaller than the one she remembered. She somehow had lost several more pounds, she appeared to be just skin and bones. Speaking of bones...

Bea couldn't tell in the dark if it was a very thin material or if Adelaide had painted her body black. Every inch of her skin was dark, with the shapes of bones, rubs, a spine, and other skeletal features glowing white.

"I love your skeleton costume!" one of the girls exclaimed.

"You have the perfect body for it," Viv said with a smirk.

"Shut up, Viv," Adelaide said, smirking back. "Oh my, is that Bea?!"

The skeletal figure ran up to Bea and embraced her. Bea returned the hug back, unsure of what else to do.

Bea was concerned, as she felt the body underneath her hands, it didn't feel like the girl she remembered. It felt weak, like her grandmother had been in hospice after fighting cancer for many years. It really did feel like she was hugging a skeleton.

Adelaide pulled away after their brief moment to look at her up close with a smile.

Something else was off about her appearance. Though hard to make out from the black and white paint that covered her face, Bea could still see a large number of wrinkles had formed around her eyes and her cheeks had become extremely sunken and sallow. She looked older, much older than she was. A little creature slowly wasting away into nothingness.

“I've been calling you,” Adelaide said with sadness in her voice.

“I know,” Bea said, not sure how to explain herself.

“And texting,” Adelaide added.

“I've been busy with school,” Bea said, using her broken record excuse for avoiding social interaction as always.

Adelaide knew the truth though, Bea could see it in her eyes. But Adelaide never betrayed anger, just sadness and longing, longing for a friend.

“Well I'm glad you're here tonight,” said Adelaide, making Bea feel better. “It's been lonely and I really had fun with you.”

Bea thought back to her memories of that night and couldn't help but smile. She did have fun after all, even if there had been unforeseen consequences.

"Maybe we could talk outside for a..." Bea tried to say but never got to finish her words.

"How'd you get in?" Mal interjected, bringing the moment between Adelaide and Bea crashing down to earth.

"Sorry," Adelaide said with a tone that sounded insincere. "I was on my way to the line and saw Harper by a side door, so he let me in early and we've been chatting. I must have missed my phone ringing."

"I see," Mal said, staring at Harper a few feet away.

Harper was dressed in his usual dark sleeveless tank top, however sticking out from this back were short and curved black feathered wings. Hanging from his neck was a pendant with an onyx claw at the end.

"Let me get you some drinks," Harper said, walking past them. It was very subtle, but he appeared to wink at Mal as he did.

Whatever anger or annoyance at Adelaide that Mal had harbored immediately passed, bubbly conversation resumed among them.

The group of girls took their seats; Adelaide, Viv, and Bea migrating toward the lounge chairs on the far side away from the main body of girls all fighting for position next to Mal on her throne.

As expected, the group of girls descended into several various conversations that crossed each other. Bea did her best to follow along but found it all too confusing and chaotic. Most of the girls made thinly veiled attempts at flattering Mal almost incessantly. Mal seemed unamused by any of it and Bea caught her staring at Adelaide several times.

"I love Halloween," Adelaide said to Bea, appearing almost giddy with excitement.

"Is it because you get to dress in an outfit that makes normal girls feel fat?" said the seemingly constantly rude and sarcastic Vivian to Bea's right.

"And what are you supposed to be?" Adelaide quipped back. "Kink queen?"

"I'm a vampire," Viv replied. She forced a smile that revealed a set of fake fangs. "Obviously."

"A vampire that likes bondage apparently," said Adelaide, content to spar with Viv. Mal knew they were both good friends. "I just love the idea of the holiday. Dressing up as your favorite scary creature, the pumpkins, the whole concept is just so much fun."

"Oh yes," Viv began sarcastically. "The great holiday invented by the candy companies."

"That's not true," Bea said instinctively. Both girls turned to look at her.

She turned red.

"How is that not true?" Viv asked directly.

"Well," Bea figured she might as well answer. "It began as a Celtic holiday, Samhain. Then when the Romans conquered, it was incorporated into a Roman festival of the dead called Feralia. Then it kind of got merged with All Saints' Day by the Pope. America didn't celebrate it until immigrants in the mid-19th century arrived and then it kind of took off."

"Are you kidding me?" Viv remarked. "You telling me all this time I thought it was some Hershey's conspiracy? Mind blown."

Viv sarcastically made a gesture of her brains being blown out of her skull and then laughed.

"What's with the sexy nun outfit?" She asked Bea directly. "Seems like you're the one who's trying too hard."

"Trying too hard to do what?" Bea said.

"This whole good girl facade," Viv said. "I can see through it, and you, girl, are just as fucked up and perverted as the rest of us."

Bea opened her mouth but no words came out.

She didn't know what to say. She had never been called anything close to perverted before. She always felt she had been too tame, too prude.

"Here you go, ladies," Harper said, startling Bea from her thoughts. He had appeared seemingly out of nowhere from behind them, like he had descended from the sky above them.

He held a black tray with several beverages. Bea recognized hers, that delicious looking amber concoction Harper had served her before. However another drink on the tray intrigued her: it was blood red, syrupy, and fog emanated from the glass.

"Let me guess, that one is for me?" Viv asked.

"Something very special actually," Harper said with a smile. He lifted the glass from the tray and presented it to Viv.

Viv reached forward and grabbed it without looking at Harper. Putting it to her lips she took a sip.

"Now that's a fucking drink," she said. "What's in it?"

"Let's call it a surprise for now," Harper said with his handsome smile. "Enjoy."

Harper spirited back to the bar.

"Oh Bea," said the overly excited voice of Adelaide as she sat down in the open seat on the other side of Bernice. "It's been too long since we talked."

"I know," Bea said with a smile. The bourbon quickly cleared the awkward feeling she had harbored when they first saw each other earlier in the night.

Bea couldn't tell if it was Bourbon loosening her thoughts, but she couldn't hold back any longer, she needed to understand what was going on with Adelaide.

"Are you ok?" Bea asked sincerely.

"Feel ok?" Adelaide questioned in reply. "I feel great, I haven't ever felt better. Between this drink and you girls, life is great."

She burped.

“Excuse me,” she said.

"I'm glad to hear that," Bea said unconvinced. "I'm just concerned, you look..."

"Great, right?" Adelaide interrupted her and turned her shoulders to show off her slim frame. "I haven't even had to diet or anything, I just keep losing weight, must be my metabolism.”

"Ya," Bea said. "Right."

They continued to chat for several minutes until...

"How are things this evening ladies?" said a deep voice from nearby.

Bea turned to see the club owner and manager Cam standing nearby, smiling at them. He was wearing jeans and a tight green v-neck shirt. Bea tried to make out the tattoos on his chest and neck, but it was too dark and he was too far away for her to determine what they were.

"Great party tonight, Cam," Mal said with a smile.

"Thank you, dear," Cam replied, his handsome smile causing Bea's stomach to do backflips.

"Mind if I take a guess at everyone's costumes tonight?" he asked.

"Go right ahead," Mal said with a smile.

"Well," Cam began walking around the group studying everyone.

He turned suddenly to Mal.

"You are very clearly a creature of the ocean," he began. "Shimmering fish scales, a fish tail..."

Mal rolled her eyes.

"I'm not a mer..." she tried to say.

"Not a mermaid," Cam said before she could finish. "The white hair gives it away, you are a seductive siren of the sea."

"Very good," Mal said, smiling at him.

The girls all clapped for him, Viv just rolled her eyes.

He guessed the rest with ease before walking to the end of the table where Adelaide and Bea sat next to the ever disinterested Viv.

Though Adelaide was closest, Cam walked right past her like she wasn't even there. He didn't look at her, much less acknowledge her. She didn't seem to mind being snubbed.

Cam smiled at Bea.

"Obviously you are a naughty nun, though you lack several of the accessories I would expect on such a seductive woman of the cloth."

He grinned ear-to-ear, Bea's stomach continued its acrobatics.

"However," he continued, "I do see one that I find most compelling. May I?" He said, touching her family heirloom.

Carefully he unwrapped the rosary from her wrist. Holding it up to the light above him, he seemed to study it closely.

"I suspect this is no costume piece," he said aloud.

"No," Bea replied. "It was my grandmother's."

"Excellent," Cam continued, "it's quite an exquisite article. Though I doubt she was the first of your family to hold it. I would say this comes from Italy...late 1800s."

"Um, maybe?" Said Bea in surprise. "She gave it to me when she died, she didn't tell me where she got it from."

"Yes," Cam said, still carefully inspecting it. "Quite an heirloom, hold onto that. It'll be worth a bit of money one day."

He handed it back to Bea.

"Oh come on, Cam," Mal said from behind him. "Has appraising the value of antiques ever worked to pick up a girl?"

Cam turned to her and smiled.

"It used to be more effective," he said with a bow.

His hands retreated to his sides, yet Bea couldn't overlook the subtle gesture of him rubbing his palm with his thumb, akin to a nervous habit someone might employ to soothe an irritated patch of skin.

"And Vivian the voluptuous vampire," Cam said, turning to the brooding dark haired girl. "How original."

"Where's your costume?" Viv replied, smirking at him.

"I haven't a moment to put it on yet," said Cam, smiling at her with eyes that seemed to glint in the club lights. "I'm going to be Twrch Tryth."

Viv burst out laughing. The other girls in the group looked to Mal for a cue as to whether they should laugh too. She sat quiet and stoic and so they did as well.

"Sounds like a Scandinavian beer?" Viv said, barely controlling her laughter.

"You'll see." Cam replied calmly.

It sounded familiar to Bea.

"It's Welsh, isn't it?" Bea asked.

All the girls turned their gaze to Bea, her social anxiety growing by the second.

"Well, well," Cam said. "I'm impressed."

"I can't remember exactly who he was though," Bea remarked. “The tales of King Arthur aren’t my specialty.”

"Well maybe when you see the rest of the costume it'll jog your memory," he replied.

His eyes were fixed on Bea, the rest of the girls' gazes melted away around her. Suddenly Bea felt like it was just Cam and her in the entire club, the world bleeding away around her like fresh paint left out in the rain.

Bea lost track of time, were they just staring at each other for seconds, minutes, maybe hours? She had no way of knowing.

"Well, is this a club or a morgue?" Mal asked from behind Cam.

Cam broke their gaze and turned, as the world around Bea returned in a snap.

"I'm sorry, my dear," he said, looking over at the stage. He raised his hand and made a short gesture to the werewolf DJ.

"I hope you all have a pleasant evening," he said, he slipped away into the crowd.

The girls resumed their chatting.

What kind of night club manager knows eccentric Arthurian legends and can date the manufacture of rosaries?

The sexy kind, the little voice in her head added.

Bea rolled her eyes at the voice, but for once they were in agreement.

"Like what you see?" Viv said with a smirk.

Bea broke from her trance. She had been staring at the spot where Cam had last been, absorbed in daydreaming about him.

"Sorry, I um..." Bea stumbled.

"Girl, be warned. He's a total hound," Viv remarked. "But he does have a nice ass."

Bea had been mesmerized by him, but not by his butt. Something about him breathed energy and heat. She felt totally intoxicated by him.

"I'd avoid barking up that tree," Viv continued as she leaned forward smiling at Bea. "You don't want to end up like that last roommate of Mal's..."

"What was her name again?" Adelaide said, her brow furrowed in thought accentuating the wrinkles around her eyes.

"Agatha," Viv said. "How can you not remember? She partied with us every night for months."

"Agatha, yes," Adelaide said in agreement. "I remember now. Nice girl, red hair."

"She was a bitch with blond hair," Viv corrected her. "I swear Adelaide, sometimes I wonder if there's anything between those ears of yours."

"Thanks Viv," Adelaide replied before sipping her drink. "Love you too."

Adelaide raised a bony middle finger towards Viv who flipped one back to show off her dark black nail polish.

“All I remember, was that once Agatha was out of the picture,” Adelaide commented between hiccups. “Cam was following me around like a poor little puppy dog.”

Bea sipped her drink nervously, she didn’t want to say anything that might betray how into Cam she really was.

"That girl was messed up," Viv added. "She had some kind of auto-immune disease or something."

"Multiple sclerosis, I think," said Adelaide.

"She was a total mess," Viv sipped her blood-like drink. "Didn't stop Cam though."

"Ughh, I know," Adelaide added. "Now he's been asking me out for months ever since. Gross."

"He's got a type," Viv said, winking at Adelaide.

"Well he's definitely not my type," said Adelaide, who was staring at the other end of the table where Harper and Mal were chatting. "I like a man who's softer, sweeter, and..."

"Has a strange obsession with birds?" Viv said with a laugh.

"Shut up, you bitch," Adelaide responded playfully. "We both know you'd fuck him in a minute if you were given a chance."

"Maybe we could share him," Viv replied. "Heard you are into that sort of thing.

Viv shot a side glance at Bea who turned bright red at the comment.

"Shhh," Adelaide hissed. "Something's happening."

Suddenly the lights in the club went out and several women screamed.

"Did they blow a fuse or something?" Bea heard Viv ask nearby with slight concern in her voice.

"I don't think so," Adelaide said calmly.

Overhead the projectors flickered back to light. A hissing sound could be heard all around them.

Dark gray clouds were projected onto the walls, fog hung low over the dance floor.

The whole club lit up as a full moon appeared from behind the clouds, shining white and silver.

Their tables and chairs vibrated as they were engulfed in the howls of a thousand wolves.

The moon shifted from silver to red, the brightest light in the club now shading everyone in deep crimson coats. Everyone looked like they were soaked in blood.

The crowd on the dancefloor howled in unison, a hellish brigade of would-be werewolves.

Adelaide grabbed Bea's hand.

"Let's go!" Adelaide said, nodding to the dance floor as she shot a look at Bea.

Bea was still awestruck by the whole scene; she did little to fight it, the allure of joining the pack was too tempting.

Adelaide danced in front of Bea, the dim light on the dance floor paired with the black lights melted away the silhouette of her body, a floating, glowing skeleton remained.

Bea tried to dance with her, moving her body in close, but found the nun outfit very difficult to dance in. She considered going back to the table and asking Viv to help her tear some seams into it so she could actually move along to the music.

Glancing back, something caught her eye. Cam and Mal were talking by themselves. Talking was a nice way to put it, it looked more like they were arguing. Mal seemed to be upset with Cam and Cam scowled as he responded. It was impossible through the dim lights and loud music to even guess what they were fighting about.

"Bea," Adelaide said, pulling her in close and whispering in her ear. "Let go."

Bea looked at the girl in front of her. Adelaide no longer resembled the young girl she had met weeks before, she looked twice her age. The sunken cheeks, the wrinkled skin, even her eyes looked dull and gray, like she had lost her youth and was quickly turning over to middle age. The only sparkle left on her was the blue and green necklace depicting a Nixie that hung from her neck.

"I'm sorry, I um..." Bea stammered.

They danced close and Bea began to forget about Mal and Cam, or concerns about preparing her thesis in time for Professor Mikkelson, or the fact that she was going to start slowly dying a painful death.

Fuck it, fuck it all, remember?

She had just begun to feel the relief of anxiety and emotion, the therapeutic effects of the club when...

A tap on her shoulder surprised her, she turned to find Mal smiling at her.

"Ready to go?" Mal asked.

"Go?" Bea answered confused. "We just got here."

"I know but," Mal replied. "I'm kind of tired. You can stay, but I'm out of here."

Bea thought for a moment, she looked at Adelaide.

Adelaide's eyes screamed STAY, but then again Mal was her roommate. She felt obliged to do what Mal wanted to do.

"I really should go," Bea said to Adelaide, smiling. "Call me tomorrow? Let's grab coffee."

Adelaide's eyes looked disappointed, she faked a smile regardless.

"Sure," she said. "Tomorrow."

Bea hugged her, Adelaide weakly hugged her back.

Bea rushed out of the club at Mal's heels. None of the other girls followed.

Bea was confused as they rode in silence in the Uber back home. Mal wasn't acting like her usual self, she seemed frustrated and angry. Even her phone, almost in her hands at all times, was face down on her lap.

Bea wasn't sure what she was supposed to do, comfort her? Ask her if she's ok over and over again until she cracks? Mal doesn't crack.

Bea had to say something, the tension in the car was palpable.

You screwed something up didn't you?

Maybe, probably, likely...

"I'm sorry," Bea said, it was the only thing she could think of to say.

"Sorry for what?" Mal asked, looking out the window with a scowl.

"For whatever I did," Bea replied. "I didn't mean to do whatever it was that I did that made you want to leave."

"You did?" Mal questioned, confused. "Girl, it was nothing you did. It's just..." She paused, like she was carefully considering what to say next. "I can't really explain it."

"You can tell me," Bea said sincerely. "You can tell me anything, I won't judge."

Mal turned to look at Bea, and for a moment, really just a half milli-second; it looked like Mal was ready to stream forth with all her deepest darkest frustrations. Mal's eyes betrayed the slightest bit of distress and loneliness.

How could a girl with that many friends ever be lonely?

It went as quick as it had appeared.

"I've been friends with Cam for a long time," Mal explained. "Sometimes though, what he does...I just can't. I can't, but I must."

"What types of things?" Bea asked.

"I don't know how to say it," she replied. "Let me just tell you this."

She seemed to pause for a long moment, as if carefully plotting her next words.

"Underneath it all," she continued. "Under the glam, under the suave exterior, he's really a good guy. He's sweet, he's caring, he's even loving. But his job, that club. He has to say things, he has to do things, has to act differently than who he really is."

"Why doesn't he just sell the club and do something else?" Bea asked.

"Sell the club?" Mal shrieked with held back laughter. "His father would murder him."

"It can't really be that bad," said Bea.

"You don't know his father then," Mal said without hesitation.

"It's more than a club really," Mal said after a silence. "The drinks, the dancing, the crazy themes. There's so much more there than people know. Cam got caught up in it a long time ago, and he knows he can never get out. Not now, not ever."

"That's kind of sad," said Bea, feeling sympathy for him.

Silence returned to the car, Bea's own thoughts were absorbed in thoughts of Cam. Mal knew him better than anyone, she had even said he could be sweet and loving.

Maybe she could be that person that helped him be that person?

Are you kidding me? Little old Bea, the deacon's daughter, with the owner of a nightclub? You're dreaming. The voice was its usual caustic self tonight.

She was dreaming, but she felt happy in that dream even as unlikely as it was to ever come true.

They were getting close to home. Bea knew in a few minutes she and Mal would be inside and back to their respective rooms. Their relationship would continue to be cordial, but this rare moment of openness between them would be lost. She wanted to know more about Mal, more about the club, but most of all, more about Cam.

Whether the bourbon was helping or not she wasn't sure, but she felt brave. Brave enough to ask Mal the question on her mind.

"Do you think he would ever be into someone like me?" Bea asked.

Mal's eyes swirled with thoughts.

"Maybe," Mal replied honestly. "He hasn't been serious with anyone, not as long as I've known him or that he's ever told me."

Bea felt disappointed.

"Don't feel bad," Mal said, noticing Bea's facial expression. "His relationships come in two flavors. Sometimes he's with someone for just a night or two, the girl usually falls helplessly in love with him only to be rejected quickly. The rejection is so sudden and devastating I seldom see the girl again. Other times though, he likes to take his time. Start things slowly, pursue the girl over weeks, maybe months. They may sleep together a few dozen times over which she slowly and slowly succumbs to his charms."

She paused.

"The end result is always the same," she continued. "The girl falls hopelessly in love and Cam rejects her. She is devastated and we will never hear from her again."

This hardly made Bea feel any better.

"It's like going out to eat," Mal said, trying to cheer up her roommate. "Sometimes you go somewhere like a fast food place."

Bea found it hard to believe that with Mal's perfect figure she frequented fast food restaurants often or at all.

"You figure out what you're starving for," she kept going. "You order it, it's in front of you in no time flat and you eat just as quickly. It's not quite satisfying, but it's nourishment. Keeps you going another day."

The car pulled up to the community, the iron gate softly creaking as it opened.

"Other times you want a bit more," said Mal. "So you go to a nice restaurant. Sit down, sip at a glass of wine, nibble on some bread, one, two, three, four, five small courses come out. You sip your coffee, you take a few bites of dessert. You really savor the whole thing."

Bea laughed, she actually had never been to a restaurant that served meals in courses before. The thought felt like a scene from a movie.

"At the end of the night," Mal said as the lights of the mansion loomed ahead of them. "The only difference between the two is how long you take to eat it. You take your time with the good stuff, rush the garbage. That's Cam's relationship philosophy."

They stared at each other a moment as the car came to a stop. Neither moving to get out of the vehicle.

"What?" Mal asked with confusion.

"Just like food, really? That's his dating philosophy?" Bea said with a growing grin.

Both girls laughed.

Adelaide lost track of time as she danced, she didn't care. She just wanted to feel the music, the heat of the other bodies around her, feel something other than pain and loneliness.

It was a loneliness she had felt ever since finding out she had stomach cancer. Triggered partially from self-consciousness at the constant barrage of symptoms: acid reflux, weight loss, just to name a few.

However, it was the knowledge and knowing that she was going to die that made it hard for her to get close to others. They hadn't caught the cancer in time, and despite the most expensive specialists, surgeries, and treatments that money could buy; every effort was as fruitless as the last attempt. She knew she was going to die, and no one around her really knew what that felt like.

Bea had been the exception, something about their connection had felt different. Yes, they had been intimate, but it was a fun fling fueled by alcohol and Tarzan's raw masculine magnetism. Their connection had been deeper, or at least she thought it had been. Seeing Bea follow Mal out of the club on a whim had hurt, hurt more than chemo had, hurt more than the third surgery attempting to remove the mass from her stomach.

However Adelaide knew it was inevitable. Mal was a force unto herself, girls clung to her laurels begging for scraps of her perfection and beauty like beggars in the streets. Their bonds of friendship were only superficial, they were more than likely to tear into one another the moment they were out of Mal's sight.

There was only one thing that made her feel better, and that was the club. The alcohol, the music, the crowd on the dance floor; she felt like it all insulated her from the pain of her loneliness even if only temporarily.

Temporarily was better than not at all.

She felt a presence behind her, a shadow even darker than the ambiance of the club.

She turned, the figure was a large man clad in fur wearing a mask resembling a wild tusked boar, he held his hand out to her as if beckoning for a dance.

She thought about it, he was easily two or three times her weight. Large men weren't really her type, but she felt something different from him that she couldn't quite explain. What the hell, you only live once right? A dance wouldn't hurt.

She took his hand, and noticed her hand looked like a child's in comparison to his. His touch blazed with a fiery intensity that sent shivers racing across her skin. Drawing her closer to his chest, the heat emanating from him felt as scorching as a blazing furnace.

Her head swirled around her as they danced. She felt his body and hers intertwine. Within minutes she felt strange sensations surging through her body, feelings of pleasure and desire.

Wanting more, she pushed herself closer to him. The fur of his body soft on her bare back, his touch strong but gentle on her hips and arms. Every moment, her body felt warmer. She closed her eyes, the lights in the club dissolved into a bright meteor shower and she danced in ecstasy.

The tingles on her skin and swimming in her blood were moving, closer and closer to her waist towards her...

She pushed him away.

She had been close, close to having a full blown orgasm right there on the dance floor. All from dancing with some stranger she had just met. It was strange, it was bizarre, it was wrong. It shouldn't work like that.

"Another drink?" asked Harper, appearing behind her and startling her.

"Harper, what?" Adelaide spun in confusion.

"Sorry love," Harper said with his shrewd smile. "Didn't mean to surprise you."

Adelaide looked around searching for the man in the boar costume whom she had just been skin-to-skin with only moments prior. He was gone.

"Where did he go?" Adelaide asked.

"Who?" Harper replied in confusion.

"The man, the, the..." Adelaide's mind was distracted and confused. "He was huge, he was just here."

"No one here but you, love," Harper said smiling.

Did she imagine him?

"How about that drink?" Harper asked.

"Um, sure!" Adelaide replied with some hesitation. She had lost count of how many she had tonight. Not that it mattered anyways, drinking made life livable.

The man in the boar costume, had she really imagined him. Maybe she should take it a bit slower. However without him, those creeping feelings of loneliness began to grow through the cracks and invade her thoughts.

What good would slowing down do? Not like she could fix anything wrong with her life after all.

Harper held out a shot glass.

She took a breath and drank it in one gulp. The creeping thwarted for the moment, but not forever. She shouldn't be slowing things down, maybe she should be taking things to another level.

"Can I get you anything else? Anything stronger?" Harper asked with his pleasant smile, almost as if he had read her mind.

She thought for a moment.

"I could go for some molly actually," Adelaide said with hopeful eyes.

"Say no more," Harper replied with a reassuring tone. "Follow me, please."

Placing his hand at the small of her back, he led her off the dance floor to a tapestry that hung against a well.

Harper pulled the tapestry to the side revealing a hidden doorway.

"Back room?" Adelaide asked.

"Can't risk it on the club floor," Harper replied.

Somewhere, in the back of Adelaide's consciousness alarm bells were going off. Alarm bells she had long learned to mute and ignore. "You only live once, so live it," she thought.

"Lead the way, Harp," she said.

They passed through the dark doorway together.

Chapter Seven

Bea woke up the next morning feeling surprisingly refreshed. The sun's radiant glow pierced the curtains, filling her room with warmth. She felt grateful for leaving the club early last night. Today, she might even inch closer to completing her thesis. But first, a cup of coffee.

She tiptoed downstairs, careful not to disturb Mal, who typically didn't rise until brunch. She paused at the kitchen entrance.

Sitting at the countertop bar was Mal, in a long gray sweater and short shorts, staring out the window into the garden. She was sipping on coffee, but her expression was sad. Here in this moment where she thought she was alone, Mal looked like something was bothering her, something was on her mind.

"Morning," Bea said.

Mal jumped and several drops of the coffee in her hand splashed to the floor.

"I'm so sorry," Bea said, rushing to the kitchen sink and grabbing a paper towel.

"No, it's fine," Mal said warmly with a smile and taking the towel from her. "I was lost in thought. Good Morning."

Bea was happy to see Mal smiling again, but couldn't help but think something was off.

"Everything ok?" Bea asked sincerely.

"Yes, everything is fine," Mal commented, cleaning up the coffee spills on the floor. "And stop apologizing so much."

"I had fun last night," Bea said, smiling. "Thank you for inviting me out."

"My pleasure," Mal said. "I had fun too."

Bea didn't find Mal's tone convincing. Still, she didn't know how to better console her friend or get her to open up.

They sat in silence both sipping on their coffees quietly.

Bea was just about to get up and say farewell so she could start on her thesis when...

"You know what," Mal said, suddenly standing up.

"What?" Bea responded.

"We haven't spent any quality time together," Mal added.

"Well, we've both been busy..." Bea's voice trailed off.

"Well, how about today?" Mal asked. "Let's go shopping, my treat."

"I don't know," Bea stammered. "My thesis..."

"You've been working on that thing like a dog for weeks," Mal commented. "Even you need a real break from it. What is one day going to hurt?"

Bea looked at Mal's beautiful eyes, staring at her with a face that was very, very hard to say "No" to.

"Ok," Bea said at last. "But only for a few hours."

"Excellent!" Mal said excitedly. "Go get ready, Cortez opens up at 10am and he makes great Mimosas."

"Mimosas?" Bea questioned aloud, not really sure what she had gotten herself into.

It didn't matter though, Mal had practically run out of the room already.

Bea sipped her coffee and took a deep breath.

Ok, let's do this.

The driver dropped Bea and Mal off in the center of downtown. Bea had only driven through the dense metropolis at night, preferring to avoid the congested throngs of people who trudged through it, day in and day out. The buildings loomed overhead and Bea found herself gazing upwards, captivated. Growing up in the suburbs, her only exposure to tall buildings had been the local church steeple and bell tower—the tallest landmarks in her hometown. Even the shortest building here would overshadow those familiar monuments.

"Come on," Mal said, leading her to the nearest tower.

They stepped into the structure through expansive glass entrances, the sound of Mal's heels echoing crisply against the polished marble of the foyer.

"Hold that elevator, please," Mal shouted.

A man inside the elevator door reached out to stop the door and it opened just in time for Mal and Bea to join him inside.

"Thank you," Mal said, smiling at him.

"What floor?" he replied. He was dressed in a suit and tie, strange for a Saturday morning. Bea imagined he was a young lawyer putting in extra hours on the weekends.

"Fortieth, please," Mal replied.

He smiled back at her, but it was his eyes that gave it away. He was attracted to her, it didn't take a rocket scientist to determine that. Who wouldn't be? The gorgeous blonde hair, the trim physique, perfect skin. Bea was surprised she wasn't a model.

"Cortez's place?" the man half-asked, half-stated. "He's amazing, the best in town."

"Oh, I know," Mal replied with a confident smile.

The man raised an eyebrow.

They rode the rest of the way in silence, Bea awkwardly observing the handsome, young lawyer, practically salivating over Mal.

"Have a fun Saturday," Mal said as the elevator bell pinged and the doors opened to the fortieth floor.

"You too," the man said, eager to catch one final glimpse of her before she disappeared forever.

The doors closed and he was gone.

"He was handsome," Bea commented.

"He was ok," Mal replied.

"He was really into you," said Bea with a smile. "Would you?"

"Would I what?" Mal asked.

"Would you have gone out with him if he had asked?" Bea elaborated.

"Oh, no way," Mal replied. "I can smell desperate social climbers from a mile away. The minute he knew where we were going he smelled money."

"Lawyers," Bea said. "The lowest form of life on this planet."

"I can think of lower," Mal said with a wink.

At the end of a hall, was an unmarked door with silver trim.

Mal rang the buzzer.

A camera hanging from the ceiling above them blinked to life and the door buzzed open.

Walking in, Bea was almost blinded by the bright sunlight.

The room was large and open, one of the walls was entirely made of glass and looked out over the bustling downtown below. The floor was marble and white, just like the walls and the furniture. Floor length mirrors and garment stands lined the perimeter.

Bea was still dumbstruck when a man emerged from behind a white curtain covering a doorway. He was tall, bald, and wore trendy square glasses. His dark gray suit, tailored to his tall, slender build, was outshone only by the vibrant maroon ascot draped around his neck. He carried a tray laden with glasses and bottles in his hand.

"Mal, so good to see you," he said warmly.

He leaned down so that Mal could kiss him on both cheeks lightly.

"Oh Frederick, it's been too long," Mal replied. "This is my new roommate, Bea."

"A pleasure my dear," Frederick said with a friendly smile. "Please, take a seat. He will be with you in a few moments."

He motioned to several large white arm chairs, both girls hurried over and sat down.

A loud pop echoed in the room as he opened the champagne and poured them both glasses.

"So," Mal said, taking hers and taking a sip. "How has he been?"

"Oh," Frederick groaned, handing Bea her glass. "He's been so insufferable. Complaining day and night about lacking a true challenge."

"You mean I'm not challenging enough?" Mal said with a sarcastic giggle.

"Dear," the man replied. "You could walk down the street wearing a garbage bag with a banana peel in your hair and men would gawk at you as if you were Venus herself."

Mal smiled deeply.

"Are you two gossiping about me again?" said a small Latino voice from behind the curtain.

Soon he burst through the doorway, his cropped black hair shimmered with a fresh layer of mousse. His beard was sculpted close to his jawline. He donned a vibrant jacket featuring reds, yellows, and blues in a coordinated pattern of varying rectangular sizes, which mirrored the design on his trousers.

"Mal, my dear," he said, walking up to her and leaning over to kiss her on the cheek. "So happy you are here. One does not find such natural beauty often enough in this world."

"Thank you, Cortez," Mal said, almost blushing. "Can I introduce you to my new roommate? Meet Bea. Bea, meet Cortez, my favorite designer."

"I'm an artist my dear, not a designer," he corrected her. "Bea, what an interesting name."

"Yes, it's short for..." Bea began to speak.

"Stand," he cut her off.

Not sure what else to do, she put her drink down and stood.

"You brought her here in flats?" Cortez remarked to Bea.

"I didn't want to tamper with her before you got a look," Mal replied, taking another sip of her drink.

Bea was confused.

"Walk," Cortez commanded.

"What?" Bea replied confused.

"Walk, or did they not teach that in whatever horrible Neanderthal cave that Mal found you in?" Cortez repeated and made a gesture with two fingers of walking across the room.

Not wanting to agitate Cortez, she followed his orders. Walking to the other end of the room and then standing there, not sure of what to do next.

"Um, turn and walk back, please," Cortez commanded.

Bea felt awkward but obeyed.

As she finished, she stood in front of Cortez who looked her up and down.

"I can't believe you thought you could bring this creature to me in such a state," Cortez commented to Mal.

"Creature?" Bea said with growing animosity towards the rude little man.

From behind Cortez, Bea could see the friendly Frederick gesturing to her to let it go.

"There's no way I can work with this," Cortez said, turning and walking back towards the curtains in the doorway.

"I'm sorry," Mal said, still smiling. "Too much of a challenge?"

Cortez stopped in his tracks.

"My dear Frederick," Cortez turned and looked at his partner, still holding the bottle of Champagne with a mischievous grin. "Have you been talking too much again? Hmm? I will have to punish you later for this."

"Fine Mal," Cortez said with a sigh. "You win, as always."

"You're the best," she replied with a flirtatious tone.

"And you," Cortez looked at Bea with a pointed finger. "Take those rags off now."

"Rags?" Bea questioned.

"Yes, rags. Off, now." Cortez said, walking to one of the clothes racks near the wall. "You can keep your panties on, but please take off that wretched medieval torture device pretending to be a bra."

Bea was frozen. Was she really supposed to strip for this stranger?

Sensing her apprehension, Frederick put his hand on her shoulder.

"Come with me, dear," he said. "You'll feel more comfortable changing behind here." He motioned towards a nearby white partition.

Once she was hidden behind the divider, she removed her clothes except for her panties as instructed and wrapped her arms around her breasts to hide them from view. After emerging nervously, she saw Cortez talking frantically to himself and throwing piles of clothes onto a nearby white Ottoman.

"Here dear," Frederick said warmly, handing her a fresh Champagne. "Trust me, this will help."

She gulped it down heartily.

"Granny panties, really?" Cortez said, turning around to look at her. "Mal my dear, she's not allowed back inside my studio unless she's wearing Agent Provocateur."

"Yes Cortez," Mal said, smiling and standing up.

Mal walked over to the mostly naked Bea and hugged her tightly.

"Thank you for this," she whispered in Bea's ear.

Bea wasn't sure if it was Mal being sweet to her or the alcohol, but she felt a little less embarrassed and nervous.

"So what's the occasion?" Cortez asked.

"Oh, you know," Mal began. "She needs a couple outfits for the club."

"The club you say," Cortez commented with a growing interest. "Any particular themes?"

"The Germans are coming to visit," Mal replied as if that statement made complete sense to everyone in the room.

"The Germans," Cortez's voice trailed off for a moment. "That means something edgy, dark, sexy, sultry. Any other audience I should know about?"

He looked at Mal who gave him a raised eyebrow reply.

"Ohh," Cortez said with a smile. "Him as well."

"Who?" Bea asked, still as confused as ever.

"Quiet," Cortez commanded again. "The canvas does not speak to the artist. Now, put this on."

He tossed a black garment at Bea.

The next several hours were a blur of being told to put on dresses and shoes and hats and jewelry and other articles of clothing she sometimes didn't know what they were called. The flow of drinks from Frederick seemed endless, Bea enjoying them in between breaks of trying on clothes and standing naked in front of Cortez as he grunted at her body disapprovingly.

They walked out of the building and into the sunlight.

"Wasn't that fun?" said Mal with giddy excitement. "He'll send it over to the house when he's done."

Bea's head still felt like it was in a whirl from all the activity. She pulled her phone from her jeans pocket.

Three missed calls from Adelaide.

"Shit," she said aloud.

"What is it?" Mal asked.

"I forgot," Bea began. "I was supposed to meet Adelaide for coffee this morning."

"Call her back," said Mal. "I'm sure she's still available."

"Ok, I just feel bad," said Bea, dialing on her phone.

"She'll live," Mal replied. "Invite her out, we can probably have a late lunch with her at that place she loves..."

"Hello," a voice on the other line answered.

"Adelaide," Bea began. "I'm so sorry, I was out with Mal and we just lost track of time. Can we have lunch instead?"

"I'm sorry this isn't Adelaide," the voice replied. "I'm her sister Marienne."

"Oh, I'm sorry," Bea said. "Is she ok?"

The voice on the other end went quiet.

"I've been on her phone," the voice said at last. "And I wasn't sure who she was friends with these days. Your name seemed to keep popping up in her outbound texts."

"What happened?" Bea's said with growing concern.

"Um," the voice replied with hesitation. "I don't know how to say this."

"What?" Bea exclaimed.

"Adelaide passed away last night," the voice said.

Bea was at a loss for words, thoughts, and actions. She remained motionless on the sidewalk..

"What? What is it?" Mal asked clueless.

The next week leading up to Adelaide's funeral seemed to slow down to a snail's pace. Bea couldn't help but feel like crying at the slightest misfortune. Dropping her pen in class, the grocery store being out of her favorite flavor of ice cream; the tears in her eyes seemed to always be on the verge of erupting, as if they were a mighty river held back by a decaying dam.

It was an odd sensation of mourning for someone she'd only met twice. Yet, in those encounters, Bea sensed a depth that elevated them beyond mere acquaintances. They shared a bond, celebrating their distinctiveness from the group, coupled with a subtle undertone of shared loneliness.

On Saturday, Mal and Bea rode together to the funeral. They both wore black dresses, Bea borrowed one of Mal's. The Uber ride was very quiet, both unsure what to say as they approached the funeral parlor.

The sky was overcast with a light drizzle. Both girls hurried out of the car, seeking shelter under a nearby awning.

"I can't believe she's gone," Bea said aloud.

"I know, I know," Mal replied.

It was difficult to discern how sincere Mal truly was. Despite the dreary weather, Mal's eyes were hidden behind dark sunglasses.

A line of people dressed in black marched slowly into the parlor, Mal and Bea joined them. At the front of the parlor was a raised platform, upon which a gold and red coffin rested like a monolith. Grand, decorative floral wreaths encircled the coffin, giving the impression it was nestled in a serene garden. A large portrait stood on an easel, a happy and smiling picture of Adelaide. From her appearance in the photo, Bea guessed the photo had been taken several years prior to meeting her.

Several other girls from the club were already there, talking amongst themselves at a cocktail table. They didn't seem to be upset at all at losing their friend, they were smiling like it was another night out.

Until they spotted Mal.

The girls erupted into exchanges of tear-soaked hugs and hollow remarks of mourning and remorse.

"It was so sudden."

"She was such a sweet girl."

"I had no idea she had stomach cancer."

"So brave."

The voices melded together in Bea's ears. She sat quietly in the chair, still not sure that the news of Adelaide's passing had fully hit her yet. One voice and face that was noticeably absent, though, was the dark haired firebrand, Viv.

It was a closed casket, something Bea found peculiar.

The sound of soft, solemn music filled the room and the chorus of voices quieted down immediately. An old woman emerged from a side room, escorted by the arm by a tall white man with gray hair. They were an odd couple to say the least, but from the tenderness he showed for her with each step you could deduce their relationship was based on long established feelings of true love. They were Adelaide's parents.

The music ceased as a young woman made her way to the lectern. She bore an uncanny resemblance to Adelaide, albeit being notably fuller. It was her sister Marienne, the one who had delivered the heartbreaking news to Bea. Marienne extracted a pair of glasses and a folded set of pages from her handbag. As she sorted and arranged the notes, Bea's mind wandered to speculate of the differences between the two sisters.

"Thank you all for coming today," Marienne began. "For those of you I haven't met before, my name is Marienne. I am Adelaide's sister."

"I know she would be happy to see all of you here today," Marienne continued. "Her death likely felt very sudden to all of you. Many of her friends here never knew that Adelaide had stomach cancer," Marienne continued.

Marienne glanced at the other girls from the club, with the exception of Bea all of them were texting on their phones and not paying attention in the slightest.

Marienne sighed.

"She had always wanted to keep her diagnosis and treatments a very private matter," Marienne continued. "My sister had one amazing strength. No matter how bad she felt, no matter how much it hurt just to exist, she still was strong enough to get up everyday and smile, hug, and continue to love."

A tear fell onto the page.

"Before we give you all a chance to say goodbye," Marienne said. "I wanted to share with you one of her favorite stories that our father told us growing up. It's a German bedtime story called, 'The Water's Edge.'"

Marienne hesitated briefly, retrieving a petite book from her bag.

"A long time ago, nestled by a mystical pond within an ancient forest, there dwelt a humble miller and his loving wife. Their lives, though filled with joy, were shadowed by poverty. One fateful dawn, as the miller sought wood for his hearth, he chanced upon an enchanting maiden, her beauty laid bare, bathing in the shimmering waters. With a voice as soft as the murmur of the brook, she promised him treasures beyond imagination, but in return, she desired that which would come to life in his home that very day.

"The miller, certain that no child awaited them, eagerly sealed the pact with the ethereal maiden. Yet, as he crossed the threshold of his abode, the unexpected wail of a newborn met his ears. To his astonishment and dread, in the time he was absent, destiny had played its hand, and his wife had brought forth a child in the warmth of their hearth."

Marienne stifled a sob.

"Adelaide always thought that part was funny," she said. "What kind of oblivious husband doesn't realize his wife is pregnant?"

A muted laugh rippled through the crowd.

“When he realized the depths of his folly, he approached the waters once more, only to discover not the elusive Nixie but a chest brimming with golden coins. With this treasure, he envisioned a life far away from the Nixie's grasp, in the bustling heart of a town.

“In that new abode, their child was raised on tales of caution, to steer clear of the treacherous pond. Yet, nature's call was potent, and the boy blossomed into a huntsman of great repute. Time, as it always does, wove its tapestry, and he found love, setting roots of his own.

“However, during one fateful hunt, as he pursued a majestic stag, destiny led him to the water's edge. Forgetting ancient warnings, he touched the waters, only to be ensnared by the vengeful Nixie.

“Distraught, his wife, in her wisdom, sought the counsel of an age-old witch atop a lonely mountain. Bestowed with a golden comb, flute, and spinning wheel, she was told that these mystical items held the power to free her beloved.

“By the haunting pond, she weaved a song of love and longing. With every note, with every golden strand she spun, her husband neared freedom. Yet, just as joy seemed palpable, the furious Nixie unleashed a tidal wave, driving them apart, erasing their memories and casting them to distant shores.

"Years trickled by, until destiny, always fond of twists, brought them face-to-face. In one shared gaze, memories surged back, drowning the Nixie's curse. Together once more, they stood testament to love's indomitable spirit, living their days in joy, forever untouched by the shadows of the past."

Marienne closed the book.

"Adelaide always believed everything has a cost," she said with tears pouring down her cheeks. "Every experience, every choice. Sometimes the cost is even bared by those you love. However, nothing can break the bonds of love that link us all."

She stepped down from the lectern and the crowd clapped quietly.

After the funeral was over, they were ushered into a side room where there was food and coffee. Bea and Mal stood in the long line to speak to Adelaide's parents and offer their condolences. It was the least they could do.

"I can't believe it," Mal said, clutching Bea's arm. "He's here."

Bea spun around to see who she was referring to.

"Ladies," Cam said with a smile. "Sorry we're late."

"Wasn't sure you'd come at all," Mal said with a raised eyebrow. "And you brought Harpy."

Harper looked bored.

"She and I were quite the best mates, weren't we?," Harper said.

Mal didn't look convinced.

"Cam told me I'd be sacked if I didn't come," he added.

Cam elbowed him in the ribs.

"Are those her parents?" Cam asked, looking over Mal's shoulder.

Adelaide's mum had tears in her eyes, yet she bravely smiled, embracing and chatting with guests by the grand portrait of Adelaide. Her dad was perched on a chair close by, quietly lost in his thoughts.

"Did you guys know she had cancer?" Bea asked Cam and Harper. Wondering if Adelaide had told anyone about it.

"No idea," Harper replied. "She was always the life of the party."

"How'd she look?" Cam asked, he seemed nervous.

"No idea," said Mal. "Closed casket."

"I see," said Cam. He seemed instantly relieved

They stood in silence.

"Hey Mal," Harper said after noticing a menacing stare from Cam. "Would you mind introducing me to her mum? I'd like to offer my condolences."

"Of course," Mal replied as they walked away together. Mal stopped and looked back at Cam.

"You coming too, Cam?" Mal asked.

"I better not, I'm awful at this sort of thing," Cam said.

"Come on love," Harper urged her forward.

Mal's eyes flashed momentary concern, but she soon yielded.

Bea and Cam were suddenly alone.

Though the room was flush with hushed voices, being alone with Cam made her feel like she was on an island. Even though he was several feet away, she felt heat radiating off him like before. He was a walking, talking, roaring campfire.

He looked at her and smiled, the overhead lights reflecting eerily in his eyes.

"Wish you had stuck around the other night at the club," Cam commented.

"Yeah," Bea replied. "Mal wanted to get out of there and you know..couldn't leave her hanging."

"Doesn't mean you have to do everything she says," he said with a grin. Bea was entranced as she traced his strong jawline with her eyes.

"So I was thinking," said Cam. "We don't get to talk much at the club. And I know you have a lot going on with your thesis. But..."

He hesitated for a moment, as though reflecting one final time on a choice or decision.

"But I really want to know more about it," he continued. "History is a kind of a hobby of mine and I'd love for you to tell me more about it."

"I don't know," Bea felt conflicted. Was he asking her out?

"Over dinner of course," he added.

He had moved in closer, his hand was now resting on her arm.

Here was the hottest guy she knew, literally her dream man. Asking her out, and she still couldn't bring herself to just say yes.

Don't be a loser.

Bea considered what she knew about him, his past with other girls. Mal's old roommate, even his obsession with Mal. She didn't know anything about him. She just couldn't, she couldn't manage another distraction. She had to say no.

She opened her mouth to speak but Cam beat her to it

"I've actually," Cam said hesitantly. "I have quite a rare book collection."

Bea's mind swirled with doubt.

"The Bonum Ruinam," Cam continued.

No, no, no. Can't do it. Bea thought to herself.

"The Daemonium Orandi," Cam began rattling off rare books that Bea recognized.

Bea did her best to focus. She needed to tell him no in a polite way, she couldn't risk losing her room at Mal's by offending Mal's friend.

"The *Filii Diaboli*," Cam added in a softer whisper.

Bea's brain stopped her there.

"What did you say?" Bea asked, her inner voice suddenly quiet.

"I have a rare book collection," Cam began.

"I know, what was that last one you said?" said Bea.

"The *Filii Diaboli*?" Cam answered with a questioning tone.

"You're lying," Bea replied, staring at him intently.

"No, I have it," said Cam confidently. "It was a gift from an old friend."

"Not a chance," said Bea. "No one has a copy of it."

"Well I don't have a copy," Cam clarified.

Bea let out a deep breath of relief.

"I have the original," Cam said suddenly.

Bullshit.

What were the chances? Almost everything she had read for her thesis thus far had been less than helpful. They all referred to the *Filii Diaboli*, however none of the authors had ever been able to get their hands on it. Supposedly, it was the source book for anything and everything demonic pre-Renaissance. It would have everything she needed to jump light years ahead on her thesis.

"So how about Thursday? My place?" Cam asked.

Bea waited a moment for her inner voice to yell at her.

Silence. Not one word.

"I'm a great cook," Cam added with his captivating gaze.

Mal's going to be pissed.

The other girls had warned her about him.

She knew what she had to do, no matter what she just needed to tell him no.

She felt a tap on her shoulder.

Turning, she saw Adelaide's sister Marienne standing behind her.

"Are you Bea?" Marienne asked.

"Um, yes," Bea replied.

"That one I spoke to on the phone?" Marienne added.

"Yes," Bea replied.

"Can I speak to you for a moment?" Marienne requested. She looked over Bea's shoulder at Cam. "In private?"

"Um...of course," Bea replied, unsure of what else she should say.

"See you Thursday?" Cam asked.

"Um...um....sure," Bea replied as she followed Marienne.

A smile of contentment filled Cam's face.

"Excellent," Cam said. He rubbed his hands together.

Marienne led her through a doorway off the edge of the reception room. She closed it behind them.

It was quiet, reserved for the close family of the deceased. Marienne sat down on a maroon velvet lounge chair and buried her head in her hands.

"I'm so sorry for your loss," Bea began, unable to think of anything else to say to the grieving woman.

"Thank you," Marienne said through sobs. "I looked through Adelaide's phone after she passed, she was texting you a lot. You and no one else."

Bea stood in silence.

"I know you two had been," Marienne said before pausing to search for the word. "Had been intimate before she had passed."

Bea turned bright red.

"It was one night, we had been drinking," Bea tried to clarify.

"I know," Marienne said. "I'm not mad, she and I haven't been close the last few years. I'm just happy she had someone with her to help comfort her."

"I didn't think she felt like that around me," Bea said.

"She felt closer to you than any of those other girls out there," Marienne continued. "I could tell."

"I don't know what to say," Bea managed to sputter out the truth. She felt speechless. Adelaide must have been extremely lonely if in her final days Bea was her closest friend.

Marienne burst into loud sobs.

Bea sat down next to her and put her hand on her back.

"I could barely recognize her," the crying woman said. "My parents were out of town, they asked me to drop in and check on her. When I saw her, her face, her body, it was so thin. She looked decades older than when I had last seen her. She had bled out, the stomach cancer had taken its toll, marking a heartbreaking end to my beautiful sister's journey."

"The mortician tried his best," Marienne continued. "To put her back together, to look like she used to. It was no use, nothing he could do, he said."

That explains the closed casket.

"I don't understand it," said Marienne as the sobs started to subside. "It doesn't make sense. The doctor had told us just a few months ago that she was starting to get better, that the experimental treatment was working.

"You saw her the night before, right?" Marienne asked, looking up through blurred mascara.

Bea nodded.

"I know it was Halloween and all," Marienne said, wiping her tears away with a wet tissue. "She always loved that holiday, especially dressing up. What was her costume?"

“Oh, she was a skeleton,” Bea answered.

“That explains the white hair,” said Marienne.

Bea's heart skipped a beat. White?

"Did you say white?" Bea asked.

"Almost snow white," Marienne commented. "It was like all the color had been drained from it. Just like our grandmother had before she died."

Bea wasn't sure what to say. Should she ask more questions? This poor girl has been through so much. It was just strange. Could Adelaide have gone home and dyed her hair after they were at the club together? It didn't make sense.

"Thank you for listening," Marienne continued. "We are going to bury her casket tomorrow. I hope that gives us closure."

Marienne stood up to leave.

"There is one more thing," Marienne said, pausing. "I know you two were close, I know she cared about you. It's just, we'd like to have it back. For closure."

Bea looked at her confused.

"Have what back?" Bea asked.

"Even if she gave it to you," Marienne said. "It would be a decent thing to do to return it. It was a present from our dad, it would mean a lot to us."

"I'm sorry," said Bea. "I don't know what you're talking about."

"Please, I beg you," Marienne said with tears welling up in her eyes again. "It was her favorite necklace, it's not worth much. Please can we have it back?"

"I'm sorry," Bea began to say. "I...I don't have it."

"Please," Marienne pleaded.

"I promise you," Bea replied. "I don't have it."

"Fine," Marienne said, turning angrily towards the door. "I should have known. You're just like all those other rich bitches."

She left.

Bea sat there a moment unsure of what to say.

"Hey," Mal said, appearing from the doorway. "Uber's here, let's go. I need a drink."

Bea remained sitting, lost in thought.

"Come on," Mal said louder this time.

"Ya, I'm coming," Bea rose and grabbed her purse, trailing behind Mal towards the exit. As they walked, they went by Adelaide's family. Her sister and parents fixed Bea with a disdainful gaze.

PART TWO

Chapter Eight

"I'm telling you, it's ok," Mal said as she brushed her hair.

"I just wanted to tell you," Bea replied. "I value our friendship and everything you've done for me. I just wanted to tell you the truth before you heard it from anyone else."

"I appreciate it," Mal said, turning around. "But not necessary."

The doorbell rang in the background.

"In fact," she said standing up. "I had been preparing for this eventuality. Don't move."

Bea sat on the side of Mal's bed wearing a sweatshirt and sweatpants. It was Thursday morning and she had taken all week to muster up the courage to tell Mal the truth. Which seemed rather silly now, given Mal's seemingly nonchalant attitude about it. Maybe it wasn't such a big deal after all?

Or maybe she's just pretending and is going to kick you out next week.

A few moments later Mal walked back in with a noticeably excited, she was almost skipping. In her hands were two white boxes with silver bows.

"I knew they'd be done on time," she happily exclaimed as she began to unravel the bows.

"The other girls, they told me you'd have a problem with it," Bea continued their conversation, not really interested in whatever gifts some admirer had sent Mal. "I thought maybe you and Cam had....had....a thing in the past."

"Me and Cam?" Mal said, stopping and looking at her. "Are you kidding me? I'm most definitely not his type. We've just been friends forever, our fathers are business partners."

"Business partners?" Bea repeated out loud.

"Ya, my daddy invested in the club years ago," Mal elaborated as she opened the lid of the first box. "Since then he's been like an older brother to me. And don't listen to those other girls, they are as much your friend as a lion is to a gazelle."

"I'm glad," Bea began to say before pausing. "I'm glad you're not mad at me."

"Oh girl," Mal exclaimed, lifting out the white tissue paper from the box. "We are more than good, check this out."

From the box, she lifted a silver shimmering dress by the straps. Under the light from the window, the silver surface danced and lit up like the lights on a Christmas tree.

"It's beautiful," Bea commented honestly. "You are going to look amazing in it."

"Oh, it's not for me," Mal said, standing up so that the dress could flow freely down to the floor. "It's for you, for tonight."

Bea was speechless.

"What? I...um...don't," she said, enchanted by the exquisite attire.

"Well try it on," Mal said.

"I...don't...I don't think I can afford a dress like this," Bea replied. She wasn't one to accept charity.

"Oh, don't worry about a thing," Mal said, handing it to her. "Think of it as a coming out gift."

Mal smiled at her warmly. Behind the smile, Bea couldn't help but sense something concealed. It lurked in the depths, obscured by layers of practiced composure and meticulous self-presentation, yet Bea couldn't quite grasp its essence.

Do you always act this way when someone gives you something?

"Do you like it?" Mal asked.

"I love it," Bea said, touching the material. It was buttery soft in her hands. "Thank you."

"Well then," Mal said, bouncing slightly on her heels. "Hurry up, try it on."

Bea carefully carried it to the changing area behind the screen in Mal's room. She took off her dirty gray sweatshirt and sweatpants, flinging them into a messy pile on the floor. She was doing her best to contain her excitement. Who was she, who was this girl who suddenly became excited over a new dress?

"And you better not even think about coming back out with a bra on under that," Mal yelled.

Bea reluctantly unhooked her discount store wire bra. Putting the dress on over her head, she was surprised at how well it fit her. It wasn't too tight in any one spot, it wasn't too loose either. It felt perfectly made for her and her body.

She couldn't wait to see it, she walked out from behind the screen and herself in the mirror wearing it for the first time.

It was like looking at a completely different person. Every part of her body seemed complimented by the dress's fit. Her breasts were held up into the most flattering position by the dress itself. Her waist and hips looked leaner, like they would if she actually exercised.

"What did I tell you?" Mal asked, now sitting on the bed watching her. "Cortez is amazing."

"He is," Bea said, still mesmerized at this stranger staring back at her with a puzzled look from the mirror.

"Cam's jaw is going to hit the floor when he sees you in it," Mal commented, smiling from ear to ear. "He's just going to eat you right up. Only question is if he'll take it slowly or won't be able to contain himself."

The doorman of the downtown high rise greeted Bea as she walked up, opening the door for her into the lobby. The lobby was like one out of a movie: marble floors throughout, mahogany wood finishes, red velvet drapes on the windows. And gold, gold, gold; glints of it trimmed almost every surface. From the banisters, to the stairs, to the elevators, to the front desk. It was surreal.

"How may I help you?" said a friendly voice.

The man behind the front desk wore a perfectly pressed suit and tie, he smiled at her warmly.

"Hi, um, I'm here to see Cam..." Bea froze as she spoke. She had just realized she didn't even know Cam's last name.

"Ah yes," the front desk attendant said immediately to Bea's relief. "Mr. Anwir told me he was expecting you Ms. Logan."

Mr. Anwir...

"You will find him in his penthouse suite," the attendant continued, motioning towards the elevators. "I'll unlock his private lift for you."

A gold double door opened at the end of the hall.

"Thank you," she managed in reply.

Bea tentatively walked over and into the small compartment.

"Um, which apartment number?" She asked.

The attendant just smiled at her in response. Though the building must have had at least fifty floors, the panel inside contained only a single floor button that was unmarked.

"Have a nice evening," the attendant said as the doors closed behind her.

She felt the elevator start to move, but something about it was strange. Uncertain if she was ascending, she noticed that there wasn't a floor indicator above the door; there was no way to track her progress up, down, sideways, or whichever way she was going. Instead, the sensation of the moving elevator almost felt as if she was being taken down into the basement. Panic struck her immediately, maybe something had gone wrong? The cable had snapped or the controls were broken?

Walls are starting to feel a little cramped, are they?

They did. Unlike most elevators she had been in, this one lacked mirrors or reflective glass to create the illusion of a more spacious environment within its confines. The dark walnut wood paneling only made it feel tighter. She imagined it was similar to what the inside of a coffin might look like from the perspective of a corpse.

The anxiety growing in her chest expanded, the sudden ominous feeling overtaking her. She took quick breaths, and began to panic.

The ring of the bell indicated she had arrived at her floor and the doors opened up to her relief.

She took a step forward to reveal a giant glass wall that looked out over the city. A continuous flow of vehicle lights resembled a parade procession along the central street, gradually diminishing into the impenetrable veil of eternal darkness enveloping the area beyond the city. Surprisingly absent was the sound of car horns honking, and other typical soundtrack of noise from the metropolis. It felt very much like she was on the outside looking into an aquarium, the fish inside silently oblivious to her observation.

"Hello?" She said, unsure if she was in the right place.

There were two open doorways next to her. The one to Bea's left led to a room that appeared only slightly darker, because she could see bookshelves and leather-clad rustic furniture. To her right, was a room with a large living space; the walls lined with art and an ultra-modern style sectional couch in the center.

"Hello?" She repeated, louder this time.

"Hey! In here," echoed a deep voice to her right.

Walking towards the living room, she was immediately floored by what she saw. It was like she had walked straight onto a page of *Architectural Digest.* A modern white table and chairs dining set matched the magnificent couch perfectly. Above the table hung an elaborate chandelier designed to look like a wind-chime. The ceilings were at least 12-feet high, making the apartment's space feel enormous. The floors were concrete-dyed white, something Bea had never seen before. They must have been recently buffed as they had almost a mirror-like reflection.

"That you, Bea?" said Cam's head poking from around the corner of a doorway.

"Hi," Bea managed to say, still in awe of the decor.

"Glad it wasn't a burglar...," Cam said, pausing mid-sentence. “You look amazing.”

"Thank you," Bea blushed.

"I mean, wow," she heard Cam say. However, his head was no longer in the doorway and had retreated back into the side room. "Can I make you a drink? Harper says you’re a bourbon fan."

Bea thought about it for a moment. She was very nervous still, nervous that she was on a date with someone for the first time in almost half a decade. Nervous that she was on a date with someone she barely knew. Nervous that she was alone with him in his fancy, uptown penthouse with no idea what would happen later.

"What are you having?" she replied back, still standing in the living room unsure if she was allowed to sit on any of the immaculate furniture.

"Just finishing up a Château Lafite I opened the other night," Cam replied. "Afraid there isn't much left. But I had planned something else. I hope you are in an adventurous mood. I may have gone a bit overboard."

Bea's heart began to race.

"Um...Why is that?" she asked.

He appeared a moment later with two small wooden trays, each with five glasses arranged on them.

He wore a white chef's apron over a maroon long-sleeved shirt and tan slacks.

Even in the apron, his attire flawlessly accentuated his shoulders and chest. Bea tried not to stare.

He sat the two trays down on the dining table.

"A beautiful drink for a beautiful woman," he said, handing her one of the glasses.

She blushed as she took it, glancing sideways for a moment at her reflection in the glass window.

It felt as if she was observing a scene from a Hollywood film, struggling to accept that the reflection was her own.

"Iechyd da!" Cam said, raising his glass.

She clinked hers against his and took a sip.

“Mmmm,” Bea said aloud. The flavor was a complex bouquet of flavors, with a subtle sweetness that didn’t feel overpowering. It was like a lush meadow had blossomed within her mouth.

Looking up she realized his dark eyes were watching her closely.

She blushed.

"Good?" Cam said with a mischievous smile, the lights from the chandelier glimmered in his dark pupils.

"Um... yeah," Bea couldn't help but reply playfully. "That was amazing."

"Old Rip Van Winkle," Cam said aloud, walking over to a nearby cabinet and pulling out a very uniquely shaped amber bottle. "Aged 25 years, almost four generations of distillers. Probably the best bourbon on the planet. Some say you should start with the worst and work your way up to the best. I disagree, I always think you should start with the best."

"And why is that?" Bea asked.

"Because if you don't like the rest," Cam said before pausing. "You can always throw it out and pour another glass of the good stuff."

He winked at her.

Bea's heart fluttered a little. She laughed.

"Oh, I'll be right back," he said, darting back towards the doorway.

With him absent from the room, Bea took special care to savor every last drop from the glass, eager not to let any of its delightful taste go to waste.

Still hoping for a little more liquid courage to face the night, she reached for the next glass.

"Not quite yet," Cam said from the other room. "That one you should save for the Amuse Bouche."

Bea pulled her hand away, intrigued that he knew.

He's probably got pervy cameras all over the house.

Bea ignored it.

Growing more curious, she strolled over to the art that hung over the table to examine it more closely. From a distance it looked rather random, a piece so abstract that an art critic might stare at it for hours trying to decipher its true meaning. Yet, as she approached, she discerned delicate brush strokes on the canvas. So fine were they that they could be mistaken for stray strands of hair adhering to the artwork. She resisted the urge to reach out and pluck one.

The strokes depicted a dragon with large curved horns and taloned wings. It was guarding something, the body of a man who lay in the fetal position on the ground. At the dragon's front, was a woman wielding what looked like a serpentine sword and a turtle shell for a shield. It was at once the most enchanting and peculiar artwork she had ever seen.

What kind of person has nightmarish art like this in his dining room?

"That toast," Bea remarked out loud with curiosity, ignoring the voice in her head. "Welsh?"

"Very good," Cam yelled from the next room. "It means 'to your health.'"

"Are you Welsh?" Bea asked.

"I am," Cam replied. "Carmarthen originally, but I've been in the States a long time now."

She examined the art a bit longer, getting lost in little details that only emerged after extended study of the piece.

"You like my painting?" Cam said, his voice suddenly right behind her. His breath was hot on her shoulder.

She jumped slightly.

"Sorry to startle you," Cam added.

"I do but..." Bea couldn't think of the right word to finish her thought.

"It's unsettling isn't it?" He found the right word for her.

"Ya," Bea managed to say, nodding.

"Art should be a little unsettling, I think," he replied. "If not, what's the point?"

Bea just nodded, not sure if she agreed or not.

"If you wouldn't mind taking your seat," he pulled the nearby chair out for her.

She sat down in it as elegantly as she could manage. She was still getting used to wearing heels, and the pair she had borrowed from Mal for tonight required a circus, acrobat-like level of balance to remain upright. Still, she managed, and Cam placed a napkin on her lap.

"For the Amuse Bouche," he began. "I had a hard time figuring out exactly what to serve. First impressions are always so important, and I needed something that would set the right tone for the rest of the meal, but still leave you wanting more."

Bea had no idea what "amuse bouche" meant, she had never been to a restaurant fancy enough to use the term. However, she didn't care. He could have served her a cold cheeseburger and she would have thought it heaven.

"I settled on something," he continued. "that you might find familiar, with a bit of my own flair added to it."

He removed the cover from the dish on the table. On it was a small round ball, dark and textured on the outside. Sprigs of thyme and mint leaned into a tepee on the steaming sphere and a drizzle of oil, cut as a perfectly chaotic zigzag, made the plate look like a piece of exotic art.

Bea sat there smiling, unsure what to do. She felt nervous.

Cam must have noticed.

He carefully picked up the fork and knife and cut into the ball.

A small jet of steam escaped, Bea jumped at the hissing noise. The blade fell swiftly, cleaving the ball into two morsels. The divided sections toppled over, unveiling a core of white and yellow.

"Scotch eggs?" Bea asked.

"The same," Cam replied.

"My grandmother used to make them for Christmas," Bea added.

"Well," Cam said with excited eyes. "How do mine compare?"

Bea pierced one of the halves, the egg yolk inside only slightly runny.

Here goes nothing...

She took a bite.

Instantly, a burst of flavor engulfed her palate. The sausage shell, surprisingly, wasn't greasy or overbearing but rather airy and delicate. The encased egg yolk was flawlessly prepared, neither too liquid nor overly dry. Hints of mint and thyme danced on the exterior. Her taste buds rejoiced, and almost at once, her stomach clamored for more. She relished each bite.

"There's another flavor there, one I don't recognize," she said aloud.

"That's a little flair," Cam said with a face of extreme pleasure. "Blodyn Aur, but more well-known in English as Rapeseed Oil. Common in Wales, but not so much here. A little goes a long way."

"I'd say so," Bea commented. Even as she swallowed the last bite from her plate she could still taste it in the corners of her mouth. "That was delicious."

"Thank you, I'm glad you liked it," said Cam, smiling.

"Where'd you learn to cook?" Bea inquired, dabbing her lips with the neatly folded napkin.

"All over the place," Cam replied. "Italy, France, Spain."

"Why didn't you become a chef?" Bea asked.

"I am in a way," said Cam. "In the club, I craft an experience akin to a chef curating a dish. Every guest has their preferred selections from the menu. Feeling parched?"

He handed her the next glass from the tray.

"Iechyd da," she declared, lifting her glass, her pronunciation reminiscent of a cat coughing up a hairball.

Cam laughed and their glasses clinked.

This whiskey was definitely not the sweet bourbon she was expecting. It was smoother than the bourbon, but it tasted more of smoke and oak. She coughed.

"Not used to scotch?" Cam said, seemingly enjoying his glass.

"No, not at all," Bea was able to say between coughs.

"Well, given you were eating Scotch Eggs," said Cam before taking a big breath to savor the flavor, "I figured a scotch was fitting. Talisker 30, one of, if not, the best scotches that money can buy."

Bea all of a sudden felt guilty at coughing through such an expensive drink.

Cam either didn't notice or didn't care.

"How'd you know I was Scottish?" Bea asked, her mind curious.

"Lucky guess, Ms. Logan," he replied with a wink. "Now for the next course I'll need to be focused in the kitchen for a few minutes. Can I invite you to check out my study? Do you like books?"

He winked again as he motioned towards the hallway by the elevator.

"Help yourself to anything you find," he clarified before disappearing again.

Bea walked down the hall and into the dark room. It was like walking into a completely different home.

The concrete floor was replaced by mahogany wooden slats. Victorian style armchairs were scattered around with a large ornate oak desk in the center. There were no windows, the walls were covered from top to bottom with wooden bookshelves. In two locations, the bookshelves had gaps where a painting hung, lit by recessed lamps.

But the books... Bea felt like Belle finding Beast's castle library for the first time. It took her breath away.

There must have been thousands of them. In the shelves, stacked on the desk or next to a chair on the floor. It would take a lifetime to read them all.

She didn't need to read them all, though, she just needed to read one.

The *Filii Diaboli.*

You know he was pulling your leg right?

She began her search through the study. Starting at the first bookshelf, she quickly read titles as she went row by row. After reading the first shelf, she stopped.

They were all history and art books about the Renaissance. Checking the next shelf, all texts related to the Dark Ages, she recognized one of the titles.

"Aha," she said aloud.

She poured through the remaining texts, which expanded into the next row of the shelf, and then the next row, her eyes felt like they were about to cross.

It wasn't there.

Told you, he's a liar. Get out now.

"Looking for something in particular?" Cam said from the doorway.

Bea jumped.

"Don't worry, you're not in trouble," he said laughing.

"Sorry, I was looking for..." she began to say.

"The *Filii Diaboli*?" Cam said with one raised eyebrow. "Do you really believe I'd leave such a precious book out for just anyone to take?"

"I guess not," Bea replied.

"I suppose it is why you are here," he said, looking at her sideways.

"No, I mean," Bea tried to clarify, she didn't want to be rude. "I'm glad I'm here, I just really, really, really would like to see it."

Cam studied her for a moment.

"Ok," he said.

Bea's heart filled with excitement.

"After the next course," Cam added, walking out of the room.

What a fucking tease.

"You got that right," Bea said aloud, following Cam..

The next course was the most beautiful salad Bea had ever seen. It was on an elongated plate, the porcelain trimmed with gold and silver. The plate itself was shaped into that of a long leaf. Sitting inside of it was the salad, full and red cherry tomatoes with the perfect amount of blistering, chunks of steaming chorizo, sprigs of cilantro. It looked as delightful as it smelled.

"I learned this one from a friend of mine while visiting Madrid," Cam began speaking, sitting across from her. "It is an autumn salad with liver and chorizo. I made the chorizo myself."

"Wow," she remarked, her eyes wide and stomach savagely growling. "It looks amazing, it's so pretty I feel bad eating it."

Cam laughed.

"The most delicious things in the world," he began. "Are usually the most beautiful."

He held up the next glass from the tray.

"Salud," he said aloud.

"Salud," Bea repeated softly. She sipped the drink, expecting another strong whiskey. She was happily surprised to taste sweet nectar.

"Oh my," she exclaimed.

"Thought you'd enjoy that," Cam said. "It's a rum from Spain. Made in the Canary Islands to be exact. It was my backup in case you weren't a fan of the scotch."

"I can do this," Bea said smiling. The sweet flavors made her cheeks and tongue tingle with joy.

For a few moments, they ate their salads in silence. Bea occasionally stole glances at Cam, uncertain if it was her innate pull towards his striking appearance or her own apprehension, seeking assurance that she wasn't messing things up.

Bea felt warm, she felt the skin of her arm. It was cool to the touch, but inside she felt like she was burning up. The salad was very good, she had never had liver before but enjoyed the rich and fatty flavors mixed with the greens.

"How are you liking your salad?" Cam asked, breaking the silence.

"It's delicious," Bea said eagerly, not realizing her mouth was still full. She gulped down what was left painfully. "Sorry."

"Not at all," Cam replied with a laugh. "Glad to see you are enjoying it. So tell me, why history?"

Bea sipped the delicious rum to help her finish swallowing her last bite.

"Well," she began. "I guess it's just something I've always enjoyed."

"How so?" Cam sipped his own drink.

"You know," Bea struggled to find the words to describe how she felt. "It's why we are here, it's what made us. Everybody comes from somewhere, somewhere came from somewhere before. Over and over and over again. Knowing how something evolved, a person, a place, a society; knowing how, it always made me happy."

"What about your family?" Cam asked.

"Um," Bea replied sheepishly. "Well they are third generation, from rural Pennsylvania. My father is a deacon with the local Catholic diocese."

Bea expected Cam to flinch, almost anyone who hears that does. He sat there stone-faced.

"What was it like growing up with a deacon for a father?" he asked with no hint of surprise at hearing about her parents. It was almost as if he already knew. Did Mal tell him? Did she tell him everything about her?

Bea struggled to find words.

"Well, I mean," she began. "I guess I grew up much like any normal kid would."

"Do normal kids where you come from go to church three times a week?" Cam asked.

How did he know that? She hadn't even told Mal that.

"Um, no I guess not," she replied. "I guess other than that it was normal."

"Were other boys and girls from your school afraid to talk to you?" Cam pressed further.

"No, I mean, maybe, I don't think," she stammered.

"Given that you're the daughter of a significant religious icon in your town," he started, taking the final sip from his glass, "I'd assume they'd be wary of him discovering their antics. Like if you caught them drinking, at parties, or taking the Lord's name in vain."

"I never thought about it," said Bea, nervously poking at what was left of her salad. "I guess you could be right on that. I never really had friends in high school, never really got invited to parties."

The happiness drained from her face, the warmth of the great food and spirits had dissipated.

"That's a shame," Cam said aloud standing up.

He paused for a long moment, staring down at the table.

"I'm sorry," he said, looking up at her and sighing.

"Sorry for what?" she asked, confused.

"Sorry about prying," he clarified. "For the intense line of questioning. I get too...bored... of the typical get to know you chit-chat that I have to partake in at the club. I want to know the real you, maybe I should have warmed you up a little bit first instead of cutting right to the chase."

Bea's heart fluttered a little.

"You warm me up just fine," she found herself sputtering out. "Oops, I didn't mean it like that."

“How did you mean it?” Cam asked.

“I don’t know?” Bea said in the form of a question.

They both laughed.

"The rum has a funny effect," he said, walking around the table. "Who knows what I might be saying by the end of the night."

He held out his hand to her.

"I believe you wanted to see a particular book," he said.

"Oh yes," Bea said eagerly, taking his hand. She felt jolts of electricity travel up her arm instantly, into her shoulder, and down her spine towards...

She rose abruptly, releasing his hand as he retreated to the study. The surges of energy that coursed through her had ceased, offering relief, yet she found herself yearning for their resurgence.

She followed.

Cam walked to the bookshelf behind the desk.

Cam held up his hand, Bea stopped dead in her tracks.

"One moment while I retrieve it," he said, looking at her.

Bea stood there staring at him.

After a few moments he held up his hand again, this time making a motion with his finger for her to turn around. She reluctantly complied.

With her back turned, she could hear the clicking sound of a safe dial being turned. The hairs on her arm stood up. Did he really have it? One of the rarest books in the world? A book that Mikkelson would gladly trade for one of his own grandchildren.

"*Filii Diaboli*, right?" she heard him say from behind her playfully, as if it wasn't one of the rarest books in human history..

She turned around. One of the bookshelves behind his desk swung away on a hinge, revealing a safe. Safe wasn't the right word, it was a vault. The walls of which were easily eight inches thick. The shelves were lined with volumes upon volumes of texts, each looking more ancient than the next.

Bea was still awe-struck, staring wide-eyed at the enormous collection. She did not even notice that Cam had walked around the desk and was standing next to her.

"They're just a bunch of books," he whispered into her ear as he slid a cloth-wrapped tome into her hands.

He closed the safe, returned the bookshelf on the wall to its original location and while exiting the room turned to her, saying, "I'll leave you two alone for a few minutes. Main course in twenty." he joked.

She barely heard him, she had melted into the closest armchair and carefully opened the cloth to reveal a faded leather bound book with the words FILII DIABOLI on the cover.

Bea did not know how much time had passed, it could have been seconds, minutes, or even hours. Her entire focus was on the stack of faded paper in her lap. It was everything she could have hoped for; the book detailed every name, date, place and ritual. Translating Latin would have usually taken her hours, but somehow she was reading it as if her parents had raised her in the ancient tongue of the Romans. With each page her excitement only grew.

"Order up!" she heard Cam yell from the other room.

Her reverie was abruptly shattered. Though a part of her yearned to continue reading, she recognized the courtesy of attending to him. She made her way to the dining room, setting the book beside her plate on the table.

"Do you always bring books with you to dinner?" Cam teased.

Bea didn't even realize it.

"Oh, I'm sorry," she said. "It was just everything I had hoped it would be, and then some."

"Well I'm glad I didn't disappoint," said Cam with a smile. "Why don't you borrow it?"

"What? Borrow? Me? I can't," she sputtered out. "It's too valuable, I could never."

"Borrow it, I trust you," he said.

"Are you sure?" Bea asked, she wasn't sure if he was joking or not.

"Ya, go ahead," he replied.

"Thank you," Bea said. It was the only thing she could think to say as she carefully placed the book into her bag.

"Now," Cam said, clapping his hands together. "How about something I can guarantee you've never tried before."

"Absolutely," Bea said, her enthusiasm unable to be sedated.

He disappeared for a moment back into the kitchen and emerged a few moments later carrying two large plates. Placing one down in front of Bea, her eyes went wide again and her mouth moistened.

The dish was a muted onyx, presenting a matte of elegance. At its center rested a steak, succulent and tempting beyond anything Bea had ever laid eyes on. Figs and carrots were intricately arranged in a spiral of color, completing the gastronomic tableau.

"Venison steak with black fig and a beetroot sauce," he proclaimed, happily sitting down in his chair across from her.

"Wow," Bea exclaimed.

"That's usually the effect I'm going for," Cam replied.

"You were right," Bea remarked. "I've never had venison before. What is it?"

Cam smiled.

"It's a game animal," he answered.

"Like deer?" Bea asked.

"Something like that," Cam replied. "This one I actually took down myself, though I have to admit I was a little bit disappointed with how lean the meat was."

Bea took a bite of hers.

"It's delicious," she said, savoring her mouthful.

"Thank you," replied Cam. "I shared some of it with others from the club, but to tell you a secret: I kept the best cuts for myself."

"I'd say so," said Bea, shoving another slice into her mouth.

"Do you like to hunt?" she asked.

"I live for it," Cam mused. "There's an unmatched satisfaction in consuming an animal you've hunted down. To have gazed into its eyes during its last moments, witnessing its ultimate surrender to destiny, that fleeting instant when it finally succumbs, almost pleading for an end."

Bea stopped chewing for a moment and stared at him, fascinated. His cheeks had gone flush, and she swore she could feel heat emanating from his end of the table.

"Dark," she said through a mouthful.

"I'm sorry," he said as his tone returned to normal. "I can get carried away sometimes."

"It's ok," she said, still enjoying every flavor.

"Oops," Cam said suddenly. "Almost forgot the most important part."

He passed Bea a glass of amber fluid and a small tray of black spherical objects.

"Caviar from Russia," he clarified. "And Vodka infused with Cognac. Also from Russia. Pairs perfectly with the dish whose recipe I learned while I was in..."

"Russia," Bea said, interrupting him. "Got it." She laughed.

"Enjoy," he said, sitting back down and slicing into his own steak with surgical precision.

Bea sampled the drink. She had believed the rum defined smoothness, but that belief was now challenged. The vodka had no sharp bite; it danced gracefully on her palate. Yet, its essence didn't vanish rapidly. The delightful aftertaste stayed, playfully reminding her of that initial sip.

She turned to the caviar, something she would usually never eat. However, the alcohol had begun to take effect on her, and she felt more outgoing and experimental than she typically would.

“Why not?” she thought.

She took a small spoonful and placed it onto a cracker, as she closed her eyes and took a bite.

This is disgusting. Bea agreed.

Out of respect for her host, Bea held still, caught between the urge to swallow and the impulse to spit. This hesitation only prolonged her exposure to the caviar's distasteful flavors and textures. Summoning all her resolve, she finally swallowed.

She quickly took another drink of the vodka, hoping to get the taste out of her mouth.

"How'd you like it?" Cam asked, staring at her intently.

Bea hesitated.

"It was good," she lied.

Cam studied her for a moment.

"Disgusting right?" he said.

"Incredibly," Bea said before drinking the last of the vodka in her glass and swishing around in her mouth a bit longer. "I could use another one of these though."

Cam laughed.

"I never understood caviar," Cam commented. "It was a gift from a Russian friend of mine, he told me it was the best caviar in the world. I'm sure it was, but I can't stand the stuff. It ruins everything."

He put his elbows on the table, his hands interwoven.

"I have a belief," he started. "Every individual has one particular taste, a singular flavor, sensation...whatever you might call it. But once you've savored it, you'd go to any lengths to relish it once more. Truly any lengths — be it lying, cheating, stealing...perhaps even committing the unthinkable, all for another chance at that unparalleled sensation."

"It's human nature I guess," said Bea with a smile.

Cam returned her smile warmly.

The rest of the night flew by. They talked for hours about history and art. He knew more than anyone she had ever met except perhaps Professor Mikkelson about the medieval times. He spoke with such calm confidence, almost as if he had lived it rather than read about it.

"I can't get over how nice your place is," she said after a spirited debate on practices of the Catholic church on punishing heretics during the Enlightenment.

"Thank you," he replied with a modest tone. "It's taken many years to get it just right."

"I couldn't help but notice," Bea's curiosity got the best of her thanks to the empty bottle of Vodka next to her. "I didn't see a bedroom."

"A bedroom?" Cam asked curiously.

"Ya, like where do you sleep?" Bea clarified.

"Bea, are you asking to see my bedroom?" he retorted, his expression morphing into a mischievous smirk.

You sound like a slut.

She didn't realize how forward she had just sounded. She checked her phone. It was definitely getting late and she had class in the morning.

"Can I help you with dishes?" she asked, breaking the silence.

Bea tried to collect her plate and take it to the kitchen. Cam quickly intercepted her, blocking the way.

"I can't allow that," he said with a flirtatious smile. "I'll take care of it."

"You sure?" Bea asked nervously.

"Yes, I can handle a few dishes," he replied.

She tried to sneak a peek into the kitchen, curious to what other surprises it may hold but Cam was making it impossible.

She wondered if he was hiding something in there, something from her. But what?

He's probably got a professional chef in there making all this and he's just pretending he did it.

Pushing the thought aside, Bea felt, deep down, that Cam had been sincere and honest with her, despite the paranoia of her inner voice.

"Perhaps we could retire to the study for a nightcap," Cam said, putting his hand on her shoulder.

She felt that electricity again, not painful but pleasurable. She wanted to pull away again, but the feeling had its own allure. She wanted more of it, she wanted to feel it all over.

You really are a slut.

"It's late," she said, forcing herself to pull away from his grasp.

Cam smiled back at her, his eyes not betraying any hint of anger or disappointment.

"And I have got to work on my thesis in the morning," she added her age-old excuse, expecting him to be furious at being led on.

But the prince did not transform into the beast.

"I understand," Cam said instead. "I'm glad you came."

He escorted her to the elevator.

"Thank you for tonight," Bea said, smiling at his understanding. "I had a lot of fun, and thank you for letting me borrow the book."

"The pleasure has been all mine," Cam said, moving a step closer to her. The heat of his body hit Bea like a wave as he drew close.

"I...I...." Bea stuttered.

Before she could finish, his lips were on hers. She felt it again, the electricity hit her. It traveled through her lips, down her neck, down her spine. Her hips felt like they were about to buckle under her.

As she broke off their kiss, she felt her whole body begin to sweat.

"Will I see you on Saturday?" Cam asked, his face just a few inches from hers.

"What's...um..." Bea's mind raced with thoughts other than her weekend plans. "What's on Saturday?"

"The club," Cam clarified. "I have some friends from Germany coming to visit, it's going to be a lot of fun. Would love to see you there."

"Sounds...sounds good," Bea said, unable to focus.

"You ok? Can I escort you down?" Cam asked.

"I'm really fine..." Bea replied as the elevator dinged. "I'll...see you." She walked into the elevator.

"Good night," said Cam, his voice sounding distant in Bea's racing mind.

What the fuck just happened? "I don't know," she said aloud. "But I wish it would happen again."

She made her way down and into an awaiting Uber, her legs and knees trembling uncontrollably, still not quite recovered.

Bea was glad to get home and fall into her bed.

Cam watched from the kitchen window as the lights from Bea's Uber became just another anonymous vehicle in the swell of downtown traffic.

Beside the sink, dishes awaited attention. Slipping the apron back on, he turned the tap to release hot water, embarking on a thorough wash. Steam clouded the room while he diligently cleaned and dried the plates, glasses and utensils.

This continued until the last remaining items were his knives. With meticulous care, he cleaned the blades before honing them on a whetstone. He did this after every meal, not content until they were sharp enough to split a hair.

Cam swung a clear plastic bag over his head, inflating it with air. Then unlocked the padlock that secured a large white deep freezer under the butcher block. He used the bag to wrap the leftover meat from dinner. Content it would not leak, he placed it carefully into the freezer unit.

However, when he attempted to close the unit's lid, it would not seal.

He sighed.

It seemed the freezer was due for some tidying up. He bent down to empty its contents, setting a hefty freezer bag onto the butcher block countertop. Inside was the frozen wrinkled head of Ilyana.

Chapter Nine

Bea woke up the next morning before her alarm was even set to go off. It was still dark outside, the sun's light only just beginning to glow on the horizon. She felt as if fueled by three cups of coffee already. After a brief shower and a quick brush of her teeth, she was eager to get started.

Content that she looked acceptable enough, she sat down at her desk and opened up the *Filii Diaboli*.

Its name was quite ominous, it translates roughly to "Children of the Devil." Yet it wasn't bound in human flesh and written in human blood as a horror fan might imagine. It was bound with leather and written by hand. No one knew by who though, its original author (or possibly authors) had never identified themselves. With the tight grip the church had on society at the time, they had never signed their greatest work, likely to avoid persecution and being burned at the stake.

For four hours she typed on her computer, writing page after page of her thesis as she cross referenced information from the book and her other sources. She reached a section that made her almost spit out her drink on the page.

PEST JUNGFRAU.

The Plague Angel. Medieval folklore mentions her often; she was the spirit that flew in the sky over Germania, spreading the Black Death with turquoise fire. She was a nightmare that scared both children and parents alike.

However in the *Filii Diaboli*, it wasn't just a legend. It was a cult-like secret society that would take plagued rats and cats, and transfer them from one town to the next. From there the city would soon be overcome with the Black Death, thousands would die. They would continue this across the countryside, hoping to destabilize the Holy Roman Empire.

She wrote her translation down by hand a second time, re-read the Latin again, and then wrote the translation a third time as she read it. She got the same result all three times.

"Summer of 1349, brought animals from Strasbourg to Cologne. Sacrificed three Jewish families by fire," she read it aloud.

She found her other notes on Cologne and the Black Death; a third of the city's population died from the Black Death.

Bea continued writing furiously, not wanting to risk losing her focus by taking a break. The Pest Jungfrau was an alliance of man and demon according to the book. Men who wanted power and demons who wanted chaos. Supposedly all sorts of creatures were part of it.

Alps, the Germanic tribes version of elves that appear in your nightmares at night and feed on your screams. They were the foot soldiers who did the dirty work. Drudes were demonic spirits, feminine in appearance but mostly ethereal. They could inhabit the bodies of town officials and guards in order to facilitate whatever course of action they desired.

For the first time in the book, an entire page had been dedicated to a single hand-drawn picture. It depicted a demon with large towering horns from his brow, covered in long fur from head to hoof, and iron chains bound around him.

Where his name had been written underneath, there was water damage and the ink had bled until his name was no longer legible. It was clear that this was the deity the cult worshiped.

"Darnit!" Bea said aloud. She scanned the next few pages but folio refused to mention the name again. Instead referring back to the creature as if saying the name would magically summon it into existence.

It was the son of Satan himself, sent to Earth as a punishment. Tormenting man was the only way to ensure his return to Hell.

Bea couldn't help but stare at the picture, it was fascinating and haunting at the same time. It even looked familiar, but then again all demons kind of looked the same to non-demons. What she found most eerie though were the creature's eyes, they were dark black opals on his face, with glints of white light reflecting upon them. She found herself leaning in closer and closer to the picture until her face was just a few inches from it.

KNOCK KNOCK KNOCK.

Bea's heart practically jumped out of her chest as she fell from her chair and onto the floor.

The door opened revealing Mal.

"Sorry," Mal said with a smile. "I was bored and wanted to check on you. Aren't you supposed to be in class right now?"

Bea looked at the time on her phone. She was already fifteen minutes late to Professor Mikkelson's class.

"Shit," Bea said aloud.

She grabbed her backpack and shoveled her laptop and books into it. Only taking the time to carefully pack the *Filii Diaboli* back into its protective wrappings before putting it in her bag.

Running at full speed down the hall, she only barely managed to yell "Thank you!" to Mal.

Professor Mikkelson scowled at Bea as the classroom door squeaked loudly on its hinges when she entered. The rest of the class turned to look at her as well.

"Glad you could join us Ms. Logan," Professor Mikkelson said sternly.

"I'm sorry sir," Bea said out of breath. She moved to the front to take her place next to the Professor. She had run to class, but she felt much more tired than she should have been. Her leg muscles suddenly felt sore and her lower back ached from the effort.

You sound like your mother. It was true, as her mother had aged she had dealt with chronic arthritis and almost constant swelling.

Bea rubbed at her knees, they did look a bit puffier than usual.

"As I was saying," Professor Mikkelson spoke as he turned his disapproving gaze back to the students who all looked at Bea with silent glee at her tardiness. "The Renaissance was a frightful time despite all the celebration over feats of art and engineering..."

Bea's attention wandered back to the image from the book. She pulled her laptop back out and began to write for her thesis again, letting the thoughts from her blitz of reading that morning drive her fingers. It was like a dam had been burst and the river of thought had finally been set free.

She didn't even notice when the students started shuffling out of class.

"A bit distracted today Ms. Logan?" Professor Mikkelson said after the last of the students had departed.

"I'm sorry sir," Bea apologized. "It won't happen again. I was caught up in..."

"Your thesis," the Professor interrupted her. "I've been doing this a long time, I know what inspiration looks like. Next time, just call me and tell me you're sick though."

He smiled at her.

Bea's apprehension melted away.

"Well," he said, looking at her with raised eyebrows.

She returned his glance with a confused look.

"What?" she managed to say after a long pause.

"Are you going to let me read the damn thing or not?" the Professor inquired.

"Of course, of course," she said, opening her laptop and handing it to him.

They sat there in silence for thirty minutes, every little while the Professor would scroll down with the touchpad. He made no facial expressions whatsoever, only pausing to rub his eyes.

At least he leaned back. Pulling his glasses off, he rubbed the bridge of his nose.

"Well?" Bea asked, unable to wait any longer for his feedback.

"I don't know what to say," the Professor said. "It's completely different than I had expected."

He hates it.

"Different in a good way?" Bea asked.

"My dear," the Professor began leaning forward towards her. "I don't know what internet hooligan was your source, but there's just nothing to support any of this."

"I know", Bea replied apprehensively. She wasn't sure how much she should divulge.

"So where did all this come from?" the Professor asked..

Bea took a deep breath and stared at the frail old man looking at her with eyes of disappointment. She couldn't stand it any longer.

"It's based on the *Filii Diaboli*," she blurted out at last.

"What?" the Professor exclaimed.

"I know, crazy right?" she said with a nervous shrug.

"Where on earth did you find a copy?" he asked.

"Not a copy," she began. "The original."

Professor Mikkelson just looked at her in disbelief with his mouth wide open.

"Here, let me show you," she said as she carefully extracted the cloth covered book and unwrapped it on the table slowly.

"Oh my God," Mikkelson said, staring at it. "The original, right here... on my desk."

He moved his hands to open it.

"I really shouldn't be sharing it with anyone," she said aloud as she wrapped the book back up. "It's not mine, I'm just borrowing it from a friend."

"Borrowing it?" the Professor exclaimed. "The *Filii Diaboli* is not some Nancy Drew mystery book to be passed around amongst friends. It's one of the rarest texts ever made, so rare many like myself no longer believed it existed anymore. And you have been carrying it around... in your backpack."

He looked shocked.

"Yes," was all she could manage to say.

"Please," Professor Mikkelson said leaning towards her. "Convince the owner to let you make a copy of it. It's the Holy Grail of Middle Age history, our Ark of the Covenant. It has the secrets to all the puzzles. It would advance our knowledge of the period more than any other discovery in my lifetime."

"I'll ask him," Bea said reassuringly.

Mikkelson sat back in his chair and took a deep breath.

"It all makes sense now," he said, looking at the laptop screen. "Historians and scientists had always found the systematic and extremely rigid pattern of how the Black Death spread through Europe so strange. It appeared faster in some cases than the methods of transportation at the time could even allow for a natural contagion. Paris, Bremen, Cologne, Venice. They all were hit exactly at the moment a momentous event in the city was planned. A festival, an uprising, a state visit. We all thought it a coincidence, but if this is genuine. You just blew the lid off the whole thing."

Bea blushed.

"There's one problem," Mikkelson said looking at her.

Bea looked up in alarm "Wh... What?"

"They'll never believe you," he said with sad eyes. "They'll never believe you had the book. They'll claim you made the whole thing up, no matter what I say otherwise. They'll want physical proof."

"I'll ask, but I can't just give the book to the school," Bea pleaded.

"I know, I know," Mikkelson said deep in thought. "This man, this book collector. How do you know him?"

Bea wasn't sure how to describe it.

"He's a friend of mine I guess," Bea replied. "He let me take it home last night when I was at his house for dinner."

Mikkelson eyed her suspiciously.

"Dinner?" he asked.

Bea nodded, trying to look as innocent as possible.

"Listen Ms. Logan," he said to her with sincere eyes. "I'm enthusiastic that you found the book. But getting involved with older men like this will not end well for you."

"Well," she said defensively. "He's only a couple years older than me I think."

"A couple?" Mikkelson asked.

"Ya, can't be more than five, maybe ten years older than me at most," she said. She really wasn't sure how old Cam actually was, he was friends with Mal and looked great but everything else about him. The places he told her he's visited, the things he knows, he seemed beyond his years.

"You were at his house for dinner, and you don't know how old he is?" Mikkelson asked.

"Well, it hasn't come up," Bea replied feeling very self conscious.

The Professor paused for a moment.

"It's none of my business," he said. "I apologize. Your acquaintances are your acquaintances. But this person, this young man you think you know, they wouldn't just have this book. It's too old, too important to the world."

He paused for another long moment.

"I have an idea that may work," he said. "Ask your acquaintance if he has any other books related to the *Filii Diaboli*. Something, anything that you can use to cross reference. You just need one tangible source to back this up and you'll be ok."

"Ok,' Bea said, unsure of how that conversation would be greeted.

Mikkelson put his hand on Bea's.

"Please, you must find a way to publish this," he said. "It's the only way this will ever come to light. It's the only way...dear there's no reason to be this nervous."

"What?" Bea said in surprise.

"Your hand, you're... shaking," he said.

"I'm what?" she looked down. Her hand was trembling uncontrollably. She hadn't even noticed.

"I...I..." she was having trouble speaking all of a sudden.

"I've got to go," she managed to sputter out finally with great difficulty. She tried to pack her bag, but the shaking had become so violent a notebook tumbled to the floor.

"Bernice, are you ok?" the Professor asked.

"I'm fine," she said indignantly, shoving the notebook back in and standing.

"Bernice, Bernice?!" the Professor yelled.

She didn't hear him, she had already made it to the hallway and rushed to exit the building. She had to see a doctor right away.

Passing through the large double doors of the history building, the University Medical Center stood tall in the distance.

"You said it started this morning?" Dr. Keeling asked as her hand held the stethoscope to Bea's chest.

"Yes, suddenly during class," Bea replied, almost panting.

"Take a deep breath please," said Keeling.

Bea closed her eyes and took as deep a breath as she could muster.

"Again," said Keeling.

Bea took another deep breath.

"It's stopped for now?" the Dr. asked.

"Yes, as soon as I got here," Bea replied.

"Interesting," said Dr. Tompkins from the spot where he leaned against the exam room wall.

"Is it?" Bea gulped. "Is it the Huntington's?"

"It's too early," Dr. Tompkins replied. "You shouldn't be having any symptoms for another ten or fifteen years. It's all in your head."

Dr. Keeling shot him a look of pure disdain.

"All in my head?" Bea replied, tears welling up in her eyes.

"Yes," Tompkins said nonchalantly. "You find out about the disease, you do some research online. When you read about the symptoms, your subconscious starts to manifest them. Textbook hypochondria."

"Hypochondria?" Bea stated as a question.

"I think what Dr. Tompkins is trying to say," Dr. Keeling said, moving her face between Bea's tear filled gaze and the doctor's face which was buried in his clipboard. "Is that worrying about it, focusing on it, dwelling on it. It could make you just as sick as the actual disease would."

"But I haven't been doing that though," Bea replied. "I've just been enjoying myself. Having fun."

"Must be the drugs then," Tompkins remarked.

Keeling cleared her throat disapprovingly at him.

Bea's tears fell to the floor. The Dr. handed her a tissue from the station nearby.

"You might want to think about therapy," Keeling said with a reassuring smile.

"Like gene therapy? You think they can fix this?" Bea said with a hopeful tone.

Tompkins let out a short laugh.

"Gene therapy doesn't exist for Huntington's yet kiddo," he said, reaching into his pocket to pull a small bag of M&Ms out before tearing it open and pouring them into his mouth.

"I mean seeing a therapist," Keeling said, turning Bea's face towards hers again. "Maybe a grief counselor. You found out you have a terminal illness, it's ok to talk about it with someone."

Terminal Illness. The words stuck in her head.

"You have some years left," Dr. Keeling's voice filtered into her head. "You still have time."

Bea heard Dr. Keeling but didn't comprehend what she was saying. Bea's mind was adrift through all her thoughts.

What was she going to do with her time left?

She hadn't thought about it at all really.

“Do you have anything that can help me with whatever is going on right now?” Bea asked. “Something to help with the tremors.”

“It's psychosomatic,” Tompkins practically chanted from the other side of the room.

Dr. Keeling looked like she wanted to throw something at him.

“Haloperidol,” she said to Bea. “I can give you a prescription, it might help.”

“Thanks,” Bea replied, glad to hear they had something that could help her other than tell her it's all in her head.

“Waste of time...” said Dr. Tompkins.

Bea made the long trek back home, doing her best to resist the urge to kick every sign post and punch every window reflection along the way. The tears of sadness had drained by now, anger filling up the crevices left behind. She walked into her room and threw her backpack to the floor, momentarily forgetting about the delicate and rare volume inside it.

She flung herself onto the bed.

"Ow!" She yelped as she landed on something hard and rigid.

Rolling over, she found a slightly crushed white box with silver ribbon on it.

Just like the one that her silver dress had arrived in.

On it was a note.

Bea opened it and read the short hand written message.

For Saturday night, time to brush up on your German.

-M-

Opening the box, Bea couldn't believe what was inside.

Chapter Ten

"So who are the Germans?" Bea asked Mal in the Uber to Club Llithium. They both wore long coats that covered them from shoulder to knee, it was starting to get colder out and their outfits for tonight were not designed to keep one warm.

Mal looked up from texting on her phone, she seemed to be thinking hard about what to say.

"They are friends and business partners of Cam's dad," she said. "Old, old friends. Big money, old money. They are kind of crazy. You'll see some stuff tonight that'll make you scratch your head."

She returned to texting on her phone.

"Oh," she remarked suddenly, adding. "They also travel with their own band."

"Their own band?" Bea repeated as a question.

"Ya," Mal replied. "When you're that loaded you can pretty much do whatever you want."

She laughed.

"Listen about Cam and I," Bea began to say.

"He told me everything already," said Mal without looking up. "Dinner, the book...the kiss."

Bea blushed immediately.

"I told you," Mal said, looking at her and putting her hand on Bea's. "It's totally fine. In fact.."

She made a long pause.

"I think it's what's best for both of you," she continued before returning to her phone.

Best for both of us? Bea thought to herself. What's that supposed to mean?

Bea considered asking her to explain her answer when...

"We're here," Mal declared, her eyes sparkling with excitement.

Bea looked out the window and for the first time since she had started coming to the Club, the street outside the old church wasn't empty and dead.

Stepping out from the car, she emerged onto a loud sidewalk that was lined with people talking and yelling to one another. Two large black tour buses were parked outside the church. On the side of one were the words "Ton Von Unten".

They bypassed the queue out front as usual.

"Hey bitch, there's a line you know," said a familiar voice.

"Only for you," Mal replied without bothering to look at who said it.

"Bea?" the familiar voice said.

Bea turned and stopped dead in her tracks.

"Hi Tess," Bea said furtively, recognizing her old roommate at once.

Tess must have been very cold, she was dressed in a black leather two-piece that showed more skin than a summer bikini. Leather bands wrapped around her wrist were connected by silver chains to a leather dog collar around her neck. Her eyeliner, lipstick, eye shadow; all of it was jet black. She wore a little black leather cap.

Mal seemed annoyed they had stopped.

"Hey Mal," Bea said, not sure how to proceed. "This is Tess, she was my roommate earlier this year."

"A pleasure," Mal said, barely attempting to hide her sarcasm.

"I never would have thought you were into Ton Von Unten," Tess said.

"Never heard of them before tonight actually," Bea said somewhat embarrassed. "We just come here a lot."

"Well it's a long line," Tess said disappointed.

"I can see that," Mal said, looking towards the line that was growing by the second as similarly dressed people continuously emerged from Ubers to join the throng in the queue.

"Come on Bea," Mal said tugging on her hand. "It's cold out and I want to go inside."

"Ya," Bea said with an awkward smile before turning to Tess again. "See you inside I guess?"

Tess just looked at her with confused eyes, her teeth chattering. She stared at them as they disappeared around the corner and into the alleyway.

"THAT was your roommate?" Mal asked with a laugh once they were out of earshot of Tess.

"Ya, she was," Bea replied with a chuckle.

"No wonder you were desperate to get out of there," Mal commented as they approached the usual group of girls standing near the front of the line. "What a freak."

All the girls wore long coats similar to Bea and Mal. Other than Viv, Bea didn't remember their names.

"Ms. Phillips," Marshall said, smiling at Mal leading the way. "Guten Abend."

"Sehr Gut," she replied with a smile. "Your German has been improving since last year."

"Taking some classes," he replied.

"At the University?" Bea asked, the girls passing quickly through to the entrance.

"At the community college," Marshall replied with a scowl.

As they entered the usual mirror lined corridor, Bea was surprised to see all the mirrors had been removed and the walls covered with hundreds of what looked like medieval torture devices. Spanish boots, pears of anguish, thumbscrews, and iron chastity belts. Items she had only read about.

She reached out a hand to touch one. Pieces of rust flaked off into her hand, it was real iron. And the tip of one of the device's spikes, it was hard to tell for sure in the dark but it looked like it was stained red with blood.

"New look?" Bea asked Mal as she rubbed her fingers together in vain to remove the powdered rust.

"Request of the Germans," Mal replied nonchalantly.

Strange indeed.

There was one more strange feature of the hallway, a doorway that Bea had never noticed before. It was sunken into the wall on one side, and a thick iron gate covered it.

"Where does that go?" Bea asked.

"Janitor's closet I think," Mal replied. "Come on, I'm excited, aren't you?"

"Sure," Bea muttered just as they burst through the double doors and the laser lights of the club immersed them.

Harper and another bartender were waiting for them just inside. Harper wore black leather shorts held up by black suspenders, and around his neck was a choker. Being practically shirtless, his very colorful and ornate tattoos of birds were on full display. Including a large phoenix on his hairless six-pack abs that didn't end at his waistline.

That boy does love his birds.

"Ok ladies," Mal said. "On the count of three. One, two, three."

All of them except Bea took off their coats at once and tossed them at Harper. With the exception of Viv, everyone was dressed in black leather from head to toe. All very similar to Mal, each one attempting to mimic her perfection.

Most nights Viv's attire would have fit right in with the theme. But not tonight. Viv wore a skin tight red latex one-piece with long sleeves, just like Britney Spears in the "Oops!" music video. The bottom barely covered her butt and the skin tight made her chest look more voluptuous than her usual outfits. Bea couldn't stop but stare at her figure, admiring how attractive she was.

"What?" Viv noticed Bea staring. "I don't do girls."

"Sorry," Bea said, looking away embarrassed.

"Your coat Ms. Logan?" Harper said, smiling at her and holding out a hand.

Bea suddenly felt self conscious as the entire group was looking at her still in her full length coat.

Reluctantly she unlatched it and slid it off her shoulders.

"You know what," Viv remarked. "Seeing you in that, I might be tempted."

Bea's black leather dress showed more skin than she preferred. The top half was more corset than traditional dress, an opening in the front ran from her neck down to her stomach and was held closed by laces. The bottom half was a short skirt with chains dangling the side. She wore calf-high leather boots with four-inch heels to complete the look.

She felt completely ridiculous. But seeing the admiring gazes from other girls, combined with the stunned expressions of several passing men, she experienced a rare surge of confidence in her appearance.

The group took their seats at their usual lounge area however the area had been expanded with some large armchairs and an extra sofa so that it could accommodate twice the usual number of bodies. In the center was a tray filled with several large bottles of Jagermeister and Schnapps, accompanied by stacks of black onyx shot glasses.

The girls sat in their usual spots, Viv and Bea at the end. Adelaide's usual seat was empty, creating a slight sting in Bea's heart.

The decor of the club was very 90's techno. Lasers punched through a thick cloud of fog that hung over the dance floor. Electronica played over the speakers, the DJ dressed like a medieval knight played from the raised VIP area. The stage was pitch black, no lasers or spotlights could penetrate its veil. The emptiness seemed alive, like at any moment the darkness would overflow and consume the unwitting dancers.

On the second floor, where the church choir would typically be performing, several large drums and strange machines lined the club from front to back. Men dressed entirely from head to toe in black latex bodysuits stood motionless next to them, ominous guardians of these enigmatic instruments. They might have been lifeless statues if not for a single zipper where a mouth might be; a single sign that they were indeed alive.

"Feels weird without Adelaide here," Bea commented to Viv who sat with her leg up in her chair despite the tight latex outfit. Viv glanced to the empty chair next to Bea, a brief moment of sadness ran across her face.

"I know," Viv said.

"I didn't see you at her funeral," Bea commented.

"I don't do funerals," Viv replied.

"Why is that?" Bea asked.

Viv stared at her, "I just don't"

Harper arrived from the shadows with a tray of drinks and handed a short glass of dark liquid to Viv.

"And what am I drinking this evening?" Viv asked him.

"Given your outfit tonight," Harper began, "I elected a Kirsch Royale for you, with extra cherries."

Viv took a sip and paused.

A moment later, a shiver seemed to pass from her head down her body like a wave.

"Wow," she said, casting a rare smile. "That's fucking fabulous."

"Thank you," Harper replied. "And for you Ms. Logan, a suggestion from Mr. Anwir. Vodka infused with Cognac. He guaranteed you wouldn't be disappointed."

Bea took the glass but noticed Viv giving her an odd look.

Bea blushed as she took a sip, the taste triggered a memory of the Venison steak from dinner with Cam..

"Interesting crowd tonight," she said aloud to Viv who was watching the scantily clad passers-by.

"Apparently the Germans come every year," Viv replied. "And it's a whole big thing at the club."

"What was it like last year?" asked Bea.

"No idea," Viv said. "Wasn't part of the group then."

"Oh, so you are new like me?" Bea questioned.

"New? We're all new," Viv said. "Girls come and join for a while, then they either leave on their own or they get into it with Mal and are no longer welcome. Happens every month or so. All the girls here? They've only joined since I've been here. Adelaide had been around longer than me, but well...you know."

The empty chair seemed to have a significance that was unavoidable.

"That's so sad," Bea exclaimed. "I mean, doesn't Mal have any long-term friends?"

"Other than Cam, no," Viv replied.

Means the clock is already ticking on you.

"Doesn't bother me," Viv said, noticing Bea's expression of unease. "All of them are fake, all of them are wannabes. They are only here so they can take pictures and put them on their Instagram and pretend they are popular and cool. Pretend they are influencers. It's a load of horse crap. They are as fake as most of their tits."

Bea choked on her drink, coughing as she tried to regain her composure.

"How'd you meet Mal?" Bea asked, hoping to change the subject. Some of the other girls must have overheard Viv and were scowling as they looked across at them.

"She found me outside the psychology building on campus," Viv replied.

"You're a psychology major?" Bea asked with excitement, realizing she hadn't done a good job of getting to know anyone in the group besides Adelaide. “I think it’s a fascinating field of study.”

"Not my major," Viv replied, looking suddenly very uncomfortable.

"Ladies," Mal suddenly announced. The rest of the group conversations all hushed.

"To Adelaide!" she continued, holding up her glass. "She was a good friend."

"That girl knew how to party,” said one of the blondes sitting next to Mal.

The rest of the girls giggled, Viv and Bea remained awkwardly silent with their glasses in the air.

They all clinked their glasses then returned to their own conversations.

"What a fake bitch," Viv said before taking a big gulp of her delicious looking red cocktail.

"What?" Bea asked aloud.

"Mal," Viv clarified, speaking more softly. "I saw her on social media after the funeral, barely any mention of her 'good' friend Adelaide."

Viv made air quotes with her fingers to emphasize her sarcasm.

"What a crock," she added.

Bea took a moment to study Viv, who stared at the uninterested Mal with those burning dark eyes.

As much as Viv seemed to hate the other girls for being fake, Bea couldn't help but feel like her bitchy demeanor was just as fake as those other girls. It was a mask, a suit of armor, to hide and insulate the girl inside.

"So why do you hang out with her then?" Bea asked, growing more curious.

"With Mal?" Viv said, looking at her.

"When she first asked me out, it was because I had heard about this place and wanted to see what it was all about," Viv said, straightening up in her chair. "Most nights it's not my scene."

"So why do you keep coming back?" Bea asked with growing surety that Viv wasn't being entirely truthful with Bea...or even with herself.

"Well..." Viv started to reply before pausing. "Well, really it's for this."

Harper had magically appeared with a fresh replacement cocktail for Viv.

"Thanks Harper," she said with a rare smile.

"You're welcome lass," Harper said, smiling back and winking at her.

Bea noticed Harper's eyes remained affixed to Viv and her's on him.

After Harper had walked out of earshot, Bea slapped Viv in the leg.

"Are you and Harper dating?" Bea asked.

"No," Viv replied.

"You should ask him out," Bea said excitedly.

"I don't have boyfriends," Viv said, sipping her drink for an extra long moment as she stared at Harper's ass.

"He's obviously into you," Bea commented.

"No way," Viv replied. "He flirts with all the girls."

"Flirting is one thing," said Bea. "But the eyes don't lie."

“Maybe not a boyfriend,” Viv continued, tilting her head. “Fuck buddy I could do.”

They both laughed.

"How's it going tonight ladies?" said Cam's voice. He was standing on the far end of the area next to Mal. He wore black slacks with stylish fake patches sewn into the knees. A white t-shirt was covered with a black button down jacket that he wore open. On the lapel of the jacket, a design of white zigzagging stripes broke the monotony of dark color. He could have been a model, his muscular jaw line always with the perfect amount of stubble.

"Hi Cam," the girls said in unison.

Though he smiled and greeted the girls individually, Bea couldn't help but feel like he was watching her out of the corner of his eyes.

Eventually he made his way to Viv and Bea's corner.

"I hope Harper is taking care of you both," Cam said.

"He’s doing alright," Viv remarked.

"And you Ms. Logan," Cam said, drawing his eyes squarely on her and smiling. "I hope you are enjoying the evening thus far."

"Absolutely," Bea found herself saying without thinking and smiling back at him. Viv gave them both a confused look.

"How's your thesis coming along?" Cam asked.

"Splendid," Bea replied. She couldn't pinpoint if it was the sight of him after two days of drifting into daydreams about him or the potent drink she was swiftly consuming, but she vividly recalled the spark they felt during their kiss.

Their eyes locked, and they stood smiling at each other for a long moment.

"Are they here yet?" Mal asked from across the area.

"Um...who?" Cam said, snapping back to reality.

Mal raised her eyebrows.

"Oh, the Germans," he said, clapping his hands together in a eureka moment. "Yes, they are just getting settled upstairs in the VIP area. They should be down shortly."

"Mal told us they are rich," said a brunette that Bea didn't remember who's name it was.

"Filthy," Cam replied with sultry emphasis.

The girls broke off into a scuttle of excited conversations.

Cam gently placed his hand on Bea's knee before ascending the nearby stairs to the VIP area. It had only been a moment, but Bea felt something different about the touch. It wasn't just the raw energy of attraction, there was something else there. Something she didn't quite understand yet.

"What was that about?" Viv asked Bea as soon as Cam was out of ear-shot.

"What?" Bea asked, still watching Cam from afar as he walked up the stairs.

"You and him?" Viv questioned.

"No, nothing," Bea lied. "So what do you think the Germans will be like?"

"Don't change the subject," Viv snorted.

Bea glanced around, pretending she didn't know what Viv was talking about.

Viv narrowed her eyes.

"The Germans," Viv started again, giving up on getting anything more from Bea. "Rich foreign men who travel to distant lands to go to clubs with young women? My guess is they are fat, ugly, old white guys who need the pill to get it up."

Bea laughed.

"You're probably right."

Viv smiled at her.

"Luk at all de pretty girls!" said a strange voice with a heavy accent.

All the girls looked up to see a party of men descending the stairs toward them.

A short plump one stood at the front, he wore a black tuxedo, an eye patch, and a round top hat that hid bushy white hair. He had his arms out wide in front of him and in one hand held a black and silver cane.

"We love America!" he yelled.

The girls next to Mal all let out a light affirming scream in response.

He immediately sat in an open seat between two very drunk blondes and put his arms around their shoulders.

"My name iz Druck," the man said.

Harper poured him a shot of Jagermeister and handed it to Druck. The girls nearby drank fancy cocktails.

"What awful drink is that," asked Druck to the girls.

"Lemon drops," said one of them. "Would you like a taste?" She waved her drink in front of the man's nose.

"Eww, lemon," Druck said with a face distorted in disgust. "I can not stand ze flavor."

He downed his shot.

"Now Jagermeister," he continued. "Zat is a magical drink, a manly drink. Make one, very... very..." Instead of speaking the word he was thinking of, he yelled a very throaty roar.

The girls giggled.

The next man to descend the stairs was of medium height and build. Unlike most of the club, he was not dressed in all black. Instead he wore white cotton pants, a bright blue shirt, and black velvet vest. His hair was auburn and his sideburns extended, hugging his jawline, down to his chin. His nose, ears, eyes, and mouth all seemed to be too large for his face, giving him a cartoon character like appearance.

"Hallo," he said, bowing to the group. "My name is Herr Kerzenflame, however please call me Kerze."

His accent was noticeable but less so than the comical Druck.

"Hello Kerze," the girls said in unison.

Kerze took a seat at the table and immediately began pouring a shot from the bottle of Schnapps.

The last German visitor descended the stairs, he was in deep conversation with Cam who accompanied him. They were speaking very fast in German, she couldn't tell if they were talking or arguing.

As they reached the bottom, Bea couldn't believe her eyes. Cam was tall, however the German man made him look regular height in comparison. He wore brown loose pants that were baggy around his feet, hiding his shoes that clopped loudly with each heavy step. Around his waist was an iron chain belt, its metal was worn and old. A sleeveless vest revealed no shirt underneath, the ashy skin of his arms and chest on full display. His beard and hair was dark brown and wild, contained only by a worn tophat and round dark sunglasses that hid his eyes well.

"Ladies," Cam said as they approached. "This is Dunkler Peter, but call him Peter please. He's visiting from Germany, please make sure he feels welcome."

The group of girls got quiet, some waved cautiously. They had sensed it too, the aura of dread that seemed to accompany

Peter as he approached. All except Viv, who laughed and beckoned him to the open seat next to her. She seemed to be enjoying how uncomfortable he made the rest of the girls.

"Shotz, shotz, who wants a shot?!" yelled Druck.

Harper began pouring Schnapps and Jagermeister into the onyx shot glasses in quick rows, the girls grabbing them from the table as quickly as he could pour them.

Peter took the seat next to Viv, Bea became immediately uncomfortable

"Dunkler Peter," Viv said with a grin. "What kind of name is that?"

Peter didn't reply.

Harper handed him a glass of a smoking drink. Not a glass actually, it was a chalice. It was ornately carved which in the dim light of the club looked like screaming distorted faces of ghosts and skeletons.

"That looks interesting," Viv said. "What is it?"

Peter was silent again, he took a large gulp from the chalice which spilled on his beard and fell to the floor in steaming drops. He finished it in one drink.

Bea noticed Cam and Harper standing nearby watching intently at the interactions.

"Hi," she said with a slight slur to her speech. "I'm Viv." She reached out her hand.

Peter turned and held out a large scarred hand that engulfed Viv's in his. His ashy skin illuminated in the club's neon lights, his fingernails were black and sharpened like claws.

"I love your tattoos," Viv said, staring at the man's arm stretched out in front of her. She seemed oblivious to all the other warning signs about him.

Peter nodded.

Bea's curiosity got the better of her and she leaned in for a better look. The man's arms were covered in a menagerie of demonic forms dragging men, women, and children toward caves and wells. Some of the poor victims were bound in chains or in burlap sacks, the creatures were grotesque. Some had teeth like swords, others had tongues as long as their bodies that wrapped around their prey like snakes.

"They are super rad," Viv commented, her voice increasingly sounding less like her normal self. "Where'd you get them done?"

Peter remained silent.

"Pardon my master, his English is not very good," the auburn-haired Kurze said leaning in.

"What part of Germany are you from?" Viv asked Kerze.

Bea noticed that in front of Viv were at least eight empty glasses. Either Harper was on his game tonight or perhaps he had something else in mind.

"Garmisch-Partenkirchen," Kerze replied.

"Bavaria?" Bea said in question form.

"Very gut,' Kerze said with a smile. "High in the Alps."

"I bet they have great skiing," said the brunette next to Kerze. "My dad has a condo in Vail, well it's actually not his. It's a timeshare, we go up every January... "

Dunkler Peter grunted and the brunette stopped talking immediately.

Viv laughed.

"Dude, you're fucking great," she said slapping Peter on the shoulder.

"You ok Viv?" Bea asked.

"I'm fine," she replied. "I'm better than fine, I feel great."

"Ok," Bea replied, completely unconvinced.

"Shhh," Druck said from the other end of the table. "Itz about to begin!"

Indeed, the lights of the club had begun to dim until they were immersed in almost complete darkness. The crowd began clamoring and yelling, partially with excitement but also with fear. Bea could feel a rumbling sound growing, like a semi was driving at top speed. But it wasn't a passing vehicle, it was the array of figures above them who had lined the club. They were playing their drums in unison.

With a loud eruption, flames appeared from the barrels next to the drums. The dancing yellow lights casting glowing shadows across the entire club.

A deep voice from the darkness emerged, "Ich will."

Several excited persons on the dancefloor echoed the chant.

"Ich will," it repeated. "Ich will."

In the light from the flame, Bea could see Peter, Kerze, and Druck turn to face the stage, like they knew what was coming.

Viv's eyes were on Peter, staring at the murals on his arms still. Her eyes looked glassy, like she was in some hypnotic state.

An electric guitar riff bellowed from the stage which despite the abundance of firelight still remained dark and foreboding.

The crowd screamed.

A column of fire shot from the center of the stage, illuminating figures with hunched over silhouettes encircling the flame. The fire column raged and grew brighter, until the darkness that had engulfed the stage lifted and men began to take form.

There were four of them and they were clad in leather briefs held up by suspenders and with black leather gas masks obscuring their faces. Each playing on various instruments, drums, guitars, and a keyboard.

The voice over the speakers repeated "Ich will,"

The noise cut out, the flame disappeared and all was silent except for the roar of the crowd.

A moment later, the flame returned as the band began playing; however front and center of the stage now stood a large, hairy, leather clad man holding the microphone. He was dressed much like the others, except instead of a gas mask his face was covered by what could have been a cow skull. The black straps of the mask wrapped around his head and held down his shoulder length blond hair.

"Ich will dass ihr mir vertraut," his voice yelled into the microphone as the heavy metal blasted from the speakers.

"I fucking love this song," Viv yelled from her seat, clapping ecstatically.

Bea glanced at her, she was alarmed to see Peter studying her closely. She seemed oblivious as she bounced in her chair watching the stage.

Without warning, the small plump man named Druck jumped nimbly onto the table.

"And now!" he yelled at the top of his lungs. "We dance!"

Grabbing the hands of the two blondes that had been seated next to them, he practically dragged them to the dance floor. They barely had time to put down their drinks.

Peter stood next, his enormous frame towering over everyone. Kerze was quick to follow. Peter leaned over and whispered something into Kerze's ear. Kerze nodded and turned to Viv.

"Mam," Kerze said. "Dunkler Peter would like you to join him please."

Viv looked at the unusual man staring down at her, his sunglasses hiding his eyes and any hint to his true intent.

She finished the rest of her drink in one gulp.

"Hell ya," Viv yelled, she jumped up and ran ahead of them to the dance floor. "Catch me if you can."

Peter grunted, however it wasn't one of disapproval or anger. It was a grunt of satisfaction. Bea couldn't for certain because of his thick beard, but she thought she caught a hint of a smile from him.

Peter, Kerze, and the rest of the girls including Mal quickly followed and soon Bea was all alone by herself watching the crowd from her chair.

"Not a fan of the music?" said Cam sitting down in the empty seat to Bea's left.

"Not really," Bea replied, smiling at him. Being this close to him again, she wished she had a way to block whatever mysterious energy he gave off that distracted her.

"As you probably realized by now," Cam said smiling. "I'm more of a fan of the classics."

"I've been to your apartment," Bea replied. "You were definitely born a few centuries late."

He laughed.

"You have no idea," Cam replied.

Harper arrived and handed him a drink.

Bea recognized it immediately as whiskey.

"Not drinking Vodka tonight?" she asked.

"Alas," he replied with a sigh. "I'm afraid I've been going a bit overboard on Russian lately. Lost my appetite for it."

"I'd say," she replied smiling. "I still wish I could get that taste of caviar out of my mouth."

"You didn't enjoy dinner?" Cam said with concern.

"No!" Bea replied. "It was amazing, I'm pretty sure I had a dream about that venison last night."

"Is that all you've been dreaming about?" he said with a wink.

She blushed as a silence engulfed the duo; both watching the chaotic dancing in front of the stage as the German band played unfamiliar song after unfamiliar song.

"I'm drinking Scotch tonight," he said at last, raising his drink to clink hers. "Much more complex flavor."

"I'd say," Bea added, remembering the Talisker 30 she had at his apartment.

"Thank you for entertaining my friends," Cam said leaning in close to her. "It means a lot."

He kissed her lightly on the cheek.

Bea felt her body quiver all over at the touch, she clenched the sides of her chair tightly.

"They are a bit over the top sometimes," he said, looking out over the dance floor again.

Bea followed his gaze. Peter could be seen clearly with the bright red latex clad Viv jumping up and down very closely to him in time to the loud guitar and booming drums.

Cam seemed to be obsessing over Dunkler Peter, though Bea could not imagine why.

"Nervous?" Bea asked.

Cam seemed flustered by the mere question.

“No, why?” he said quickly.

Though their acquaintance was brief, she could easily differentiate between his confident demeanor and his moments of doubt.

“Fine,” he said, giving in to her prying. “My parents are coming to visit in a few weeks. It's always a big affair when they come."

"Your parents?" Bea asked. “I’m sure they are wonderful.”

"That’s not the word I would use," he replied. "My father is a bit overbearing, he wants to control every aspect of my life.”

Bea could relate, her deacon father was not exempt from committing the same mistakes as any other parent.

“What about your mother?” Bea asked.

“After all these years,” Cam sighed, he seemed less stressed as he opened up to her. “She hasn’t forgiven me for not settling down and starting a family."

"All these years?" Bea said with a raised eyebrow. "You are still so young, plenty of time for that."

"Right," Cam said, nodding with a smile. "I think we both know how time can get away from us if we aren't careful."

Bea looked at him carefully. Did he know?

Of course he doesn't know.

A hint of sorrow crept back into Bea's heart as she recalled her diagnosis. It felt as if an internal hourglass had been flipped, its sands rapidly depleting, leading her towards an inevitable and agonizing conclusion. The medication prescribed by her doctor could only mitigate the symptoms, offering no true reprieve.

"Best we enjoy the time we have been given," he added at the end, almost as if he could sense her thoughts. “Better with someone by your side than alone.”

He smiled at her, her worries about her future melted away.

A stillness returned to the space, the dancing bodies nearby feeling far away and distant.

"Enough sad talk," Cam said with a more upbeat tone. "I've got tell you a secret."

"A secret?" Bea replied, curious to what kind of secret he would reveal.

"Come here," he said, leaning closer to her and gesturing with his finger for her to do the same.

She nervously leaned in.

"Closer," he whispered.

She moved in another inch. His mouth was right next to her ear, his hot breath like fire on her bare neck. With each second, his body pulsed with heat and energy; like the heartbeat of a gigantic furnace.

"You are by far," he began softly. "The most beautiful woman in this entire club."

Tingles ran down her body, from the hair on her neck down to her toes. The energy, the electricity that somehow Cam exerted on her had returned despite her attempts to mute it.

"Maybe a little later we could get away for a few minutes," he added.

She was drunk in erotic emotions, her sex hormones spreading like wildfire throughout her body.

"Get away? Where?" she managed to say, unable to focus or concentrate on any one thought as she swam in her senses.

"There's some quiet and comfortable places in the back," he said. "I know a guy."

Bea laughed, her body and mind feeling foggy and drunk.

"I bet you do," she managed to say as she giggled.

"Just what the fuck do you think you are doing?" said an angry voice.

Cam and Bea turned to see Viv standing with her hands on her hips, staring at the two of them.

"We were just talking," Bea said, unsure why Viv sounded so angry.

"That's Adelaide's chair," Viv said, staring with furious dark eyes.

"Oh, I'm sorry," Cam said, standing up suddenly. "I had forgotten..."

"You forgot?" Viv interrupted him.

Kerze and Peter emerged from the crowd several yards behind Viv.

"My mistake," Cam apologized again.

"And what are you doing talking to her?" Viv yelled.

Mal emerged from the crowd as well and ran to Viv's side.

"Viv, calm down," Mal said, tugging on her arm.

"Don't tell me to fucking calm down," Viv yelled jerking her arm away. "Adelaide's been in the ground barely a week and he's already hunting for his next piece of meat. What a fucking asshole."

Bea just looked at her stunned, unsure of what to say.

"I was just talking to Ms. Logan for a moment," Cam began to say calmly.

"You shut your mouth," Viv said, stopping him. "I don't want to hear another word of bullshit from you."

"Viv..." Mal tried to say before being interrupted again.

"Come on Bea," Viv said. "Let's get out of this fucked up place."

Bea was still too stunned to move, she sat speechless unsure of what to say or do.

"Wait..." Viv said as if she had just realized something. "You're fucking him aren't you?"

"No, no I'm not," Bea pleaded. "We were just talking."

"You are a fucking slut," Viv screamed.

"That's not fair," Mal said, coming to Bea's defense.

"Shut up you brainless twit," Viv snarled at Mal. "I can't believe this. Adelaide's gone and before her body's cold you already jump into bed with the biggest asshole in this entire fucking fucked up club."

Mal, Cam, and Bea were all stunned speechless.

"Fuck you," Viv said walking to her chair and collecting her purse and flipping off Cam along the way.

"Fuck you," she repeated towards Mal.

"And you," Viv said, turning to Bea with the beginnings of tears in her eyes. "Fuck you, I thought you were different than the rest of them."

With that, she turned and walked briskly toward the exit. Harper attempted to step in front of her to block her way.

“Now settle down, love,” he tried to say.

With a swift strike, Harper fell to the ground, crunched into the fetal position.

“Fuck you, you sexy...” she yelled and then grunted in frustration.

She disappeared through the double doors.

They were all frozen in silence.

Bea glanced at Cam, expecting him to be watching Viv leave.

Instead, she saw something in his eyes she didn't recognize, something she had never seen before in him. It looked like he was afraid, and he was staring straight at Peter.

The momentary fear was replaced by anger.

"Harpier," he practically yelled.

Harper groaned as he stood.

"The bitch punched me in the nads," he exclaimed.

"Shut up! What are you waiting for?" he said, gesturing in the direction she left. "Go talk to her, bring her back. Now!"

Harper hurried away at a limping jog, still clutching his crotch.

Bea looked at both Cam and Mal. Both seemed equally alarmed at the series of events. Peter stood forebodingly in the background.

Cam approached Mal and they began chatting quietly, Bea couldn't hear what they were saying.

Cam was visually distressed, clutching at the bridge of his nose as he spoke.

Bea approached.

"Why'd you call him Harpier?" Bea asked, hoping to break the tension.

"What?" Cam said, looking at her, distracted. "Oh, um. It's his real name. Everyone just calls him Harper around here."

"Oh," Bea said.

Something about the name Harpier sounded familiar, she just couldn't quite put her finger on it.

"I've got to go with him," Cam said at last. "Stay here, I'll be back."

He put his hands on her shoulders which comforted her only slightly, before rushing off to follow Harper.

Mal and Bea collapsed into the two nearby chairs.

"I need a fucking drink," Mal said.

"Did someone say, drink?" yelled Druck from nearby. He quickly ran to the table and began pouring shots of Schnapps into the onyx shot glasses.

Bea just stared at the shot glass in her hand.

"She was always a fucking bitch," Mal said gulping down her shot. "Don't let what she said get to you."

"I know, I just..." Bea's voice trailed off.

"Take a drink," Mal encouraged her. "Shake it off, let's go back out there and have some fun."

"Ein Frau after my own heart," said Druck, bowing.

"I should go talk to her," Bea said, putting down her drink and trying to stand up.

Mal grabbed her arm.

"Harper and Cam got it," Mal said. "Just relax."

Druck held out her shot in front of her.

"It's very tasty!" he exclaimed.

Bea thought for a moment before pulling her arm from Mal's grasp and standing.

"I'll be back," she said and she ran off to catch up with the others.

Mal followed her with great concern.

Emerging into the cold night outside the club, Bea found the throng of those waiting to get in still lined up around the corner. Many shivering in their scantily clad attire.

Harper and Cam stood halfway down the alley, they seemed to be arguing.

She approached slowly, as she got closer they did not notice her but she could hear what they were saying.

"You know what happens if we don't deliver right?" Cam said angrily to Harper.

"I know, I know," Harper replied, looking distressed.

"I wouldn't be the only one here to suffer," Cam continued.

"She got into a cab," Harper pleaded. "I don't know where she went, I don't know what you want me to do."

"Find me someone else then," Cam said.

"How are we going to find someone like that on such short notice, his terms were extremely specific..." Harper said his voice trailing off as he noticed Bea nearby listening.

"Bea," he said with a smile. "What are you doing here?"

They both turned to face her.

"I was looking for Viv," Bea said cautiously. "I wanted to try to talk to her."

"She's gone already," Harper said. "Couldn't catch up to her in time."

"Let's get you back inside," Cam said approaching. He pulled off his jacket and wrapped it around her shoulders where her skin was turning red from the cold.

Bea was going to walk back inside when...

"Bea, Bea!" yelled Tess's voice.

Bea looked over to see her former roommate standing only a few yards farther forward in line then when she had last seen her. Her cheeks and ears bright red from the cold, the two men she had arrived with looking equally close to hypothermia.

"Hi," Bea said half heartedly, her mind still confused and unsure of what was going on.

"Who's your friend?" Tess asked through chattering teeth.

"This is Cam," Bea replied instinctively.

"Hi," Tess said, raising a hand to wave at him.

Cam just stared at her without expression, like he was studying her.

"Listen," Tess began to say. "I know we didn't quite get along as roommates. But I've been dying to see this band since I first heard them. Do you think you could help me get in?"

"Get in?" Bea repeated out loud. "I don't know."

"Oh, ok," Tess sounded most unlike her normal self.

"I can get you in," said Cam, whose expressionless face and stare had changed to a warming smile.

Bea gave him a confused look.

"Really?" exclaimed Tess.

"Sure," Cam said. "But only you."

Tess looked back at the two men she had arrived with.

"Sorry boys," she said, jumping out of line. "No dice tonight."

Both men groaned in collective disappointment.

"Where are you from Tess?" Cam asked as they walked towards the entrance.

"Grand Rapids," she replied.

"Never been, is it nice?" Cam continued the conversation.

"It's a shit hole to be honest," said Tess, giddy and happy to be getting in.

Bea walked with them but her mind was far away, thinking about Viv and where she could have gone.

"Sir," said Marshall as he opened the door for them to enter.

"Thank you Marshall," Cam replied.

Cam looked back at Harper who was still standing in the alleyway watching them re-enter the club, he nodded.

Harper nodded back and grinned.

Bea sat back down in her usual chair, the band had stopped playing and the DJ was playing techno music again over the speakers.

Mal and the rest of the girls were busy chatting with Druck, who was balancing a shot glass on his nose before dropping it into his mouth. The girls laughed and cheered at the jolly little man.

"Where did Peter go?" Cam asked Druck as he approached.

"He went upstairs," Druck said suddenly, no longer grinning. "He was not glücklich."

"I'll go talk to him," Cam said. "If you'll excuse me."

Cam addressed the group, but his eyes were fixed to Bea who understood he was really talking to her.

Harper arrived with a fresh round of drinks and led Tess to the empty nearby chair where Viv had previously sat.

"Oh my God," Tess squealed with excitement as she sat in the warm comfortable seat. "I've been wanting to see these guys live for years, but they never tour in the U.S."

Harper draped a thick fur jacket over Tess's shoulders.

"Don't want you catching cold on us, would we?" he said with a flirtatious smile.

"Thank you!" Tess exclaimed in return, downing the shot of alcohol he handed her. "How did you know my favorite drink was Jim Beam?"

"Call it a lucky guess," Harper replied. "Enjoy."

Tess seemed to warm almost instantly, her flushed cheeks returning to her normal pale white complexion.

"I can't believe I'm here," Tess said excitedly. "I was afraid I was going to be out there all night."

"Ya," Bea said, still lost in thought.

"Are you a fan of Ton Von Unten too?" Tess asked.

Bea wasn't really listening.

"Ya, sure," she replied.

"Oh my God, their music," Tess began to talk in a flurry. "It's so dark, it's sexy, it's hypnotic. So raw! I know it's mostly in German but when I looked at the translated lyrics, it just spoke to me. I felt like they wrote it all for me, for what happened to me."

Bea continued to only listen partially.

Tess didn't seem to notice her disinterest.

"When I was younger," Tess continued wiping the excess liquid from her lips. "My father. He was not a good man, he did things...to me."

"I'm sorry," Bea said, her subconscious talking for her.

"Thanks," Tess replied. "I guess I haven't really had anyone to talk about it with."

Maybe you'd have more friends other than all those guys you made us wait outside while you... Bea didn't want her voice to finish the thought.

"What about those men you've been dating?" Bea asked.

"Dating?" Tess said with a loud laugh. "They are all just dicks with legs to me. Men are pigs, they should be treated as such. I guess the music is the only thing that I've had to keep me sane all these years. I feel angry sometimes, at my dad, at what he did, at men in general. The music helps me channel it, let it out."

"I'm glad you found something that works," Bea responded.

"And now," Tess grew giddy and drank another shot. "They are right here, in this club. And I'll finally be able to see them! Speaking of which, when do they go on?"

"Oh Frau," exclaimed Druck who had been listening nearby. "They will be on again shortly. Schnapps?"

"Sure!" Tess exclaimed and drank the shot glass he offered happily.

Bea still didn't feel right about what happened with Viv. She looked over at Mal who was watching Tess intently, studying her.

The DJ's last song ended and the lights of the club dimmed.

"Oh my God, it's time!" Tess yelled, jumping up.

"Yes, Fraulein," Druck said, joining her. "Shall we?"

He held out his hand and Tess took it eagerly.

Mal also stood and the rest of the girls except Bea joined her.

Druck led the procession of girls to the dance floor, where the crowds parted to let them to the front of the stage.

Mal hung back, looking at Bea with concern.

"Coming?" Mal asked.

"I don't think so," Bea replied. "I think I'm going to go home."

"Come on," Mal said, tugging on her arm. "It'll be fun, once in a lifetime experience I promise."

"No, I'm tired," Bea said, standing and collecting her purse. "Will you tell Cam thank you for a wonderful time from me?"

"Sure," Mal said with a reassuring smile.

Harper had appeared behind Bea holding her long coat.

"There's a cab outside waiting for you Ms. Logan," he said.

"Thank you Harper, but how did you..." Bea said, putting her coat on.

Harper just nodded.

Mal hugged Bea tightly.

"Next time, it'll be more fun," Mal whispered into her ear. "I promise, don't let her ruin your night."

Bea hugged her back.

Mal returned to join the rest of the girls on the dancefloor and Bea left the club and got into the cab. The entire drive back to the house, all Bea could think about was what Viv had said and what she had overheard Cam and Harper discussing outside. It didn't feel right, and she was determined to make sense of it.

Tess screamed as Ton Von Unten ran back onto the stage. Though she had watched every music video, their interviews, their live shows; none of it compared to seeing them in the flesh just a couple yards in front of her.

However tonight was something she had never seen before from them. All five band members had three foot long black Dragon heads strapped to the front of their briefs. Running from their backs was a thick rubber hose that disappeared backstage.

"As the instruments began to play, Tess's joy was palpable when flames burst forth from the Dragon's maws, cascading above the audience like blazing jets. With every fiery eruption, the assembly responded with a mix of shouts and applause."

The music was heavy, Tess jumped and screamed. Her arms waving in the air, bodies pressed up all around her. The small German man Druck was singing along drunkenly to the lyrics. It was everything Tess had hoped for.

After what felt like only a few minutes, Tess looked at her watch only to realize that the band had been playing for over an hour. The lights went out on the stage and the crowd went wild.

"Zu-ga-be! Zu-ga-be! Zu-ga-be!" the crowd chanted, the echoes reverberating off the walls of the old church.

Suddenly a drum beat began to resound through the halls, the crowd grew excited to get their wish.

Tess looked up at the great fires that lined the second floor, and saw over a dozen fully latex clad men beating on drums. Their faces hidden behind masks with closed zippers, but somehow all beating the enormous percussion instruments in harmony.

Her body resonated with the rhythm of the drums, vibrating with each pulse.

The spotlight lit up the stage and the lead singer of the band stood there in his demon mask.

"This last song," the band's singer said in a heavy German accent. "Is for the Fräulein."

A chorus of feminine screams erupted from the crowd, in which Tess joined.

As the song began, Tess recognized it immediately. A cover of Dead or Alive's "You Spin Me Round (Like a Record)".

"If I, I get to know your name," the song began.

Tess jumped high as the song continued, oblivious to several sets of watchful eyes from high above her on the second level that were intently focused on her every move.

"All I know is that to me," the song continued. "You look like you're lots of fun. Open up your lovin' arms. Watch out, here I come."

Tess felt like the singer was speaking to her directly. His mask hid his eyes, but she felt his gaze on her.

"I set my sights on you, and no one else will do," he continued. "And I, I've got to have my way now, baby."

She felt warm, hot; and it wasn't just the flamethrowers shooting above her head. She wanted him, she wanted him badly. Hell, she wanted the whole band, all to herself.

"You spin me right 'round, baby, right 'round," the song continued.

Tess was right in front of the stage, the lead singer's dragon swaying to music right above her.

"All I know is that to me, you look like you're lots of fun," he sang out. "Open up your lovin' arms. Watch out, here I come."

Dragon flames burst forward ten feet into the crowd over their heads.

Tess was sweating but loving every moment.

As the song ended and the stage was blanketed in darkness again, Tess wanted more. More of the music, more of the feeling, more of the band. Even if only temporary, it made her feel complete again.

Tess had long used music as her escape, drowning out the noise of the demons of her past. Whatever nightmares the metal she played while she slept gave her, they were a welcome break from her horrific memories of her childhood that played back on endless repeat when her world was quiet.

"Fräulein!" yelled Druck.

"Little," Tess began to say, unsure of what his name was. "German, man!"

"Would you like to meet the band?" he asked.

"YES!" she replied without hesitation, practically screaming at him.

"Follow me please," he said as he bustled off through the crowd with Tess in tow. Walking to the stairs that lead to the VIP area, the bouncers stepped aside immediately and Tess practically ran up the flight of steps.

From his perch at the top, Cam watched Tess disappear into the VIP area. He breathed a weary sigh of relief. Looking over, he caught Mal's eyes as she sat sipping on her drink also watching the events unfold.

He nodded at her and she nodded back.

Crisis averted.

Chapter Eleven

Bea left Professor Mikkelson's class, making her way to the library. She had a couple of books she needed to check out as cross references for her thesis. It had been almost a month since the Germans had visited. She had made incredible strides on her thesis, so much so that she had gone from being far behind to being almost done. All that was left was for her to tidy up a few references.

Aren't you forgetting something?

The voice wasn't wrong. She still had one major hurdle that she wasn't quite sure how to overcome yet. That being how to convince Cam to release the *Filii Diaboli* to the academic community. The Professor had been right, even if he vouched that he had seen it with his own eyes, without a copy of the mythical text available no one would believe that anything she wrote wasn't just fantasy.

Bea cared about Cam, he made her feel something that she hadn't felt with anyone else before. Their casual dates over the last several weeks had only deepened their relationship. He wasn't constantly pressuring her into sex like her high school boyfriend had, Cam showed phenomenal patience. Something she admired greatly.

He also was incredibly intelligent, they could discuss and debate several topics of interest related to accounts of historical events; trading valid points with civility like two Olympic fencers locked in a never ending draw.

It was because she cared for him, that asking him to give up likely one of his prize possessions was impossible. Imagine how hard it had been for him to obtain it, how much it had cost...

If unveiled to the public at this moment, if duplicated, its worth could drop by millions, perhaps even tens of millions of dollars.

As she nervously thought about how she would ask him, finding no good answer she heard the ping of her phone indicating a text message.

A sliver of hope sprung from her heart, perhaps it was Viv texting her back.

After the night with the Germans, Bea had tried to contact Viv in multiple ways. Countless texts and voice-mails; she even had tried to find out where Viv lived from Heather O'Connell with the campus housing group. Apparently Viv lived off campus making it impossible to locate her without the help of some kind of private investigator.

Bea had almost given up hope.

Fishing her phone from her bag, she read the alert.

The message was not from Viv, Bea's heart sank.

Instead, it was from her Mother.

She sighed and unlocked her phone lazily.

That woman has the worst timing.

No kidding, she began to read the text then stopped in her tracks.

JUST LANDED, EXCITED TO SEE YOU TONIGHT. RESERVATIONS AT 6, SEE YOU THERE!

What?

You forgot, didn't you?

Bea's heart raced with anxiety.

She had forgotten, forgotten that her parents were attending a conference for the Catholic Diocese downtown. That this had been planned months ago, including dinner tonight.

After she had been diagnosed with Huntington's Disease, the only way she could avoid being angry with her family was to push every thought of them from her mind. It was the only way to avoid hating them for giving her a death sentence, for not being the ones to tell her and leaving that to assholes like Dr. Tompkins.

If she had been asked what living with Huntington's was like, Bea wasn't sure she could answer. The drugs from Dr. Keeling had helped with the physical symptoms like the trembling and the shakes; and even with some of the cognitive lapses that came and went. They didn't go away entirely but were less frequent and momentary. However it couldn't do anything to help with the sadness and depression that creeped in when she was alone with her thoughts.

Her only method of stopping herself from falling into a deep depression had been to pretend like she didn't have the disease at all. The evenings with Cam and the days engrossed in her thesis provided a comforting escape from solitary moments when thoughts of her own impending mortality consumed her.

Every time she felt her fingers twitch involuntarily, knocked something over clumsily, or when she sometimes even struggled to find the right word, she would try and pretend it never happened. It was manageable at the moment, at least for this moment. Tompkins had been convinced it was in her head, that symptoms didn't develop in someone her age. That she had at least ten more years of freedom from the disease.

Bea wasn't so sure.

Her body was changing faster than she had ever noticed before, beyond just the symptoms. Wrinkles were slowly forming at the corners of her eyes, aches and pains were ever present in her joints, her cheeks had become more sunken. Mal had reassured her she looked great, that she just needed more beauty sleep; but Bea felt like something else was happening to her.

Bea didn't realize she had started crying, several onlookers noticed her standing in the middle of the sidewalk sobbing. The library could wait, she needed to get home before she really put on a show.

"Hey Bea," Cam's deep friendly voice greeted her from the speaker on her phone.

Bea sat on the edge of her bed, staring at the mirror as she spoke.

"Hi Cam," she said. "Listen, I..."

"I'm glad you called," Cam said before she could finish her sentence. "I was thinking that tonight we could go to that new place downtown, Château Bien."

"About that," Bea replied.

"I know," said Cam. "Too bougie for you, but the chef is supposedly amazing."

"Cam," Bea said, more forceful.

"Ya, what's up?" Cam asked.

"I need a favor," Bea said.

"Sure, anything," Cam responded, not realizing what he was getting himself into.

"I need you to come to dinner with my parents tonight," Bea said.

"Your parents?" Cam questioned.

"Ya, I forgot they were in town," Bea clarified. "I'm having dinner with them tonight and need you there with me."

"I don't know Bea," Cam said, sounding flustered. A rarity.

"I know we are still new," began Bea. "But I'm going to need you with me tonight. Holding my hand, I have to tell them something. And you. Without you there with me, I don't think I will have the strength to do it. Cam, please."

The line was silent, with each passing moment Bea's heartbeat grew louder in her chest.

She wasn't sure how much time had passed before she heard him finally speak.

"Where are we going?" Cam replied.

"Thank you," Bea said.

Relief rushed over her body at once, the moments of silent tension disappeared entirely and she felt happy to see her request for support reciprocated.

She told him the name of the chain steakhouse next to the airport where her parents had arranged for them to meet.

"Really?" Cam said with a questioning tone. "I mean I can get us reservations somewhere downtown that serves food that didn't come from a processing plant..."

"I don't want to hear it, young man," Bea said playfully to him, a behavior she was growing more comfortable with as they had become closer. "And my dad is going to pay, don't even try to pick up the bill."

"Ok, I guess," Cam said. "Pick you up at 5:30?"

"Sounds good," Bea replied, smiling once again.

She paused.

"Oh, and Cam," she said into the receiver, a tear of relief forming in her eye. "Thank you for this."

"It would be my pleasure," Cam replied.

Bea smiled as she heard the line click.

She looked at the clock, it was 2:30. She had plenty of time before dinner.

Talking to Cam had made her feel flushed.

She crawled into bed and pulled the covers over head. Her thoughts filled with images of Cam's.

It was 5:15PM. She was panicking as she was still wearing sweatpants and a t-shirt. Standing in front of her closet completely distraught at the realization that she had nothing suitable to wear. None of the outfits that Mal had given her over the last few months to wear at the club were remotely appropriate for dinner with her parents. On the flip side, none of her old run down wardrobe seemed to be worthy to wear while out with Cam. She had nothing to wear.

"Hey Bea," Mal's voice rang from the hall. "Cam's outside already. I guess he's here to pick you up..."

Her voice trailed off as her head appeared in the doorway.

Bea glanced over at her with a look of terror.

"Oh," Mal said, realizing the situation. "Can't find anything to wear?"

"I'm stumped," Bea said, sitting back down on the bed and burying her head in her hands.

"Why not wear that sexy black thing you borrowed a few weeks ago?" Mal asked.

"Can't, it's dinner with my parents," Bea replied.

"Parents?!" Mal exclaimed.

For a long moment, Mal looked totally perplexed.

"I mean," Mal continued, unsure of how to respond. "What, how, why?"

"I forgot they were coming to town," Bea clarified. "And I asked Cam to join me, please help. I'm desperate, nothing I have seems right."

Mal seemed to take a long moment to process this.

"Ya, um..." she said at last. "I think I know what you are looking for. Come with me."

Together they ran to Mal's room where Mal pushed Bea behind the changing screen.

"Try this," Mal said as she flung two articles of clothing at her.

Bea stripped her ratty sweatpants and t-shirt and frantically put on the flying garments.

Walking out from behind the screen, Mal smiled.

"I am a genius," Mal said with a smirk.

Bea looked in the mirror. The sleeveless black top with the crew neck made her look slim and fit. Meanwhile the white skirt that stopped an inch above her knees showed off her legs perfectly. Once again, Mal had saved the day with the perfect outfit for the occasion.

"Thank you so much," Bea said, beginning to put her tennis shoes back on.

"Uh-uh," said Mal, walking over.

She handed Bea a pair of white open toed shoes.

"You aren't wearing those scuffed up tennis shoes in Cam's car," Mal said. "It would be a crime."

"What? I'm not..." Bea started to speak, but paused when she recognized the designer brand of the shoes. Her eyes widened in surprise; her time with Mal had shifted her perspective over the recent months. The temptation of getting to wear high-end shoes was now irresistible to her. Eagerly, she took the shoes from Mal and slipped them on.

Standing up, she enjoyed the woman looking back at her in the mirror.

"Hmm.." Mal said with her finger on her chin staring at Bea. "Maybe a thicker heel..."

"No, this is perfect," Bea replied. The shorter heel still made her figure look sexier without feeling like a stripper.

She ran out of the room, but stopped in the doorway.

"Change your mind about the shoes?" Mal said with a laugh.

"No," Bea said looking at her.

Without warning, Bea rushed over to Mal and gave her a deep warm hug.

"Thank you so much," Bea said. "For this, for everything you've done. I don't deserve you."

Mal seemed stunned by the gesture.

"I...um..." Mal stumbled with her words for once. "Go, he's waiting."

"I'll see you later," Bea said smiling at her after breaking the hug. She practically ran out the front door of the house.

Mal sat down on the edge of her bed alone and let herself do something she didn't do often, she let herself truly smile.

Cam was standing outside of his red Jaguar F-type coupe, leaning on the sports car with his hands in his pockets.

"You always find a way to look so beautiful," he said with a smile as Bea approached. Her heels clicked lightly on the stone pavers of the walkway.

"Couldn't do it without Mal," Bea replied, turning red.

"You probably could," he said, taking her hand and kissing it lightly.

"Red sports car huh?" she said, peering behind him. "A little avant guard for you isn't it?"

"You mean this old thing?" Cam said, peering over his shoulder. "I just keep her around because I like the color."

Bea laughed.

He grasped her chin lightly in his hands and lifted her face up towards his.

They kissed.

Bea didn't know how long, she just knew her knees were getting wobbly with each passing second.

Finally, he pulled his face back and smiled at her.

"We're going to be late," he said.

Bea took a breath to regain her composure.

"Do we have to?" she replied.

Cam playfully pushed her into the car.

The entire drive to the restaurant, Cam drove at a brisk pace. Never once did Bea feel like he wasn't in complete control. His right hand lightly rested on her exposed knee, a touch she found comforting. It provided a temporary distraction from the impending challenging discussions of the evening.

Classical piano played over the Jaguar's speakers, only interrupted by the soft rev of the engine as they accelerated almost effortlessly along the city streets. The car was fast and smooth, giving Bea the impression that they were driving on a cloud in the sky.

Bea felt safe with him, like the rest of the world could fall into flame and ruin around her. Just as long as he was next to her, she would be fine. It was a feeling that she had never felt before in her life, and the more time they spent together away from the club the more it only grew inside her.

The clock on the dashboard had just ticked to 6:00PM when they pulled into the parking lot of the restaurant. He had made record time.

The parking lot was packed, there wasn't a space in sight. They were going to have to park across the street at the shady looking hotel and then walk over which would make them late.

Then, if by magic somehow, a car in the space closest to the front door backed out. Cam pulled in immediately.

"Wow, that was lucky," Bea remarked as he opened the door and helped her out of the car.

"It happens," Cam said with a mischievous look that Bea wasn't sure how to decipher.

Bea's parents were waiting for them in the waiting area.

Her father was wearing jeans and a gray collared shirt, his large belly stretching the fabric around his abdomen and extending over his belt buckle. His white hair had thinned, his bald spot conquering more territory than when she last saw him.

Her mother was still just as small and frail as Bea remembered. She wore a red long-sleeved top and a matching calf length red skirt, a short black jacket covering her shoulders. A large pearl necklace around her neck made her look like she belonged in the 1960s. Her auburn hair was up and set into a beehive like form on top of her head. Her thick black glasses hid her dark eyes, the same eyes that Bea had inherited.

"Bernice!" her mother said, stepping forward and hugging Bea.

"Hi Mom," Bea replied awkwardly from her mother's shoulder. "Hi Dad."

"Hello pumpkin," her father said, stepping forward to hug her as well. "And who is this?"

"This is Cam," Bea said, stepping to the side.

Bea's father stepped forward and held out his hand to Cam.

Cam shook it confidently.

"Hello Cam," Bea's father said with a deeper than normal voice. "I'm Martin, this is my wife Adelia."

"Nice to meet you both," Cam said warmly.

Bea noticed something strange in her father's eyes. He eyed Cam suspiciously.

"I'm afraid, dears, that the restaurant gave away our table already," Bea's mother announced. "It'll be another half hour until they can seat us."

"Let me see if I can talk to them," Cam said. "One moment."

Cam broke away from the group and approached the hostess.

"I didn't know you were seeing someone," Bea's mother said once Cam was out of earshot. "He's very handsome."

Bea wasn't sure what to say, so she fell back on her usual tactic when someone said something nice around her. She blushed.

Cam returned with the hostess.

"Your table is ready," said the hostess carrying menus in her arms. "This way please."

From behind her, Bea caught a wink from Cam.

"Well that's a pleasant surprise," commented Bea's mother.

They were seated and a very tired looking waiter greeted them at the table.

"Can I get you something to drink?" he asked in a monotone.

"I think I'll have a glass of your red," said Bea's mother. "Is that alright dear?"

She turned to Bea's father Martin who still was glancing at Cam with a peculiar expression.

"Ice Tea," he said, not breaking his concentration.

"Same as her," Bea added, referring to her mother.

"What kind of whiskey do you have?" Cam asked when it was his turn.

"Um..." the waiter said cluelessly.

"You know what," Cam interrupted him. "That's alright. I'm driving. I'll have some water please."

"You got it," the waiter said before shuffling off.

"So," Adelia began. "How's school been Bernice?"

"It's been good," Bea replied, always uncomfortable talking about herself. "Professor Mikkelson keeps me on my toes."

"And your thesis?" Adelia added.

"Going well," said Bea. "Thanks to Cam's help I've been able to almost finish it."

"Oh really?" Adelia exclaimed.

Bea father grunted and scowled with his arms crossed.

"And exactly how has he helped you?" Bea's mother added, visibly embarrassed at her husband's less than friendly demeanor.

"I have a rare book collection," Cam replied with a smile. "Luckily one of those books happened to be exactly on the subject of Bea's thesis."

"And what is your thesis about dear?" Bea's mother asked as she tore off a chunk of the stale bread the waiter had dropped at the table and proceeded to smear large portions of butter onto the chalky object.

"Demonic worship during the Black Death..." Bea purposely let her voice trail off.

"Oh..." Bea's mother said, sounding almost startled. "Isn't that...interesting. Right dear?"

She turned to Martin who just grunted in response.

"We thought you were writing about the church," Bea's mother asked.

"I know," said Bea knowing that her thesis topic was going to go over like a lead balloon with her parents. "Professor Mikkelson convinced me to do something a little...different."

Her father scowled, Bea immediately regretted her comment.

"So, Cam," Adelia jumped in. "What are you studying in school?"

Cam turned to her and smiled, he seemed completely oblivious to Bea's father's stares. In fact, he seemed to almost be enjoying the optical sparring match they were engaged in.

"I'm not in school," Cam replied.

"You already graduated?" Adelia asked.

"No, school wasn't really for me," Cam clarified.

"So what do you do then?" her mother's voice not betraying any hint of judgment, only supreme sincerity.

"I'm a manager at a nightclub," Cam replied calmly and confidently.

"A night club..." Martin repeated with huff.

"Yes, Club Llithium," Cam added. "If you'd like we could drop in for a drink after dinner."

"No, I don't think that would be necessary," Bea's mother quickly said. "We have a big day tomorrow. Conference for the diocese and all."

"Another time then," Cam said smiling.

"I've never been to a nightclub before though. How late do you stay open?" Adelia asked, fiddling with her napkin in her lap.

"All night long," Cam replied. "We typically don't close until the sun comes up."

"Oh dear," Bea's mother commented. "I always told Bernice, nothing good happens after midnight."

"Let's hope so," Cam said with a wink.

The waiter returned with their drinks and took their meal orders. Bea's mother ordered a Cobb salad and Bea's father ordered a cheeseburger.

Bea herself, who was becoming uncharacteristically picky after weeks of only eating at fine dining establishments, settled for a familiar pasta dish. Cam ordered a steak, extra rare. The waiter informed him it's the chain's policy to not serve any meat cooked less than medium rare. Cam gave in to the offer of a medium rare steak though he seemed perturbed by the constraint.

A round of rubbery fried calamari quickly circulated the table, of which Bea took only a "no thank you" helping and Cam pretended to eat but after one bite quietly didn't touch it again.

"Great Calamari," Adelia commented. "Right dear?"

She was looking at Bea.

"It's delicious," Bea said as she took a sip of her wine to get the taste out of her mouth.

Cam's knees brushed up against hers, his way of playfully letting her know he knew she was lying to be polite.

The dinner conversation continued, venturing into the mundane. Bea's mother talked at length about the parish back home and tame church gossip. Martin grunted when prompted by Bea's mother but otherwise didn't speak a word. Bea and Cam listened intently, both smiling and doing their best to appear interested. Meanwhile they held hands under the table and their fingers wrestled playfully with one another to pass the time as the conversation droned on.

To Bea's grumbling stomach's welcome relief, the waiter arrived with their entrées. The dish in front of her steamed with the smell of freshly microwaved frozen pasta. Bea glanced over to see Cam trying to cut with frustration through his tough and over cooked steak. Peering inside, there was not a speck of pink flesh inside. She could practically feel his disappointment.

Bea's father cleared his throat loudly. Both Cam and Bea looked up to see both of them clasping their hands together in front of them with bowed heads.

Bea quickly did the same, Cam placed his hands in his lap and leaned back.

Bea's father shot him a foul look before closing his eyes.

"Our father, who art in heaven," Martin began to speak, the most words he had uttered all night. "Please bless this food which is about to nourish our bodies. Please give us the strength to fight against the agents of evil that bar our path to righteousness. Please give us the vision to see who amongst us are truthful and who are false, for the demons of hell take many forms, Amen."

Bea's father glanced at Cam at the end. Her mother repeated the Amen. Both Cam and Bea were silent.

They sat in silence as they finished their meal. Bea had taken a bite to appease her empty stomach, but found herself no longer hungry and grasping for her water to compensate for the over abundance of salt that had overwhelmed her dish. Meanwhile Cam had proceeded to cut his steak into many shapes and sizes, frantically searching for any part that wasn't completely well done. His efforts were fruitless.

"Please excuse me for a moment," Cam said standing up. He must have grown tired of wrestling with the steak and he disappeared towards the restrooms.

"I like him," Bea's mother said with a sweet smile.

"Thank you," Bea squeezed her mother's forearm. Her mother was kind, very passive but always kind.

"He kind of reminds me of that one fellow," Adelia scrunched her face together for a moment while she tried to think of his name. "Oh what's his name... Channing Tatum?"

"How do you know who Channing Tatum is?" Bea asked while holding back laughter.

"Well, I don't get out much but the other women do like to talk," Adelia replied. "They keep telling me I need to rent that movie Magic Mike."

Bea almost spit out her drink.

Bea's father's eyes narrowed.

"Really I'm just happy you found someone," Adelia continued. "We just want what's best for you, for you to be hap..."

This would have been a sweet moment if not for Martin's loud grunt cutting her off. Adelia put her hands back in her lap and stopped talking. Bea's heart sunk, she recognized the look her father had. It was the one he had before launching into a long-winded sermon about hell and damnation, his two favorite subjects.

Bea's heart was lifted when Cam returned to the table and took his seat, his hand finding hers under it immediately.

They sat in a silence for a few minutes, her father's subdued anger turning him puffy and red-faced. Bea considered asking the waiter to bring the dessert menu to try and diffuse things, but it was too late.

"So what kind of man has a rare book collection with texts on demonic worship?" Bea's father asked bluntly, breaking the silence, the only remnants of his burger being a few ketchup smears.

"My collection is actually quite diverse," Cam replied calmly, putting his steak knife and fork down. "It was just luck that I happened to have the one that Bea needed for her thesis."

And if we could just lend it to the academic board too. The voice in Bea added, reminding her of her ongoing dilemma.

"And how did you obtain it?" Martin asked with an accusing tone.

"In my travels of my younger years," Cam replied. "I was able to procure it in a wager with a fellow I met in Romania."

"You obtained a book about demons through gambling?" Martin repeated with judgemental eyes.

"How was your pasta dear?" Bea's mother asked, hoping to change the subject.

Bea was about to respond when her father interrupted.

"I know a sinner when I see one," he said.

"Father, I don't think," Bea began.

"Quiet," her father replied sternly.

Bea put her hands in her lap and recoiled into her seat. She had argued with her father for many years, so she knew that fighting him only provoked him further.

"That wasn't very nice," Cam said, leaning forward onto his hands and staring at Martin.

Bea's father leaned forward as well, he looked like he was about to jump over the table and grab Cam by the collar.

"Don't tell me how to speak to my daughter," Martin commanded.

Cam gave him a sly smile.

"Your daughter deserves more respect than you've given her," Cam said calmly. "Her thesis is going to be groundbreaking."

"Damn the thesis," Martin replied, the anger in his voice growing more noticeable. "I want to know what she's doing with a shifty night club owner like yourself."

"Shifty?" Cam said with a questioning tone.

"You've been lying since the moment you sat down at this table," her father remarked.

Several other tables had gone quiet, their own curiosity peaking at the raised voices.

"I haven't told a single lie," Cam replied.

"You have secrets, I can tell," her father's voice grew more hoarse in his anger. "Dark ones I bet."

"How does the Bible verse go," Cam began. "Why do you look at the speck of sawdust in your brother's eye and pay no attention to the plank on your own?"

"Don't quote the Bible to me, young man," Bea's father replied.

"Enough, both of you," Bea said at last.

She turned to face her parents.

"We need to talk," she said with confidence to her parents. Cam's hand returning to hold hers under the table, it made her feel ready for anything.

"Oh dear," Bea's mother exclaimed. "You're pregnant?!"

"No, I'm not pregnant," Bea replied.

"Oh thank God," Bea's mother replied. "You had me worried for a minute there."

"Listen..." Bea began saying before taking a deep breath. "I have Huntington's disease."

Silence fell on the table, she pulled her hand away from Cam's in order to wipe her swiftly watering eyes with her napkin.

"The Doctor's did a DNA test earlier this year and confirmed it," she continued.

"What is Huntington's my dear?" Bea's mother asked innocently.

"It's a debilitating illness," Bea explained. "In my thirties or forties, I'm going to start losing the ability to walk, to talk, to do anything really. Until I slowly die."

"Oh my God," Bea's mother exclaimed. "That's horrid. I'm sure they have treatments for it..."

"There's nothing they can do about it," Bea said, glancing at Cam who just stared at her father intently.

It was Cam's first time hearing the news as well, she wasn't sure how he would react either. He didn't seem to react at all, almost like he already knew.

"So how did you get it?" Adelia asked.

"It's genetic," Bea replied. Sensing her mother didn't quite fully understand she decided to elaborate. "It means it was passed down from one of you."

"Well I've never heard of it before," Bea's mother stated. "No one on my side has ever mentioned it. Are you sure they are right about this? I mean Doctors, can you really believe what they say? They just want something to bill you for."

"They are sure, mother," Bea said coldly. She sat there watching her parents as she took deep breaths to keep herself calm.

Silence engulfed the table, no one moved. Passersby might think that four realistic wax figures had been placed at the table as a display.

Her mother broke the silence at last.

"Well, there's nothing about it from either of us..." she began.

"He knew," Cam said, interrupting her, staring directly at Bea's father.

"What?" Bea exclaimed looking at her father.

Martin Logan, the deacon of his parish, sat at the table perfectly still. His eyes fixed on the young man across from him. Cam returned his gaze with equal parts intensity.

"Your grandfather, my father was diagnosed with it," Bea's father said, lowering his eyes.

"You told me he died of pneumonia," Bea exclaimed.

"He did," Martin clarified, burying his face in his hands. "His lungs stopped working."

"Why didn't you tell me? Why didn't you warn me?" Bea addressed her father angrily.

"I didn't want to worry you," he replied. "He wasn't diagnosed until much later in life, after the symptoms had already shown. After he found out, he was...well he was a different man. I didn't want that for you, the burden of knowing..."

"That I was going to die young?" Bea interrupted him.

"Yes," Martin replied flatly. "This world, it's a gift from God. You needed to see it through innocent eyes, not tainted ones."

"Some gift," Bea replied. "Why did you even have me? Knowing you could pass on the gene to me? Why not adopt?"

"When Adelia got pregnant," answered her father. "We knew that we couldn't do anything about it, God would never allow us to."

Bea's mind swirled with thoughts on what to say next but she soon realized she had nothing to say. Her anger, her frustration, no matter what she said or did would mean nothing. She would still die young, she would still never see a day past fifty years old. Never get to retire, grow old, see her children grow up.

"I thought talking to you would make me feel better" Bea said through held back tears. "I was wrong."

She turned to Cam.

"Let's go," Bea said sternly.

“Wait,” Martin said, holding up a hand.

For a moment, Bea thought he was going to say something redemptive. That he would put away his religious fundamentalism, his helpless clinging to ideas of nuclear family, and for once just be genuinely empathetic to her.

She was wrong.

“You need to come home,” he said. “Forget this silly thesis, forget grad school. Forget the other students who surround you with sex and drugs and alcohol. Forget whatever lecherous lair you found this sorry excuse for a soul at...”

He motioned with his hand at Cam who stood stoically at Bea’s side.

“Come home, you can work at the church,” he continued. “I’ll find you a nice man, a good man. One who won’t lead you to your eternal damnation.”

“I’m not being led anywhere dad,” Bea replied. She felt different with Cam at her side, she felt more confident than she ever had before. “I want to finish grad school, I want to finish my thesis, and I want to be with Cam.”

“I forbid it,” Martin replied, slamming his hand on the table.

Bea thought hard about how to respond.

“I don’t care,” she said at last.

"Bea, we are..." her mother tried to plead.

"We're done mother," Bea interrupted her before she could finish her sentence.

"Would anyone like to see the dessert menu?" The waiter asked, appearing at the most inopportune time.

"No," Bea replied, crossing her arms in front of her.

"I'll take the check," Bea's father said with a growl.

"It's already been taken care of," the waiter replied before retreating. He must have known it was wise to get out of there before things escalated further.

"We're leaving," Bea declared.

"Bea, please don't," Adelia pleaded.

Bea couldn’t bear anymore, she needed to leave.

She stood, as Cam followed suit.

“But he’s a sinner,” Martin practically yelled.

Eyes around the restaurant flicking towards them at the outburst.

“We all are dad,” she replied. “You taught me that, in your sermons.”

"It was lovely meeting you both, good luck at the conference tomorrow," Cam said with a grin as they hustled away. “And don’t worry, I’ll let you get the next one.”

He winked at Bea’s father, his face flushed with embarrassment and mouth agape.

And with that, Cam placed his hand, warm and caring, on Bea's arm, and they left. Before she knew it, Bea was in the car with the windows down and watching the lights of the nearby airport disappear into the distance. The chilly night wind blew through her hair and dried the tears to her face, but she didn't mind.

Cam's hand was holding hers on the center console and that was all that mattered right now.

"Sorry I didn't tell you sooner," Bea said, closing the window and wiping the last of the tears from her face.

"I already knew," Cam replied calmly. "I could tell since the first time I met you."

"What? How?" she replied.

"Just a feeling," Cam responded. "I knew something was wrong."

"If you knew," Bea began before thinking of a different way to phrase it. "If you felt that I had a terminal illness or whatever. Why on earth did you ask me out? Knowing it would never go anywhere, we could never be together forever?"

Cam was quiet for a moment.

"Beauty isn't encapsulated in the perfect and the immaculate," he said before pausing. "I've lived long enough to appreciate enough art to know that real beauty lies in the flawed. That's where love truly lies. So I don't care if you have twenty years to live, one year to live, hell even if you had only ten more minutes. I'd still want to be with you."

Bea didn't know what to say, she didn't know how to process it.

"So maybe instead of worrying about twenty years from now," Cam continued glancing at her with his signature smile. "Let's just worry about the next twenty minutes."

Bea nodded as she smiled.

"For example," Cam continued. "Let's find out if I can still get us into Château Bien."

He grinned wide.

"Oh my God, please yes," Bea said. "I'm fucking starving."

The sports car sped off down the road, the lights of downtown growing large as they approached.

“You know what this means though?” Cam asked.

“What?” Bea asked, clueless.

“Now you owe me dinner with my parents,” Cam said with a wink.

Chapter Twelve

Bea awoke to sheer darkness. The sheets against her bare skin, the soft pillow comforting her head...were all foreign to her. Even more alarming, she heard deep and rhythmic breathing next to her, and felt on her naked shoulder, hot like fire.

As the fog of sleep was dissipating and she started to remember. It was Cam.

She had gone home with him after a late dinner at Château Bien. In fact, they had closed down the restaurant. The restaurant staff had kept it open late after Cam left a generous tip, and they had enjoyed hours of conversation.

And then? The voice said.

And then they had gone home and though it was still kind of a blur; she remembered hours of... something else but equally enjoyable.

It wasn't her first time, that had happened with her long time boyfriend from high school years ago. However her only recent rendezvous for comparison purposes was a vague black out memory with Adelaide and Tarzan. None of the previous times even compared to her first time with Cam. His furnace-like body pressed against hers. Passionate yet controlled, strong but gentle, attentive however also connected. It had been amazing and she didn't feel an ounce of guilt or regret.

However she did feel something else, panic.

What time was it?

Professor Mikkelson had an early class today and she was already skating on thin ice. She could not be late.

Bea rolled to her side and fumbled on the night stand until at last she felt the outline of her phone. Lifting it up, the back light lit up immediately revealing the time. She was relieved that she still had an hour and a half till class started. Enough time to shower and make herself presentable.

Trying not to wake Cam, she carefully crawled out of the enticing bed and stumbled to the bathroom. The bright light caused her eyes to burn. Covering them with one, she felt her way to the toilet.

Once her eyes were adjusted, she saw that Cam had put out a toothbrush for her, still in its new packaging and some toothpaste.

When did he do that?

Must have been after she had fallen asleep.

Bea turned on the shower, it instantly poured out a jet of hot water and the bathroom began to fill with the clouds of steam in the cold autumn morning. The shower was large and surrounded on two sides by glass walls. They steamed up quickly until they had the opacity of frosted glass.

She enjoyed the warm water on her skin, washing away the leftover drowsiness.

Thump.

She thought she heard a noise, but she ignored it.

The water rushed over her face and she closed her eyes under the stream.

It was then that she felt a presence behind her, someone else was in the shower with her. A large pair of hands wrapped around her hips.

Her instinct was panic, she spun around.

All fear and foreboding dissipated immediately as she felt the familiar lips of Cam pressed against hers. Jolts of pleasure shot down her body to her toes.

Somehow he felt warmer than the shower.

He pulled away from their kiss and smiled at her.

We have time, right?

Bea almost nodded in agreement.

Cam had put out a hair dryer for her and Bea spent the next twenty minutes doing her best to look presentable for class. She hadn't planned on getting her hair wet, but the moment had gotten away from her in the shower. She kept glancing at the clock on her phone nervously, trying to gauge exactly how much time she had left before she had to order her Uber.

Content that she had thread the needle on time long enough, she finished getting dressed and walked to the living room. Cam was waiting for her there with a steaming hot cup of coffee.

Thank God, said the usually more atheistic voice in her head.

"Thank you," Bea said, taking the cup and sipping the hot liquid.

"My pleasure," Cam replied.

He was dressed in designer blue jeans and a dark gray turtleneck. Somehow he had found the time to make her coffee, get dressed, and do his hair.

Forgetting her rush, she sat next to him on the couch and took a moment to enjoy the moment.

It was a long, silent pause as they both just looked at each other grinning.

"Thank you for last night," Cam said at last. "I know it didn't go as you wanted, but I was just happy to spend it with you."

"No, thank you," Bea couldn't help but reply enthusiastically. "I wasn't sure I would have had the strength to face them alone. I appreciate you being there for me. And I appreciate dinner...and what happened after that. And what happened this morning..."

She trailed off and they both laughed.

"Listen,I wish I could stick around, but..." Bea said after their laughs dissipated and were replaced by grinning expressions at one another.

"Professor Mikkelson's class?" Cam interrupted her.

"Ya," Bea replied as she sighed. "I've got to order an Uber..."

"Nonsense," Cam said, standing up and walking to the kitchen. "I'll drop you off."

"It's fine," Bea pleaded. "I don't want to impose on you..."

"Not at all," Cam replied, returning with two paper to-go coffee cups. "It would be my pleasure."

Cam got her to class in record time, his red Jaguar flying through traffic effortlessly. They made such good time that she was actually ten minutes early as they pulled up outside the university building.

"Thank you for the ride," Bea told him with a smile.

"Any time," he replied.

He leaned in and they kissed.

Bea only pulled away when she saw the crowd of passers by admiring them and the flashy sports car. A couple she recognized as students from the Professor's class.

"See you soon?" Cam asked softly.

"Ya, I think so," Bea replied, stepping out of the car.

The sidewalk outside felt so cold compared to the warm interior of the Jaguar. She waved as he sped away, the engine purring loudly.

"Ms. Logan?" asked a familiar voice behind her.

She turned on her heel to see Professor Mikkelson standing behind her, one hand on the door to the building.

"Morning, Professor," she replied, turning red.

She stood there unsure of what to say next.

"Coming in?" he asked in his old frail voice, breaking the awkward moment.

"Oh yes, of course," she said, hurrying after him.

They walked silently down the hall.

"You know, I've been thinking about your thesis," the Professor said aloud.

Bea panicked, she wasn't sure what he was referring to.

"Yes Professor?" she managed to ask.

"With enough outside sources to corroborate your primary source," he began.

Bea breathed a sigh of relief.

"You might be able to get away with not having to release the book to the public," he continued.

"You really think so?" Bea said with growing hopefulness in her voice.

"Absolutely," the Professor replied. "Try Bradley's take on Demons and Demonology, 1962. He had alluded to having read the *Filii Diaboli* in his works, but didn't cite it directly."

"Thank you, Professor," she said.

"I met him, you know," Mikkelson said.

"Met who?" Bea asked with confusion.

"Bradley," the Professor continued on. "He was a brilliant student, prone to his bout of partying, too."

The remark stung Bea a bit.

"He claimed to have met someone who shared it with him," the Professor said. "I didn't believe him at the time, thought he had been fooled by some charlatan. But now, after seeing the book in the flesh. I'm not so certain."

His voice trailed off.

"Where is he now?" she asked. "Maybe I could speak with him?"

"Dead I'm afraid," replied the Professor solemnly. "Bad heart, got him a few years after he published. Do you mind?"

Professor Mikkelson was gesturing toward the locked door.

"Of course," she replied, fishing into her purse for her keys. The keys fell with a jingle to the floor.

Bending down, she tried to pick them up again only to have the same result.

"Are you alright Bernice?" The Professor asked, concerned.

"Yes, yes, I'm fine," she said, successfully picking up the keys this time. "Just a little clumsy this morning, coffee hasn't kicked in yet."

"I see," said the Professor, he did not sound convinced.

Bea sat through the lecture taking notes on her yellow legal pad as always. When the Professor wasn't looking, she took the medication for her Huntington's. She had forgotten earlier that morning.

She grew frustrated as she caught herself dropping her pen twice. When the lecture had ended, she tried to read through her notes of what the professor discussed so that she could include it in the next quiz. Her handwriting was borderline ineligible.

Usually the medication took care of the symptoms quickly.

Was she just tired? Was it just the byproduct of a night and morning of amazing sex with Cam?

She thought back to Dr. Keeling's warning, that as her symptoms worsened the medication would become less and less effective.

She chose to push it from her mind, she needed to focus on her thesis today. Don't worry about ten years from now, worry about just the next twenty minutes. Just like Cam had advised.

The library was quiet, with midterms over many students must be taking a break from studying. This was perfect for her, she was determined to pour through Bradley's work as the Professor had suggested. With enough supporting inference, maybe, just maybe, she could get away with not having to release her primary source to the academic board. She could avoid having the dreaded conversation with Cam to ask him to let her have the book.

His prize possession...

Bea tried to ignore the voice.

After finding Bradley's book using the index system, she sat at a table next to a large clear window that looked out over the hustle and bustle of students walking around campus. They could of course see into the library as well, however many walked past, oblivious to her or the fountain of knowledge the building contained.

She was thankful for the Professor, the book by Bradley had exactly what she needed. It was like a field manual to demons and other mythical creatures.

"ON INCUBI AND SUCCUBI", the next chapter was titled.

"The Incubus and Succubus are the masculine and feminine forms of the same demonic species. Though the Succubus is much better known in legend, likely due to their fulfillment of a male fantasy archetype, the Incubus is just as important as a creature of folklore. Both operate under the same desire, to absorb the life force of others via sexual intercourse."

"Scholars have often equated this as a fable warning about engaging with those who are sexually promiscuous; further reinforcing puritanical beliefs of sex and marriage. The fact that the Succubus is the more well known of the two creatures is tied to thousands of years of shaming women who do not save themselves for marriage."

Referring to us are they?

She ignored it and continued reading.

"However I believe they represent something different. They were more than just sex monsters, they were a key cog in the mythical army of darkness. A front line spy of sorts, designed to infiltrate the enemy and find out their weaknesses. The emphasis on sex to do so is not something alien to any of us who have watched a James Bond film. The sex is just a means to an end, a way to sustain themselves and their purpose. In actuality, they were sent forth by Satan in order to establish footholds on the mortal Earth, whereas more demonic activity may be launched upon unsuspecting humanity. Or so the legends would have us believe."

This statement was almost exactly as described in the *Filii Diaboli.* Bea couldn't help but think that somehow Bradley had read this book. Maybe there were more copies floating around, maybe whomever had it before Cam had lent it to Bradley. Regardless, the chance of her thesis being accepted grew with each passing sentence. She read on.

"This was evidenced by the pro-creation with mankind by Incubi and Succubi. Their offspring were called..."

The page had a printing error, the word was strange computer symbols she did not recognize. She continued.

"These creatures retained many of the power and abilities of their demonic mother or father. However it was their half-human nature that made them particularly dangerous, as they could pass for ordinary more-so than their flashier parents. Their only flaw it seems, being that they were born typically grotesque and ugly. A by-product of their mixed breeding, it also made them more likely to be overlooked or ignored. Living in the shadows, they could watch and influence mankind for their own devices."

A chill ran through her spine, how creepy.

Something else was bothering her though, a nagging feeling. A feeling that...she was being watched.

Bea glanced behind her and to her sides, the library was empty except for her. The light shined brightly through the window...except the shadow of a figure was partially blocking it.

She looked up, her fear rising.

The figure was covered in black from head to toe, black shoes, black pants, black shirt, black jacket...and black...lipstick.

Bea was filled with both alarm and relief simultaneously.

It was Viv.

"Oh my God," Bea said as Viv approached. "I thought I'd never see you again."

"I know," Viv replied. "I didn't plan on talking to any of you ever again."

Bea rushed forward and embraced Viv tightly.

"I'm so sorry," Bea said, squeezing her friend. "I should have talked to you about it."

"It's ok," said Viv. "I was just...angry...really angry. For a long time. Losing Adelaide hurt a lot."

"I know," said Bea. "Tell me, what have you been up to?"

They both sat down.

"Brooding mostly," said Viv with a smirk. "I went home for awhile, talked to my mom. She helped me find someone to talk with."

"Like a therapist?" Bea asked.

"A trauma counselor actually," Viv clarified. "I've been holding onto a bunch of anger for a long time at my dad."

"Your dad?" Bea questioned.

"Yes," Viv said, pausing for a moment. "He did things to me when I was younger..."

"Oh my," Bea replied. "I'm so sorry, I didn't know."

"No one did," Viv continued. "Not even my mother. It wasn't until I talked to the counselor that I was comfortable talking about it with anyone."

"Is your mother going to divorce him?" Bea asked.

"Divorce? Oh no," answer Viv. "Not necessary. He's dead."

"Oh," Bea said, not sure what to say.

Viv paused to think, she opened her mouth as if to say something but seemed to think better of it and changed her mind.

"It's ok," she said at last. "My mom and I, we got through it together. Working on your thesis?"

"Yea," said Bea, happy for a subject change.

"Last time we talked you had barely scratched the surface on it," Viv said. "How is it now?"

"Almost done actually," Bea explained. "Cam let me borrow one of his books..."

She stopped herself, not sure how Viv would respond.

"Cam huh?" Viv asked, looking down uncomfortably.

"Ya," Bea replied.

"So you two are...dating?" Viv said unsure.

"Kind of," Bea answered honestly.

Silence engulfed them again.

"Listen," Viv said, breaking it. "You seem like a nice girl, not like the rest of them."

"Thank you," Bea responded.

"But you need to get out of there," Viv continued. "They are bad news. I was looking into it. Adelaide wasn't the first."

"The first what?" asked Bea.

"The first to die in the group," Viv answered. "I tried to look up a few of the girls, the ones that disappeared before Adelaide. They are all either missing or dead."

"Missing or dead?" Bea repeated. "I don't understand."

"I don't either," Viv replied. "At least not fully. I only came back to finish the semester, then I'm transferring to a college closer to home."

"I don't understand," Bea said, feeling confused. She began to pack up her books into her bag. "This doesn't make any sense."

"You don't think what happens at the club is weird?" Viv asked. "Crazy expensive parties, strange visitors from foreign countries? It's obviously a front of some sort."

"A front?" replied Bea.

"Yes, a front for something like..." Viv paused to think. "Human trafficking."

Her words echoed uncertainty and paranoia.

"No, I don't believe it," Bea said, finishing putting her books away. "Cam would never be involved in anything like that."

"Are you really that sure?" Viv asked.

"Yes, I am," Bea said standing up. She started to walk away.

Viv grabbed her hand.

"I know you care about Cam," Viv said, holding her hand tight. "But I know you aren't stupid. Take a closer look, something about that place isn't right. You see it right?"

Bea looked at Viv's eyes, the usual strong eyes of defiance had been replaced by ones of concern.

"I don't know what you're talking about," Bea said and she pulled her hand away from Viv's.

Bea didn't even turn around to see Viv staring at her with tears in her eyes as she left.

Chapter Thirteen

Bea walked downstairs from her room and enjoyed the warm sunshine beaming through the monstrous foyer windows. Peering outside she noticed a thin layer of snow covering the ground. It sparkled in the morning sun, and would likely melt by the afternoon; regardless, there was still something magical about the first snow of winter.

Bea could hear Mal talking on the phone in the kitchen, she had the phone on speaker. The other voice on the line was hard to hear, but Bea thought it sounded like Cam.

She walked through the doorway into the kitchen and almost ran into Mal who was wearing a soft pink bathrobe and holding a hot cup of coffee and her phone.

"Oh!" Mal yelped as she steadied herself.

"Sorry," Bea replied, stumbling backwards.

Mal must have exceptional balance, as she avoided spilling a drop of the steaming hot liquid.

"It's ok," Mal said smiling. "No harm, no foul."

“Was that Cam?” Bea asked, curious.

“Yes,” Mal replied. “He was asking for my advice about how to keep his parents... entertained.”

"Oh, he told you about that," Bea said. "Did he tell you about..."

"That you were going to be there?" Mal said smiling. "Yes, he did and I think..."

Here it comes, the statement of disapproval.

"I'm so happy for you," Mal said smiling.

"Really?" Bea exclaimed in disbelief.

"Absolutely," Mal continued. "He's never introduced anyone to his parents as long as I've known him. When they come to visit his dad usually has him holed up in the back office. For you to be going to dinner at his place with them, well that's really neat."

"What are they like?" Bea asked.

"His parents both are...interesting," she mused. "Kyla, his mother, is beautiful and elegant," Mal gushed.

"Is she kind?" Bea wanted to know everything.

"Kind..." Mal said contemplating. "I wouldn't use that word. She is fierce, very fierce. Especially when it comes to Cam. She would do anything for him, anything to protect him. With few exceptions, anyone who has ever tried to hurt him...well, she made sure it didn't work out for them."

This made Bea nervous.

"What about his dad?" asked Bea.

"Morfran," Mal's voice kind of lingered as if she was searching for the right words on how to describe him. "He's a bit of an acquired taste. He mostly just cares about the club and how the VIP clients are doing. He rarely talks with Cam about anything else, much less a personal life. He can be a tad... aggressive."

"Is he tall and handsome like Cam?" Bea's curiosity getting the best of her.

"Oh God no," Mal replied as her smile melted away. "He's about the scariest looking man I've ever met. Makes Dunkler Peter look like Brad Pitt."

Bea stood quietly, feeling a bit discouraged.

Mal noticed.

"But don't worry," Mal said, her smile returning. "You're going to do great, Cam cares about you. That's all that matters, they're going to eat you up."

Bea smiled back, feeling better.

Thinking Mal was going back to her room as she usually did in the mornings, Bea was surprised she instead lingered in the doorway.

"Plans this weekend?" Mal asked.

"Just working on my thesis," Bea replied, almost instinctively at this point.

"Still plugging away on it?" added Mal.

"Almost done actually," Bea answered.

"When's it due?" Mal took a sip of her hot coffee.

"Next semester," Bea said flatly.

"Then you are ahead of schedule," Mal said excitedly.

"I guess you could say that," Bea replied. She knew full well she held a deep anxiety about being late for anything, especially due dates. This made her often neurotic about finishing things ahead of schedule.

"That's great news," Mal said before pausing. Her eyes seemed to be thinking about what to say next carefully.

"That means you won't have any excuses this weekend," Mal continued.

"Excuses for what?" Bea asked, confused.

"Excuses for why you can't join me," Mal said with a mischievous grin.

"Join you where?" Bea was lost.

"You'll see," Mal replied. "Let's say, be ready in an hour and pack an overnight bag."

She walked out of the room.

"But my thesis..." Bea pleaded.

"No excuses!" Mal yelled from her room before shutting the door loudly behind her.

Bea poured her cup of coffee and thought about her next move.

She really should be finishing up her thesis.

The coffee cup fell out of her hand and fell a few inches to the counter top. Thankfully it didn't break, but the hot liquid splattered over the surface.

Bea rushed to clean it up with a towel, her hand still trembling out of control.

She immediately wanted to cry.

Probably the Huntington's.

I know, she thought to herself. Her prescription was in her bathroom but it had become so ineffective, she wondered why she bothered taking it all anymore.

Dr. Keeling had warned her it started with the involuntary movements but only got worse from there.

How much longer could she still walk? Drive? Type?

Everything was progressing so fast, it should take years for it to get this bad. However, her symptoms seemed to get worse every day.

She felt depression sweep over her.

Bea just wanted to go back upstairs and lay down in her bed. Maybe all day even. The reminder of her impending mortality only made the world around her seem so bleak.

"I said no excuses!" Mal yelled from the next room.

Bea jumped.

What's more important? Living out your remaining days the way you want...or writing some paper for a bunch of high and mighty academic assholes who won't believe you anyways.

Bea hated when the voice was making sense.

Why not though? Why not enjoy something spontaneous and fun with Mal? Mal hadn't led her astray so far, in fact she can thank Mal not only for her current living situation but also for meeting Cam.

What harm could it do?

Exactly.

She finished cleaning up her mess in the kitchen and ran up the stairs. Packing a bag with some sweatpants and other comfy clothing. What was she going to wear?

It was a question that she faced every day of her life of course, but for some reason when Mal was involved it carried much more pressure than she cared to admit.

Frantically looking through the clothes in her closet, something caught her eye.

There was one outfit hanging from the rack that was completely foreign and out of place. It was a light blue jumpsuit.

How did that get there? Bea certainly hadn't purchased it.

She picked it off the rack to take a closer look, there was a note attached and in big bold letters were written.

NO EXCUSES

Bea couldn't believe it, the only way that Mal could have snuck this into her closet undetected would have been when she was at the library the day before. Which means...

She's been planning this for days.

Bea couldn't help but laugh.

"Ready?" she heard Mal yell from downstairs.

"Coming," Bea yelled back.

She slipped on the very comfy jumpsuit and finished packing her toiletries.

Much to Bea's surprise, Mal was waiting downstairs with a small light blue designer weekender bag and wearing the exact same jumpsuit as Bea.

"How did you do?" Bea asked in bewilderment as she walked down the stairs.

"I have my ways," Mal said, grinning. "Come on, the driver's waiting."

They hurried out the door to the waiting black SUV.

During the drive, Mal typed furiously on her phone. She was reviewing Twitter, Instagram, and SnapChat pages; commenting and posting at a dizzying pace.

Bea had never subscribed herself to social media, it never held an appeal for her.

Showing off pictures of herself? No thanks, she had a hard enough time looking in the mirror.

Sharing her thoughts and opinions? A lifetime of living with two hard-line Catholic parents had already made that an uncomfortable practice to even think about.

Scrolling endlessly while liking and commenting on others posts and pictures? When would she ever find the time between studying and work.

In Bea's opinion, it took a certain type of personality to excel on social media. A personality like Mal, someone who was instantly popular no matter where she was or what she was doing. Beautiful, confident, able to win over anyone in a heartbeat with a simple smile.

The exact opposite of you.

So why did Mal invite her to wherever they were going? Bea wasn't sure, but she knew better than to ask questions when Mal was on her phone.

Bea looked out the window and was surprised to see the car heading out of the city. In the distance, tall mountains grew large with each passing mile. Condominium complexes slowly gave way to small suburban houses. Then the houses became more and more sparse, replaced by a white Aspen enveloping forest.

The bright sun glistened on the trees, the snow shimmering like glitter. The forest was still and quiet, nothing moved or swayed. It was as if she was staring at a static painting of the scenery, only the light giving it any appearance of life whatsoever.

As twenty minutes passed, then an hour; Bea was growing anxious to their surprise destination. They had reached the base of the mountains, when the driver took a turn onto a side road paved in concrete and stone. The vehicle subtly vibrated as it drove up the long driveway that disappeared into the white forest.

At last their destination appeared before them, a large warm and inviting lodge nestled at the base of the mountain. It was decorated in a Tuscan style, concrete roof with a warm pastel exterior. Though blanketed with a thin layer of snow, Bea could identify large rosemary, lavender, and Italian cypress bushes meticulously sculpted and perfectly placed in the front entranceway that accented two oversized wooden doors; it reminded her of a medieval castle.

Bea glanced over at Mal who, much to her surprise, put her phone in her purse.

"We're here," she said with a tone of relief.

"Great," Bea commented before adding. "Where is here?"

"Why the Bellezza of course," Mal replied with a smile. "The best spa in the entire country."

"Oh," Bea said, pretending to sound like she knew of the place already.

The driver opened the door for Mal.

"Come on," Mal said, stepping out. "You're going to have fun, I promise."

Bea followed both anxious and curious.

The inside of the lobby was breathtaking. The small plaza was flanked on both sides by two waterfalls that poured from rock formations built into the wall. An elderly man played a calm melody on a strange flute while sitting cross legged on a large white pillow.

"Ms. Phillips, Ms. Logan, welcome to Bellezza," said a very attractive attendant standing behind a large mahogany desk facing them.

"Hey Jan," Mal replied with a smile.

Two women dressed in white togas appeared from a side door and took their purses and bags.

"We'll get these taken to your room," said Jan as she walked from around the desk to stand in front of them with her hands behind her back.

Bea was taken by surprise.

"Wait," she said in a sudden panic. "I just need to grab my phone."

"I'm sorry Ms. Logan," Jan said calmly with a smile. "We don't allow any mobile devices inside. We believe it misaligns your energies and prevents you from healing."

"Ok..." Bea replied trailing off.

Mal won't last long here.

"Sorry Bea," Mal said next to her. "No phones, it's the rules."

Bea was confused but handed over her purse without further discussion.

"Now if you are both ready," Jan said walking to another doorway. "Please join me in the Intentions room."

Mal wrapped her arm around Bea's as they walked.

"Intentions room?" Bea repeated aloud to Mal in a whisper.

"Just you wait, you're going to love this," Mal replied.

Walking into the doorway they were greeted by warm sunlight shining through several large windows with plantation style shutters. In the center of the room was a small circular pond that swirled clockwise in a gentle current. On the edges of it were large soft pillows.

"If you would, please take your seats around the Waters of Intention," Jan said gesturing for them to sit on the pillows. "We can begin your healing journey today by ensuring we have the right intentions."

"Come on," Mal said.

A male wearing an orange robe approached them carrying a large box. Kneeling next to Mal first, he opened it to reveal a large assortment of smaller wood boxes.

"Please state your intention," Jan said.

"Malachite," Mal replied quickly, clearly knowing exactly what her intentions were.

The man opened up one of the boxes and produced a large green stone. Mal held out her hands and he placed it into the cradle her hands had formed. Mal then leaned over the pond and gently placed the stone on the surface. Within a moment it began to sink and rested on the bottom.

"Excellent choice," Jan commented. "Ms. Logan?"

"I...I...don't...." Bea stuttered.

"Perhaps you would like the stone to choose you?" Jan asked.

"Yes," Bea replied, unsure what that meant.

The man proceeded to place the wooden boxes into the water, they floated on the surface and became caught in the current of the pond. After all the boxes had been placed, they swirled in a mesmerizing dance where each bumped and jostled with one another for an unknown position in the hypnotic parade.

Suddenly, one box broke from the group and floated out of the current. It softly stopped against the edge of the pond right in front of Bea.

"Excellent choice," Jan said and gestured for Bea to reach for the box.

Lifting it out of the water and placing it in her hand, Bea opened it to reveal a shining black and white stone.

"What is it?" Bea asked.

"Snowflake obsidian," Jan replied warmly.

"What does it mean?" asked Bea, having never heard of anything like this before.

"Snowflake obsidian is a special stone," Jan said, placing her hand on Bea's shoulder. "It represents your intention to obtain spiritual protection and acceptance."

The words stung a little bit closer to her heart.

Was that really what she was searching for, some sort of acceptance of her own mortality? She couldn't remember a single day in the last few months that she hadn't cried about her diagnosis. Maybe there was something to this. Maybe, just maybe, she could heal.

Drop the stone in the damn pond stupid.

She followed suit, it made a loud plop and splashed water onto her knees. The stone spun as it slowly sunk to the bottom.

"Now that intentions have been stated," Jan said, reaching down to help Mal and Bea stand. "We must cleanse ourselves before continuing the journey."

Jan led the way as the man in the orange robe collected the other wood boxes from the pond behind them.

"What did your stone mean?" Bea whispered to Mal as they walked.

"What?" Mal said, pretending to not notice.

"Your stone, what did it..." Bea said before being cut off.

"In this room," said Jan, opening the door for them. "You must allow the cleansing power of the quartz crystal to wash over you."

Bea was awe-struck. At the far end of the room was a waterfall. The water flowed over a ledge made entirely of crystal and disappeared into a gap in the floor.

"Quartz has been a prominent purifying stone since the beginning of time," Jan explained. "Here at Bellezza, we have the largest unbroken quartz crystal. It infuses natural mountain spring water with the ability to purge negative energies from your bodies.

You may change here, I will meet you on the other side when you are ready."

Jan disappeared out the door, shutting it behind her.

"Change?" Bea asked with confusion.

"Can't go through the waters in our jumpsuit," Mal said. They approached the quartz edge, shoulder-height walls sparkled on both sides of them. It felt like they were traversing a crystalline cave.

Mal was quick with her jumpsuit, zipping it down the front and letting it fall over her shoulders.

"So I just what... strip?" Bea asked.

"Ya, why not?" Mal replied.

"Well, I..." Bea stammered searching for a reason to protest, however seeing Mal's nude figure caused her to flinch.

Mal was completely naked, she apparently hadn't been wearing any underwear.

"Are we doing this or not?" asked Mal with her hands on her hips. She was smiling at Bea, who stared dumb struck back.

"Ya, ya, one second," Bea clumsily pulled at the zipper of her own jumpsuit.

Here goes nothing, the voice actually encouraged her.

Bea pulled the zipper down and awkwardly removed the clothing from her body, leaving her in her bra and panties only.

"No way," Mal said. "If I'm going through naked, so are you."

Mal screamed and jumped through the waterfall, disappearing through the liquid wall.

Bea quickly removed her undergarments and faced the waterfall with hesitation.

Thinking of how cold the water was going to be, she stood there completely naked for a few moments.

"You can do this," she said to herself.

Almost running forward, she finally leaped through the water.

The water was not cold, it was refreshing and warm. The water flowed momentarily over her face,

As she emerged from the opposite side, a novel sensation of tranquility washed over her. Whether it was the cool touch of water on her skin or the sheer freedom of her unclothed state, she felt as though she had crossed into an entirely different realm. The weight of Professor Mikkelson, her thesis, familial expectations, and her diagnosis that had oppressed her for so long now seemed distant, no longer weighing heavily on her thoughts or emotions.

Wiping the water from her eyes, she realized that the room where Mal stood nearby drying herself with a towel was full of stars. They weren't real stars of course, instead the purple walls glinted with small lights that gave the effect that she was standing in the middle of space.

Something soft hit her face, it was a towel.

"Get dry," Mal said with a small laugh. "You look like a wet dog."

Bea grinned despite her confidence that her tangled mane of hair was strewn all over her face.

They quickly put on a pair of white bathrobes that hung from the nearby wall and wrapped their wet hair in towels.

Stepping out from behind the curtain that concealed the room, they entered a spacious circular chamber, its glass ceiling flooding the space with light. There were five other doors in the room, each with strange symbols that Bea couldn't decipher.

A man appeared at their side, dressed in a white shirt and pants and holding a tray.

"Thank you," Mal said as she pulled a champagne flute full of bubbly orange liquid from it.

The other drink was also in a champagne flute, however it was pinkish in color and several blueberries floated in it.

"But I didn't order anything..." Bea remarked.

"I told them what you liked," Mal said smiling. "Go ahead, try it."

Bea tentatively took the glass and held it to her nose. It smelled sweet.

"It's a bit early don't you think?" remarked Bea.

"Nonsense," Mal replied, as she raised her glass. "To us, may we enjoy this much-deserved day of healing."

Bea clinked her glass to Mal's and they both took a sip.

"What is this?" Bea asked with a smile. Whatever they had given her, it was amazing.

"You like it?" Mal said smiling. "It's called a Knoxville Smash."

"I do," Bea replied as she eagerly drank the rest of the glass.

She looked around embarrassed, realizing she had chugged the drink.

"Don't be embarrassed," Mal said with a wink. "It's time for us to let loose a little bit. Jan, another one please for my friend."

"Of course Ms. Phillips," Jan said after somehow appearing from a side corridor that Bea hadn't noticed.

A moment later, a line of men and women all dressed in white shirts and white pants appeared from one of the doors. They were a diverse group, encompassing nearly every major ethnicity. However, they all shared one striking similarity: their undeniable attractiveness. The men stood tall with pronounced muscles, while the women boasted height and an athletic build.

Jan returned with a fresh drink for Bea and handed it to her.

"Ms. Phillips, would you like to choose first?" Jan asked Mal.

"No, I think I'll let Bea go," Mal replied.

"Choose what?" Bea said bewildered.

"Why your personal attendant for today of course," Mal said with a grin. "Go ahead, they are all quite good. Pick your favorite."

"I...uh.." Bea stepped forward to look at the line. They all indeed looked capable, however there was one particular large tanned male with dark hair on the end that particularly caught her eye.

Of course, you want the one that looks just like Cam.

"Him, I guess?" Bea said pointing.

"Sergei, excellent choice," Jan said.

Sergei stepped forward, still standing at attention and looking straight forward.

It was Mal's turn, Bea watching her closely. Mal paced the length of the line, studying each attendant carefully.

Bea wondered which one she would pick. She hadn't seen Mal with anyone yet, but she assumed Mal would prefer the most handsome of the men of which there was plenty of choice.

Maybe Mal would pick the tall African-American male or the handsome Polynesian one with the chiseled jaw.

"You," Mal said at last, pointing to a blonde female who stepped forward immediately.

"Anastasia," Jan said aloud. "I believe you've enjoyed her before."

"I know," Mal said. "She is just the best."

Bea was confused, she had been sure Mal would have picked one of the handsome strong men.

"I'm glad to hear so," Jan replied. "Ladies, this way please."

Jan gestured towards a teak door, its wood grain appearing authentically natural, yet uniquely arranging itself into a series of spiral patterns.

Bea hurriedly joined Mal who had approached the door without the same hesitation as Bea.

The next few hours were filled with some of the most amazing sensations of Bea's life. It began with deep tissue facials that left Bea's normally dry skin glowing followed by manicures and pedicures. At lunch they enjoyed light salads next to a private indoor pool that looked out into the forest while their feet were massaged by Sergei and Anastasia.

The entire time though, Bea and Mal talked and talked and talked. They had been roommates for months and had never spoken this many words to each other in that entire time. They drank, joked, and they laughed together.

After lunch they were led to a terrace where Sergei and Anastasia proceeded to give them side-by-side, sensual massages using lavender oils and wax from eucalyptus candles. Bea was nervous at first, the melted wax was hot but it cooled quickly on her skin and left behind a sensation of ecstasy where it dripped.

Bea couldn't help but melt away herself as Sergei cleared out what felt like twenty years of anxiety from her muscles. She found herself nodding off to sleep.

When she awoke, Sergei was gone. She was still on the massage table, face down and considered moving to sit up when she heard the sound of soft giggling nearby. She opened her eyes to see the table where Mal had been sitting was empty. However on a bench behind it, Mal and Anastasia sat next to one another.

Her sleepy eyes struggled to adjust to the light but as they did she was able to more clearly see the two women in the distance.

Whoa.

Bea stopped herself from echoing the exclamation. Anastasia and Mal were locked in a deep kiss, Mal's arms wrapped around the back of Anastasia's neck holding her close. They'd both break the kiss for a moment to smile and giggle at one another before continuing on.

To say Bea was shocked would have been an understatement. She was straight flabbergasted. Mal, the untouchable icon of male desires...was a lesbian?

Looking back now, it actually kind of made sense. Mal surrounded herself with beautiful women, was extremely comfortable with the naked female body, and showed zero interest in any male that she ever met despite being beautiful enough to land any man in the entire world. I mean, how could she have remained just friends with Cam for so many years unless she just wasn't into men?

Bea suddenly felt something, a cramp in her leg had formed. Likely from sleeping for however long she had been face down on the massage table. However she didn't dare move, not an inch. Not wanting to give away to Mal and Anastasia that she was awake and watching them.

Speaking of which, the two women had begun to touch themselves more than along their faces and necks, but hands were traveling farther down each other's bodies. Bea didn't want to interrupt, but the cramp was getting worse.

When she couldn't take anymore, she moved her leg slightly, hoping she was subtle enough that the two wouldn't notice.

They did, both immediately stood up at attention.

Bea closed her eyes tight, maybe they would think she was still sleeping and she wouldn't have interrupted them.

Several minutes passed, the soft sounds of the music playing on the terrace the only thing she could hear.

Opening her eyes slightly, she found Mal face down at her own table again and Anastasia gone.

You know you've always been pretty good at that.

Good at what? She asked herself back.

Ruining perfectly beautiful moments.

Shut up.

Later that evening, Bea and Mal sat at a candlelit table overlooking the mountains on the terrace as the staff brought them drinks and dinner. Both had changed back into their light blue jumpsuits and were quietly staring out into the rapidly dwindling sunlight as it set, casting brilliant oranges and reds across the mountain stone scape.

"Thank you Mal," Bea said, breaking the silence. "You've been more than kind, more than sweet, more than helpful to me since I met you."

Mal smiled at her.

"It's been my pleasure," she replied.

"I just...I just..." Bea began to say.

Don't do it, don't be that person who looks a gift horse in the mouth.

"Why me?" Bea asked, ignoring the voice. "You have so many beautiful friends already, why bring me into your home...and dress me in beautiful clothes...and take me to amazing places like this. I don't get it."

Mal laughed.

"My friends?" Mal commented with sarcasm. "They only like me because my dad's rich and I can get them into places they couldn't get into on their own. They suck up to me, they lie to me, they tell me all sorts of crap. But they don't like me, they don't love me. They just want to be me. That's not friendship, that's followership."

"Well don't you have real friends then? Others like Cam?" Bea asked.

"I wish," Mal replied, looking back at the mountain and taking a sip of her drink again. "Cam's been a good friend over the years, but he's still Cam. I can't talk to him about certain things, certain things he would never understand."

"Like what?" questioned Bea.

"Like.." Mal began to speak before pausing to think harder on it. "And you can't say a word of this to him."

Bea nodded.

"He knows nothing about love," Mal continued. "I mean he thinks he does. Lord knows he's read more books about love than anyone else I've ever met. Thinks he's some suave Casanova type that can swoop in and lift anyone off their feet. But when it comes to real love, true love...he knows nothing."

"What do you mean?" asked Bea.

"He's good at the charming part," Mal said, taking another sip. This had been the most Bea had seen her drink, by far in their time together. "He knows what to say, he knows how to impress. That's just not enough."

"So what is true love then?" Bea said.

"I don't know if we should be talking about it," Mal said, putting her drink down. "You and Cam, that's between you two."

"No, it's ok," Bea replied. "I want to talk about it, it's important. To you, to me. I have to be honest...I'm not sure I know what true love is either. And nothing you say leaves this...Room? Terrace? I don't know what to call it."

They both laughed.

"Well, true love," Mal began. "It's something that doesn't come from words, it doesn't come from things, it comes from something else. Sure, it starts with that kind of stuff, but that's not what it really is. It's an action, a consequence...a sacrifice that one makes for another without any expectation of reciprocation or reward. It's something born of truly putting that other person before yourself. That's true love."

Bea nodded and they sat in silence a few minutes longer, both quietly watching the colors fade from the mountain and it turn white and gray once again.

"So you," Bea said before pausing for a moment. "So you were in true love once?"

Mal looked at her for a moment.

"Yes, I mean, no," she replied.

"I mean you sound like you know all about it," Bea answered. "So you must have been in true love before, right?"

"I was, well I wasn't," Mal seemed to struggle to find the answers. "Someone was truly in love with me, they had sacrificed it all for me. But when the time came for me to do the same for them...I hesitated."

"I'm sorry," Bea said softly.

She watched Mal carefully, the slightest glint of a tear had formed in the corner of Mal's eyes.

"Don't be," Mal said, wiping the tears away quickly with her napkin. "It's my own fault, I wanted to but when the time came...I just couldn't. I wasn't willing to sacrifice it all for them, that's why I say it was true love, but not for me."

Silence engulfed them again.

Bea was stunned to see this level of vulnerability from Mal. Mal the beautiful, Mal the perfect, Mal the impenetrable. Bea was quickly realizing that all of those things that other women flocked to Mal for, all the traits that made others want to be her. They were all made believe, a facade, a show for the world to hide the sad lonely little girl sitting at the table next to her.

Well, Bea wasn't going to allow such a creature to suffer alone.

She reached out and put a hand on Mal's shoulder.

"What was her name?" Bea asked with a reassuring smile.

"What? Uh...umm.." Mal stuttered for the first time since Bea had met her.

"I saw you and Anastasia," Bea said. "It's ok, it doesn't bother me. You can be you, I don't care."

"But, no...um...I'm not..." Mal continued to stutter and stammer her words as tears began to flow freely from her eyes.

Bea just looked at her and smiled, squeezing her shoulder softly.

Mal at last looked at Bea in the eyes, with tears streaming down her cheeks.

"Her name..." Mal said in between sobs. "Was Monica. She was my best friend in high school. She begged me to come out to my parents, to run off to some backwoods college together. I just didn't want to disappoint Mom and Dad. They had already bought this place for me and donated a ton of money to the university guaranteeing my acceptance. I couldn't let them down, they would have disowned me. Cut me off, I would have been buying my clothes at Goodwill. I just couldn't do it."

"What happened?" Bea asked.

"She came over, to be with me when we told them," said the sobbing beautiful blond with her makeup running down her face. "I told her to leave...and never talk to me again."

"Where is she now?" asked Bea.

"I don't know," Mal replied. "I haven't seen her since that night."

"I'm sorry Mal," Bea said.

"Silly right?" Mal said as the sobbing began to subside. "Everyday I pretend to be something I'm not, something my parents told me I needed to be."

"Not today you don't have to be," Bea said with a smile.

"Thank you," said Mal, smiling back.

Silence returned to their table, Mal continued to wipe her tears away as best she could with her napkin.

"Listen Bea," Mal said at last, turning to face her. "There's something I need to tell you. It's about the club, it's about Cam..."

"Sure what is it?" Bea replied, her curiosity growing.

"Would you ladies like another bottle?" Jan asked, appearing from behind them very suddenly.

Bea jumped.

"Yes, um...another bottle would be fine," Mal replied.

Jan walked away.

Turning back to Mal, Bea noticed something strange happening to Mal's face. Maybe it was just the makeup smear, but her face wasn't looking like it always did. Bags had formed under the normally beautiful girl's eyes, pock marks emerged from her cheeks, somehow her teeth appeared crooked and her nose was larger than it normally looked.

"Oh my God Mal," Bea exclaimed. "Are you ok?"

Mal felt at her face and immediately her expression turned to horror.

She grabbed her purse and began to shield her face with it.

"No, I'm fine," she said from behind the bag. "I'm really ok, it's just my makeup is running. And I may be having an allergic reaction."

Mal stood up and quickly shuffled off to the restroom.

Bea sat there watching in disbelief at the strange transformation that had begun before her.

Several minutes later, Mal re-emerged from the bathroom and sat down back in the chair.

"Sorry about that," she said with her perfect smile once again shining.

"What was that?" Bea asked.

"Nothing, just allergies," Mal commented nonchalantly. "I'm fine now."

"Are you sure?" Bea pushed. "You didn't look fine."

"I'm great, just forget it," Mal assured her.

"Ok," Bea said suspiciously. "You were talking about Cam and the club?"

"What? No, nothing," Mal said, putting her purse down.

Jan reappeared with a fresh bottle of champagne and poured it for them.

"No really, you were just about to say..." Bea began.

"You know what, I never told you what Malachite was for," Mal interrupted her.

"Oh no, you didn't," Bea replied.

"It's for wealth and beauty," Mal answered with a smile before taking a long drink from her champagne flute.

"Seems like you have enough of that already," Bea commented.

"Trust me," Mal said, putting her hand on Bea's. "You can never have enough of either."

She smiled at Bea, but Bea didn't believe it. She was hiding something, something about the club and Cam. But what could it be?"

They continued to drink and talk the rest of the evening, however every time Bea tried to bring up Cam or the club, Mal expertly avoided the question.

Later that night, Bea went to sleep in their room with mixed emotions. Feeling comfort and relief that Mal had opened up to her regarding a major secret she had been keeping for years. Bea also felt unease though, that Mal also kept one more secret somehow far more dire and desperate to protect. A secret Mal would keep at all costs, as if her life depended on it.

Chapter Fourteen

Bea's Uber pulled up to Cam's building. Before she could open the door, the driver had already jumped out and ran around to open it for her. He opened an umbrella and shielded her from the cold pouring rain outside as she stepped with her kitten heel to the curb and straightened the cocktail dress Mal had let her borrow.

It had been a week since she and Mal had gone to the spa together, a week since the first snowfall of the year. The weather had thankfully warmed back up, melting the thin layer of pristine snow that was nothing but a distant memory now. Today's torrential rain storm had blown in suddenly and caught the entire city by surprise.

Everyone in the city seemed to be on edge. They had passed several accidents on the way from the university to downtown, including one in which both drivers were screaming at each other while soaking wet outside their mangled vehicles. Even the Uber driver who was escorting her from the car to the front awning of the building wasn't in a friendly or talkative mood. They had barely spoken three words the entire drive.

"Thank you," Bea said with a smile as she reached the awning.

However she might as well be speaking to a ghost, the driver had already run back to his car and had disappeared into the driver's seat; cloaked behind the pattering of rain on his windshield that his wipers with much futility tried to sweep away.

Thankfully for Bea, the door man at Cam's condo was in a much better mood than the rest of the city.

"Hell of an evening Ms. Logan," said the friendly man as he opened the door to usher her in.

"You said it Thomas," she said with a smile as she ducked inside.

"Mr. Anwir and his guests are upstairs already," Thomas said, taking her rain jacket and shaking the water from it onto a nearby mat.

"Is that Ms. Logan?" said a friendly voice from behind the desk.

"That it is Clarence," replied Thomas.

Bea had developed a friendly relationship with Thomas and Clarence, the two old gentlemen who worked the lobby at Cam's building. She had been visiting Cam several times a week for months now and they always shared a few short but warm conversations when she visited. They seemed to be the only two employees of the building.

"How'd your football teams do this year?" asked Bea, who knew nothing about football except that the pitcher threw the ball and the goalie tried to catch it.

"I don't want to talk about it," replied Clarence with a scowl.

"You Chicago fans are always such sore losers," chided Thomas with a smile.

"Your team didn't do much better," mocked Clarence back.

"We beat you twice," responded Thomas.

"And still didn't make the playoffs," Clarence said with a laugh.

"Sounds like you two are a match made in heaven," joked Bea.

Both men laughed.

"You got that right, Miss," Thomas said with a grin.

"I'll open her up for you," Clarence said, pressing buttons on his keyboard.

Cam's private elevator opened at the end of the lobby.

"Have a good night now," Thomas said, waving.

"You too," Bea said with a smile and walked into the elevator.

"You would sell your soul to the devil for a winning season," Bea heard Thomas exclaim as the doors of the elevator closed behind her.

She had grown accustomed to the cramped space of the elevator, it no longer made her feel claustrophobic like it had the first time. In fact, she and Cam had shared many passionate moments in it since; too impatient to wait to get to his penthouse before their clothes were off and hands all over each other. She smiled at the memory.

The only unsettling thing that remained about the elevator was that each time she used it, it always felt like it was going down and not up. Likely a strange result of the older building and the quirks that go with such outdated technology.

Tonight though, something else gnawed at the back of her mind. In the week since bonding with Mal at the spa, Bea had tried countless times to bring up the conversation regarding Cam and the club again. Mal, each time, successfully diverted the conversation to other topics. Between that, and what Viv had told her...she knew something was wrong, she just wasn't quite sure what it was.

Human or sex trafficking were the most likely of possibilities. Dangerous narcotics were also a thought. However, Bea didn't see any evidence of it. Everything so far was strange coincidences and gut feelings. Bea knew about Viv and her past trauma, it could all be in her head and they were just sharing in the baseless hysteria.

Besides, what kind of nefarious criminal mastermind invites someone to meet their parents?

The elevator slowed and the doors opened in front of her.

She stepped forward onto the familiar threshold of Cam's apartment. Soft music played in the background, a mix of an orchestra and Scottish bagpipes. It had a very old world sound to it.

Cam usually greeted her when she arrived but he was nowhere to be found. She made her way to the living room near the kitchen. Maybe he was busy preparing dinner.

Turning the corner, she saw the most beautiful woman she had ever seen sitting on the couch.

"Hello Bea," said the woman with a confident and sultry voice.

The woman rose and Bea almost couldn't believe her eyes. The woman had long and luscious platinum blonde hair that stretched almost to her lower back. She was very thin, her chest, waist, and hips well defined and accentuated by her silver cocktail dress. Her shoulders were barely covered by the thin straps of the dress that showed off her perfectly shaped collarbones. Her legs were long and she wore high heels that matched her dress perfectly. She was tall, she could have been a model.

"Hi," Bea managed to say as she soaked the woman in.

"I'm Kyla," the woman said, striding forward with a walk that made her look as if she was floating on a cloud. She held out her hand.

"Cam's mother," she added.

"Nice to meet you," Bea replied, her eyes awestruck. She shook Kyla's hand more aggressively than she had planned, the woman's slender fingers much more elegant and well-manicured than her own.

"I like your dress," Kyla said with a smile.

"Thank you," Bea said suddenly feeling inadequate in her simple black cocktail dress. "I like yours, too?"

She hadn't meant to end that in a question.

"Oh the boys," Kyla said with a shrug. "They are still working up dinner in the kitchen. Would you like to join me for a drink?"

"Um, sure," Bea said, gaining back some of her wits.

Kyla took Bea's hand in hers and led her to the couch. Kyla lowered herself smoothly and effortlessly onto the cushion, her shoulders back and knees together. In contrast, Bea kind of fell onto the couch and was hunched over. A pair of glasses filled with a blood red colored wine were already waiting for them on the side table.

"Try this Chateau Lafite," Kyla said, handing Bea her glass. "It's to die for."

They both took sips, Bea concentrating to avoid spilling a drop like her usual clumsy self would.

"It's great," Bea said.

"It's from 1787," Kyla commented. "They really knew how to make wine back then."

Bea nearly choked.

"This wine is over 200 years old?!" she exclaimed.

"Oh yes," Kyla replied calmly. "It's quite special. Much like you."

Bea blushed immediately.

"You know in all these years," Kyla remarked before taking another dainty sip. "Cam has never once introduced us to one of his girlfriends."

Bea took a sip, her eyes wide.

"So you must imagine our surprise," Kyla's eyes narrowed, they were a brilliant emerald green. "And curiosity when he informed us you would be joining us for dinner this evening. So Bea, tell me a little about yourself."

Bea panicked, she wasn't quite sure what to say.

Kyla must have picked up on this.

"Let's start with, where are you from?" Kyla asked with a smile.

"Pennsylvania," Bea replied. "A small town outside of Pittsburgh. Very rural, lots of farms, some Amish communities."

"And what do your parents do?" Kyla questioned further.

"My father is a deacon of our Catholic parish and my mother stays at home," Bea responded.

"Very interesting," Kyla remarked. "So how does the daughter of a deacon end up in a big city like this?"

"The university," Bea replied. "I'm working on my master's thesis."

"Oh yes," Kyla exclaimed. "Cam did mention it, he loaned you a copy of the *Filii Diaboli.*"

Loaned.

"Yes," Bea said. "That's been very helpful."

"So what do you think?" Kyla asked.

"Think about...?" Bea replied with the open question.

"The book of course," Kyla answered. "It's truly an eye opening volume, full of the inner workings of a part of society that's often...suppressed in history."

"Suppressed, yes," Bea commented. "It's been very helpful for my thesis, however it's quite dark and horrific at times."

Kyla eyed her cautiously.

"I see," Kyla said at last. "Well as the daughter of a deacon, I'm sure you've seen first hand the hypocrisy and fascism of the church."

Bea's heart skipped a beat. She took another long sip of the wine until her glass was empty.

Did Cam tell her about dinner with her parents?

“And your history studies,” Kyla continued. “You are of course well-educated on how the church has scorned outsiders, those who believe in other theologies.”

She had emphasized the word “other”.

Bea gulped.

“Yes,” Bea wasn’t sure what to say. “I’m well aware.”

“Good,” Kyla said, her eyes narrowing as they pierced Bea.

Bea felt something from Kyla, the same warmth Cam gave off. It was off-putting but something about her was irresistibly attractive. A feeling, a scent, maybe a pheromone. Whatever it was pulled at strings inside Bea that she did not want tugged.

"Can I fill that up for you dear?" Kyla asked with a smile.

"Um...yes please," Bea responded, feeling relief as Kyla’s gaze left her.

As Kyla stood and took her glass elegantly to the nearby counter where the open bottle of the wine sat, Bea felt herself beginning to feel something ominous draw closer. Kyla’s glass had started to subtly ripple in rhythm to the steps of some enormous beast approaching. When the footsteps stopped, a shadow had overtaken the room.

Standing in the doorway from the kitchen stood the largest man Bea had ever seen. He must have been seven feet tall or maybe more. His shoulders were broad, barely able to fit through the doorway without turning sideways. His features were dark, difficult to see while silhouetting the light from overhead.

"Is dis her?" said a loud, deep, booming voice.

"It is, my dear," replied Kyla who returned to the couch with the glass of wine and handed it to Bea.

"Bea, let me introduce you to my husband," Kyla said as she glided over to the enormous man. "Bea, this is Morfran. Morfran, this is Bea."

Kyla must have been half his height, her waist thinner than his arm. Yet Kaya wrapped her petite hand around his elbow and guided him with what seemed like little to no effort.

As he came closer, his face became less obscured by the light and came into better view.

He had short black hair that connected down his cheeks into a short beard. His face was as large and square as the rest of him. One of his eyes was dark brown while the other was completely silver. A long scar stretched from his forehead, over the silver eye, and down his cheek disappearing into the beard. His large nose was crooked, like it had been broken several times but never set right. Pockmarks and other scars lined his cheeks and his lips drooped on one side at an awkward angle.

Morfran held out his hand.

Bea had the urge to flee; the man's presence sent a chill down her spine. His imposing stature and unsettling appearance made him appear less human and more like a monstrosity.

Bea swallowed hard and mustered all of the courage she could to reach out and grasp his.

His hand, which was easily twice the size of Bea's, was strong. She felt like she was grasping the hand of a stone statue in a museum, the skin unrelenting to the pressure from her own fingers. His skin didn't feel like skin. It was ice cold and felt like sandpaper, it scratched at her and made the hairs on her arms stand up.

Thankfully, he let her hand go quickly.

"Nice to meet you," he growled.

"Nice to meet you too," Bea squeaked in response, her heart racing in fear.

Kyla must have sensed it.

"I'm afraid my dear husband isn't much for social graces," Kyla said, leading Morfran to a seat on the couch and ushering Bea to do the same on the opposite side.

"However, I must assure you," Kyla added. "He's much friendlier than he looks."

Morfran forced a smile at Bea, revealing a mouth full of crooked and brown-stained teeth.

As the enormous Morfran and the thin petite Kyla sat next to each other holding hands, Bea's mind raced to understand how they fit together. She couldn't imagine a more mis-matched pair.

Bea felt the tension of silence growing in the air.

"Can I get you a drink my dear?" Kyla asked, smiling at her husband.

Morfran grunted in affirmative, all the while staring intently at Bea.

Kyla returned with a large mug. Morfran drank it sloppily, the dark amber liquid spilling into small streams as it ran down his beard and the subsequent drops absorbed by his coat.

"Chwisgi," Kyla said as if she could sense Bea's curiosity. "It's the only thing he drinks."

"What's it like?" Bea asked.

"Oh, um..." Kyla seemed to think for a moment. "It's a traditional Welsh whiskey. Quite unrefined in fact, not quite as elegant as the Chateau Lafite."

"Cam had mentioned he was Welsh," Bea said more comfortably, Kyla's presence balancing the room against Morfran's. "I'm quite partial to whiskey as opposed to wine. Do you think I might try some?"

Morfran and Kyla looked at each other for a moment.

"I'm not sure it's quite your taste..." Kyla began to say.

A grunt from Morfran interrupted her and she stood to pour Bea a glass and handed it to her.

"May I propose a toast?" Kyla said.

They all raised their glasses.

"To family, to new friends," she said before pausing and glancing at Bea. "And to our health."

Kyla and Bea gently tapped glasses, Morfran meanwhile guzzled the last of his mug.

Bea took a sip of the whiskey.

It did taste unrefined, nothing like the bourbons or scotches she had tried before. There was something primal about it, an ingredient she couldn't quite nail down that gave it a flavor that caused burning but also pleasure as it poured over her tongue. She suppressed the urge to cough.

"Afraid I warned you," Kyla said, once again sensing Bea's discomfort before it could even be expressed. "Quite unrefined."

"I like it," Bea said enthusiastically. Drinking the last of what Kyla had poured.

Morfran grunted in what Bea hoped was a sign of his approval.

"Getting started without me I see," Cam said from the kitchen doorway.

Cam wore a white apron that was covered in red smears, something not altogether strange as Bea knew Cam's preference to butcher his own meat to his very specific preferences.

Bea stood and rushed over to him, not minding the stains at all. She hugged him tight.

"It's good to see you," she whispered in his ear.

"You too," he whispered back. "My mom hasn't been grilling you has she?"

"Just a little," she replied.

"Well don't mind them," Cam said reassuringly. "They aren't as scary as they seem."

They released their embrace, Bea looking back to the couch to see Kyla's pleasant and inviting smile next to Morfran's lopsided scowl.

"I'm going to change real quick," Cam said to the group. "If you would like to take your seats, the first course will be out shortly."

As usual, Cam's meal was exquisite. Though it might have been considered traditional for most kitchens, he always dropped in the perfect amount of flair to turn the mundane exotic.

Bea utilized the time to watch Cam's parents carefully, studying their unique and very paradoxical natures.

For example, Morfran refused to touch the garden salad that Cam had prepared. Cam didn't seem the slightest bit perturbed by it, likely a result of years of such behavior. Meanwhile, when Cam brought out steaks, Morfran's portion was easily four times the size of the one that Bea had eaten. Kyla seemed to eat very slowly and daintily, taking a break to set down her utensils and make conversation between each bite. Morfran, on the opposite side of the spectrum, ate his steak as if it would disappear from his plate and be gone forever at any moment. Devouring it with speed and aggressiveness that might better suit a grizzly bear or mountain lion.

The conversations seemed tamer than Bea had expected, mostly revolving around the club, the club's finances, and other mundane aspects of operating the business. That was until...

"So tell me the story of how you two met," Kyla asked.

Morfran sat next to her, seemed uninterested and proceeded to begin eviscerating his fourth serving of meat.

Bea wasn't sure how to begin, she was beginning to panic while trying to think of what to say when Cam put his hand on hers.

Immediately her mind calmed and her anxiety dissipated.

"Well I was visiting the club with my friend Mal," Bea began.

"Ah yes," Kyla interrupted. "Wonderful girl, her family and ours have been in business together for years."

Morfran's attention seemed to perk up momentarily at the mention of the word business but when Kyla urged Bea to continue he quickly returned to his meal.

"And well," Bea wasn't quite sure how to continue.

Try, I saw the sexiest man I've ever met and immediately wanted to jump his bones.

"He was very charming," Bea found the more appropriate words to describe it. "And so when he asked me out to dinner..."

"When I finally worked up the courage to ask her out to dinner," Cam interjected, winking at Bea.

Bea couldn't help but smile.

"There was no way I was going to say no," Bea added.

"Were you seeing someone else at the time?" Kyla asked.

"Mother," Cam's voice said, trailing off to try and stop her.

"It's an honest question," Kyla asked. "I'm just being curious."

"You're being rude," Cam replied.

"Oh come on," Kyla said leaning forward onto the back of her interlocked hands. "Girl to girl."

She winked at Bea and that strange sensation from the couch returned to Bea's stomach.

How was she supposed to respond?

Were you seeing someone? Well, depending on your definition Adelaide and well Tarzan too...

"Nothing serious at the time," Bea replied.

"Wonderful," Kyla said, turning back to her meal.

Silence descended on the table, well relative silence. Morfran's cutting and chewing had formed a steady background noise that they all had grown accustomed to by this point.

"How did you two meet?" Bea asked.

Morfran stopped chewing and the table went silent.

Oh no, the voice echoed her panic in her head.

The silence continued. Bea shot a nervous glance at Cam but he was staring at his mother intently almost as if he was just as interested in her answer as Bea was.

"I'm sorry," Bea stammered. "Did I say something I shouldn't have?"

"No, not at all," Kyla replied quickly. "It's just..."

She searched for a moment for how to continue.

"We haven't been asked that question in a very long time," Kyla added.

Morfran sat back in his seat and crossed his arms, his scowl as disapproving as ever.

Kyla looked at Cam one more time, her eyes asked a question but what it was Bea couldn't be certain.

Cam knew though, and he nodded back at her.

"We met in Wales," Kyla said. "A small little village named Aberdaron. I was working at the time and my dear Morfran was a soldier in the army. He courted me, relentlessly."

She smiled as she took another sip, losing herself to a fond old memory.

"He went off to war," she continued. "And I never expected him to come back, much less survive. But he did, more or less in one piece."

Cam, Kyla, and Morfran all chuckled.

"Excuse me," Bea interjected. "But is that where you lost your eye?"

Morfran let out a loud laugh, it bellowed around her and shook the table.

"No," he said, suddenly ceasing his laughter. "I was born with this face and none other."

“So when he returned,” Kyla continued her story. “He asked me to marry him.”

“Which she refused,” Cam added with a smile.

“Yes, but,” she replied. “He was very convincing and after a short while we were married and then pregnant and then...”

She held her open palm out towards Cam who nodded his head and shoulders in a quarter bow.

“Which war did you fight in, sir?” Bea asked Morfran, hoping that if she could get him talking he would be less scary of a figure. Her guess based on his accent and likely age was that he had fought for the British in the gulf war or maybe Eastern Europe.

Kyla looked at Morfran for a moment and raised her eyebrows before hiding her face in her wine glass.

Morfran leaned forward, his eyes darkened as he did so. His hands gripped the table tightly.

“The last war that mattered,” he growled, his brown and broken teeth on full display in an unnerving grin.

Bea felt frightened in the moment, Cam’s hand on hers giving her just enough strength to avoid recoiling.

The sound of the elevator opening surprised Bea and she turned to see their visitor. Walking from the hallway was Harper, strutting towards them with his characteristic confidence and swagger.

"Harpier," Kyla exclaimed, clapping her hands together.

"Mrs. Anwir," Harper replied with a smile and a bow.

She hugged him and kissed him on the cheek.

"Sorry, I'm late," Harper said sitting down at the open seat. "I'm not a big fan of the rain, I was waiting until it finally broke."

"We completely understand," Kyla replied. "It's been too long my dear."

Bea gave Cam a curious eye, she had not expected Harper to be joining them that evening.

Cam caught her eye and quickly jumped in.

"My parents have known Harper since he was very young," Cam said.

"A fledgling really," Kyla added. "We asked him to join us.

Harper pulled up a chair and placed it between Cam and Kyla.

"Harpier's family is very dear to us, "Kyla continued. "They've long been loyal servants to us for as long as I can remember."

"Proud and loyal," Harper said, pouring a glass of wine for himself.

"Hungry Harpier?" Kyla asked. "Cam just finished making us the most amazing meal. I'm sure there's a few scraps left."

"No thank you Mrs. Anwir," he said with his signature smile. "I already ate."

He took a sip from his glass.

"So Harpier," Kyla continued the conversation. "Have you thought about settling down? There must be someone in your life who is special?"

"Alas Mrs. Anwir," Harper said downing the last drop of wine. "There's just too much special in this world. I feel spoiled for choice."

"I see," Kyla commented with a grin. "Sounds to me you are much like the Saltmarsh Sparrow, a perennial bachelor."

"Cam must have inherited his eye for the truth from you Mrs. Anwir," Harper said with a wink.

Kyla laughed.

Bea glanced at Cam who stood there smiling awkwardly, also not entirely enthusiastic about the conversation topic.

"Now," Cam said, intending to change the subject. "For dessert I have prepared..."

"Mhmmmm," Morfran grunted loudly, interrupting him.

"Yes father?" Cam said, turning to the large creature that lurked at the end of the table, forcing his best smile.

"I tire of the charade," Morfran said with his booming voice. "Business, now."

Cam smiled and tilted his head.

"Yes, I understand," Cam began to say. "However, maybe it would not be polite to discuss business in front of Bea..."

Morfran's large fist slammed the table loudly, the glasses, utensils, and plates all jumping up an inch.

"Mhmmmm," Morfran grunted again.

Cam sat speechless.

"It's ok my dear," Kyla said, patting Cam on the shoulder. "Why don't Harpier, you, and your father retire to the study to discuss. I'm sure I'm more than capable of entertaining your new friend in the meantime."

Cam seemed to panic for a moment.

Bea looked at him, she rarely saw him so out of sorts. It must be some skill that all parents seem to possess, an innate knowledge of how to strike sheer social terror in your child in front of their friends. Cam, who seemed so perfect at all other times, was just as nervous when his parents met his girlfriend as a normal person. The chink in the armor only made her feel more warmth and affection for him.

"It's ok Cam," Bea said reassuringly. "We'll be here when you get back."

She smiled at him, and his face changed to one of relief.

The three men left the table, the large Morfran's steps causing reverberations throughout the apartment until they disappeared behind the library door.

"Finally," Kyla said standing up. "Care to join me on the balcony? I'm dying for a cigarette."

"Sure," Bea said, standing up as well and picking up her glass.

"Here, let me get that for you," Kyla said, bringing over the crystal decanter filled with the dark Chwisgi whiskey and pouring Bea's glass almost to the brim.

"What is it with men and discussing 'business' behind closed doors?" She asked rhetorically with air quotes. She picked up the bottle of wine. "We all know we ladies are the true brains around here."

Kyla pulled the sliding door that opened out to the balcony open, the howl of the wind poured in.

The rain fell hard outside, the balcony roof shielded them well from the cold water. However, it didn't do much to stifle the cold wind that blew in from the storm that bit at Bea's exposed skin. Kyla started the gas fire in the nearby pit much to Bea's relief. Bea pulled the sole blanket from the couch and offered it to Kyla.

"No thanks dear," Kyla said. "I'm fine."

"It's pretty cold out," commented Bea.

"I burn hot," Kyla said with a smile as she fished into her purse.

Bea wrapped the blanket around herself, she immediately smelled Cam on it. Memories of their last sexual foray underneath it ran rampant through her mind.

She didn't even realize that Kyla was watching her closely.

"My son likes you," Kyla said with a grin.

Bea nodded.

"And you him," Kyla continued.

"Oh yes," Bea said without even stopping to think of the answer. "I like Cam very much."

"I'm happy for you," Kyla said with studying eyes. "When I first met Morfran, well the world didn't quite care much about him. He was feared and mostly misunderstood."

She pulled out a cigarette.

"Do you mind?" Kyla asked.

"No, not at all," Bea replied. She did mind in fact, she hated the smell of cigarettes. Yet she agreed, unsure if it was the fact that Kyla was Cam's mother or that Kyla's gaze made her impossible to deny.

"You see Morfran has a strange gift," Kyla stated.

Bea's eyes grew wide, Kyla's cigarette was lit but she could not see a lighter. Perhaps it was just the dim light of the patio playing a trick on her eyes.

"He was cursed as a child," Kyla continued. "Cursed to some, a gift to others. He has the ability to predict the future, pretty accurately actually."

"Predict the future?" Bea repeated back to her.

"Oh yes, well not exactly," Kyla replied. "He's not always right, but he has a strong instinct as he calls it. You and I may call it intuition. But he always has a feeling on how things are going to end. You've probably noticed the same in Cam."

"He does have a strange way of knowing things, now that I think about it," Bea said.

"Exactly," said Kyla. "Like father, like son. When Morfran was a young man back in Wales, this made the people of his village quite afraid of him. That and his fearsome reputation as a soldier."

"What kind of reputation?" Bea asked.

"Well, it's hard to separate the facts from the rumors," Kyla clarified. "But let's just say that there was never a fight he didn't win by any means necessary."

"I see," Bea said. "What wars did he fight in?" She was still curious from dinner.

"Oh you know," Kyla commented. "The last ones that mattered."

They both laughed as Kyla took a puff from her cigarette.

A loud crash could be heard from the room nearby.

"Oh my," Bea said, startled. "What was that, are they ok?"

"I'm sure they're fine," Kyla replied calmly. "The boys will work it out in their own way I'm sure."

She took another puff from her cigarette and exhaled. The smoke seemed to move as if it had a mind of its own and swirled around Bea like a snake coiling around its prey.

Bea coughed.

She was amazed Kyla wasn't freezing to death. The wind and cold was blasting them on the balcony, and the woman wasn't shivering or showing any sign that she was feeling the winter's bite in the slightest.

The voices grew louder, Bea strained her ears to listen. She wasn't sure but it sounded like Morfran was yelling about the Germans' visit.

"So what are they talking about in there that is so heated?" Bea asked.

"This and that," Kyla responded. "I guess the visit from the Germans didn't go as swimmingly as we had all hoped. Though I applaud Cam for his resourcefulness, he does seem to have a knack for pulling through in tough situations."

"I'm not sure what you mean," Bea replied, confused.

Kyla laughed.

"Of course dear," Kyla said. "Why would you? Maybe some aspects of the business are better left for them to handle."

She leaned forward and squeezed Bea's knee playfully.

Immediately a jolt of electricity shot through Bea's body, the same jolt she felt sometimes when Cam touched her. Tingles of warmth and pleasure, mixed with the alcohol in her head it made her vision blur momentarily and her head swim.

What the hell was that?

Bea sat there befuddled.

Kayla removed her hand from Bea's knee and took another puff of her cigarette.

"I see what my son likes about you," she said with a smile. "You've got something, it's hard to understand, but it's something unique about you."

"What?" Bea answered, still trying to focus her thoughts once again.

"It's a conflict of sorts," Kyla clarified. "You straddle two worlds at once, one of the deacon's daughter, the other the mischief maker. One instinctual and suppressed. I'm sure it's quite difficult at times."

"I really don't know what you mean," Bea replied.

"Yes you do," Kyla said playfully. "You just don't want to admit it."

The voices from the library grew heated again, this time over another topic. They were still muffled but it sounded like they were discussing Bea.

Kyla leaned forward and flicked her cigarette into the fire.

"Come on," she said with a smile and held out a hand. "Let's get you inside, you'll catch your death with a chill out here."

They walked inside.

The door of the library had barely slammed shut when Morfran turned to Cam with a fuming expression.

"How dare you invite her?" he boomed loudly.

"Shhh," Cam said. "They'll hear."

"Let them," Morfran spoke loudly again.

"Drink anyone?" Harper asked as he made his way to the small bar set up in the corner.

Neither of the other men acknowledged him.

"I've grown tired of your arrogance," Morfran stated as he loomed large over Cam.

Cam seemed immune to the enormous man's foreboding frame. He turned calmly and walked around to the window. He looked out to peer at his mother and Bea sitting on the balcony.

"It's not arrogance, father," Cam said at last. "It's just good business. And it's been very lucrative for us I think."

"Lucrative?" Morfran replied angrily. "You call that stunt with the Germans good business? He was ready to take your head."

"But he didn't, did he?" Cam stated as he turned to face his father. "I know you've been doing this a lot longer than I, but the old ways...they just don't work anymore. Society has changed, the world has changed, the clientèle has changed."

Harper appeared at his side holding a crystal glass and handed it to Cam.

"The world has grown more sophisticated," Cam continued after taking a drink. "People don't want the generic, they want a more nuanced experience. If you go out to eat, you don't have to order what's exactly on the menu anymore. The best restaurants, the most successful ones, give the client exactly what they want, menu be damned. I believe we've been able to deliver that swimmingly thus far."

"Swimmingly, excellent word choice sir," Harper said as he began mixing another drink.

"Shut up, parrot," Morfran growled at Harper who shrunk away.

"I know it's hard to accept, father," Cam said. "I took your dying old business model and turned it into something that's more than quadrupled our clients. Not only that, I've created extremely loyal clients who come back year after year. It's not some airport deli where any old traveler passing through stops in, it's the most talked about and exclusive harvest in town now. Perhaps in the whole country."

Despite being shorter and much less bulky than Morfran, Cam stood facing his father with just a few feet separating them. He stood with all the confidence he was capable of mustering.

Harper approached and handed Morfran a drink.

Morfran reached with his enormous hand to take the glass and just stood there holding it staring at his son. His false silver eye burned with the same gaze as his good one.

"Most talked about..." Morfran growled.

Without warning the giant of a man threw the glass at the wall and it shattered into hundreds of shards that rained down on the carpet. The lamps began flickering in the room.

Harper hung back in the shadows, like a mouse trying fruitlessly to distance itself from a serpent in a cage.

Cam alone stood facing his angry father, unflinching.

"We have always operated out of the shadows youngling," Morfran boomed. "The shadows are where we live. The shadows keep us safe."

"But why?!" Cam yelled back. "Why must we live this life of solitude and seclusion?"

"You know why," Morfran replied through gritted teeth.

"This isn't the 17th century anymore," Cam said, his face showing no sign of a retreating nerve. "They embrace us now; our symbols, our idolatry, our wickedness. We are the mainstream, we are fools to not tap into it!"

"And what about the girl?" Morfran growled. "Bee, or Be-a, or whatever her damn name is. Does this deacon's daughter embrace all this?"

"Yes," Cam replied. "She has enjoyed it with me, and I with her."

Morfran narrowed his one good eye.

"I see," he began. "But does she see?"

"What do you mean?" Cam replied, his voice showing the first signs of doubt.

"Has she seen the real you?" Morfran asked, his mouth contorted into the most unsettling of grins.

"Yes, no," Cam stifled. "I mean, I think she doesn't care."

"Ha!" Morfran laughed, his hands slapping at his stomach. "She knows nothing, you have shown her nothing. Not of you, not of the real you. You think this mortal will still want you when she knows what you really are?"

"Yes, you hypocrite!" Cam shouted as anger boiled over into his face. "Were you not broken and fallen on the field of battle, facing your own extinction when mother saved you?"

Cam and Morfran's noses were inches from one another now, their fiery stares intense. Like two roman statues, they stood there silent, motionless. Neither wanting to be the first to flinch.

Suddenly, Morfran's gigantic arm swung forward and the back of his hand hit Cam squarely across the jaw. Cam didn't realize it until it was too late and found himself flying across the room and hitting a nearby wall.

"Extinction you mutter, boy?" Morfran said, stepping forward and leering over Cam.

"Do you even know how many men have tried to kill me?" Morfran growled. "Thousands, millions even. None have succeeded and none ever will. Their souls haunt the halls of the damned, their blood staining my hands, their screams falling upon deaf ears. I will not be defeated by them or by some arrogant welp eager to prove a worth beyond his capabilities."

Morfran's silver eye turned bright red, blood began to drip from it onto his cheek and then down onto Cam's nicely pressed shirt.

"Your shenanigans have cost us more dearly than you know," Morfran continued. "That girl out there has clearly clouded your judgment. Since when do we allow outsiders into our homes?"

"She's not some outsider," Cam exclaimed, wiping at the blood. "She's different, she's special."

"She's the daughter of a deacon," Morfran said, almost frothing at the mouth. "You think she's stupid? That she doesn't realize something is going on here?"

"She does, but I think she can be persuaded..." Cam pleaded.

"Persuaded? Ha!" Morfran's single laugh echoed in the room. "She's going to be the end of you. I have foreseen it."

"You're not always right, father," Cam said.

This only seemed to infuriate Morfran more.

"You have become delusional in your decadence, boy," Morfran yelled. "I will not see my empire demolished by such foolish actions of a juvenile."

"But father," Cam tried to say, his voice disappearing into a whisper.

"You will cease this foolish game at once," Morfran said. "Liquid the stock, sell the building, and re-establish operations overseas once again."

"Leave? You want us to leave?!" Cam couldn't believe it.

"Yes, this country corrupts all who enter it," Morfran beamed. "Including you. We will leave it and return to the homeland. Dunkler Peter..."

"What about him?" Cam interrupted, his voice shrill with fear.

"Dunkler Peter has graciously agreed to allow us a prominent foothold in Germany," Morfran began. "In exchange for what was promised."

"He got what was promised..." said Cam.

"You delivered some pathetic creature to him," Morfran continued. "Not what you had paraded in front of him. He's not pleased."

Cam was breathing heavily, fear in his eyes.

"I understand," Cam said. "We'll find a way to deliver. I'll make it right with Peter."

"You better," Morfran replied. "For if you do not, not even I can protect you."

Cam's expression morphed into one of terror, for he knew the power that Dunkler Peter held. The power to reward or the power to punish.

"We will begin making the preparations immediately," Cam said. "I'll move my plans forward for Bea..."

"She will not be joining us," Morfran growled.

"But..." Cam seemed to lose the words in his mouth.

"She will be liquidated like the rest," Morfran said, turning around.

"But, father," Cam pleaded.

"I have spoken," Morfran said, facing the door, his voice low and angry. "My orders will be obeyed."

"....Yes....sir," Cam said at last after a long pause.

"Harpier," Morfran growled. "Make me another drink and try not to muck it up this time."

Harper's face appeared from behind an armchair where he had been hiding.

"Right away sir," Harper said, his face almost white with fear.

Morfran's heavy footsteps echoed on the library walls as he left the room.

Kyla and Bea were laughing on the couch, Kyla sharing a story of Cam as a baby.

“You wouldn’t believe how ugly a child he was,” Kyla was saying.

“No way,” Bea said laughing. “I don’t believe it. Do you have any pictures?”

“Unfortunately no,” Kyla replied. “Wasn’t the fashion back then.”

Bea was startled when the enormous frame of Morfran emerged from the hallway.

"Mmmhmmm," he grunted as he stomped past and disappeared into the kitchen.

Bea looked back at Kyla who had turned pale.

"I better go check on him," Kyla said with feigned composure. "It's been lovely to meet you my dear."

She stood and Bea did as well.

Kyla hugged Bea tightly, Bea enjoying the seemingly genetic furnace of warmth that both Kyla and her son seemed to share.

"You too," Bea said, her head starting to swim from the whiskey.

She stood there quietly in the living room, swaying slightly in her drunken state when Cam and Harper appeared from the hallway.

Cam looked different, for one he had a bruise forming on his right cheek. Secondly and actually much more noticeable, was that his calm and cool demeanor was completely gone. He didn't look at Bea, didn't dare make eye contact. His eyes were affixed to the floor.

Harper hung at his side, Cam whispered something into his ear.

"Well love," Harper said, approaching her with her jacket. "Looks like tonight's over. Cam here has asked me to take you home."

"Home?" Bea looked up, confused.

"Yes, sorry," Harper continued for Cam who didn't make any motion to look or talk to her. "Everyone's a bit tired you see, jet lag and all."

"Ok..." Bea said as she was helped into her jacket.

Harper tried to lead her to the elevator.

"Cam, what's going on?" Bea said defiantly, stopping them in their tracks.

Cam didn't respond or acknowledge her.

"Come on," Harper said. "Best not to make a mess of these types of things you see."

"Cam, talk to me," Bea repeated, resisting Harper from leading her to the elevator.

"Just go," Cam growled quietly under his breath. It was a tone and voice Bea had never heard before.

"Cam, tell me," Bea pleaded. "What did I do wrong?"

"Just go!" Cam yelled loudly this time.

His voice boomed in the apartment, much like that of Morfran's.

"I don't," Bea said as being startled by Cam's loud yell momentarily broke her ability to stop the pulling of Harper. "Please...talk..."

Before she could speak another word, she was in the elevator with Harper and the doors were closed.

Harper let her go at last and leaned backwards against the wall.

"Tough luck, love," Harper said with a smile. "But I'll get you home safe and sound. Just need to stop at the club for a moment to drop something off."

"I don't want to go to the club, I want to talk to Cam," Bea said with tears pouring down her face.

"Don't you fuss now," Harper continued. "Everything will be alright."

The elevator doors opened and Harper led the stumbling and crying Bea out towards the front door.

"Ms. Logan!" Clarence exclaimed, jumping up from his post at the sight of Bea crying. "What's wrong?"

"Nothing's wrong," Harper said for her, as she tried to speak through the tears. "Just a little too much to drink. I'll be taking her home now."

"Ms. Logan," Clarence repeated standing up. "Are you sur..."

"She's fine, mind ya business," Harper said sternly.

"Ahh Ms. Logan," Thomas said, appearing from the door. "Your car is here for you."

"What?" Harper exclaimed in confusion.

"The car she ordered," Thomas clarified confidently. "It's waiting outside."

"No need, I'll be taking her home," Harper said, pulling her arm.

Instead of opening the door for them, Thomas stood still.

"The car is waiting for her," Thomas repeated. "For just her."

He blocked the exit, arms wrapped in front of him. Though his nature thus far had been sweet and friendly, he was glaring at Harper with fiery defiance.

"What is this?" Harper asked aloud. "I'm taking her home."

"Let me help you to your car Ms. Logan," Thomas said, ignoring Harper.

Bea rushed to Thomas, Harper reached to try and grasp at her arm but Clarence had grabbed his shoulder, holding him out of reach.

“Let go of me you...” was the last thing she heard Harper say as the lobby door closed behind her. Thomas opened the door to a black SUV and guided her inside.

"What, why, I don't..." Bea stammered.

"This car will take you home," Thomas said. "We'll make sure he doesn't follow."

"Th...th...thank you," Bea said, her makeup running down her cheeks from the tears.

"Stay away, Ms. Logan," Thomas said as he took a step back onto the curb.

The rain was pouring, water beaded on his bald head. "Just stay away, please. For your own good."

He closed the door.

The driver took off in the night and before she knew it, the lights of downtown were small and distant.

PART THREE

Chapter Fifteen

It was Saturday, and even though the sun was just starting to creep in through her bedroom's drapes, she had been awake for hours staring at her phone. Still no new texts.

It had been a week, and for what felt like the thousandth time she felt the tears swell in her eyes and her emotions of heartbreak take over. When it would pass, her pillow would be soaked.

Final exams were over and Christmas break on campus had officially begun. That meant many of the students had started to depart to return to their homes and a general aura of eerie silence had descended on the university.

That same mood seemed to extend into Bea and Mal's house. Bea could count on one hand the amount of times she had actually seen Mal in the last week, and each time Mal was in too much of a hurry to stop and chat. Bea's texts and calls went unanswered, it was like Mal was cutting her out of her life.

What was worse was that Bea wasn't sure what she had done wrong.

Was it because Mal had opened up to Bea and spilled her dark secrets at their little retreat together? Not that Mal had any reason to be embarrassed, her secrets were safe with Bea regardless of their friend status.

Or maybe it was because she and Cam were officially over. Mal did say that Cam was one of her oldest friends. When people break up, they end up having to divide friends like kids in a divorce, right?

Except you don't have any friends left anymore.

Bea hated when the voice was right.

Except...maybe the voice wasn't this time.

She picked up her phone and hit the button marked NEW MESSAGE.

Bea nervously twirled the wooden stirrer in her cup of coffee. She had ordered it black from the barista, so there weren't exactly any ingredients to mix but the action seemed to make her feel better.

She was nervous, would they show?

Bea hadn't spoken to another adult other than Professor Mikkelson in over a week, and even then that conversation was strictly professional. He had asked for a fresh copy of her thesis for him to read and make notes on over winter break. She had provided it, and then he left. Off to his home, to his family, not to speak to her again until the new year.

She had called home of course, but her mother and father hadn't called her back yet. They were typically busy at this time of year with church activities: planning Christmas Eve Mass, putting up decorations, planning nativity plays. Bea couldn't help but feel resentment at their seeming purposeful and deliberate neglect of her, just weeks after she revealed to them her terminal diagnosis.

The wooden stirrer fell to the table, splattering a small amount of coffee onto the lacquered surface accordingly. She grabbed at her hand that was twitching uncontrollably and looked around nervously. No one noticed, no one cared. Her loneliness only compounded.

She's not coming.

Bea looked at her phone, no response to the text she had sent several hours ago.

What was she thinking? She wouldn't show, they didn't care about her. No one did. And in a few years, if her Huntington's continued to degrade at this rate, she would die alone in a hospital. With no one to talk to, no one to hold her, and no one who cared about her. Maybe her parents might be there.

Maybe not.

She began to pack up her things into her purse. She was being stupid, she was being naive.

"Hey," said a familiar voice from behind her.

Bea spun around in her chair excitedly.

Viv was standing there, staring nervously at the ground. She wore dark black jeans and a black jacket with the hoodie covering her head. However Bea immediately recognized those dark eyes under the hood.

"You made it," Bea said standing up.

Viv joined her.

"Ya, I guess I did," she replied.

"I was worried that you didn't..." Bea began to say.

"I've been here awhile," Viv said, sitting down. "I just wanted to make sure someone wasn't following you."

"Why? Why would that..." Bea's voice trailed off. She quickly realized what Viv was worried about.

"So I'm guessing you've realized it too," Viv stated, fumbling nervously with a napkin on the table in front of her.

“Kind of,” Bea began. "I met Cam's parents and.."

"His parents?" Viv interrupted her. "What were they like?"

Bea thought for a moment.

"Well his mother was elegant," she began. "And beautiful. His father was not a nice person. I think you were right about the club."

Viv's eyes lit up.

"I was?" Viv asked aloud.

"Yes," Bea replied. "Something is wrong there, but I don't think it's Cam. I think it's his father."

“Bea,” Viv said with an exasperated breath. “If there’s anything wrong with the club, Cam is in on it. Perhaps even orchestrating it. You know this.”

"Well," Bea took another sip of her coffee. "Nothing is for certain, but it just seemed like his dad was forcing him to do something he didn't want to do."

"I see," Viv said with narrow eyes. "What about Mal?"

"I don't know," Bea said.

"She's a bitch," Viv replied. "Of course she's involved."

"I think she's nice," commented Bea. "If you only got to know her..."

"Jesus, Bea," Viv exclaimed. "Don't you get it? These rich fucks aren't your friends. They want something from you, something they think their money, houses, and flashy cars can buy. Mal, Cam, his parents...they aren't good people."

Bea felt the tears try to force their way forward but she took a deep breath and held them at bay.

Silence overtook the table like a pesky fog that would blow away in a slight breeze but resettle as soon as the air had calmed.

"So are you and Cam still," Viv asked tentatively. "You know, seeing each other?"

"We haven't spoken since Harper tried to..." Bea trailed off, she wasn't sure how to explain it.

"Harper tried to do what?" Viv asked.

"Harper tried to kidnap me I think," Bea managed to say aloud. Something about saying the ridiculous thought lifted a weight off her heart immediately.

"Have you spoken to the police about it?" questioned Viv, she was growing curious.

"No, there's nothing I can say that's concrete," Bea replied. "He said he was just going to take me home, but..."

"You knew better," Viv finished the statement.

Bea stared at her coffee cup, the memories of that night at Cam's apartment flooding back and clouding her thoughts.

They both sat in silence for a moment.

"What does Mal have to say?" Viv asked with a snooty tone.

"She's not really talking to me either," said Bea.

"Have you thought about going home for the break?" Viv asked. "Get a break from this place, a break from living with that queen b..."

"My parents," Bea stopped her. "They haven't replied back to me about anything. Not since I told them about it."

Her voice trailed off.

"About what?" asked Viv with curiosity.

Bea wasn't sure how to say it.

"About being diagnosed with Huntington's," Bea said at last.

Viv's expression didn't change, she stared at Bea with blank eyes.

Bea wasn't sure if telling Viv about it made her feel better. She really barely knew this girl, they had exchanged superficial conversation at the club a few times. Saw each other at the library once but that didn't end well. And now she had told her two secrets in less than five minutes.

She thinks you're a psycho.

Bea crossed her arms and began to clutch at her elbows nervously. She wanted to run out of there, run back to her bedroom, ruin another pillowcase with wet mascara.

Viv reached across the table and rubbed Bea's arm, squeezing her.

"I'm sorry Bea," Viv said with sad eyes. "I didn't know."

Bea let out a whimper, the touch of another human after a week of utter loneliness somehow melted away her sadness.

"No one did, really," Bea answered, the weight lifting off of her chest. "It was kind of my secret."

"From what I know about Huntington's," Viv continued. "You still have plenty of years left to enjoy life. It won't really hit you until you're in your late thirties or forties, right?"

"That's the thing, though," Bea interjected. "I feel...older."

"Older?" Viv repeated.

"I feel like I'm actually getting older more quickly," Bea continued. "It's been hard to sleep, I have tremors, the muscle spasms are so bad I can barely hold a pen. The doctor doesn't believe me, he thinks it's psychological. That somehow because I know I have it now I'm manifesting this. But it's not just that. My muscles ache more, I have wrinkles, even my hair is graying."

Viv stared at her for a long moment.

"I know," Bea started again. "You must think I'm crazy."

"No, I don't," Viv replied, stopping her.

Viv leaned over and rolled up the leg of her jeans.

Bea's eyes grew wide. On the pale skin of Viv's bare calf was a purplish spider web of blood vessels clearly visible.

"My mom had varicose veins," Viv said before pulling her jean leg back down to cover it. "My doctor thinks I must have developed them early. But for three generations of women in my family, they all got it after their 45th birthday. I'm not even 23 yet."

Bea retreated into her own thoughts, not sure how to respond.

"Something about that place," Viv continued. "Something about Club Llithium is making us older. I don't know if it's drugs in the drinks, radiation, whatever. But it's happening. And there's only one way to find out the truth. We've got to go back and find some real evidence. Let's find it and bring it to the police. Let's bring those fuckers down."

"I don't know if I can go back," Bea said.

Indeed, returning to Club Llithium was the last thing she wanted to do.

"You must," Viv stated.

"I'm sorry Viv," Bea explained. "But I just can't. It's too much, I can't see him again. Plus, what if something happens to us? Can't we just call the cops, let them deal with it?"

"I already tried Bea," Viv exclaimed. "After the Germans came to town, I was pissed off. I called the police and told them they were putting GHB in the girls' drinks at the bar. They went to the club, searched the place, and found nothing."

"Well, that explains it then," Bea replied. "If the cops looked into it, then there's probably nothing going on. It's all in our heads."

Viv leaned back and crossed her arms disapprovingly.

"But I guess," Bea said aloud after her mind had taken a moment to think. "It's an old building, there are dozens of passageways and rooms. There was a door in the entrance hallway. I noticed the night we met the Germans, it's blocked by a mirror most nights. The cops wouldn't know to look for it if they had covered it back up."

"See, now we're talking," Viv said, leaning forward and putting her elbows on the table.

They both jumped as Bea's phone suddenly buzzed, the vibration causing it to slide away on the table. It must have been just as afraid of the plan they were hatching as she was.

Bea reached for it instantly and answered without even looking to see who it was.

"Hello," she said into the receiver.

The voice on the other line spoke.

"No, I haven't seen her," Bea said with growing concern in her eyes.

The voice continued.

"No sign at all?" Bea asked. "Have you tried her parents? Any of her boyfriends?"

The voice spoke frantically.

"Of course, if I hear anything from her you'll be the first to know," Bea stated.

Viv's eyes were narrow, watching and listening closely.

"Bye," Bea said as she hung up the phone.

"What was that about?" Viv asked with fierce curiosity.

Bea just sat in silence thinking.

"Hello? Earth to Bea?" Viv asked.

"What? Oh," Bea exclaimed, regaining her focus on the moment. "That was...um...Heather from campus housing about my old roommate, Tess. She missed her finals."

"Oh," Viv replied. "Party girl? Likely to drop out?"

"Yes, but," Bea paused. "Last time I saw her was at the club."

Viv's eyes grew wide.

"Something's definitely wrong," Bea said. "We should go tonight."

"Now we're talking," Viv replied with a mischievous smile.

They spent the next hour at the coffee shop, planning what they were going to do next.

Later that evening, the driver pulled up to the old church building and let them out. It was cold outside, Viv and Bea's jackets doing little to warm them from the brisk night air. They hurried to the side alley where the usual crowd of people waited in the long line to get into the club. As they had many times before, the two ladies ran to the front of the line where the bouncers diligently stood guard.

"Can I help you?" Marshall asked when they arrived at the door. He seemed to be in a sour mood tonight, not his usual self.

"It's us Marshall," said Viv as she smiled at him. "Let us in, it's freezing outside."

"Where's Mal?" Marshall asked, looking around for their usual ring leader.

"She's running late," Viv replied. "But our Uber already dropped us off. Please let us in, it's cold."

"I don't know," Marshall replied. "I'm supposed to not let anyone in unless Mal's with them."

"Come on Marshall," Viv said, sliding the zipper of her jacket down six inches . "As you can see I'm shivering."

Marshall's eyes grew wide.

"Yeah, um," Marshall stammered, seemingly embarrassed at being caught ogling Viv's breasts. "Go on in."

He stood aside.

As they walked through the warm hallway filled with the mirrors, Bea turned to Viv.

"I wasn't sure that was going to work," Bea said.

"Men," Viv replied. "As predictable as ever."

They both laughed.

"Now where was that door?" Viv asked, slowing to study the mirrors on the wall.

"It was dark," Bea stammered. She frantically studied the hall and tried to recall exactly where the opening had been.

"Here I think," Bea said at last.

Viv stepped beside her, and together they stood before a massive, intricately adorned mirror. The frame was carved with figures the entire length, demonic monsters feasting on men trying to flee into pits of fire.

"Creepy," Viv said.

Viv was the first to act, she pulled at the mirror but it didn't budge.

"Let me help?" Bea asked.

Bea joined her and together they pulled and pushed on it with all their strength, but it remained affixed tight to the wall.

"You sure there's a door here?" Viv asked.

Bea suddenly felt filled with doubt.

"I mean not 100 percent," Bea said nervously. "I thought I saw one."

"Well if it's here it's locked tight," Viv said, turning around.

"Check this out," Bea exclaimed. "No smudges."

Viv turned back to the mirror, "Ya they probably cleaned it."

"No I mean," Bea said curiously before continuing. "We were just pushing and pulling on the mirror glass. There's no fingerprints or anything on the mirror."

"So what?" Viv asked.

"It's just strange I guess," Bea commented aloud.

"Come on," Viv said. "I think there's a door by the stage that leads to the back rooms. We should try to sneak into that."

Bea stared at the mirror a second longer before turning and joining Viv as they walked back toward the double doors from where the loud booms of music were faintly emanating.

"Ma'am, your bag?" The man at the coach asked her.

"No thanks," Bea replied. "Going to keep it to myself."

"Suit yourself," he said before handing her a ticket for her jacket.

Though she was no longer cold, her outfit was not something she would ever have imagined wearing in public. Viv had looked online and found out that the night's theme at the club had been announced as a Lingerie Party. So both were dressed in their skimpiest and sexiest lingerie. Bea in a pink bra and lace panties that Mal had given her, Viv was head to toe in black lace.

Are you sure this was a good idea?

No, Bea wasn't sure. She had been so caught up in trying to figure out what was going on at the club, she hadn't stopped to think about what would actually happen tonight. What would happen if she saw Cam for the first time since their breakup?

When you see Cam you mean. She tried to hush the voice.

Bea and Viv had planned for the eventuality of course, but it was still just a plan in her head. Execution would be another story.

Bea was relieved when she realized almost everyone else in the club was dressed in similar attire.

Most of the men wore tight boxers that left nothing to the imagination. The women meanwhile wore a more diverse array of undergarments. Chemises, babydolls, teddies, corsets, and bustiers. Many also donning matching garter belts and hosiery. A few even wore body stockings that were practically see through. Most of them were items Bea had only seen on websites that she had clicked on "by mistake."

Bea glanced over to the right, where their usual table was and confirmed it was empty. No one else from Mal's group had arrived yet.

"There's that rat," Viv muttered with a snarl.

Bea looked over to see a shirtless Harper throwing bottles into the air and pouring drinks at the bar. His bird tattoos seemed to flutter as he did his well-choreographed bartending routine. Several women were watching intently and uttering "ooooh"s and "ahhhh"s.

"Quick, before he sees us," Bea said, grabbing Viv's arm and dashing out of sight to the far side of the club where the crowd of patrons blocked them from the line of sight of the bar.

"When I get my hands on him," Viv uttered with clenched fists.

"Remember why we are here," Bea reminded her.

"I know," Viv said through her gritted teeth.

They found a secluded spot next to a table that had a good view, scanning the large space carefully.

"There's the door," Viv said, pointing to the left of the stage.

Bea spotted it as well.

"Shit, they have someone guarding it," Bea said.

A large doorman stood in front of a curtained opening.

"Hello ladies," said an unfamiliar voice from behind them.

Both Viv and Bea froze.

Slowly they both turned with looks of terror at who it might be.

Then they both let out a sigh of relief, the person addressing them was no one they recognized.

The man was about Bea's height. He had spiked hair with frosted tips and faint stubble on his chin. Without a shirt it was rather obvious that he was an obsessive weightlifter. His pectorals and biceps were clearly over-developed, likely from years of focusing only on the muscle groups that men think attracts women. The look of disgust on Bea and Viv's faces clearly proved that theory wrong.

"How are you two hotties doing tonight?" he said. Based on the slurred speech and his flushed cheeks, he was clearly very drunk.

"Fine, until you showed up," Viv replied with a frown.

"Whoa, no need to be rude," the man said. "I'm Frank. You guys want a drink?"

"No, tha..." Bea began to say.

"Yes, please," Viv said, moving to the side. "Right now, two martinis. There's a bartender, right there. Go."

She pointed over Frank's shoulder to Harper who had appeared at a nearby table to deliver drinks.

"You got it," Frank began to walk towards Harper, who hadn't noticed them yet, then Frank stopped.

"What are your names?" he said, turning around.

"Pam and Peggy," Viv said quickly. "Drinks, go now."

"Cool," Frank said as he walked away.

Viv grabbed Bea's arm and rushed to cover behind a nearby group of people taking shots. Peering from around them to watch as Frank approached Harper.

"I hate his fake smile," Viv said. Bea could practically feel the anger in Viv boiling over.

"Why do you hate him so much?" Bea asked.

"You mean other than the fact that he was likely going to kidnap me and tried to kidnap you?" Viv asked sarcastically.

Bea gulped.

She's got a point.

"You know how many times he flirted with me?" Viv said after a while. "He brought me cool drinks, he gave me sly looks, he treated me differently than the rest of the girls. All that time I thought it was because he liked me."

Bea listened attentively.

"And it was all bullshit," she snarled. "Just fake bullshit to make me trust him so that he could take me into whatever crazy shit this place is into. That's why I hate him. He made me feel special, but I wasn't."

Bea couldn't help but feel there was more to it, but this was neither the time nor the place.

"He's coming back," said Viv and they moved out from behind the group of club goers as Harper turned to walk back to the bar.

"What an asshole," Frank commented as he approached. "Said I was too drunk for him to bring me booze. Does he even know who I am? My dad, he could buy this whole place in an instant."

"Yeah whatever," Viv said, content that Frank's usefulness had run its course. "Piss off then."

"Screw you, too," Frank said, turning. "There's a million bitches in this place who want a piece of Frank."

He wandered off into the crowd.

Viv and Bea both let out a collective groan. Turning back to the curtained door, they hoped for an opportunity to enter the mysterious backrooms.

"Doesn't this guy ever have to pee?" Viv asked aloud.

"Seriously," Bea replied in agreement.

"Well, I have to pee," Viv said. "Keep an eye out till I get back?"

"Sure," Bea said, nodding.

Viv walked away.

Bea continued her vigilant watch but found herself distracted by the nearby dance floor.

Bea couldn't help but remind herself that she had been out there just a few months ago. Dancing with Adelaide, the alcohol in her bloodstream driving her thoughts and actions. It had been fun, that was for certain, but it had also been something else to her: hollow. The partying, the booze, it was always fun in the moment. The next day though, it was always a different story.

How many people waste away their nights in places like this? Drop out of school, cheat on a partner, cause irreversible damage to their bodies. It was like they were exchanging some part of themselves in order to get that short-term moment of bliss their everyday lives couldn't provide them. It made Bea sad, to think how many lives would be better spent giving back to the world and society around them instead of wasting away in places like this.

Several members of the crowd didn't fit in with the rest. They weren't clumsily dancing, they moved seamlessly and carefully. Their eyes reflected the lights that illuminated the dance floor, flashing white.

One dancer in particular was a woman with jet black hair and black lingerie. Black wings were attached to the back strap. She was watching the crowd at first then she seemed to narrow in on one individual in particular, Frank. She moved so smoothly that she appeared to glide towards him as he danced drunkenly by himself.

Bea watched as they exchanged greetings, the woman's seductive smile seemed to snare Frank instantly. Before long they were dancing together, Frank doing his best to grind his crotch against the woman. She however didn't seem to mind, in fact she was moving her body in a way that seemed to urge him on.

The longer they danced like this, the more excited Frank seemed to become. Until at one last moment he seemed to jerk his body up uncontrollably and the blood drained from his face. The woman seemed content with him at that point, she turned and kissed him lightly on the cheek before walking away and disappearing into the crowd. Frank staggered to the nearest wall and leaned up against it. He seemed heavily labored by the whole ordeal.

"Bea?" said an all too familiar voice behind her causing her to jump.

She turned, knowing that she was about to face the exact moment she had been dreading the entire evening.

Cam stood there, a perplexed look on his face. He wore jeans and a blazer with a white t-shirt underneath.

"Hi," she managed to say, preferring to stare at the floor rather than look into the eyes of the man she still felt a lot of strong feelings for.

"I didn't think," Cam started before reconsidering his comment. "I couldn't imagine you'd come back here after everything that happened the other night."

"I know," Bea replied. "I wasn't planning on coming back. There was something I needed to do before I left."

She fished into her bag and pulled out a large dusty tome. It was the *Filii Diaboli* that she had borrowed from him. She looked at it a moment before holding it out for him.

"I wanted to give this back to you," she said.

Cam just stared at her and the book for a moment.

"I don't know what to say," he said after a long moment. "You didn't have to return it. You could have given it to the library or sold it for millions of dollars."

"I know," Bea replied. "But I wanted to do what was right. It doesn't belong to me."

"What about your thesis," Cam asked.

"I'll write a new one," said Bea through held back tears.

Cam held out his hand and grasped the book.

They both looked at each other, both holding the book for a long moment. Then Bea released her grasp and Cam took it.

"Thank you," he said with uncharacteristic humility. His eyes were studying her intensely.

He turned to walk away before stopping mid-stride.

"This is why you are here tonight?" Cam asked, staring her straight in the eyes.

Bea did her best to force a smile.

"Yes, I just wanted to give it back before I went home on break," Bea tried hard to tell a convincing lie.

Cam just continued to stare, then his eyes narrowed.

"Very well then," he said in a cold and distant voice.

"Goodbye Cam," Bea said.

Cam didn't reply, he just nodded and walked away.

As soon as he was out of sight, Bea placed her hand over her mouth to stifle a desire to begin sobbing uncontrollably. She wanted to leave, run away from there. Run back home.

Viv appeared.

"Sorry it took so long," Viv began. "The line was... what's wrong?"

Bea took a deep breath and tried to calm herself down.

"Oh shit," Viv said. "Was it him? Did you give him the book?"

Bea managed to nod in reply.

Viv hugged her tightly.

"I'm sorry," Viv said, trying to comfort her.

They hugged for the moment but then Viv's voice grew frantic.

"That means we don't have much time," Viv said. "Do you still want to find out what they were doing here? Why did they try to take us?"

Bea took a deep breath and wiped away the tears streaming down her face. She nodded.

"Then we need to hurry," Viv said. She scanned the crowd intently, looking for any ideas. Then she saw him, Frank was still resting with his hand on the wall trying to compose himself.

"I've got an idea," Viv said. "Follow my lead."

Together they approached Frank but as they got closer Bea noticed he looked different. It wasn't just the paleness of his face, but several subtle gray hairs that had formed around his sideburns. Maybe she just hadn't noticed before, but Bea just couldn't help but feel like Frank, who was so obsessed with his looks, wouldn't go out to a club like this without trying to mask any signs of his age. It was definitely peculiar.

"How's it going Frank?" Viv asked him.

Frank seemed startled by their sudden appearance and immediately tried to stand up straight and flex his muscles tightly for them.

"Oh, um, hi Pam? Or was it Peggy?" Frank asked as he wiped sweat from his forehead.

"So is it true?" Viv asked, ignoring his question.

"Is what true?" Frank said with a perplexed look.

"Well you see that guy over there?" Viv pointed to a random man on the edge of the dance floor who was talking to several very attractive women.

"Yeah, so what? Looks like some scrawny pussy to me," Frank said with bravado.

"Well we overhead him telling those girls," Viv began. "That he saw you blowing some guy in the bathroom."

"What? I would never," Frank said very defensively.

"Yeah, well that's what he was telling them," Viv continued. "He said he thinks you're gay."

"I am not gay!" Frank said with growing anger in his voice.

"I mean," Viv took a step closer to Frank. "I don't think you're gay." She traced a finger across his chest and down to his abdomen before pulling away suddenly. Frank seemed momentarily entranced.

"But if I was you," Viv remarked. "I wouldn't be too happy to have someone telling everyone that you blow dudes. Unless you actually do."

The comment seemed to only throw gasoline on the fire that was burning across Frank's face.

"I absolutely do not," Frank practically yelled. "I'll show him."

Frank stomped towards the dancefloor.

"This is your plan?" Bea asked as soon as Frank was out of earshot.

"When the clock is running out," Viv replied. "Sometimes you just gotta throw the Hail Mary."

Viv winked.

The chaos that ensued was exactly what they needed.

Frank ended up throwing the first punch, but in his inebriated state he only managed to stumble forward and knock the drink out of the man's hand that sprayed all over the nearby women. They screamed in response, and before long Frank and the stranger were entangled in one another on the floor wildly flailing around.

"Bingo," Viv said.

Bea saw it too, the guard at the door immediately rushed forward to try and break up the fight.

"Let's go," Viv said, and Bea followed her through the doorway.

Please don't get caught, please don't get caught, please don't get caught.

Bea had never snuck in anywhere in her life, trespassing being a sin that her parents' endless quoting of Leviticus had warned her plenty about. They moved fast and the lights of the club blurred as the curtain that concealed the doorway whooshed around her. However it ended in a moment, as if she had passed through a portal into a completely different world.

The loud music was muted inside the dimly lit corridor, only a few incandescent light bulbs hanging from the ceiling showing them the way forward.

"Where are we?" asked Bea out loud.

"Shhh," Viv hushed her. "Do you want to be caught?"

"No, I just," Bea began.

"Shhh!" Viv hushed her louder.

Slowly they crept down the hallway, the fearless Viv leading the way.

This was crazy. Bea wasn't even sure what they were looking for.

On their right was a door. On it was a placard that said MANAGER.

Viv put her hand on the doorknob and looked back at Bea.

They both nodded to one another and with a turn of the knob pushed their way into the office.

Shutting the door behind them, they stopped to breathe.

Much to their relief, the office was empty. The walls of the room were bare brick, no pictures or paintings. There was very little furniture. A single desk sat in the center of the room, scratched up and old. It was out of place compared to the immaculate decor of the nightclub interior. In front of it were some plastic chairs. The leather chair behind it was torn at places, tilting awkwardly to one side.

"Are you sure we are in his office?" Bea asked as they separated to look around.

Viv leaned over the desk and began to read the loose papers, turning through them frantically.

"I think so," she remarked. "His name is on these invoices."

"What are they for?" asked Bea.

"Liquor license paperwork," Viv began to read them off. "Invoices for alcohol, tax paperwork, and more and more bills. Shit, nothing here."

"Well I don't think he'd leave anything incriminating just sitting in the open right?" said Bea.

"You're right," Viv replied.

She started rummaging through the drawers of the desk.

"Aha," Viv said after arriving at the last drawer. "This one's locked. It's got to be it."

"How are we going to get in?" Bea asked.

Viv reached into her bra and pulled out a small slim object.

With a click, a switchblade knife sprung forward from her hand.

"Always come prepared," Viv said with a smile.

Bea was impressed.

Viv wedged the blade into the gap in the locked drawer and began to pry it open. She tried for several minutes before at last...

"Got it!" she exclaimed.

Bea was growing nervous. How long had they been in there? Long enough to break up the fight? Long enough for the guard to return to his post? How long before Cam would go back to his office?

"We've gotta get out of here," Bea said, stepping away. An ominous feeling of dread began to overtake her.

"Just chill," Viv said as she reached into the drawer and retrieved a small jewelry box.

Setting it on the top of the desk and opening it, her eyes grew wide.

"Holy shit," Viv exclaimed.

"What is it?" Bea asked fearfully.

Viv slowly lifted a small metallic object out of the box and unfurled a pendant necklace which hung between Viv's hands. The pendant was blue and green, and depicted a creature that Bea recognized at once. A Nixie.

"Why would he have Adelaide's necklace?" Viv asked aloud.

"I don't know," Bea replied.

"Unless he was behind what happened to her," Viv stated.

"But how, she died of natural causes," Bea stated.

"I don't know, but there's tons of other jewelry in here," Viv said, putting the necklace back into the box and closing it. "There must be others like her. Is it enough to go to the police with?"

Bea was still thinking, trying to process how this could have happened. Could Cam have killed Adelaide and done something to make it appear natural? If he did, why? And why keep the necklace? The box was full of other pieces, were they all trophies from his victims? Was he a serial killer?

The questions swirled in her head.

"Hey Bea!" Viv exclaimed. "We've got to go, gotta find a way out of here."

Bea managed to grunt in the affirmative.

Viv walked to the door and put her hand on the knob.

"As soon as I open the door," Viv said. "Be prepared to run. We're going to run for the nearest exit and keep going until we are far away from here."

Bea nodded.

"Ok," Viv said. "One, two, three."

She swung open the door.

Blocking her way were three silhouettes.

Two very tall bouncers including Marshall stood on each side, and in the middle...

"Hello love," Harper said, stepping forward.

"Fucker!" Viv yelled, she tried to kick Harper in the crotch, but before she could she was grabbed and lifted off the ground.

"Ain't gonna get away with that shit again I tell ya," Harper said with a snarky smile.

"Bea, run!" Viv yelled as she struggled and kicked futilely.

Bea looked for somewhere, anywhere to go. But the room had only one door and there was nowhere for her to escape to.

"And you," Harper said, turning to Bea. "Boss said I'd find you back here snooping around."

Bea began to cry, Harper and the other bouncer approached slowly. Each flanking her on a side, she had no way to escape.

"Dear, dear," Harper said mockingly. "You should save some tears for later."

Bea looked up at him.

"You'll need 'em," he said, smiling down at her.

She wanted to scream.

His eyes had turned completely black.

Chapter Sixteen

Outside the Village of Aberdaron, Wales.
Year of our Lord 537 AD

Morfran's horse slunk to the ground and died. He had been riding the chestnut mare for three days straight without rest or food and its last bit of will had been spent.

"Pathetic," Morfran spat on the creature's corpse as it lay on the side of the crude road just outside the village.

It was another one hundred yards to where the little wooden houses of Aberdaron seemed to sprout from the oceanside clifftop.

He adjusted the battle ax strapped to his back and slung the pack containing his armor and provisions across his back; it was heavy and the worn leather straps relented as they stretched. Much like the horse, Morfran had pushed the pack to the length of its endurance yet still asked for more. He would have to find new ones in the village, both a pack and a horse.

He marched forward.

The gray sky over Wales had been an ominous presence for over a year, the sun peaking through on only the most blessed of days. The limited light that did make its way to the frozen ground had a bluish hue. Seasons no longer existed, when it should have been summer, it was winter. When it was winter, it felt like Hell hath frozen over. Many of the crops had died, food was scarce, and the king was in France hunting his bride and her lover, one of his knights with whom she had run off. Times were dark.

It was August and the clouds were shedding thin flakes of snow that turned immediately to gray water upon landing. It made his clothes damp.

But Morfran didn't mind the cold, he never had. Not since he was a boy and his father had left him outside on a winter night in hopes of being rid of him once and for all. Morfran had endured, his father had not.

The path quickly turning to mud, Morfran increased his pace.

As he ventured into the village, it appeared abandoned. None of its inhabitants ventured out from the comfort of their ever-burning hearths, the sole refuge from the relentless winds that assailed the cliffside town.

Morfran smelled death.

The body of a dog lay under the porch of a home. Either frozen or already succumbed to rigor mortis, Morfran could not tell. The flies feasted regardless.

It was a good time to be a woodcutter or a carrion-feeder.

The wood sign for the inn flapped in the wind, Morfran did not bother to read its name. He entered and found a scene very different from the exterior.

The room was bright and warm, a large bonfire in the center was burning with full magnificence. It had been piled high with several freshly cut logs.

Around the tables sat various townspeople and travelers, discernible by their dirty faces and baggy clothes that masked their thinning and malnourished bodies. They sat in silence and drank wooden mugs of thick brown ale, their eyes lifelessly staring at the spectacle in the back corner of the room.

It was there that half a dozen knights sat at a long table cheering and making merriment with several ladies of ill-repute. They wore pristine white tabards with brilliantly colorful house crests embroidered on them. Some still wore their chain mail, untarnished and sparkling in the firelight. All had scabbards hanging from their waists, concealing their deadly weapons of war.

They cackled with laughter, making jokes and challenging each other to feats of revelry. They chugged their mugs of ale and threw spare bits of food at each other, some falling to the ground where a cat or dog would quickly leap forward to devour and fight over them.

Morfran sat at an empty table on the opposite side of the inn, though he was also a fellow knight and soldier in Arthur's army he had no desire to mingle with those of noble and prominent families. Not that they would accept his company either.

The barkeep approached him and dropped a mug of ale at the table. Morfran looked up to ask him how much but the man took one look at him and scampered away without asking for payment.

Morfran was thirsty.

He drank the entire mug all at once. Not because he liked it though, he detested the mud-like flavor and consistency. He yearned for something stronger, something that acted faster to help him sleep.

Someone was watching him.

He peered from under his dark brow at the knights. None had noticed him enter, but one of the girls they were playing games with had. She might have been the most beautiful woman he had ever seen. She was tall and thin, with long golden locks of hair that stretched down her back. Her skin was perfect, immaculately smooth. But it was her eyes that were most remarkable, emerald green jewels that struck you with their gaze.

Morfran had been used to the cold, he had lived in it his entire life. It didn't bother him. But her gaze filled his body with a warmth he had long forgotten. It filled him with thoughts of her body on his, the impossible entwinement of their limbs.

A knight moved in front of her and their line of sight was broken.

Morfran felt his body drain immediately, the lonely bitter cold returned.

He returned his focus to his empty mug of ale.

Why would she be staring at him? She was a prostitute after all, maybe she saw him as an easy mark for business.

Morfran had traveled all over Wales, approaching countless women of the night like her; all had rejected him. His coin purse bulged with gold like many soldiers of fortune did, yet no amount of gold was enough to compensate a woman for a night alone with him. His features were apparently too grotesque to withstand even in the pitch black of night. A blind whore had once turned him down.

Most babies at birth are ugly, their parents ignore this and swoon over even the most ill-formed of child with confidence that as they grow the features would reshape into more desirable forms. Morfran had been the exception, an ugly newborn that grew into more of a monstrosity with each passing of the seasons. He had been born with only one eye, his head was shaped like a block of stone, his hair was dark and bushy even at a very young age and his cry was like the wailing of a goat more than of a human.

As a grown man, this served as an advantage on the battlefield. Many opponents were so put-off by his appearance that they were distracted in battle, some had turned and ran at his very approach. His broadaxe eventually found them all, ending their lives, whetting his appetite for revenge on humanity, and filling his pockets.

But this woman at the bar had not merely glanced at him like he was a freak oddity of nature. She had not stared at him in horror. She had watched him closely, with eyes that betrayed more than just mild curiosity.

Morfran pushed the thoughts from his mind as the barkeep returned with two more mugs of ale.

Morfran sat and drank in silence until he felt eyes on him again, this time they were different. They were accompanied by the clinking of chain mail and the dragging of a longsword scabbard across the wooden floor.

He began to reach for his broadaxe propped against the table.

"I come in peace dear warrior," a voice said behind him.

Morfran held his hand on the pommel, knowing better to trust a voice he did not know.

A knight dressed in white appeared from his side and proceeded to take a seat at Morfran's table facing him.

He was young, couldn't have been more than a boy of seventeen. The embroidery of his tabard was gold and red, his family crest featuring both an Eagle and a Lion's head. He was handsome, but of course anyone was when compared to Morfran.

"Sir Morfran, right?" The boy asked. His eyes twinkled with fool's courage.

"Just Morfran," Morfran replied. "The king has bestowed upon me the title of knight, but I have yet to be granted a presence for the ceremony."

"A pity," the boy replied, smiling. "I am Sir Valurhart, son of Lord Bedwyr."

Morfran didn't respond, he drank from his mug.

"I bet you are wondering how I know you," Valurhart stated.

Morfran grunted.

"I was at Badon," the boy continued. "I was only a squire then but I got to watch the battle with my own eyes. You left quite an impression."

The ale from the mug spilled down Morfran's beard and drips fell to the table.

"Was it ten or fifteen men I counted you slaying on the field that day?" Valurhart asked.

Morfran looked up at him.

"Twenty-seven," he said.

"Twenty-seven, amazing," Valurhart repeated. "I believe it, you and that ax of yours were quite a sight to behold."

The boy had begun to reach for the handle, Morfran followed his hand with his eyes.

"Careful boy," Morfran snarled.

"Right," Valurhart said, recoiling his hand. "You know what we called you right? After the battle?"

"What?" Morfran asked with his social patience growing thin.

"The Butcher of Badon," Valurhart said smiling.

Morfran grunted.

"I hope to get my own chance soon," Valurhart continued. He awkwardly fondled at the hilt of the longsword on his belt, like a boy who had just become an adolescent.

Sir Valurhart paused then leaned in close and began to speak in almost a whisper.

"You know the king's returning, right?" he said softly.

Morfran glanced around, none of the villagers nearby were listening. When you had nothing in life, secrets of over-privileged knights were of no value.

"Arthur is in France," Morfran replied, not bothering to whisper. "He's still chasing after that fool Lancelot and his whore Guinevere."

"No, no," Valurhart replied, growing excited. "Mordred has pronounced himself king. Arthur is on his way back from France right now, ready to rouse an army of his loyal knights to usurp his brother-son."

Morfran was skeptical.

"So what about you?" Valurhart asked.

"What about what?" Morfran replied.

"Which side will you be fighting on?" the boy said. "The infamous Morfran, who's never fallen on the field of battle. Whose foes tremble in terror at the mere sight of him. Whose ax has tasted the blood of hundreds of men. Who will you side with, King Arthur or the would-be King Mordred?"

"Whoever will pay more," Morfran replied as he finished the last of his mug.

Lord Valurhart seemed taken aback for a moment, then something perked up in his eyes.

Morfran felt it too, someone was approaching from behind him. He heard no footsteps or creaks from the rotted hollow floorboards, he heard no scraping of burlap clothes or shoes either. Whomever approached, approached silently, as if they were floating through the air like a wisp.

Morfran felt the warmth return as the beautiful whore who had locked eyes on him earlier appeared next to them.

"Oh my," exclaimed Sir Valurhart. "Such an elegant beauty."

"Hello dear knight," the woman replied in a supple and seductive voice.

Morfran kept his head down and his eyes fixed on his drinking mug. He did not dare risk scaring the woman away with his ugliness. He enjoyed her presence immensely, even if her attention was on the pretty and young knight.

"My lady," Valurhart continued, his voice growing excited and short of breath. "I would be honored if you would lie with me tonight for you are by far the prettiest woman in all of Wales, nay all of Britain."

"The prettiest?" The woman said playfully. "I can't just lie with anyone then, can I?"

"I am not a mere anyone," the boy boasted. "I am Sir Valurhart, son of Lord Bedwyr, heir to vast lands and a brilliant keep to call my own."

"Hmmm," the woman said with an unimpressed tone.

Sir Valurhart seemed flustered but undeterred. Standing, he reached for his belt and unhooked his coin purse, dropping it onto the table. The pinging sound of hundreds of gold coins filled the air of the room. Several desperately poor villagers looked over, their eyes reflecting the bulging purse that was easily more money than they had ever seen before in their lives.

"I'm rich as you see," Valurhart continued. "I can pay, handsomely."

"Oh dear," the woman said, feigning distress. "I'm afraid I'm already spoken for this evening."

"By who?" Valurhart exclaimed. "I will challenge whomever they are for the right to a night with a lady as exquisite as yourself. Point me in their direction, no man can stand before me in battle."

"Why Sir Morfran of course," the woman said.

Morfran's ears perked.

Sir Valurhart's chest deflated and his eyes drooped.

"I'm sure you are mistaken," he began to speak, his voice trembling.

"I am not," the woman replied. She took the empty seat between Morfran and Valurhart. "However, if you would like to spar with the Butcher of Badon, that would be quite entertaining."

Valurhart seemed to weigh his chances in his head. His mind was occupied in a tug-of-war between his brain and his balls.

Fortunately for Lord and Lady Bedwyr, their son chose the former.

As Sir Valurhart retreated back to his knight friends who hollered and cajoled at him as he approached, Morfran did not dare look up and into the eyes of the gorgeous damsel that sat next to him. She was a delicate flower, that he worried even the slightest breath of his might cause to wither and wilt into nothingness.

"Youth is wasted on the young," the woman said, her voice like silk. "Do you agree, Sir Knight?"

"I'm not a sir, I was..." Morfran began.

"I know," she interrupted him. "You were never formally knighted by the King."

Something brushed Morfran's beard, something completely unexpected. He thought at first it was an insect of some sort that had attempted to nest in his beard, but it did not flail like it was caught in a web. It was her hand, soft and smooth. She was stroking his coarse dark beard, attempting to soothe him.

Morfran, son of no one important, Butcher of Badon, a knight so ugly many an enemy thought him a demon, was trembling.

"I... can... pay," he managed to sputter out as he reached for his coin purse.

"That won't be necessary," the woman replied. "I am Kyla."

"Kyla," Morfran repeated slowly. "Where are you from?"

"Somewhere very far away," she replied.

Then he did the one thing that he had been torturing himself by holding back for not doing already. He looked into her eyes.

The gaze penetrated him in ways he could not imagine.

They spent that night together, locked in a lover's embrace. And the next night. And the next night.

It was on the eighth night together that Morfran snored in a deep sleep, Kyla's naked body wrapped around him tightly like an octopus holding onto its prey.

He awoke with a start, sitting up so suddenly that Kyla was nearly thrown to the floor.

"What is it my dear?" Kyla said recovering.

"I saw, I saw," Morfran struggled to find the words.

"What did you see?" Kyla asked, drawing close to him.

"I saw King Arthur," Morfran began, his chest rising and falling in heavy breaths. "His crown lay in the mud, split in two. An ax stuck out from his skull. My ax."

"Your ax?" Kyla exclaimed.

"Yes," Morfran replied. "I was standing on the battlefield, surrounded by dead bodies. The lone survivor of a battle, a river running nearby, dyed red with blood."

Morfran fell silent, afraid that his horrific vision would scare her away where his ugliness had not.

"Was this a dream?" Kyla asked, not sounding afraid at all.

"I don't know," Morfran replied. "It didn't feel like one. My dreams are filled with fog, I saw this clear as I see you now."

They laid in bed another hour, she asked him question after question about his vision. She wanted more detail than he wanted to provide, but there was no rejecting her inquiries. Her soft voice could make him do anything she asked. It lingered in his head after she spoke, whispering at his thoughts over and over again.

They were interrupted by a loud knock at the door.

Morfran went to answer it, naked except for his battle ax in hand.

"What is it?" Morfran said angrily as he opened the door.

A trembling boy stood before him, he was a squire.

"Sir Morfran," he said with a mouse-like voice.

"Not sir," Morfran snarled.

The boy yelped and recoiled a step.

"I've been told to fetch you," the squire continued using whatever courage he could muster.

"Fetch me for what?" Morfran asked. "I do not like being interrupted."

Morfran began to close the door.

"It's the King sir," the squire yelped. "King Arthur has returned."

Morfran stopped and stared at the boy.

"He's mustering his knights," the boy sputtered out. "He's asked for you specifically. They are assembling on the road to Cornwall. Mordred is marching."

"Will he pay?" Morfran asked with a booming voice.

"Yes, handsomely," the squire said, his eyes fixed on the ground.

"Stay here," Morfran said, returning inside and shutting the door behind him.

He quickly began rummaging through his pack, putting on his clothes and armor. Kyla watched naked from the bed.

"You are going," she said softly.

"Yes, to battle," Morfran replied.

"With Arthur?" she asked.

"Yes," Morfran said as his voice trailed away. The vivid memory of his vision running through his mind.

"Will you return?" She asked.

Morfran paused to look at her.

"It is not assured," was all he could manage to answer. He finished putting on his armor. The familiar iron heavy on his shoulders and chest.

He thought for a moment.

"Marry me," he said flatly to the beautiful woman still warm in their bed.

"Marry you?" She answered with a question. "You are about to go to war, perhaps never to return."

"Marry me anyways," he said.

She fell silent as she thought about his proposal.

"No," she said at last.

Morfran looked at her for a moment before standing and opening the door. The squire was still standing there, afraid to move.

"What are you still doing here?" Morfran boomed. "Find me a horse and a new pack for my belongings."

The boy shrieked as he ran out of view.

Morfran turned back to Kyla.

"You will marry me," he said, stepping through the threshold. "Upon my return."

He closed the door and was gone.

Most women would have cried at their lover's departure. Most women would have chased after him seeking one last moment together before their likely death in battle. Kyla was not most women.

She lay back in their bed, still heavy with the fragrance of their love making and grinned.

What would be known as the Battle of Camlam was quickly taking shape. Mordred's forces had assembled opposite Arthur's. Lines of peasants holding spears had begun to organize on the field. Huntsmen with their bows stood close behind them ready to rain death upon the charging opponents. The beautiful river Camblam flanked the soon to be scene of slaughter, its blue water like a pure spring of hope below the eternally gray sky above.

Morfran assembled with the other knights on horseback, he had long shaken the pre-battle jitters. His blood burned hot and began to boil in his veins, his grip on his ax tightened, and the iron armor felt like an extension of his own skin. Yet today it was different, he carried something else with him into battle.

A voice, a sweetly elegant voice lingered in his mind. It spoke softly in a language Morfran did not know, and yet, he understood. He did his best to ignore it, but with each beat of the war drum it grew louder, thundering in every part of his being.

When the battle commenced, Morfran charged in with the other knights like he had at Badon, like he had at countless nameless battles before. His ax swung through the air with elegant purpose, simultaneously crushing and slashing anyone stupid enough to not move out of its path.

Despite his success, the battle raged as an even contest. Corpses with the colors of both Mordred and Arthur were strewn across the field; blood, guts, and shards of bone forming a swamp-like ground that squished and crunched under the feet of warriors still battling.

Morfran did not care, he knew only one thing at that moment: pure, unending, unquenchable, rage.

It wasn't until he had killed every living thing around him that he stopped to observe the aftermath. The field had almost cleared but neither army had retreated. Instead, only a sparse handful of soldiers on both sides were engaged in hand-to-hand combat with one another.

The silhouettes of two figures stood out on a hilltop against the red-tinted setting sun quickly retreating behind the mountains. Morfran approached, hungry for more battle and bored at the lull in violence.

However, he stopped as he got close. Upon the head of the two soldiers were not typical helms. They were both adorned with beautiful gold crowns. One that Morfran did not recognize and one that Morfran had fought alongside many times .

Arthur and Mordred, the last men standing of their once mighty armies were dueling to the death. No doubt the final death in the battle that would signify the end to another war in Britain for the title of King. It wasn't the first, and it would not be the last.

Morfran considered stepping forward to help Arthur, his king and employer. However the voice in his head was louder than ever, and it stopped his ax from joining the fray. Instead he watched.

Both Kings were exhausted.

Their blows glanced off each other's armor, neither able to wield enough force to puncture the thick forged iron. They both moved slowly, like they were stuck in a thick mire and each step took insurmountable energy.

Mordred however was the younger of the two, and his strength won out. With a mighty swing, he knocked Arthur's legendary sword Excalibur from his hands. It landed with a thud at Morfran's feet.

Arthur reeled back and fell onto the ground near a pile of soldiers' corpses.

Morfran kneeled down to try and retrieve the mighty King's weapon, but everytime he grasped the hilt of Excalibur it slipped through his fingers like they were coated in thick oil. He eventually gave up, his ax anyways.

Mordred yelled as he charged forward with his sword high above his head, ready to swing it down onto Arthur's defenseless head.

Youth may have speed and strength, but age will always breed more cunning.

At the last moment, Arthur brought up a fallen soldier's spear that had been discarded on the ground.

It caught Mordred square in the eye, impaling his face. However, it had not been enough to stop Mordred's thrust and the false King's sword had found the weak spot in Arthur's armor, embedding itself in the King's shoulder. Blood sprayed from both men and mingled in the soil.

Mordred's body slunk and fell to the side, the battle was over and Arthur had won.

There was no one there to celebrate, no one there to cheer. Arthur himself lay on the ground spitting blood and cursing.

Morfran approached, he should give aid to the King.

But he did not.

The voice in his head told him something else entirely.

Morfran stood above King Arthur holding his ax.

The man below him, the person who all in the land answered to and revered as a near god lay before him. Tears ran down the poor bastard's face, he alternated between cursing and crying out for his dear Guinevere.

Morfran knew the look in King Arthur's eyes. He had seen it countless times in battle, it was the helpless realization that death approached. The reaper sows all in the end.

You are that reaper, a voice sang to him.

Morfran raised his ax, Arthur's eyes flashed with fear. He begged for mercy. The King of Britain begged Morfran, son of no one important, Butcher of Badon, a knight so ugly many an enemy thought him a demon; begged for mercy and the right to live.

Morfran did not believe in such a thing.

It was over quickly, Morfran's appetite for blood finally satisfied as the crown of the King lay in two on the ground. His ax had sunk deep into Arthur's skull, the King's eyes no longer showing fear or anything for that matter.

He removed his ax and faced the rest of the battlefield. Those who had not died yet lay in agony, wishing they had followed their brothers into the afterlife. He stood alone, the river Camblam ran red with the blood of the soldiers.

However, something else watched him from the other riverbank. A purple mist had formed and a figure stood in it, but it was no man nor woman. It was a creature unlike any Morfran had ever seen before. It had horns on its head, large glistening teeth, and numerous tentacles that danced and swayed. However, Morfran did not fear it, he did not run away from it. For the creature's striking emerald green eyes watched him closely.

A sound was forming in the still air, it started softly at first but grew only stronger as the last light of the sun faded.

The creature was singing to him, it was singing him a love song. It was in no tongue he knew, but he again understood the meaning of it immediately. He took one step forward, then another.

He walked through the red river Camblam, his armor and clothes turning crimson as he became soaked in the blood of thousands of men. He walked and he walked until he was engulfed in the mist.

If anyone had been left alive to watch, they would have seen the creature's tentacles ensnarl him as he gave himself up willingly to it.

Bea felt groggy as her eyes opened.

She was in a run-down room with no windows and only a single door. The walls were red brick and the only light emanated from two small candles sitting on the ground. Large globules of melted wax forming at their bases.

"Bea, are you awake?" a voice said in the dim light.

"Who's there?" Bea asked, the voice sounded familiar.

"It's me, Viv," said her friend.

Bea could see the silhouette of Viv strapped to an old wooden wheelchair nearby.

Bea looked down to realize that she was in a similar state, she struggled against her restraints.

"I'm so glad you're awake," Viv said with slight relief in her voice.

"Where are we?" Bea asked.

"Somewhere under the club," Viv replied. "I think at least. I just woke up here, same as you."

"Are you alright?" Bea asked.

"Other than being kidnapped and strapped to this old piece of shit chair?" Viv said sarcastically. "Just peachy."

Loud footsteps could be heard coming from the door.

"Someone's coming," Viv whispered.

"What do we do?" Bea asked.

"I don't know, I'll think of something," Viv said.

They both stared helplessly while the handle on the door turned slowly and then opened inward.

"Right this way sir," said a familiar voice.

A monstrous silhouette stood in the doorway. As he came into the glow of the candlelight, they could see he was a man or at least man-like. He wore a sleeveless doublet and dark linen pants that hid tufts of thick dark that covered him from neck to foot. The iron chain around his waist jingled with each step, a cane and several hooks hung from it. His feet were not feet at all, but large cloven hooves like that of a goat. On his head was a tophat that required him to crouch so that he could clear the doorway without knocking it off.

Dunkler Peter had returned.

He was not wearing sunglasses like he had been when they had first met him, though they wished he was. His eyes glowed orange and red, burning like a smoldering bonfire. Their gaze unmistakably focused on Viv.

Behind him another figure emerged, this one small and petite. A woman wearing a silver cocktail dress. It was Mal.

"Told you that you wouldn't be disappointed," she said with a perkiness voice.

"You fucking bitch!" Viv yelled at the top of her lungs.

She struggled and tried to jostle free of her restraints, but she only managed to cause the wooden wheelchair to creak and wobble.

Mal watched from the doorway, ignoring Viv's cries as Peter stepped forward.

He looked down at her with ferocious eyes. A large hand with long sharp fingernails stroked Viv's face.

Viv tilted her neck as far as she could stretch.

Peter grunted loudly, not sounding like a man, but more like the grunt of a bear or wild boar.

He grabbed Viv by the cheekbones. She tried to scream but her mouth was smothered by Peter's palm. The claws dug into the flesh of her cheeks. Streaks of red blood ran down the jawline and began to drip from her chin.

"Shhhh," Peter said, his other clawed finger pursing his lips.

He leaned in closer to Viv until his face was right in front of hers.

He removed his tophat, and Bea could see two ashy horns sitting on his bushy scalp.

"What the hell are you?" Bea shouted.

Peter ignored her. His focus remained completely on Viv who was frozen and motionless in his grip, her tears tinting red as they mixed with the blood running down her cheeks.

With a guttural growl, a long snake-like tongue emerged from Peter's mouth. It twirled and twisted violently in the air then lapped at the bloody tears, smearing them.

Peter seemed to grow excited, his breathing grew faster and heavier as it engulfed Viv's face with each exhale.

Mal noticed it too.

"Now, now sir," Mal said, stepping forward and placing a hand on his shoulder. "It's not time yet. No need to rush."

Peter's tongue retracted back into his mouth and he let out a deep growl in defiance.

"You have no reason to be concerned," Mal said with a calm voice. "Sometimes waiting just makes it all the sweeter."

Peter grunted in frustration before standing up and releasing Viv from his grasp.

"Soon," said a twisted and unnatural voice.

"They have a special room prepared for you downstairs," Mal said, taking him by the arm. "Let me escort you. You're going to have such a good time, we guarantee it."

He ducked through the doorway and disappeared into the darkness of the hallway.

"See you ladies soon," Mal said with a wink as she closed the door behind them.

"Oh my God," Bea said with a gasp. "What was that? Are you ok?"

Viv sat in her chair nearby, her head down, her breathing shallow.

"Viv, stay with me," Bea pleaded. "I'm right here."

Silence was Viv's only response.

"We'll find a way out of here," Bea said, trying her best to be positive. "We just need to..."

"He showed me things," Viv said as her voice cracked. Her fierce eyes hidden by her dark bangs, droplets of blood falling onto her lap.

"Showed you things?" Bea asked.

"He showed me what he would do to me," Viv replied, trembling. "How he would hurt me, over and over again. It was like living in a nightmare, I felt everything."

"I'm sorry," Bea pleaded. "We have to think about how we are going to..."

"He showed me what happened," Viv continued, not listening. "What I did."

"It doesn't matter," said Bea.

Viv's stare looked past Bea, through the walls, towards some distant far off horizon where the memories and visions seemed to play through her mind.

Viv sobs deepened.

"I don't know what he is," Viv said in a close whisper. "But I saw what he wanted. He wants me, to punish me, for what I did."

"Is he a demon?" Bea asked, it was the only thing she could think of that made sense.

"No," Viv replied. "He was a man once, a long time ago. I sensed it in him, but he's changed into something else."

They both looked up as the sounds of footsteps approaching echoed from the door. It sounded like the clopping of hooves on the stone floor.

"Shit," Viv said aloud. "He's coming back. Coming back for me."

"We won't let him take you," Bea said with no idea if it was even possible.

The footsteps stopped just outside the room and the handle turned.

Viv braced herself, ready for the worst.

The door opened, the darkness of the hallway looming on the other side of the threshold.

However, the faint silhouette wasn't large and ominous like Peter's.

It was Mal, she entered with her high heels clopping on the stone floor.

"You," Viv snarled. "You dare come back in here after,"

"Shhh," Mal said quickly. "They'll hear."

"Let them," Viv said without bothering to lower her voice. "Let them know I'm not going to let them lay a finger on me. Not without a fight."

"Can you just shut the fuck up for once in your life, Viv?" Mal exclaimed. "You don't get it. They can do whatever they want to you. We've got to get you out of here."

Mal started tugging on the ropes securing Viv to the chair.

"What is this? A trick?" Viv asked.

"No, all of us," Mal replied. "We need to get away before they come back."

Bea watched Mal, her eyes and facial expressions weren't their usual calm and collected self. She looked sad and worried, like she did when they had talked at the spa.

"No way, I don't trust you," Viv continued. "This is just another trick to get our hopes up before..."

"Viv," Bea said, interrupting her. "I think Mal's trying to help us."

Viv looked at Bea as if her head were upside down on her shoulders.

"Be quiet," Mal said nervously. "These nails make untying these knots almost impossible. We don't have much time."

They let her work.

“Shit,” Mal exclaimed.

“What is it?” Bea asked with concern.

“I broke a nail,” Mal replied.

Viv’s face contorted into an angry scowl.

“You better get me out of...” she stopped as the rope fell loose to the floor.

"Thanks, I guess," Viv said as she rubbed her wrists where the ropes had bruised them. "I still don't trust you."

Mal moved to Bea's chair and did the same.

"You don't have to trust me," Mal said quickly. "You just have to run."

Bea, free from her restraints, couldn't help herself any longer. She wrapped her arms around Mal and hugged her tight.

"Thank you," Bea whispered in her ear.

"No," Mal replied. "This is my fault. I have to set it right."

Neither wanted to let go of the other.

"If you two don’t mind, I’d like to get the hell out of here right now," Viv said from the doorway.

Bea and Mal separated reluctantly, Bea noticed Mal’s eyes had formed bags and her makeup had mixed with tears.

But it wasn’t just that, her nose had changed as well.

"Mal," Bea said with alarm. "Your face, what's happening to it?"

"I'll be fine," Mal said, turning away before Bea could get a better look. "Quick, follow me."

Mal plunged forward and was engulfed in the darkness of the hallway. Viv and Bea quickly followed.

"Not sure how you sneak out in high heels," Viv remarked as they crept. "It sounds like the Kentucky Derby here."

Mal sighed and reached down to unclasp the straps of her shoes.

"They're all I brought," she said, slipping both shoes off and leaving them on the floor.

"Where are we?" Bea asked.

"Deep under the church," Mal replied.

"How deep?" asked Viv.

"I don't know exactly," said Mal as they walked. "But really deep."

They wandered forward in a column. Each with a hand on the person in front of them so as to not lose each other in the darkness as Mal led them forward. A faint light from the yellowish glow of a candle formed at the end of the hallway.

"Those are the stairs," Mal whispered. "They lead up to the church and down to who knows where."

Bea noticed a metal door to their right.

"Where's that lead?" Bea asked.

"No idea," replied Mal. "This isn't the kind of place you explore for fun."

Bea tried to examine Mal's face again but she kept turning everytime Bea got close, purposely avoiding Bea.

They all stopped dead in their tracks as they heard voices forming, voices that echoed from the stairwell ahead of them.

"Shit, they're coming," Mal said.

"Can we outrun them?" Viv asked.

"I don't know," Mal replied, her nervousness evident in her voice.

"Well we better figure it out, they are almost here," Viv said.

"We can hide," Bea said. "If they come looking for us and we're gone, maybe they'll think we escaped and search for us outside. Then we'll have a chance to make a break for it."

The voices grew louder, loud enough to hear them speaking in a language Bea didn't recognize.

"What do we do?" Viv said aloud.

"In here," Bea said as she unlatched the metal door and slid it on its rusty bearings to the side.

"Shhh," Viv said frantically. "Quiet!"

"I'm trying," Bea said. The gap that had formed from the sliding door was dark, pitch black inside. "It won't stay open."

"That's wide enough, come on," Mal said.

Bea held the door open as best she could as Mal and Viv squeezed under her arms and into the side room. The voices from the stairwell were very loud, she pushed herself the rest of the way through the gap and the door slid shut behind them with thankfully a soft thud.

"Where are we?" Bea whispered.

"I don't know," Mal said in the darkness. "I can't see a thing."

Suddenly a small flame clicked into existence near them, it illuminated Viv's bloodied and scarred face.

"Where'd you get that?" Bea asked.

"Had it in my bra," Viv said nonchalantly.

Bea looked at Viv for a long moment.

"What?" Viv said defensively. "I like to sneak a smoke now and then."

"Thank God for your disgusting habit," Mal said.

She lingered just outside the range of the lighter's flame.

"Where are we anyway?" Viv asked, happy to change the subject.

"I don't know," Mal replied. "I've only been down here a few times."

"Ya," Viv said suddenly loudly. "What have you been doing down here? What is this place?"

"Calm down, Viv," Bea said defensively. "She did help us escape after all."

"Yeah, I know," replied Viv, taking a step forward towards Mal. Mal seemed to take a step backwards instinctively. "But we wouldn't be down here at all if it wasn't for her. I want to know what this place is."

"It's a really long story," Mal said with a stammer. "I'm not sure this is the best time to explain it all."

"She's right," Bea said. "We can figure that out after we get out of here and find the police."

"If we get out of here," Viv corrected her, taking another step.

Mal couldn't retreat this time, she was up against a wall and there was nowhere left to hide from Viv's lighter.

"I want to know right now what they are doing with all the girls," Viv stated.

"I swear," Mal exclaimed, hiding her face with her hands. "I didn't know exactly what was going on. I was just doing what I was told."

"Doing what you were told, huh?" Viv said with growing anger in her voice. "Sounds like bullshit to me."

"I really didn't know," Mal pleaded.

"Well I'm not taking another step," Viv stated, until you explain everything and it all makes sense to me. Seems like this place is some creepy perverted sex slave dungeon."

"It's not, it's..." Mal stammered.

"It's what?" Viv snarled.

"It's," Mal stammered again.

"It's what?" Viv practically yelled.

Suddenly something large fell from the ceiling and landed next to Viv, hitting the ground hard with a loud thud.

She fell backwards and dropped the lighter from her hand, they were plunged into utter darkness

Bea screamed and fell backwards.

"What was that?" Bea asked in a whisper.

"I don't know," Viv replied. "But it scared the shit out of me. Where'd my lighter go?"

"I got it," Bea said, feeling it on the ground beneath her fingertips. She flicked it back to life and the faint glow illuminated something lying on the ground at her feet.

"Oh my God," Viv exclaimed. "It's a body."

"Whose is it?" Bea asked.

Bea knelt closer to it. Whoever it was, was very thin. The limbs and torso were almost skeletal and wrapped in wrinkled, pale skin. Long white hair covered the face.

Viv lifted back the strands to reveal an old woman. Her eyes were open, but her pupils were dull and white.

"It's some old hag," Viv stated, letting the hair fall back over the woman's face.

"She looked familiar," Bea said, trying to think where she saw her before.

"Have you seen her around campus?" Viv asked. "Teacher or librarian, maybe?"

“I'm not sure," Bea replied. "Just something about her looks..."

"It's Tina," Mal stated, interrupting her.

"The blonde that never shuts up?" Viv asked.

"It can't be her," Bea commented. "This person looks older than my grandmother."

"Trust me," Mal said with shame in her voice. "It's her."

Viv took the lighter and held it close to the woman's face as she lifted the hair again.

"Holy crap," Viv said after a moment of intense studying of the woman's features. "It is her. Why does she look so old?"

Her voice trailed off. Both Viv and Bea looked up at Mal.

"What the hell is going on?" Viv asked for what felt like the hundredth time that night.

"I told you it's too much to explain here," Mal said from the edge of the light.

Viv rushed forward and pinned Mal to the wall.

"Viv, no!" Bea pleaded.

But Viv had already recoiled and released Mal, like she had seen a ghost.

"Oh my God Mal. Your face, it's," Viv said but couldn't find the words to finish her thought.

"Don't look at me," Mal covered her face with her hands.

Bea approached to get a closer look. The beautiful perfect model of beauty and fashion was gone, instead someone barely recognizable was cowering in her place. Her teeth had become crooked, her nose resembled the shape of a hawk's beak, and her hair was thin with dark brown roots.

"What happened to you?" Bea asked.

Mal whimpered a response.

A foreign sound penetrated the darkness.

"What was that?" Viv asked, looking around wildly for the source.

A loud heavy wheezing was steadily growing louder and it was accompanied by shuffling steps.

Viv frantically used the lighter to search the room for somewhere to hide.

Bea ran back towards the steel door they had entered from. Feeling with her hands for a handle or other way to slide it open, she found none. There was nothing to grip, they weren't going to be able to go out the way they came in.

"Over here," Viv whispered as she waved her arms in the dim light beckoning them over to a wooden table she had found pushed against one of the walls. Its surface was covered in what looked like blood and other body parts.

Beggars couldn't be choosers, and they scrambled under the table and huddled close to one another.

A door on the far side of the room opened, an orange glow emanating from inside it. The rectangular glow fell onto poor Tina's body, which lay over a rusted drain.

The light dimmed when something passed in front of it. Bea could hear the creature better than she could see it. Its breaths were heavy and labored like those of a man dying of pneumonia. They could only see its shadow, and whatever it was could barely fit its waist through the frame before it closed behind it.

However it didn't close all the way, a faint sliver of orange light shone through where it sat slightly ajar.

The creature moved to where Tina's body lay on the floor and stood above the corpse.

From where they hid, they could see it from the waist down. Its legs were round and the skin stretched against bulging calves that overtook where its ankles would have been. It did not wear shoes, its feet were human but with orange toenails that would make a nail technician shudder.

It wore an apron over the front of its body, stained with brown, black, and red streaks, which Bea was thankful for as it wore nothing underneath. One arm hung at its side but where a hand should have been, a butcher's cleaver had been crudely sewn to a stump at the end.

All three girls covered their mouths, stifling a scream, or risking even the slightest gasp alerting the creature to their presence.

What's it doing? Bea watched the creature intently.

All three of them jumped when the creature's other arm sprung forward and struck Tina's body.

Slowly it walked towards them, Tina's body dragging lifelessly behind it and a steady smear of blood trailing them.

Bea could feel the other two girls tense up as it approached. They all wanted to run, but with it just a few feet in front of them it would certainly see them.

It swung Tina's body onto the table, the wooden legs shook violently as the corpse landed with a loud thud. All three girls covered their mouths tight with their hands, again holding back screams.

The creature stood in front of the table, still wheezing heavily with each breath. Its other hand hung loosely at its side. Like the other arm, there was no hand but a meat hook hung down dripping blood.

The table above them began to bang over and over again as the creature's cleaver went to work on what was left of Tina. Bits of blood, brain, and bone splattered like rain all around them. The small pools of blood that formed gave way to small streams and rivers that ran like tributaries toward the center drain.

Bea looked over at the others, Mal's head was buried in her knees and far too afraid to face whatever had cornered them. Viv meanwhile was the opposite, she had found an old sliver of bone about the length of a ruler. One end of it had broken off at an angle forming a sharp point. It wasn't the same as having a firearm handy, but it was better than nothing.

They all jumped when Tina's head fell to the stone floor next to them, the old woman's face staring at them with dead eyes that Bea would never forget.

Bea began to panic.

The creature had stopped butchering Tina's body, crouching to retrieve the head when it suddenly froze.

The room was dead silent, the only sound being the sound of the creature's sniffing like a dog following the scent of its kill.

It was down on one knee now and its head was now in view, they were discovered.

Well they would have been, if the creature's eyes hadn't been sewn shut. Whatever it was it looked like it had been cobbled together like Frankenstein's monster.

It had no hair, just tufts of sparse fur on its otherwise bald head. On one side, a pig's ear had been stapled into the skull and on the other a dog's. Where a nose should have been, two gaping holes were all that were left. Its mouth was open and a forked tongue lapped at the air from a gap in the creature's black and crooked teeth.

Every second its face inched closer to them.

Bea pushed her body against the wall, futilely trying to put distance between her and this horrific butcher. Mal didn't dare look up and face it. Viv however, her eyes burned with the same ferocity and defiance that Bea had seen when she had stormed out of the club during the Germans visit.

Mal and Bea may have been afraid to act, but Viv was not.

"Die fucker," Viv screamed as she pierced the creature's neck with the wayward bone she had found.

It fell back immediately onto the floor, with a loud squeal, as putrid green liquid spurted from the hole in its neck.

"Hurry," Viv yelled over the squealing. "The door!"

Bea, still in shock, tumbled out from under the table with Mal close behind, and together they darted toward the strip of orange glow in the distance not knowing or caring what lay beyond it.

Viv was the first through it, however she came to a sudden and abrupt stop. Bea ran into her and would have been able to keep them both standing if not for Mal knocking into them and sending all three tumbling to the ground.

Temporarily stunned by hitting the ground, Bea's mind swirled. Putting her hand to her face she felt the wet trickle of blood from her nose. Her vision was blurred and foggy; she heard Viv groan next to her, and Mal whimpered.

The creature's screams were still faintly audible in the room behind them, but something else entirely now drew her attention.

A shadow loomed over her, a blurry dark mass outlined in brilliant orange light. She struggled under the weight of Mal to get back to her feet. The featureless face only grew closer, and closer, until it was right in front of hers.

"I understand why he liked you," said a deep gruff male voice. "You are tenacious."

Bea's eyes adjusted to the light and the man's face began to take shape. A black beard and scruffy hair, then an old scar running the length of the face, and a dead, silver eye; it was Morfran, Cam's father. He leered over her grinning with brown stained teeth.

Chapter Eighteen

The three girls shuffled along a dim stone corridor under the club. Their hands were chained together in iron shackles connected to a long chain leash. The rusted metal clinked and clanked out of rhythm as they moved, jagged edges cutting at their wrists. At their lead was Morfran, who for his own amusement would periodically tug on the line causing them to stumble forward.

The little light that did illuminate their march came from a few sparsely arranged candelabras, held to the wall by bronze fixtures that resembled human arms and hands. As they passed one, Bea thought she saw one slowly move to follow them with the light.

From cell-like doorways that they passed, glowing green eyes watched from the safety of the shadows; betraying both curiosity at the new captors of this dungeon but also recoiling in fear at the enormous man leading the procession.

Viv and Bea were still dressed in the attire they had arrived in, albeit now covered in a mixture of grime and blood. Whatever feelings of vulnerability Bea had felt wearing lingerie in front of strangers at the club was only intensified as the faceless eyes stared at her near naked body.

Mal was not spared the same treatment.

Morfran had stripped her of her silver cocktail dress, leaving her in expensive designer lingerie. Bea couldn't help but notice Mal's body had changed as significantly as her face had since their escape attempt had begun. Her hourglass figure was gone; large mounds of fatty cellulite had grown around her waist, hips, and stomach. Her skin had become freckled and she even looked shorter than Bea remembered.

The woman who had originally been perfect enough to be a fashion model had transformed into someone else entirely, someone very, very ordinary looking.

However it was Mal's eyes that may have transformed the most. They were brown and haggard looking with sunken bags underneath where tears had ruined her mascara. The sparkle of confidence and pride was no more, replaced by an agonizing fear of her fate.

Her spirit had been broken, whatever courage she had mustered to help them escape in the first place was spent, and Mal had given up all hope of ever leaving this place.

They reached ten-foot tall double doors at the end of the hallway and Morfran knocked three times, his immense fist like a battering ram trying to break through a castle gate.

The sound of gears and other machinery grinding emanated from the other side. As the door swung open slowly, Bea could see Harper was waiting for them on the other side.

Morfran grunted as he yanked on the chain, all three girls forced to lunge forward.

Viv was the first one through.

"I really am sorry about this, love," Harper said with a smile. "But ya know, orders are orders."

"Fuck you," Viv muttered.

"Was that an offer?" Harper replied with a laugh.

"In your wildest dreams maybe," Viv replied, Bea found it reassuring that she hadn't lost hope yet like Mal had.

"Or maybe yours?" Harper said as he winked at her.

She spat back at him but missed and it hit the floor.

Morfran grunted and Harper took a step away.

Bea thought she was hallucinating, for the vivid tattoos of birds that adorned his chest, back, and arms weren't static images. The birds moved, their wings flapping as they darted across his skin. It might have been just a trick of the light, but either way, she did not have time to linger.

Bea followed by Mal were the next into the room.

Expecting another low-ceiling, dungeon-like space, Bea was stunned to see ceilings thirty or forty feet high above her and painted from corner to corner in an intricate mural depicting imagery of angels and demons locked in some kind of voracious battle. At the center of the mural was a skylight, the bright full moon and stars visible high in the night sky.

The walls were rounded, giving the room a circular shape. They were lined with tall bookshelves that held an immense library of dusty tomes mixed with decaying human skulls. A bronze brazier in the center of the room, the only source of heat or light.

On the far end of the room, sat three raised platforms in front of a long banquet table with high-backed dining chairs extravagantly upholstered in a maroon and gold pattern. The tabletop was a single slab of marble, and it was covered in bowls, plates, utensils, and serving platters. All of which overflowed with steaming cuts of roasted meat.

Seated at the table were many Bea had seen before. Bea shouldn't have been surprised to see Cam and Kyla. Next to Cam sat the ominous Dunkler Peter, who was joined by his cronies, the rotund Druck, and the feeble Kurze. The remaining seats were occupied by those she presumed were other associates of the club like Dunkler Peter. Many were old and fat, with hungry eyes that watched as she, Mal and Viv were forcibly brought, half-naked into the room.

"What is this?" Viv asked as they grew nearer to the platforms.

"Dinner and a show," Morfran replied with a sinister tone of amusement.

Bea's growing fear was only stalled by the distraction of seeing Cam again. She studied his face as best she could through the flickering flames but she could read no reaction. No sign of emotion whatsoever. He was stone faced, staring at them as if they were nothing more than cattle being delivered to the slaughterhouse floor.

One by one, Harper separated the chain link that strung the three girls together and pulled them each to separate platforms where he fastened their shackles to an iron ring attached to the floor.

"What do you even want you motherfuckers?" screamed Viv, but no one responded or acknowledged her except Peter who's serpentine tongue wetted his lips.

Bea was the last one and after stepping onto her stone stage winced in pain as something sharp cut into her heel. She knelt to stem the squirting blood with her hand and saw what she had cut herself on. The platforms were indeed made of concrete, however instead of mixing it with gravel it had been made using human bones as the aggregate material that stabilized and strengthened it. A shard of femur was tinted red where it had cut her.

Bea's eyes were filled with tears, Cam's indifference to her plight stabbing at her heart worse than she could imagine. She looked away, searching for anything that would take her mind off of him.

Unfortunately, she got her wish.

Being this close to the table, she realized the feast laid out on the platters was not as it seemed. What she had thought was a leg of lamb, resembled a human thigh roasted on the bone and still steaming. The bowl of apples were actually human hearts, some still beating.

"I must say Cambion," Druck spoke while cutting into a large cut of meat on his plate. "This venison is just delightful. Can you tell me what type it is?"

"A chef never betrays his secrets," Cam replied calmly.

Cambion? Did he just refer to Cam as Cambion?

"No need to be so secretive my dear sir," Druck said.

"Don't keep the poor fellow in suspense my son," Kyla said.

For a moment, Bea swore she saw a nervous expression fly across Cam's face. But it was gone before she was sure exactly what to make of it.

"If you must know," Cam said, returning to his cool and calm demeanor. "It's Russian. The poor creature wandered into the club a few months ago, a ballerina now that I remember it."

"That explains the lack of fat," Druck said as he shoved another over-sized portion into his gaping mouth.

That meat looks familiar.

Cam glanced at Bea one more time, this time his apprehension was unmistakable.

It finally clicked in Bea's mind. It was exactly the dish that he had served her months ago.

Her stomach turned over immediately and she felt the desire to retch.

"Dear, dear!" The little Druck man was yelling at Bea. "Do you mind? I'm trying to eat here."

Bea looked up, feeling very pale.

Morfran took his seat between Cam and Kyla.

"I believe it is time for a toast," he bellowed, his voice projecting off the walls.

A large gold goblet sat in front of him at the table. It had white horns for handles and it was engraved with a wide arrangement of markings. He lifted it and a splash of dark red liquid spilled to the table.

"First, to our honored guests," he turned to Dunkler Peter and his entourage. "For centuries, we have brought you the finest entertainment and you have kept us well fed. Thank you, to many more centuries of fun and delight!"

The entire table raised their glasses, Peter grunted and the others cheered.

Morfran turned to Kyla.

"And to my wife," he continued. "When she chose me, I was merely a bloodthirsty lost soul on the corpse-littered fields of Camlann. She saw something more in me, a purpose that even I didn't know existed."

The table cheered again and Kyla nodded gracefully as she sipped at her goblet.

"And lastly," Morfran turned to Cam. "To my son Cambion. Though young and foolhardy at times."

Cam fidgeted in his chair.

"With this unique establishment," Morfran continued. "He showed an entrepreneurial spirit and vision that will doubtlessly provide valuable lessons in our next endeavor."

The group cheered once again, except for one.

Dunkler Peter did not raise his glass, he appeared most displeased at the speech.

"I must say," Druck said as the cheers subsided. "I found the establishment perfectly enjoyable."

A loud grunt of disapproval erupted from Peter, Druck immediately stopped speaking and guzzled at his drink instead.

Kyla seemed to grow alarmed at this, as she quickly nudged her husband.

"We understand your experience didn't go exactly as planned," Morfran added, sounding uncharacteristically nervous. "Though the substitution was less than satisfactory and the subsequent delay most unfortunate..."

The substitution, is he talking about Tess?

"As promised," Morfran's voice boomed with confidence again. "We have delivered on your original request and you are free to do as you wish with her."

Oh no.

Bea turned her head so she could see Viv.

Viv's fiery glare was gone. Her rebellious and contentious expression erased. All of it replaced by a look of utter terror. She was petrified, her body tensed in anticipation of a fate that had already been revealed to her.

Dunkler Peter rose slowly from the table as the rest of the guests grew quiet. The fire in the brazier magically followed suit, dimming to just a few glowing embers.

In the dim light, Bea could see his body dissolve into a foreboding cloud of thick, black fog that flowed over the table towards Viv. She could hear a voice coming from it, speaking a language that Bea did not know but found unnerving regardless.

Viv whimpered as she uselessly strained against the chains that bound her to the platform, afraid to look at what approached her.

When the onyx cloud had met the platform, the brazier burst back to light. A flame rose high into the air and temporarily blinded Bea.

When her eyes had readjusted, the cloud was gone as Peter stood leering over Viv.

Viv stared at Bea, tears in her eyes. The light of hope all but extinguished in them, except for one last sliver that still burned.

Viv swung her leg and kicked Peter in the crotch.

Peter let out a loud snort, but otherwise was unfazed.

He reached down and with savage glee, tore at her under garments with his sharp claws until she was left completely naked. The few remaining bits of clothing fluttered to the floor. Viv screamed as splatters of blood flew to the ground.

Peter removed what looked like a tree branch from the chain around his waist. Lifting it up and into the light, Bea shuddered to see that it was covered in gnarls and thorns.

Without warning, he swung it down hard and the snap of the branch whipped across Viv's bare thighs. She yelped and a dark streak of red painted the floor. Peter swung again and this time hit her across the ribs, where the thorns caught and tore at her flesh. Blood gushed as Peter continued to thrash her.

Viv's screams echoed on the walls, repeating an endless sound of torment that haunted Bea. Except Viv's mouth was closed, she wasn't screaming. Bea was the one screaming, unable to handle the horror of seeing her friend tortured and mutilated before her eyes.

Viv curled into a ball on the floor, Peter's whips slashing at her bare flesh until every inch of her body was soaked in her own blood.

He raised his hand to strike her again but paused, instead looking at her curiously.

Her weeping subsided, Viv had passed out from blood loss.

Bea noticed for the first time that the platform had grooves carved into the floors that routed the streams of blood towards a single point at the front. Here, Viv's blood drained steadily into a small wooden cask.

At least her suffering will be over soon. Bea realized that the cask was almost filled to the brim. No one could survive that.

Peter lowered his arm and fastened the blood stained switch back to his chain belt.

"Oh, I do love this part," Druck commented from the table; his eyes glistening with excitement watching the scene.

What worse could he do to her? Bea wished the thought never entered her mind.

Peter glanced sideways at her and grinned, as if he heard the voice too.

His clawed hand reached down and pulled Viv's head up by her hair. Her body lifted off the ground and soon her toes were dangling in the air. His face was only a few inches from hers, she held her eyes closed tight afraid to look at him.

"No, please no," whimpered the weakened Viv.

Peter emitted a satisfied grunt.

Without warning, the brazier erupted, this time spraying embers and bits of flame that spread on the ground. She expected the party at the table to express alarm, but none moved.

Bea could see why.

The wildfire on the floor was forming itself into the shape of a person, a little girl of six or seven years old. The rest of the flames danced and showed phantom images of a couch, a television, and a rug.

The little girl was watching something on the television, as several loud voices erupted from the crackling fire. The little girl turned, Bea could feel the girl's emotions. Fear and dread emanated from her like heat from the flame itself.

The fire had formed another shape, definitely masculine. Bea could feel his emotions as clear as the girls; anger, rage, and both fueled by a relentless self-loathing and feelings of inadequacy. He stomped up to the girl and grabbed her by the arm, dragging her away.

A fiery hand reached out to stop him, feminine and petite.

The man let go of the girl who fell to the ground.

The flaming man disappeared, his fire snuffed out like a match in water.

Just the girl remained, Bea examined her and with each passing moment felt something more familiar about her. It was her eyes.

As she focussed on them, Bea felt her body drift away from her. She felt like she was floating closer and closer towards the flames. Their light grew brighter, she shut her eyes against the intense burning but it did little to stifle it. She wanted to scream in pain until suddenly her whole world went dark.

When the burning ceased and she could open her eyes again, she was no longer in the room under the club. She was in a living room, on her knees, on the floor, while a nearby television played cartoons. It wasn't the house she had grown up in, it wasn't a house she had ever stepped inside before.

On the wall was a line of framed family photos, two parents and a dark-haired girl. The parents she couldn't recognize but the girl, she was sure by her eyes, was Viv.

She had somehow been transported to Viv's childhood home, and she knelt on the floor exactly where the little girl had been, which meant she was somehow seeing this through Viv's eyes.

There was no time to marvel at the mystical circumstance that had brought her there, a loud scream pierced the silence from the kitchen.

There the man stood, his chest rising and falling with each heavy breath like he had just ran a marathon. At his feet on the floor lay the body of a woman, her neck was twisted at an impossible angle. Bea knew the truth immediately this woman was dead, beaten to death at the hands of the rage-filled man. Her face was bruised and bloody, contorted into a horrific death scream but Bea recognized her regardless. It was the woman from the family photo, Viv's mother.

As the man turned to face her, she recognized him as well from the same photo.

If Bea had been in control, she would have screamed or cowered in fear, unable to muster enough courage to fight back. But Bea was not in control, Viv was running away from her father and Bea watched through her childhood eyes unable to stop her.

Viv dashed down a hallway, the heavy breaths of her father following her until at last she flung herself into her parents bedroom and slammed the door behind her before locking it.

Not a moment had passed before Viv's father slammed into the door which rattled on its hinges.

He screamed and yelled obscenities, then false promises of reconciliation, followed by lies that her mother was just sleeping and would be just fine in the morning. Viv believed none of it, and neither did Bea.

Bea would have called the cops, hid and hoped for the best. But she could still feel Viv's emotions as clear as if they were her own, and Viv had no desire to see her father in prison. She was angry, just like him. Her own rage fueled by the deep wound of seeing her mother's destroyed body on the ground. An image that was seared into her mind, never to be removed.

Viv's rage only fueled her action.

She went to work as her father continued yelling and banging on the door. First checking the bedside tables of their room, then the closet. Clothes were flying as she searched relentlessly for her father's firearm–protection or retaliation for killing her mother, it didn't matter now.

The screws on the door were beginning to fail, with each thump of her father's fists they gave way to more and more bend. It would not be long now before the door would no longer be an obstacle, no longer a separator between father and daughter. Viv only could think of one last place to look, feeling around in the gap between the mattress and the box spring she held out one last string of hope.

Then she found it.

She pulled it from its hiding place and gripped it tightly in her hands and shakily pointed it in the direction of the door.

Just in time, the door fell forward as the frame had given in at last.

Her father's silhouette against the hallway light stood in the door frame.

Except Bea saw in a blink of time, the silhouette of Peter, his orange eyes like two flames in the darkness of Viv's father's shadow.

The moment passed as a gunshot rang out. Bea felt pain as the force of blast recoiled and sent jolts up Viv's young body. Bea could see a thin line of smoke escaping from the barrel.

Viv's father lay in a heap on the floor.

Viv stepped forward, the gun still shaking, but ready in her hand.

Evident the shot had hit its target, a steady stream of red flowed from the man's chest and spilled onto the carpet. A red dot growing in size by the second.

They stood over the body, Viv's father's eyes were filled with tears. Viv's had long dried, replaced by shock.

He pleaded with Viv for his life. Said he was sorry for what happened to her mother. Begged for her to call a hospital before it was too late.

Viv heard him but did not listen.

She raised the gun again and aimed at this chest.

His eyes reflected images and memories of all the awful times he had hurt her and her mother. The beatings, the violations, the million sins for which he deserved death.

He begged for her mercy, that he would live.

Viv was not interested in mercy that day.

Three more shots rang out and the world around Bea went black.

When the room under the church rematerialized around her, she was still on the platform. The flame from the brazier had died down, a few mere embers remained. Everyone at the table was standing and clapping enthusiastically.

Viv's body lay collapsed on her platform, so still that Bea wasn't sure if she was even still breathing.

Peter patted her head softly, then left her there, returning to the dining table.

"Bravo!" Druck yelled, food splattered from his mouth.

Kurze met Peter next to the table and helped him put on a long black trench coat that concealed the splatters of blood soaking into his body.

Peter leaned down and whispered something into Kurze's ear.

Kurze nodded and turned to the guests still seated at the table.

"My lord is satisfied," Kurze said.

Morfran nodded and patted Cam's shoulder with encouragement.

"However," Kurze added. "What of the other two? My lord is intrigued by their fate."

Cam glanced at Harper who took a step forward.

"My dear sir," Harper said as he clasped his hands together and approached Peter. "I'm afraid both of them are already spoken..."

He did not finish his sentence. Peter's hand had swung around and backhanded him across the face. Harper fell to the ground immediately and cooed like a wounded dove.

"My lord does not allow familiars to speak to him as such," Kurze said, stepping forward and looking down at Harper. "Now fly away, frail little fowl."

Harper crawled away on all fours and out of sight.

"Then allow me to speak, my lord," Cam said, brushing away his father's grip and standing. "Our agreement was for the one, and the one we have delivered. I believe payment is due."

Peter seemed to mull this for a moment, staring at Cam who did not flinch or cower before those two orange fires that burned from under the tophat.

Peter grunted and then put on his sunglasses. He then unhooked a brown sack from his chain belt and dropped it on the table with a loud thud.

"Then business is concluded," Kurze said. "Until next year."

Morfran nodded.

Kurze and Peter swiftly left the room.

Druck waddled as he followed them.

"Oh, what a mess," he said as he stepped around the large pool of blood at Viv's feet.

It wasn't until the door clanged shut that Morfran turned to Cam and slapped him across the face. Cam fell back into his chair while Kyla watched without flinching.

"You reckless fool," Morfran snarled. "That is not the person you say no to. And neither am I."

Cam looked back at him with furious eyes.

"You plebes," Morfran said, gesturing towards the others at the table. "Get out there, start packing up. Tell the Butcher to burn what's left of the bodies. I want this building to be nothing but cinders by the morning."

A chorus of "Yes, sir" was replied as the men shuffled out of the room.

Morfran sat back down into his chair and drank the last of his cup.

"My dear," Kyla said softly from next to him. "What should we do with these two?"

Morfran looked up again and turned his gaze towards Mal, who was still curled up in a ball crying.

"Ah yes," Morfran said. "What to do with the traitor."

He stood and walked around the table till he was next to her.

His large hand thrust forward and grabbed her left breast.

"Floppy tits," Morfran exclaimed. "The skin of an aging whore, flabby thighs."

He lifted her head up to look at her tear streaked face.

"Ughhh," he said, dropping her head down. "A face only a mother could love."

"Now dear," Kyla said from the table. "Sometimes beauty exists on the inside."

"Must be deep inside," Morfran commented before spitting on the back of Mal's head.

He pulled a cell phone from his coat and dialed a number. It wasn't long until a voice answered.

"It's me," Morfran said into the phone. "I'm afraid we have a problem."

Morfran paused as a voice on the other line spoke loudly and with much worry.

"Well, it seems your daughter has betrayed us," Morfran explained. "The deal is off."

More angry yells erupted from the other end of the line.

"There's no need to be angry," Morfran continued. "It was your blood that was your downfall. Say goodbye to your daughter."

Morfran held the phone to Mal's face.

"Daddy," Mal said through a whimper. "I'm sorry."

Morfran laughed and pulled the phone away, tossing it in the fire.

"Oh daddy," Morfran repeated in a mocking tone of Mal. "You should have known better than to betray us. And for what? Some brat child of a deacon and patricidal emotional dung heap,"

He paused, turning back to the table.

"And you," he said pointing at Cam who stood motionless glaring at his father. "I expected better of you. My only son, my dear Cambion. You got sloppy. I should have offered you up to Peter instead of going through this ridiculous circus to bring these pathetic females here."

“About them,” Kyla said, trying to intervene. She had been seated last Bea had seen, but now was suddenly at Morfran’s side. “Cambion and I have discussed it. The traitor’s fate is sealed, we know that. But Bea. She might be of use to us.”

“Use, how?” Morfran said unconvinced.

“Much like the man I found at Camlam,” Kyla seemed to float on air as she circled Morfran with her hand on his chest. “We see something else in her, something special.”

“Look at her,” Morfran exclaimed. “She’s nothing, she’s trembling.”

“I remember another who trembled once under my touch,” Kyla replied with a smile. “A man who was lost but that I knew held much promise. A man who when offered the gift, knew what the joys of immortality could bring him.”

Morfran glanced at the brown bag Peter had left on the table.

“Why not offer it to her?” Kyla continued. “Trust in your son’s judgment, that she could be one of us. Maybe even more.”

Kyla drifted away and returned to her seat.

Morfran stared at Bea, his silver eye almost twinkling as it looked at her, through her, like he could see far in her future.

The chamber was submerged in this silence, not even Mal's sobs penetrating it.

"No," Morfran said under his breath.

"What do you mean no?" Cam exclaimed.

"I say no, son," Morfran said through gritted teeth. "She shall not be one of us."

"It's my time to choose a partner," Cam said, standing up from his chair and reaching for the brown bag. "It's not your choice, it's mine. And I chose her."

Morfran grabbed Cam by the collar and pulled him over the table, slamming him to the ground by the brazier.

"I said no," Morfran snarled. "Now you will do as you are told, you will eliminate your mistakes."

Morfran released him.

"Starting with her," he added, pointing squarely at Bea.

"But Father," Cam pleaded.

"No excuses, no way out, kill her and be done with it,"

"Mother," Cam said, turning to the table.

"This does not involve her," Morfran said as he grabbed his son's chin and forced him to face him. "Do your duty to your family."

Cam hesitated.

"If you won't," Morfran added, noticing Cam's increasing hesitation. "Then I will, and believe me when I say that I know many ways to make it most excruciating and unpleasant for her."

This caught Cam's attention, he placed himself between her and his father.

"That's better," Morfran said, returning the table and taking his seat.

Bea watched with tear filled eyes as Cam marched slowly towards her. His face was devoid of expression. He had something hidden beneath his coat.

As he got closer, she could smell the scent of his body. She felt the heat radiating onto her skin. He was close enough that she could feel his breath on her skin.

"Best to make it quick dear," Kyla said from the table. "For her sake and yours."

Cam remained motionless. He just stared at Bea with eyes whose coldness slowly melted, revealing something else entirely. Sadness.

Bea thought about her life. She would never get to finish her thesis. She would never see her parents again.

Those weren't the things that saddened her the most. Despite all of the evil that she had been drowning in over the last few hours, she was most saddened to think about not being able to see Cam again. That this would be her last moments with him.

The tears in her eyes were no longer ones of terror or fear, but mourning and loss.

"I'm sorry," Cam muttered softly.

"Me, too," Bea replied.

He wrapped his arms around her and kissed her. As their lips and tongues met, Bea felt nothing but warmth and pleasure. It pulsated through her body in waves of joy. She had never felt this good before.

She opened her eyes and looked deep into Cam's eyes. Her own face reflected in them.

However, she didn't recognize the person that stared back at her. Her face looked dry and wrinkled, her hair was somehow gray and thin. She looked almost exactly like her grandmother before she had passed.

Yet that didn't sadden her, she had known for months now that she would never get to see herself grow old. Yet here she was, in the arms of the man she loved aging without the joy of living a fruitful life.

It's better this way, isn't it? The voice was probably right; she was ready, she was ready to go.

She lost the ability to control the muscles in her legs and arms, her body began to slink to the floor. Her wrists had become frail and thin, slipping from the shackles which clanged onto the floor. Cam slid with her, holding her tight and looking deep into her aged and dying eyes as they embraced.

"Cam," Bea muttered softly under her shallow breaths. "I love you."

Cam stared at her back and for the first time ever, she saw the glint of a tear form in his eye.

"I love you, too," he whispered back to her.

He leaned again and kissed her once more and for the last time.

From the table, Morfran grunted.

"Well that's that then," he commented. "Now the other one."

Cam didn't move, he remained on his knees still embracing Bea's motionless body.

"Well, we don't have all night," Morfran spoke again. "Get along with it."

Cam carefully let Bea's body fall to the ground.

"Now dear," Kyla began. "I know this may hurt now, but this type of thing fades with time."

Cam turned and faced them.

Kyla gasped.

Cam's face was no longer one of an attractive young man, it had turned a puke-like green color. His cheeks bulged as bulbous jowls expanded and grew over his cheekbones. Hair from his head and beard began to fall to the ground. His skin was wrinkling and cracking, his face began to resemble wet clay drying out on a hot day.

The rest of his body changing with it, he hunched over onto all fours. The buttons of his jacket popped off in quick succession like a gun as his belly grew out and tore at his clothes.

"What the hell did you do," Morfran said, standing up.

"This is who I am," Cam replied. "Or do you not remember?"

"I had long pushed this hideous form out of my memory," Morfran snarled in disgust.

"It was how I looked as I came into this world," Cam said solemnly. "Before your magic and schemes turned me into something I was not. I choose to leave this world as I should have been. Me."

"Leave this world?" Kyla exclaimed in horror, rushing over the table towards him.

"You do not have my permission to do such a thing," Morfran yelled. "Reverse whatever it is you have done."

"No," Cam said in the same voice that his father had used to reject his own pleas.

"Please, dear," Kyle pleaded as she held Cam's weakening form. "Don't do this, don't leave us."

"This is what I want," Cam muttered. "She loved me even as I betrayed her, even as I tried to take her life."

"They are just cattle," Morfran snarled.

"They are more than that," Cam's voice grew weaker with each word. "They are better than us, they deserve their place here. Not us."

Kyla cried over her boy's body.

Morfran was practically breathing fire.

"No!" Morfran yelled, grabbing his son by the shoulder and slapping him across the face. "I did not make a deal with a demon to obtain the powers of hell, just to watch my only son throw it all away because he fell in love with some unremarkable mortal!"

"But father," Cam's voice barely above a whisper, his broken nose bleeding. "She is remarkable."

"This is madness," Morfran continued.

But it was too late, Cam's eyes no longer reflected the light in the room. His body no longer radiated infernal warmth. His physical form was dead. Though he had walked the world as the handsome, well-dressed suave club owner, he left it the grotesque form he had been born in.

A faint whimper escaped Kyla's lips.

Morfran grabbed the table with one hand, flipping it on its end. The plates and platters crashed to the ground.

"The fool!" he yelled, his voice blood curdling.

Black tears poured down Kyla's face, sizzling as they landed.

"What do we do now?" Morfran asked with frustration. "This whole thing was his stupid, idiotic, pig-headed idea. We must salvage this and start over..."

"Shut your mouth at once," Kayla said. Her voice was suddenly loud and cutting. The flame from the brazier flashed purple. "He just wanted to be like you. He built this place for you. He did all of this so that you would be proud."

A purple fog began to swirl at her feet.

"What? No, he..." Morfran stuttered, stumbling backwards.

"Silence!" Kyla yelled, her eyes darkened to the point of being almost pitch black. From under her dress, slithering, purple tentacles appeared and pulsated as they inched towards Morfran.

"Kyla, my love, please," Morfran said with his voice cracking in fear. "I didn't, no it wasn't me, it was her..."

Despite centuries of battle, facing some of the most horrific monstrosities in history; his eyes reflected something they hadn't in years, genuine fear.

A tentacle grabbed his leg and moved up his body. He squirmed with futility against it.

"Kyla, please," Morfran pleaded. "Let's talk about this. You need me, remember?"

The mist reached the last bit of fire in the brazier and extinguished it. The room became tinted in the faint purple glow.

Morfran did not get to speak again. The tentacles had wrapped tight around his body and were constricting tighter with each passing second. The echoes of cracking bones bounced around the chamber and as the purple glow faded, the room was plunged into utter darkness. The only sound that lingered was Morfran's muffled scream coming from deep under the ground.

Bea opened her eyes slowly. The chamber was dim, the light of dawn only barely shining through the hole in the ceiling. She could hear several birds chirping to greet it.

She felt like she had just woken from a long sleep. Her muscles were tired and sore. She stretched her legs and wriggled her toes.

She thought about the last moments of her nightmare, of turning old in Cam's eyes. She put her hands to her face. Her skin was smoother than she had ever remembered it to be.

She remembered her thin and frail bones. Sitting up, she felt no aches, no pains. Even her arms where the shackles had been rubbing against her wrist were completely healed and there wasn't any bruising.

She remembered her hair turning gray, but when she looked down she saw long beautiful brown locks flowing over her shoulders. Not only that, her hair was more bright and full than she remembered.

She stood up and steadied herself, wondering if all of it and hopefully the worst parts had all just been a bad nightmare. That the danger had in fact passed.

Bea was startled when something flew out in front of her.

“Whooo,” the barn owl hooted at her as it flew just above her in circles. She swatted at it but it was fast and evaded her swings.

It began to dive bomb towards her head, its sharp talons extended. Bea side-stepped to avoid but stumbled on something that lay on the ground, falling backwards.

She landed with a thud onto a pile of dishes, utensils, and glasses from the table.

“Ow,” she said aloud, propping herself.

What did you trip over?

Bea looked down at her feet and saw a brown sack. The same brown sack that Peter had given to Morfran in payment. The same brown sack from her dream.

It was real.

A whimper emerged from the darkness.

"Mal!" she practically screamed.

"Is that you Bea?" Mal's voice replied.

"Yes, let me help you," Bea rushed towards the voice and found her friend still chained to her platform. She struggled at first but eventually was able to wrestle the cuffs free from around Mal's wrists.

Bea knelt and wrapped her arms around her, holding her tight.

"I'm sorry I got you into this," Mal said, sobbing uncontrollably. "I should never have let my dad convince me this was ok."

"It's over," Bea said.

"I passed out," Mal said between sobs. "Is Viv ok?"

"No, Viv's dead," Bea said.

Bea helped Mal to her feet and together they walked over to Viv's platform. Neither could hold back tears as they saw her body lying on the ground, pale and drained of blood. Bea wasn't sure how long they had been standing there when she heard something rustling behind them.

She turned to find the barn owl had landed and was tugging at the brown sack, trying with all its might to fly away with it.

"What is it doing?" Mal asked.

"I think it wants whatever is inside," Bea replied.

"We should get out of here," Mal said, turning towards the door.

Bea didn't move, she stared at the struggling bird which seemed to grow more frustrated with each failed attempt at liftoff.

"Leave it be," Mal said. "We should call the cops."

"Wait," Bea said as she stared at the sack with growing curiosity.

"Don't you want to know," Bea asked. "Why did they give Viv up to Peter? What all of this was for? It has to be something of value, and I want to know what was worth her life."

"Come on Bea," Mal pleaded, she was clearly still uncomfortable being down there. "Please let's go."

"Not yet," Bea grabbed a glass on the ground and threw it at the bird.

It hit the owl square in the side and a flurry of feathers erupted. At this, the bird finally gave up and flew out of the hole in the ceiling.

Bea picked up the sack and brought it over to Mal. It was heavy in her hands.

"What is it?" Mal asked.

"Only one way to find out," Bea replied.

She untied the knot that held it shut and pulled the drawstring open. The morning sun had grown stronger and a bright beam of light now shined down onto where they stood next to Viv's body.

Inside the sack was what looked like black sand, Bea reached her hand in but pulled it out quickly.

"Ow," she said. "It shocked me."

"What do you think it is?" Mal asked.

"I don't know," Bea replied. "But I don't think it's something we should leave for the police."

"You want to take it with us?" asked Mal.

"Yes," said Bea. "At least until we know what it is."

Sirens were blaring outside, it sounded like someone had already called the police.

"We better go," Mal said. "But what about Viv?"

"I don't know," Bea replied, kneeling over her friend's body one last time, however she slipped and dropped the sack.

It landed on Viv's body and spilled everywhere, littering the platform and Viv with the little onyx granules.

"Damnit," said Bea.

The sirens sounded closer.

"We really should go," Mal said, looking anxious.

"Wait," Bea said. "I just want to say goodbye."

Bea put her head on Viv's chest and closed her eyes.

"Goodbye Viv," she whispered.

She couldn't explain it but she thought she heard the faintest sound of a heartbeat.

Chapter Nineteen

Bea reached with her hands, her fingertips trailing along the soft silk sheets of the bed. It was dark, too dark to see where he was laying next to her. The only proof of his existence was the radiating warmth of his skin.

"Getting warmer," Cam's voice said softly.

"Where are you?" Bea asked.

"Just playing a little hide and seek," Cam replied in kind. "Warmer."

Her arms stretched and fingers probed for any sign of him.

"Red hot," Cam's voice said in the darkness.

Indeed, she could feel it. The flame like heat radiating from him.

Her fingers found him at last, his skin like fire.

"Found me," Cam said.

"I missed you," Bea replied, scooting her body closer.

She could feel his skin with her palm. It was his chest, his muscles sculpted and hard to her touch.

Her hands continued their path up towards his shoulders, then to his neck, and then to his lightly stubbled cheek. She tried to pull herself in close to him and was relieved to feel his strong hands and arms reach out and grasp her first, bringing her in close.

"I never left," he whispered.

Bea's body felt each pulse of the blood pumping in Cam's veins, as if they pulsed in her own. It was still dark, but she knew it was his lips that closed on hers.

"I love you," he whispered.

"I love you too," she whispered back.

Just as soon as it began, it stopped.

Suddenly she felt nothing. Cam was gone. His body was replaced by empty space.

She opened her eyes. The bright sunlight burst through the drapes that hung from the window. Bea covered her face with her sheets, her mind still lost in the daze of a pleasant but cut-all-too-short dream. Her hands reached blindly, still in search of Cam in her bed, but they would find no such prize this time.

She took a deep breath and tried to calm down, her heart still beating at a mile a minute.

It wasn't long before a loud clanging sound from the kitchen began to concern her.

She's not trying to cook again, is she?

Bea forced herself to roll out of bed and her feet touched the carpet. She squeezed the threads between her toes and let out a deep exhale. It was strange but somehow she appreciated the feeling of the cheap apartment carpet under her feet.

The moment of appreciation was over, and she walked to the bathroom. Along the way she had to carefully avoid the moving boxes full of clothes and other personal items that were littered across the floor. She moved into her new place a few days prior and hadn't had time yet to fully unpack.

Turning on the light in the bathroom, her eyes stinging as they adjusted, the girl staring back at her came into focus. Even though it had been months, she still didn't quite recognize herself. The bags under her eyes from late nights of studying were completely gone. The beginning of crow's feet, something her mother must have passed to her genetically, had also smoothed and disappeared. Her hair was once again lush and full like it had been in high school. However the strangest change of all was her eyes themselves. They seemed to be more reflective than she remembered, reflecting the faintest glimmer of light in the room.

Washing her face and brushing her teeth, she prepared to meet the disaster that was quickly coming together on the first floor.

As expected, something was burning. Bea opened the oven and a wave of bacon smoke hit her immediately. Turning the heat off, she pulled the pan from the oven and put it on the stove top. Then opening a window, she grabbed a nearby dishrag and like a conductor for a symphony, waved it with purpose trying to usher the smoke out of the room before the alarm went off.

Um, did you just pull the pan out of the oven with your bare hands?

She thought for a moment. Yes, she had. She looked at her fingers in the light, expecting to see signs of a burn but there was none. They were as perfect as ever, her nails strong and unbroken. Her palms, soft to the touch.

It was just one of several strange new phenomena that occurred since her escape from the club. She had sworn when talking to Professor Mikkelson that she could hear his thoughts, even when he wasn't talking.

"Now where is that girl?" Bea asked aloud.

It didn't take her long to see why her roommate had abandoned breakfast so haphazardly. The newspaper was wide open on the kitchen table. The headline was large and unmistakable.

BILLIONAIRE HEDGE FUND MANAGER ARTHUR PHILLIPS DECLARES BANKRUPTCY

It was something both Bea and Mal had expected for months, Mal's income from her father had dried up shortly after their escape from Club Llithium. Notice of foreclosure on the "Barbie Mansion" soon followed.

It appeared that Mal's father had made some sort of deal with Morfran, for throughout his career every business he started, every investment he had made, seemed to turn to gold. Until now.

But without Morfran, all of his firm's investments had suddenly gone sour. Like dominoes each had fallen into ruin under increasingly strange and coincidental circumstances.

Bea wanted to feel bad for him, after all it was Mal and him that had allowed her to live in their beautiful mansion last semester, even if they had planned all along to pass her along to Cam's machinations at Club Llithium. However it was Mal who she had felt worse for, her friend who was soon to be homeless and had no job history to speak of, with a family name that was publicly in a free fall.

Bea snatched the paper from the table and tossed it into the nearby open trash bin.

Now if we can just get her to stop trying to cook.

Mal walked into the kitchen, her eyes dark and red from crying in her room alone.

"Morning," she said before sniffling hard and reaching for a paper towel.

"Sorry to hear about your dad," Bea said, hugging Mal.

Mal nuzzled her head into Bea's shoulder.

"I'll be ok, I think," Mal said. "Are you hungry? I am making us break..."

She saw the burnt tray of bacon sitting on the oven top.

"Shit," she said.

"It's ok," Bea replied, rubbing her shoulder. "It's just bacon."

"I know," Mal said. "Bacon is just so expensive."

"Don't worry about it," Bea said, walking to the tray and dumping it into the trash. "I'll get some more while I'm out today. How about some fresh fruit?"

"Sure," Mal replied, wiping away a tear from her face. "How's your book doing?"

"Great," Bea said as she pulled a knife from the block and began to chop at several apples and bananas. "The publisher is telling me that it'll be top of the best seller list by next week if it keeps going at this rate."

"That's such great news," Mal said smiling, her crooked teeth jutting out awkwardly.

So modest.

Her book was selling well, even better than she told Mal. It was already at the top of several best seller lists and was showing no signs of slowing.

It was titled, *Conversations with Demons,* and though her publisher considered it a work of fiction, both Bea and Mal knew that every word of it was true. Bea changed names of people and places, of course, and kept out several key details that some may find disturbing, but otherwise it was her story from the moment she met Cam until the moment she said goodbye. She had written it shortly after the events and the first agent to read it immediately snatched her up to get it published.

The timing couldn't have been better. The advance had allowed Bea to find them a house. It was a cute little cottage, short on square footage by comparison to the mansion, but abundant in charm and coziness. More importantly it felt less lonely, it was impossible for Mal and Bea to avoid each other in the tight confines, but the constant interactions only strengthened their bond of friendship.

"Bea!" Mal exclaimed suddenly in alarm.

"What?" Bea replied instinctively.

Mal's eyes were wide and staring at Bea.

Bea looked down, following the line of Mal's gaze and jumped when she realized she cut a large gash into the palm of her hand by mistake. She didn't feel any pain and there was no blood. Bea slowly removed the blade from her hand and Mal rushed to the sink to grab a dishtowel.

Wrapping it around Bea's hand, they both expected large gushes of blood to absorb into the cloth but after several tense moments, none came. They removed the towel and found her hand completely and utterly fine. There wasn't even a scar or mark where she had sliced at her palm.

"Well that's new," Bea said curiously.

"It's so crazy," Mal said, throwing the dry towel into the sink. "Their magic, the things they could do, somehow you absorbed some of it and now you can do what they can do."

"I don't know about that," Bea said, feeling guilty.

"I know what it's like," Mal said with a hint of sadness in her voice. "That feeling of invincibility, that everything will go your way. That everyone will like you no matter what."

Bea blushed.

"It's ok though," Mal added. "You deserve it, after all you've been through."

Mal hugged Bea tightly.

They both jumped as the loud beep of Mal's phone receiving a text message pierced the silence of the kitchen.

"Shit, sorry," Mal said, rushing to silence it.

Bea watched her from across the small room, grinning.

Mal nervously peered at the screen then began typing a response back. Content, she pressed enter and smiled.

Bea smiled too.

"So, how is Jill?" Bea asked playfully.

"She's amazing," Mal said.

"I don't understand how you make any money in tips," Bea said with a grin. "With all the time you spend staring at her at work rather than serving your tables."

"She doesn't seem to mind," Mal replied. "Besides, the best is when we close the diner up early and we finally get a chance to be alone."

A loud car horn blared from the front driveway.

"Damn," Bea said, startled. "She's here early today."

Both girls walked to the front door and opened it just in time as the motorized wheelchair drove up the ramp and over the threshold.

"Slow down, Mad Max!" Bea exclaimed, jumping out of the way at the last second. "Be careful with my door."

"Meh," said Viv from the wheelchair. "You can afford another one."

Bea rolled her eyes.

Mal leaned over and squeezed Viv tight.

"How are you doing?" Mal asked.

"Great," Viv said weakly in reply. "Better if you let me breathe a little."

"Right," Mal said, blushing and letting go of Viv.

Viv lifted her nose to the air for a moment.

"Burnt bacon," she said. "My favorite breakfast."

"I think we've got some croissants in the pantry," Bea said with a smile.

"Great," replied Viv. "I'm fucking starving."

Viv rolled up to the kitchen table, Bea brought the bowl of fruit and the tray of croissants.

"How's rehabilitation going?" Bea asked.

"It sucks," Viv said flatly.

Bea shot her a disapproving look from behind the cabinet.

"But it's getting better," Viv added with a fake smile.

"They still asking you all sorts of questions?" Mal questioned as she sat down.

"You mean like how did you survive losing eight units of blood?," Viv replied, raising her eyebrows.

"I tell them the same thing every time," Viv continued. "I don't know, now stop asking me."

“Want one?” Mal asked, opening a jar of jam and holding up a croissant.

"Oh yes," Viv said. "I'm starving. Can you believe the therapist had the balls to tell me today that the difficulty walking is in my head? I just about slapped her right then and there."

"Well, we can't expect them to understand," said Bea. "I still don't really get it and I was there."

Both Viv and Bea shot a glance across the table at Mal.

She was midway through shoving a croissant in her mouth and managed to mumble what sounded like "Me too."

"Anyways," Viv said. "I saw a plastic surgeon yesterday. He said he can graft some skin from my ass to clear up all the damage that asshole Peter did."

"That's great news Viv," Bea exclaimed.

"I told him to fuck off," Viv replied.

"What? Why?" Mal said in utter bewilderment.

"Cause it would only be hiding who I am," said Viv. "It would be like getting all dressed up and going to that club all over again. I was hiding who I was. The scars, they are part of me. Reminders of what I've gone through. I wouldn't let anyone take that away from me just to fit some male ideal of what beauty should be."

Viv snatched a croissant and took a bite.

"Besides," she added through her mouthful. "Scars are supposed to be sexy on a guy, why not for a girl?"

"Cheers to that," Bea said with a smile.

All three raised their glasses of orange juice and clinked them together.

"Enough of talking about me," Viv said as she brought her glass back to the table. "I want to hear what kind of naughty things that you and Jill are getting into, you little slut."

Mal smiled and turned red.

The three continued their chatting for another two hours before Bea looked at her watch.

"Damn, if I don't get ready soon I'm going to be late," Bea said.

"What for?" asked Mal.

"I'm meeting Professor Mikkelson for coffee," Bea explained. "He wants to try and convince me to reconsider publishing my thesis and releasing the *Filii Diaboli* to the academic board."

"Haven't you told him you don't have it anymore?" Viv asked.

"Of course," Bea replied. "The damn thing disappeared from my room after we escaped. I told him I gave it back to the original owner. But for some reason, he doesn't believe me."

"Well good luck with that," Viv added.

"Shit," Mal exclaimed, looking at her watch. "Me too, I gotta get to work."

Viv put two fingers to her mouth in a v-shape and flicked her tongue playfully at Mal.

"Oh shut up," Mal replied and tossed her napkin at Viv before standing.

"Oh Bea," Mal added. "Would you mind taking the trash out? It's starting to smell."

"I didn't realize that Bea was your housekeeper too," Viv said mockingly.

"No, I," Mal stammered.

"It's ok," Bea said smiling. "I got it covered. I'll walk you out Viv."

Viv's motorized wheelchair whirled as they walked to the door.

Once outside the door, Viv unlocked her car and a ramp came out to help her back into it.

"Did you send it?" Viv asked.

"Of course," Bea replied. "Adelaide's sister called me last night to thank us for returning her necklace back to them."

"Did she ask any questions?" Viv added.

"No, she was genuinely just happy to get it back," Bea said with a smile.

"Good," Viv said as her voice began to trail off.

They both paused in silence.

"Listen, I," Viv said with uncharacteristic hesitation.

"It's ok," Bea replied to her. "You don't have to."

"No, I do," Viv continued staring at the ground and then took a deep breath. "Thank you for saving me, for bringing me back."

"I didn't do that," Bea said. "I think it was whatever was in that bag."

"It's more than that," Viv continued. "I've been a bitch, I've said awful things to you. I've done nothing to endear you to me, yet somehow you still only saw the good in me. You really are a good friend. I'm lucky to have you."

Bea smiled and put her hand on Viv's shoulder.

"Are you sure that you didn't save yourself?" Bea asked.

The ramp whirred as it lifted Viv into the car.

"Maybe," Viv replied. "But even if I had somehow managed to keep myself alive and it wasn't some magical dust crap from some demon's fanny pack. I don't think I could have done it without you."

Bea hugged Viv.

"Next week?" Bea asked into Viv's ear.

"Wouldn't miss it for the world," Viv replied.

The door closed and the car started up.

Bea waved at Viv as she backed up and drove off.

Bea took a step towards the door when she realized the full trash bag was sitting on the driveway next to her.

"Oh, you," Bea said aloud to herself.

Lifting it and carrying it to the side of the house, she was frustrated to find that the dumpster was already full to the brim. It was filled with boxes of all sorts, no doubt remnants from the move.

"Damn," Bea said, trying to figure out how she was going to fit it in the bin.

At last she gave up on making it neat and hurled the bag into the air and to the top of the pile. Hoping that would stay steady until the garbage company came by to empty it.

She walked up to the door of their house and found the mailbox stuffed full with letters but also a brown package.

Bea walked back into the kitchen and sat down at the table, content that she had a few more minutes until she had to finish getting ready for coffee with the professor.

The first several letters were pre-approved credit cards for Mal, who obviously needed to be talked to about personal finances and managing her credit, now that she didn't have a trust fund to live off of.

After that, a letter from her doctors who undoubtedly were imploring her to return to the clinic for more tests. They were convinced that she was the key to finding a cure from Huntington's after recent tests had come back that the gene variant that causes the disease had somehow altered itself back into a healthy version. What she couldn't tell them though was that it was very unlikely that they would ever be able to explain or recreate what had happened to her, at least scientifically.

She tossed the letter to the side.

All that remained was the small brown package. It didn't have any postage on it, nor an address. Just Bea's name affixed to the front. It was thin and square, wrapped in what looked more like brown butcher paper and tied in twine.

I wonder what this is.

Pulling the threads of the twine bow, it came loose quickly and she tugged at the paper ripping it open.

The contents of the package thudded as it fell to the surface of the table.

Bea immediately recoiled back in her chair.

Sitting on the kitchen table was *Filii Diaboli*. A fresh streak of blood lay across its cover and a small white note stuck out from the pages.

Bea slowly pulled the note from the book and found it had writing on one side. The ink was crimson red, the same color of the bloody streak on the cover, and it read:

One of the lessers pilfered this from your room, and after reading your book, I thought it only fair that it was returned to you. As far as I'm concerned, Cam wanted you to have it.

P.S. Pardon the blood, the thief who took it wasn't too keen on returning it to its rightful owner.

- Kyla

Bea wondered if she should be concerned, but she shrugged it off. The sun was steadily rising in the sky and the morning was quickly escaping her.

Well, there's one nice thing about all this.

"What?" she said out loud, not caring that she was just talking to herself.

At least you can give the book to Mikkelson now so he'll leave you alone.

Bea laughed.

"Ya right," she said aloud to the empty room.

"Hey Bea!" Mal yelled from the room down the hall.

"What?" Bea yelled back.

"Can I get a ride to work?" Mal asked.

Bea rolled her eyes.

"Sure," She called back with a reluctant smile.

She walked to her own room to finish getting dressed and put on some makeup, leaving the *Filii Diaboli* on the kitchen table.

The white barn owl watched from the shade of the tree branches. From his perch he could see the front driveway and into the window of the small kitchen of Bea and Mal's cottage. He had watched the girls intently all morning, like he had every morning, and every day, for the last several months.

Content that Bea had left, he made his move.

He swooped down, gliding silently on broad wings until he landed on top of the pile of garbage.

Sinking his talons deep into the bag that was carelessly piled on top of the bin, he flapped his wings in strong, powerful movements until at last the top bag from the pile lifted off the ground. Hovering for a few moments in the air holding it, he dropped it to the grass where it landed with a clink of aluminum cans banging into one another.

Landing on top of the bag which had already begun to tear and rip. A few minutes of clawing later and the bag was wide open, its contents spilled across the ground.

The owl nipped hungrily at the slices of burnt bacon, swallowing them without hesitation despite the coal-like texture.

He hadn't eaten in weeks, his hunting skills somewhat diminished since his absence from this form for over a century. So he was glad to take such a welcome source of protein regardless of the taste.

Sorting through the various pieces of bacon grease soaked garbage, he found the newspaper. Pulling it from the mess and laying it out neatly on the grass.

Carefully he turned the pages, doing his best to avoid rips and tears. This was made all the more difficult by the bacon grease spots that made most pages stick together.

Then at last, he stopped, having found the thing for which he was searching.

The owl appeared to be reading the LOCAL NEWS section of the paper, reserved for only stories that the community cared about. One in particular in the bottom right hand corner.

A neighbor's cat just happened to be prowling the wall nearby and spotted him. In an instant, it pounced onto the unsuspecting bird.

The barn owl narrowly escaped, flying off into the sky with only a few blood soaked feathers left behind on the ground as penance for its foolishness.

The newspaper, having survived the ordeal still very much mostly intact, lay open still to the same page where the owl had been reading. In the bottom right corner, an article headline read:

ABANDONED NIGHTCLUB, FORMER CHURCH, TO BE CONVERTED TO ART GALLERY

About the Author

C.R. Allen, is an Arizona native. He balances life as a dad, business professional specializing in A.I. software, and a passionate author. A proud alumnus of Arizona State University, where he completed both his undergraduate and master's degrees. His fascination with storytelling began early, crafting his first screenplay at age 10. Today, he is known for his compelling works in horror, historical fiction, and science fiction, drawing inspiration from the rich landscapes and technological advancements surrounding him. Allen's writings stand out for their dark and mysterious narratives that explore profound sociological and technological themes.

Other titles by C.R. Allen

Short Stories-

Overclocked

Anna King

Novels-

Case 355: Stonehearth, TN

My Friend George (coming Summer 2024!)

Made in the USA
Las Vegas, NV
19 January 2024